A Public Nuisance

Publisher's Acknowledgement

Dr. Leslie Harris, President of Memorial University of Newfoundland, assisted the publication of this book with a subvention from the University's Publication Fund.

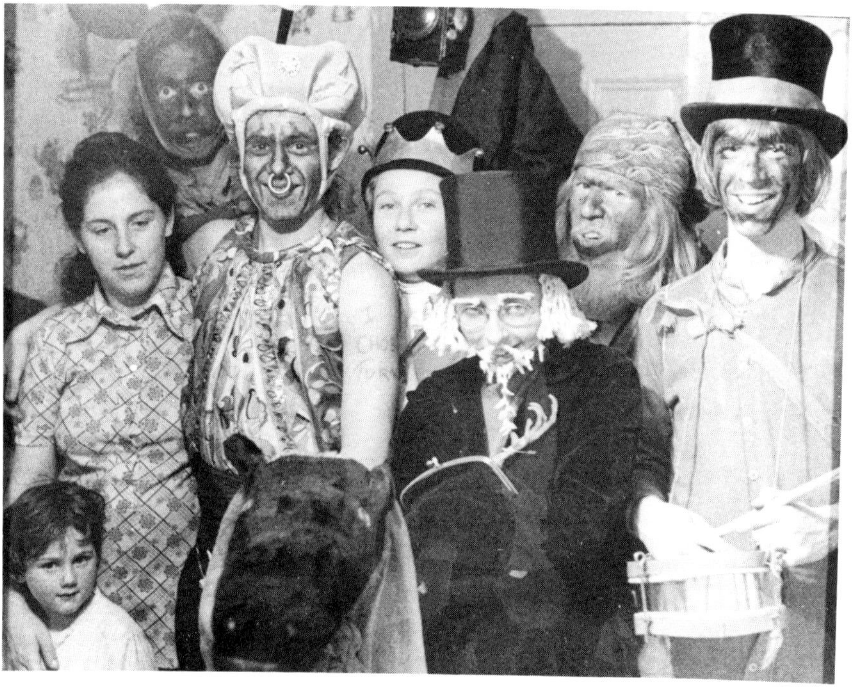

The Christmas mummers pose in Mary O'Neill's kitchen, Port Kirwan, Newfoundland, 1973.
Left to right: Lisa O'Neili, Mary O'Neill, Chris Brookes, Bembo Davies, Lynn Lunde, Jan Henderson, Bob Pot, Paul Collins.
Photo: Don Wright.

Any Person who shall be found, at any Season of the Year, in any Town or settlement in this Colony, without a written license from a magistrate, dressed as a Mummer, masked, or otherwise disguised, shall be deemed guilty of a Public Nuisance, and may be arrested by any Peace Officer, with or without a warrant, and taken before any Justice of the Peace in the District or Place where such person may be found, and on conviction, in summary manner, before such Justice, be committed to Gaol....

The Act to Make Further Provision for the Prevention of Nuisances, Government of Newfoundland, 1861.

For George Ryga

A Public Nuisance

A History of the Mummers Troupe

Chris Brookes

Social and Economic Studies No. 36
Institute of Social and Economic Research
Memorial University of Newfoundland

Published by the
Institute of Social and Economic Research
Memorial University of Newfoundland
St. John's, Newfoundland, Canada
ISBN 0-919666-59-0

Canadian Cataloguing in Publication Data
Brookes, Chris, 1943-
A public nuisance
(Social and economic studies ; no. 36).
Bibliography: p.
ISBN 0-9191666-59-0
1. Mummers Troupe -- History. 2. Mumming
-- Newfoundland. 3. Theatre -- Newfoundland.
I. Memorial University of Newfoundland.
Institute of Social and Economic Research.
II. Title. III. Series: Social and
economic studies (St. John's, Nfld.) ; no. 36.
PN2305.N6B76 1988 792'.06'0718
C88-098602-6

Contents

Acknowledgements

I am indebted to many people for making this book possible. To the members of the Mummers Troupe itself, without whose talent and perserverance there would have been nothing to write about. Rhonda Payne, Donna Butt, Rick Boland and Bembo Davies were particularly kind to wrack their memories and filing cabinets for the manuscript's benefit.

Alan Bolt showed me the reason to write this history. Dorothy Anger, Alan Filewod, and Diane Humber provided spiritual nutrition and editorial insight. Gerry Hallowell and Angela Ribiero encouraged me in my darkest hours.

I am indebted to Cam Mustard for the cover design, to the Institute of Social and Economic Research for its many favours, and to Robert Paine, George Story, Gordon Inglis, and John Widdowson for their criticism and support. Copy-editors Jeannie House and Sara Carter beat my prose into readability. Jeanette Gleeson painstakingly guided it through ISER's computer, and Susan Nichol and Beth Ryan guided it safely through the many intricacies of manuscript preparation. Thanks are also due to Gerry Porter for layout, and to Mannie Buchheit, Warren Brownridge, Kent Barrett, Derek Butt, Michael Schmidt, Don Wright, Memorial University Extension Service, Newfoundland Archives and AP/Wide World Photos for the photographs, and to Pat Byrne and Al Pittman for permission to reproduce the song, "The Government Game." The 17th-century illustration of the Doctor is reproduced with permission of Dover Publications, Inc. Mummers Troupe Playscripts are excerpted with permission of the authors.

Preface

The activities described in this book spanned the decade from 1972 to 1982, or in Cosmic Time, the period roughly from the breakup of the Beatles to the death of John Lennon. I write this account for several reasons.

Theatre is the art of the immediate. It breathes with the actor, and vanishes with that breath, surviving only in the present. This here-today-gone-with-the-curtain-call quality gives the art its particular power. Unfortunately it also makes it difficult for many of us who practise and study theatre to profit from the experience of our predecessors. Visual artists today are still able to see how Reubens managed his effects, writers may read Tolstoy, and filmmakers can watch *Metropolis*. But the theatre artist, at best, scans yellowing scripts and faded production photographs. What 16th-century *Commedia dell'Arte* was *really* like, how Deburau moved his audience to tears or how Kemp rolled them in the aisles are secrets we can only imagine. Yesterday's performance is over. Want to know what it was like? You had to be there.

It is always a privilege, although sometimes a painful one, for artists to live and work during remarkable times. Newfoundland in the 1970s was not Chile, Nicaragua, Poland or South Africa. Nonetheless, it fired its artists with an intensity common to any people raging against threatened death and indignity. In Newfoundland's case, the indignity was social and economic; the threatened death was cultural. The Mummers Troupe flourished during a peculiarly vibrant period for Newfoundland's indigenous artistic expression. While it was happening, we were all riding the crest of the wave and had little time for analysis. Now perhaps some useful lessons can be drawn from putting that period in perspective. Many groups contributed to the outpouring of artistic creativity, and obviously this is a description of only one of them. But I hope it can illuminate the wider experience which we all shared, and the current of cultural electricity which fired it. The Great Newfoundland Artistic Revival of the 1970s didn't happen because people like Al Pittman, Gerry Squires, Mike Jones, Codco and Figgy Duff all got together and decided it would be a Good Thing; it was somehow triggered by the temper of those times.

During most of its ten-year life, the Mummers Troupe was the leading edge of the political theatre movement in English Canada. Some theatre critics compared our work to the Canadian Workers Theatre Movement of the 1930s, and although there was no historical connection, both the Mummers and the CWTM developed a theatre intended primarily for community development and social animation. Our work was far less doctrinaire, more similar to the kind of "theatre for development" methodology used today in areas of the Third World. I hope that our successes and failures—the lessons learned and ignored by one small theatre company working in one particular social geography—can be of value to other artists elsewhere working toward social change. Please steal any good ideas.

The history of the Mummers Troupe is the history of the work of many people. Since for most of its ten-year life the company was the central focus of my own work, my way of telling this story is autobiographical. It is traditional for autobiographical accounts to style the author as the Good Guy. I have obliged accordingly, and divided the rest of the characters neatly into Heroes and Villains as well. Readers should therefore easily deduce that they are reading low farce, not high drama. They should not, however, conclude that I was the star of the show. The show had 106 stars. They were (in order of appearance) The Mummers:

Lynn Lunde
John Doyle
Kevin Pittman
Diane Olsen
Tom Sexton
Sam Hedge
Sandy Cantwell
Jane Dingle
Paul Sametz
Mary Walsh
Chris Knight
Andy Thompson
Donna Butt
Jan Henderson
Bob Pot
Bembo Davies
Paul Collins
Don Wherry
Judy Marshak
Marsha Coffey
Michael Fahey
Heather Earle
Rick Boland
Rhonda Payne
Lee Campbell
Howie Cooper

Allen Booth
Connie Kaldor
Alan Filewod
Michael Schmidt
Derek Butt
Connie Brissenden
Maddy Williams
Ron Hynes
Steven Bush
Jane Foster
Wayne McNiven
Ray Landry
Pam Morgan
Jeff Pitcher
Frank Lapointe
Bob Banfield
Judy Parsons
Ron MacEachern
Ann Narvaez
Susan Perly
Bill Maloney
Don Walsh
David Ross
Jeannie Becker
Brenda Devine
Mavis Penney
Terry Reilly
Geoff Butler
Jules Drake
Joan Brownridge
Bob Joy
Brian Hennessey
Janet Michaels
Michael Kearney
William Roberts
Sheila Zisman
Kelly Russell
Jim Payne
Pierre Beaupre
Glen Tilley
Ann Budgell
Gay Hauser
Steven Osler
Kent Barrett
Charles Tomlinson
Mark Manson
Charlotte Jewzyk
Wanda Crocker
Mac Furlong
Denis Parker
Brian Downey
Paul Steffler
Warren Brownridge
Laine Lunde
Christine Lewes
Henry Chaulk
Betsy Erving
Colin Quigley
Beni Malone
Glenn Rockwood
Greg Thomey
Caroline Ford
Jim Maynard
Stephanie Squires
Michelle Fleiger
Jacquey Ryan
Pat Byrne
Janis Spence
Kevin Noble
Ed Keilly
Sheilagh Guy
Sherri Smith
Gerry Squires
Clyde Rose
Kay Anonsen
Ian Wallace
Mary Lynn-Bernard
Merle Matheson
Michael Wade

Chris Brookes

Maddox Cove
August 1988

Getting it off the Ground

Whenever I hear anyone talk of culture I reach for my revolver.

Hanns Johst (popularly but incorrectly attributed to Hermann Goering)

Cultural Concussion

1

> Every colonised people—in other words every people in whose soul an inferiority complex has been created by the death and burial of its local cultural originality—finds itself face to face with the language of the civilising nation; that is with the language of the mother country. The colonised is elevated...in proportion to his adoption of the mother country's cultural standards.
>
> Frantz Fanon

When I was growing up in St. John's it never occurred to me that I could become an artist. I wanted to be an electrical engineer. Years later I did briefly become one and I wonder if my eventual commitment to an applied, useful theatre originated from my foray into applied science. I have never been able to separate discipline from purpose.

At age thirteen I decided to demonstrate my technological precociousness. If microchips had been invented back then, I might have tried to build a computer like Captain Crunch (the teenage hero who accessed long-distance telephone and data-communication circuits with a cereal box whistle). They hadn't, so I assembled a homemade tape recorder from old Meccano parts, string, and bits of wire. It looked pretty funny, but it worked, more or less. And for the first time I listened to a playback of my own voice. The sound that warbled from my red-and-green mechanical triumph was the broad brogue of a Newfoundland townie.

I knew what that meant. I went to school in 1950s Newfoundland. I listened to the radio. Sometimes I even sneaked over to a friend's house and watched television. I was a fast learner. I knew that Newfoundlanders were supposed to be some sort of second-class Canadians. We were a national joke. Canadians laughed at accents like mine.

> Say, did you hear about the Newfie with the terrible inferiority complex?
> He thought everybody else was as good as he was!

Haw haw. It was no laughing matter to me. At thirteen I'd never heard of cultural imperialism. I concluded that an electrical engineer with a thick Newfoundland accent would never be able to get a decent job up on The Mainland. (I don't think it ever occurred to me that I might not have to go to the mainland to get a job. That's where the jobs were supposed to *be*.) So for the next few months I worked feverishly trying to change my accent to that "mid-Atlantic" standard which the CBC, and presumably the mainland job market, seemed to prefer.

I eventually discovered that "class" is not always something you get let out of every day at 4 p.m. And my vocabulary eventually discovered "imperialism" and a few other "isms" guaranteed to stop chit-chat at uptown art gallery wine and cheese openings for the latest high-priced egg temperas by what's-his-name. By then, the '60s were well under way. That was the era which believed that the quickest way to create a radical was to send a student out on a peace march: after he got his head split open by the police he'd come back a radical.

In my case, the tape recorder got to me long before the cops did, although it was a while before I realised the extent of the wound. The foundations of the Mummers Troupe were initially laid by the cultural billyclub which busted my head, and the heads of many of my peers.

2

The Countryside is the Basic Area for Fighting

> 1. Popular forces can win a war against the army.
>
> 2. It is not necessary to wait until all conditions for making revolution exist; the insurrection can create them.
>
> 3. In underdeveloped [societies] the countryside is the basic area for fighting.
>
> Che Guevara

I emerged from the 1960s with a theatre degree from an American university, which I had earned, and a temporary place in the American immigration computer's "undesirables" file, which I hadn't. It was the era of the Living Theatre, the San Francisco Mime Troupe, and the Chicago Seven, an era of theatre moving off the stages and into the streets. A time for decisions. Some of my fellow students decided to arm themselves and go underground to become urban guerrillas. I decided to go back home to Canada.

Things weren't quite the same here. For one thing, being an urban guerrilla wasn't such a popular career choice in this country, at least for English Canadians. In Toronto Jim Gerrard had just founded Theatre Passe-Muraille with support from Rochdale College and was keeping it alive with productions of new American plays. It was a harbinger of what later became the truly *Canadian* theatre movement of the later 1970s, but in 1969 not much else had gotten into gear. I floated around the Toronto theatre scene as a director and taught university in British Columbia for a while, but my theatre didn't seem to mesh with my politics. So in 1970 I took the Whole Earth Catalogue's advice and went Back to The Land to raise chickens in the small outport community of Maddox Cove, fifteen miles south of St. John's.

There was no running water, no indoor toilet, no central heating. But there was this girl I'd met in Vancouver: Lynn Lunde. And I learned a way of living that my townie upbringing had ignored. My teachers were haystacks and horses and good neighbours. And a four-horsepower Acadia make-and-break marine engine that had to be taken apart so many times I could still do it in my sleep.

A year later Lynn and I had realised two things in particular. One was that nobody in their right mind can enjoy raising White Leghorns. Because White Leghorns are not exactly in their right minds themselves. The other was that nearby, at the Memorial University of Newfoundland, there were some interesting experiments going on in the Extension Department.

They were feeling around for new ways to use art and media in community development. Extension and National Film Board filmmakers produced documentary films as vehicles of community animation. Extension visual artists like Don Wright inked up tools of people's daily work— barrel stencils, stove parts, fish— creating a kind of labour landscape art, visual documentaries of work. All this plugged into a field staff network of rural development workers around the province.

We eventually met most of that field staff during the summer of 1971. The neurotic Leghorns had gotten to us. We gave ourselves a rest with inanimate objects: puppets. I'd wanted to experiment with puppets ever since seeing Peter Schumann's Bread and Puppet Theatre a few years earlier in New York, and was curious about the dynamics of small street shows. We decided to build a Punch and Judy show and tour it around the province. It was a perfect way to get to know rural Newfoundland audiences, a self-contained, portable performance we could do by ourselves. This was just as well, since our year with the Leghorns hadn't warmed us up to the local theatre scene. The province had no professional theatre, and its amateur theatre movement was on a very different wavelength. It seemed to me that the movement would never get out of its cast-party-and-society-culture syndrome as long as it based itself on middle and upper-class urban audiences.

There has long been a standoff between "townie" (St. John's) and "bay" (outport) culture in Newfoundland, a result of the relationship that evolved between the two over the last century. Townie culture considered itself superior. Bay culture resented that. In the early '70s, the most graphic evidence of the relationship usually showed up in washroom graffitti wherever the two cultures mixed, such as the university. You sat down, expecting to see the usual girls' telephone numbers and "shithouse poet strikes again" rhymes, and there it was:

BAYMEN SUCK COCKS!
TOWNIES SUCK COCKS
BAYMEN SUCK COCKS
TOWNIES SUCK COCKS
BAYMEN SUCK COCKS
BUT TOWNIES ARE BIGGER!
YEAH? YOU'D KNOW!
...et cetera.

The name-calling bespoke economic, not anatomical disparity.

I hoped that a scruff puppet show for children, performed outdoors on wharves and meadows (not in halls belonging to the school or the church, echoing of catechisms and homework) might present itself as just plain fun, far from the pretentious smell of Art and Culture with which townie audiences liked to perfume themselves. Half the theatre of anything is how it comes *at* you before the show even starts; the clothes it wears and the expectations it arouses in an audience.

The script of Punch and Judy is a far cry from perfumed art. Probably *the* most popular show in the history of Anglo-Saxon drama (Shakespeare and Agatha Christie notwithstanding), its appeal has always been to the working class, children and adults alike.

The plot is basic. A roguish Punch bumps off first his own wife and child, and then a series of bourgeois authority figures. After he finishes off the figureheads of Law and Order, the Devil appears, to carry the transgressor off to the Fiery Furnace. Aha, you think, Righteousness triumphs at last. But Punch then demolishes the Devil as well and proclaims the demise of the whole system: "Now we are free to do as we like!"

You probably remember Aristotle. His Poetics, which are so beloved of freshman university English classes, advance the idea that the seed of tragedy is sown when an individual conflicts with the ethic of his society: The Tragic Flaw. According to this analysis we, as spectators, feel empathy with the tragic hero, a relationship which permits us to share the character's life, albeit now a short and miserable one. Sooner or later he's gonna get his, we just know it. When we experience his eventual come-uppance we undergo a kind of projected anguish, *Catharsis*, by which we are supposedly purged of the negative social characteristic which we vicariously adopted. Hoorah for the Status Quo. This idea of catharsis underlies virtually everything from Great Masterpieces to television westerns. It is an insidious concept. It assumes the ruling sociopolitical structure to be fixed, given and impervious: the setting against which the Hero tragically flings himself— and fails. Far from inciting social action in an audience, it is designed to inhibit it. If Punch and Judy had met Aristotle, they would have beaten the shit out of him.

Performing in various locales, Lynn and I noticed that our Punch was much more of a hero in poor neighbourhoods than in wealthy suburbs. When the Devil died, rich kids sometimes looked as if they'd swallowed a prune, but poor kids always knew what it was about: they cheered. Upper-income parents sometimes protested to us that the show was improper, and too violent for children. This often led to discussions of revolutionary criminality.

Although Punch and Judy is not native to Newfoundland, the show appears to have been well known to some outport audiences of the nineteenth century. In 1971, its hoary old chestnuts of British Victoriana were still familiar, and Punch's cutthroat demolition of them still appealed to all ages. Our show was historically accurate, but we interspersed the old script with impromptu quips, depending on the audience. In centuries past Punch and Judy street shows were sometimes used as a vehicle for extemporaneous political com-

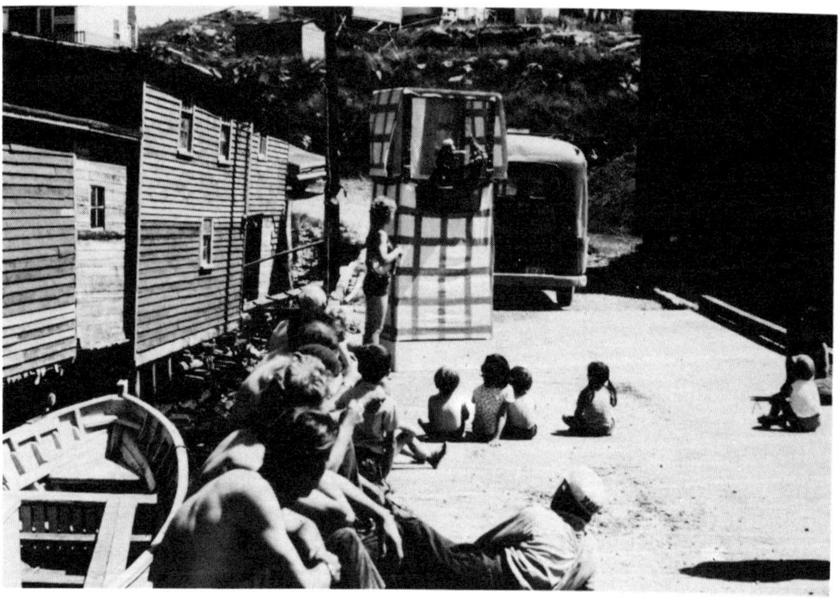

Punch and Judy performance in New Bonaventure, Trinity Bay, July 1971. Photo: Don Wright.

ment to adults in the audience, asides slipped in while the youngsters squealed at the action. Usually we inserted a Smallwood puppet, who of course got beaten up. (In fact, Lynn and I had done a precursor to this show nine months earlier, at the 1970 St. John's Regatta, entitled *The Punch and Joey Show*. The plot involved bashing the Joey puppet repeatedly over the head— Smallwood was then still in power— with the sole educational objective of getting crowds of children to chant "Down with Joey! Get rid of him! Knock his block off!")

The Punch and Judy tradition had developed and survived for four centuries in the street without ever having been enshrined in the schoolbooks and opera houses, as had happened, for instance, to Shakespeare. So it never represented school, or intellectual foppery, or the boss. Like mummering (the Newfoundland folk theatre tradition we were later to explore), it was never considered "proper." It survived as a form of popular theatre which works precisely because it does *not* exemplify the classic Aristotelian dramatic mechanisms.

The little wooden hunchback and his twelve fellow players took Lynn and me, an old delivery van, a dog, and a propane stove all over the island that summer. We seldom drove on paved roads and seldom played a community with a population of over a thousand. Aside from the flat tires it was terrific. We performed for free, or for the occasional fish or free meal. Kids loved our show, and we fell in love with our audiences in return. We met a lot of good people, listened to a lot of stories, heard a lot of history, and got to know something of the distinct regional and community identities of rural Newfoundland. We saw some communities proud and prosperous, and many others victimized by fishery, resettlement and development policies over which they had no control. Much of what we learned later formed the backbone of the Mummers touring work.

After the island tour we kept on singing for our supper, panhandled the puppets up to Toronto, and settled into Rochdale College where Lynn researched her anthropology thesis on communes. Rochdale was at that time a collectively-owned fifteen storey residential high-rise described by those who believed in it as an experimental institution of higher learning, and by those who didn't as "that high-rise hippy haven," "a doped-up den of iniquity," and "the Blot on Bloor Street." The police and every decent middle-class Torontonian hated it. It housed the most incredible, ingenious, and inspired collection of crazies I've ever met.

In 1971 the Federal government had just announced their new LIP (Local Initiatives) grant programme. It provided a transfusion for the (by now) distinctly visible Canadian theatre movement—notwithstanding the fears of some critics that LIP was designed to buy out the leftist fallout from the '60s. ("Assimilation is the secret weapon of the bourgeoisie," American theatre director Herbert Blau had warned a couple of years earlier.)

The fears were not without foundation. During the winter of 1972 I was directing a LIP puppet project in downtown Toronto. The crunch came when the local LIP bureaucracy hauled us up and demanded to know why some of our built-with-federal-funds giant puppets had been seen at the head of an anti-Vietnam War demonstration outside the U.S. embassy. Canada Manpower was not about to support politically visible theatrics.

I found it hard to appreciate officialdom's concern. Demonstrations outside the U.S. embassy were old hat. They might have been visible, but aside from justifying the salaries of a few RCMP photographers they were pretty ineffective. Change is never that easy, petitioned by a handful of well-intentioned but politically powerless people on the sidewalk. It has to be *built*, brick by brick. Picket lines are useless without a strike on the factory floor.

The only piece of the factory floor that I knew well was two thousand miles East. I was wasting time pacing the pavement in Toronto. So I returned to Newfoundland in the spring of 1972 determined to build a theatre. Not a theatre passing out plays like pamphlets to an anonymous audience of passers-by, but a theatre which would engage in constructive dialogue with a people I knew intimately. The experiences of the previous year fell together. I envisaged a full-time professional ensemble, able to work indoors or outdoors, flexible and mobile enough to go into Newfoundland communities and create original shows about local issues. It would be wired to its society: if there was a crisis in Labrador or a strike in Burgeo it should be able to get there quickly and roll up its sleeves, providing a community mirror in which residents could get a clearer look at their needs and their problems.

> The art of the poet...consists in separating from the fable whatever does not essentially belong to it, whatever in the daily necessities of real life...interrupts the progress of important events (Schlegel 1808).

For Lynn, this was applied anthropology. For me, it was a theatre based—unlike psychological melodrama—on a *social* rather than on a *private* definition of the individual. For both of us the objective was to animate social change.

We both felt that it would be crucial to focus on the rural working-class audience. Rural because it is in The Bay, not in St. John's, where the real essence of Newfoundland culture lies. Working-class because that kind of audience base would develop our art as a practical, useful tool, rather than as a status symbol for sophisticates. We could not ignore the city, but it would not be our prime interest.

There was no time to waste. Newfoundland's indigenous identity was already drowning in the cloned plastic-wrapped homogeneity of North American consumer capitalism. The waters were rising. And although I was never naive enough to think that one small socialist theatre would single-handedly turn the tide, I believed that it could contribute to the work of those who can. My cultural doomsday scenario gave us five or six years at most. Faced by an enemy with vaster cultural firepower, we would have to be resourceful, quick, and adaptable. We would build a cultural base for progressive social action.

It is important to realise that we weren't starting from scratch. We were extending an unique tradition of people's theatre in Newfoundland, applying its objectives to the Newfoundland society of the 1970s.

It is a tradition I'd like to dust off for you.

Newfoundland Theatre: Looking Under the Colonial Cabbage Leaf 3

The history of art is often presented as a sequence of random inspirations suffered by individuals, catalogued into stylistic "trends" devoid of social meaning and removed from any political or economic environment, drifting in and out of fashion like hemlines. And appreciated, like fussy table manners, by the well-bred and well-fed.

There are those, for example, who like to think that the professional Newfoundland theatre of the 1970s developed out of a refined thespian tradition generously bequeathed to us by the aristocratic elements of our British colonial heritage.

Don't you believe anything of the kind.

"There is," said that non-Canadian playwright in whose festive honour (in Stratford, Ontario) the largest single share of Canadian public funds for theatre is annually consecrated, "a tide in the affairs of men...." The history of the Newfoundland theatre has had much more to do with the tide of socio-economic affairs than with the arrival of any stork from Drury Lane.

> The real question is: to whom does the meaning of the art of the past properly belong?...When we "see" a landscape, we situate ourselves in it. If we "saw" the art of the past, we would situate ourselves in history. When we are deprived from seeing it, we are being deprived of the history which belongs to us. Who benefits from this deprivation? In the end, the art of the past is being mystified because a privileged minority is striving to invent a history which can retrospectively justify the role of the ruling classes, and such a justification can no longer make sense in modern terms (Berger 1972).

Newfoundland theatre history mystified? "Tsk," you say. Well, my way of seeing may not sandblast that history into dazzlingly precise scholastic detail. But I hope it will at least blow away the fog sufficiently to allow a quick peek at the general shape of the architecture. Let me start this way:

The cultural values and theatre traditions of the working class and those of the middle and upper classes are by no means the same. The work of the Mummers Troupe during the 1970s did not grow out of the theatrical fashions practised in St. John's in the late 1960s, but out of a primarily working-class tradition which rooted itself in Newfoundland almost five centuries earlier: "mummering," "janneying," or "fooling." It is not as easy to spot, however, in our historical theatre landscape. That's because the authorities tried to paint it out of the picture. Mummering was officially banned in 1861, and although elements of the tradition continued in some parts of the island more or less until present times, they did so illegally. In St. John's, the mercantile centre of Law and Order, and in most larger towns, the custom ceased entirely. Our theatre history was thus pulled up by the roots. After that, "official" Newfoundland theatre, rather than evolving from an ancient working-class tradition in the outports, began by implantation via the middle and upper-classes of St. John's and the new industrial towns. In spite of this, it was still dragged off course from time to time by the tide of events rolling in the streets, outside the drawing rooms of privilege.

The Mummers Play is where Newfoundland's theatre history begins. At least, it's where it begins for white folks. In the culture of Newfoundland's native peoples, (unlike present-day Western white culture) neither theatre nor religious ritual were activities split off from everyday life. But relatively little remains of Newfoundland's native cultures today.

When the island was officially "discovered" by Western European economic interests it was already populated by a native race, the Beothucks. The Beothucks may have practised a variety of performance rituals. But the invading whites were more interested in genocide than in theatre research, and wiped out this entire indigenous race without discovering anything of their culture. The Beothucks' theatre, whatever it may have been, died with them.

In Labrador, the arrival of Moravian missionaries in 1771 began the systematic repression of Inuit cultural forms (which the Moravians, a German Protestant sect, considered heretic). By the twentieth century, most traditional Inuit music, dance, and theatre had been replaced by German brass and string music, church choral singing, and American movies. (As late as 1975, a well-known English-Inuktitut dictionary published by a Moravian missionary distinguished between *imgerut*, which it defines as the Inuit word for "hymn," and what it calls "heathen Eskimo song": *pissek*.) A Spanish influenza epidemic introduced accidentally to the northern coast by the Moravian supply ship *Harmony* in 1918 helped wipe out any dance-theatre tradition which may have survived surreptitiously in the memories of the elders. Subsequently, one of the last *angakoks* (shamen) who may have held substantial knowledge of Inuit ritual was publicly tortured by the white authorities to break his "conjuring." In mid-winter 1938, in the northernmost settlement of Hebron, Jefta Jeraruse was imprisoned in solitary confinement for a month in an unheated Hudson's Bay Company icehouse until his spirit broke.

The Naskapi of Labrador were by comparison more recently and less zealously infiltrated by the white man's church than the Labrador Inuit. Many of their rituals are remembered, but seldom practised.

The suppression of mummering amongst Newfoundland's white settlers continued this pattern. Destruction of indigenous culture is the best insurance against militant resistance.

Whites (predominately English, and later Irish fishermen) first began to settle in Newfoundland over four centuries ago. For three of those centuries, independent settlement was officially illegal, and harsh persecution of settlers commonplace. The reason for the ban was starkly simple: England saw Newfoundland as one great natural resource to be pillaged. As the British Under-Secretary of State, William Knox, phrased it in 1793: "The island of Newfoundland has been considered...as a great ship moored near the (Grand) Banks during the fishing season for the convenience of English fishermen."

He might more accurately have said "for the convenience of English fish *merchants*." The British crown decreed settlement to be illegal in order to protect the economic interests of the powerful West Country fishing merchants, thereby guaranteeing them full control over the exploitation of their migrant fishermen-workers and the Newfoundland saltfish industry. The merchants feared that if settlement were legalised, it would permit the development of a class of more independent resident worker-fishermen who would be in a price-bargaining position, thus threatening industry profits. The prohibition was zealously enforced by the British navy, which torched any settlers houses it found around the coastline.

But despite the atmosphere of persecution and hardship, the numbers of settlers slowly increased. These early settlers, of necessity building their homes in isolated bays and coves, hiding from all officialdom and from both the British and French navies, brought with them a traditional folk drama with which they leavened their lives until the early twentieth century. It was the Mummers Play.

Out of respect to those ancestral actors I should point out that they themselves never actually called it the Mummers Play—that is the title bestowed upon it by modern folklore scholars. To those who practised the custom it was never "theatre," "art," or a "play." In some communities it was referred to as "the rhymes," but in most outports it was simply *done*. Passed down through the generations as an oral tradition, it was performed in the kitchens and front rooms of Newfoundland homes during the twelve nights of Christmas (26 December - 6 January). But one of the interesting things about the play is that as a Christmas tradition, it has absolutely nothing to do with the birth of Christ. To the extent that the ritual is religious, it may belong to a much older folk religion than Christianity.

Its basic dramatic structure consists of two characters who declaim rhyming lines and knock sticks or wooden swords together. One of the characters is killed. A Doctor rushes in and "cures" the dead man, who jumps up alive again.

That's all. Hardly Tennessee Williams, is it? From a dramatic standpoint it sounds simplistic and dull, and this is exactly how most post-Confederation Newfoundlanders, if they knew of the custom at all, considered it: dusty old historic stuff, irrelevant and *boring*. Yet it was popularly performed for hundreds, perhaps thousands of years, not by stuffed-shirt culture-vultures but by ordinary folk who liked to have a good time at Christmas. Obviously it wasn't a dry old piece of obligatory heritage for them. What was it, then? To find out, we have to approach it a little differently from *Night of the Iguana*.

First of all, the Mummers Play is not a drama in the literary sense. It is theatre. And theatre is not a literary art amenable to the laws of grammar and syntax. Theatre is what makes your spine tingle in the back of the balcony; an art whose essence is to be found in the moment-by-moment relationship between performer and audience. It can be as perfectly present in a union meeting, a street demonstration, or a kitchen conversation as in a production of Othello at the Opera House. Julian Beck of the Living Theatre used to say that the most perfect form of theatre is revolution.

Any play is a conjuring, a ceremony of symbols and incantations designed to summon forth an unique and unnameable presence. The ceremony of the Mummers Play chalks its particular pentagram. What is the name of the presence it summons? Light? Luck? Change?

I won't pretend to lay out a definitive analysis of mummering or of the Mummers Play. For one thing, I can't. No one knows for sure how the tradition originated. For centuries ordinary folks just went out and practised the custom without taking any notes at all. This was very thoughtless of them, making things extremely difficult for latter-day scholarship. And if the historians and the folklorists can't agree on how mummering originated, then its unlikely that actors like me will solve the puzzle. All I can offer is an opinionated practitioner's analysis. At least, analysis is what I call it. You may call it superstition. Regardless, it provided the groundwork for what the Mummers Troupe was eventually to become, which is why I outline it here. I believed that the prototype for the kind of theatre we set out to construct in the 1970s had been around for a very long time. We merely tinkered with the contraption, changed the timing and the transmission ratios, and ran it down the road of the twentieth century. The result was that even later Troupe plays having nothing on the surface to do with folklore or mummering drew their roots from an attitude towards art and audience that was formed by the theatre of the ritual Mummers Play. Or rather— for those of you taking notes— by the following opinionated *interpretation* of that ritual and its function in society. It goes like this.

When the Mummers Play arrived in Newfoundland in the sixteenth century, it was already ancient. It may have evolved from early solstice ritual. If so, then its original practitioners, feeling the days grow colder and shorter, and seeing the sun growing weaker and weaker in the sky at the time of the winter solstice, conceived the event as a cosmic battle between light and darkness— a battle which the sun was clearly losing. So, in order to give the sun a helping hand, they performed a ritual with characters representing light and darkness. Light was killed by darkness, but miraculously rose back up to life again. The idea, of course, was that the sun in the sky would follow this example and renew itself too. For in this theatre, performers did not *symbolise* light; they *were* light. A modern Western concept of character representation did not exist.

Such basic solstice ceremonies can be found in many cultures. They date from a time long before theatre and religion were isolated from the rest of life and relegated to Saturday nights and Sunday mornings. A time when the practice of ritual was believed to influence the course of events in the natural world. And the proof was in the pudding: after the solstice performance the sun did indeed start to revive. (Even in recent times, the performance of the Newfoundland Mummers Play was considered to bring "good luck" to the household and to help ward off disasters during the coming year.)

Suppose for the sake of argument that the Newfoundland Mummers Play was an evolutionary hand-me-down from this kind of ritual theatre. Then what interests me is this: politically speaking, its premise lies in the collective belief that *reality* is transformable. This is quite different from Aristotle's vision of a cathartic theatre purging our Pity and Fear for some Tragic Hero who challenges the established order and fails, thus eliminating the revolution before it catches hold. Neither is it the familiar notion of theatre as a "willing suspension of disbelief," a diverting interlude in escapism offering temporary relief from the fixed reality to which the audience must return after the curtain call. Solstice ritual assumes just the opposite: that the extra-theatrical reality actually *can be transformed* by collective effort of will. The whole purpose of its theatre is to mobilise and focus that collective will.

Over the centuries, some of the basic solstice symbolism found its way into Christian ritual: a God of Light in constant battle with a Prince of Darkness for men's souls, the death and miraculous resurrection of the God of Light as a symbol of eternal hope, etc. In present-day Newfoundland, the colour of the Devil is generally believed to be not red, but black, the same as the colour of one of the protagonists in the Mummers Play. And while some of the dramatic imagery of earlier beliefs was co-opted by mainstream Christianity, other ceremonial elements of those beliefs continued as "folk tradition" long after their official religious status had been supplanted. Slowly, their original meanings became forgotten, and they were practised "for good luck," or simply because "that's what we always done, boy." Ritual became custom.

Exactly how primitive ritual might have evolved into the Mummers Play is anyone's guess. Mummering was mainly a custom of the peasant classes, and ruling-class historians didn't record it. But looking at the play as it survived in the British Isles and Newfoundland, it is possible to imagine in it elements of that old solstice ritual, gussied up and decorated by later history. It wears a few more sophisticated articles of theatrical clothing, of course.

Firstly, it developed a "script:" a simple set dialogue of rhyming couplets.

> And if there be any Man who
> Before Me stand,
> Bring Him in and I'll cut Him down
> With Sword in hand!

In an oral custom handed down through generations of illiterate peasants and fishermen by word of mouth, the adoption of rhyming couplets was probably as much a practical way to remember lines and action as an attempt at poetry. Because the custom survived in relatively isolated communities, over the centuries some of the lines (although rarely the rhythms) developed idiosyncratically in different communities. Some versions of the play, for example, have a character called The Turkey Snipe instead of The Turkish Knight. Try the old parlour game of passing a whispered message sequentially around a circle of people and you'll get similar results.

In performance the rhyming boasts and challenges become almost musical as the two protagonists prepare for the inevitable battle. A heavy, measured rhythm underscores the importance of the ceremony taking place. It is a ritualistic encounter, and in some Newfoundland communities (Renews and Port Kirwan area, for instance), no attempt was made at naturalistic acting. The protagonists marched to and fro, rhythmically stomping their feet, and knocked their wooden swords together at prescribed intervals.

Secondly, the two protagonists, Light and Dark, are personified. The Mummers Play features the Prince of Darkness, Turkish Knight, Slasher, or the King of Egypt (performed with the face painted black) in battle with Saint George, the King of England, or Alexander (with a white face.) Perhaps Crusade era audiences wanted up-to-date characterization and appropriated the identities of popular contemporary superheroes?

> In Comes I, the Turkish Knight;
> Come from 'cross the sea to Fight;
> To fight Saint George with Courage bold.
> If his Blood runs Hot,
> It will soon run Cold....

Thirdly, a Doctor character appears after the battle to "cure" the dead man, providing a more modern dramatic motivation for the miraculous resurrection. Interestingly, when he appears the whole style of the performance changes. It's like a different play. The Doctor delivers a rapid-paced burlesque comedy routine which differs totally from the measured rhythm and rhyme of the two main protagonists. Unlike them, his part traditionally features improvisation and interplay with the audience.

> ...I can cure all aches and pains, hiccups, chilblains and migraines. The itch, the stitch, the gump, the gout, the pain within and the pain without. If the devil's in a man I can drive him out. Give me an old wife of fourscore and ten, and I can make her young again. I can make the blind to hear, the deaf to see, and the lame to walk

and fly. Why, I can cure the lovesick maid—I takes her home, rubs her o'er and o'er, then if she dies, never believe me more.

FATHER XMAS: How came you by your knowledge?

DOCTOR: By my travels. I've travelled high, I've travelled low, I've travelled the land of ice and snow; Icaly, Picaly, France and Spain, around the world and back again. I don't go about like them half re-rafty-sham doctors—neither kill nor cure. I goes about for the good of the country...rather kill than cure.

Where did this character come from? He sounds remarkably like a similar character in the sixteenth-century Italian *Commedia dell'-Arte* tradition.

DOTTORE: Yes, sir, I practice medicine out of pure love for it. I nurse, I purge, I sound, I operate, I saw, I cup, I snip, I slash, I smash, I split, I break, I extract and tear and cut and dislocate. I dissect and trim and slice and, of course, I show no quarter.

PANTALONE: You are a veritable avalanche of medicine.

DOTTORE: I am not only an avalanche of medicine, but the bane of all maladies whatsoever. I exterminate all fevers and chills, the itch, gravel, measles, the plague, ringworm, gout, apoplexy, erysipelas, rheumatism, pleurisy, catarrh, both wind-colic and ordinary colic, without counting those serious and light diseases which bear the same name. In short, I wage such cruel and relentless warfare against all forms of illness that when I see a disorder becoming ineradicable in a patient I kill the patient in order to relieve him of his disorder....

Commedia dell'Arte was a zany physical theatre generally performed in the open air. The shows satirised establishment figures, and often played "close to the wire." But because most dialogue was improvised without a written script, the authorities were commonly frustrated in their attempts to censor the plays. Professional *commedia* companies such as the *Gelosi* were enormously popular, and toured throughout Europe in the sixteenth and seventeenth centuries. Their character stereotypes caught popular imagination and were widely borrowed. (Punch, the character of the British magazine and puppetshow, for instance, developed from Commedia's Pulcinella.)

Like Commedia's Dottore, the Mummers Play Doctor is a satire of the professional classes, with the dead man becoming the unfortunate working-class victim.

Fourthly, a retinue of extraneous characters often appeared at the end of the Mummers Play, reminiscent of the parade of the Seven Deadly Sins from mediaeval morality plays. The mummers' parade usually included topical figures, each of which declaimed a short

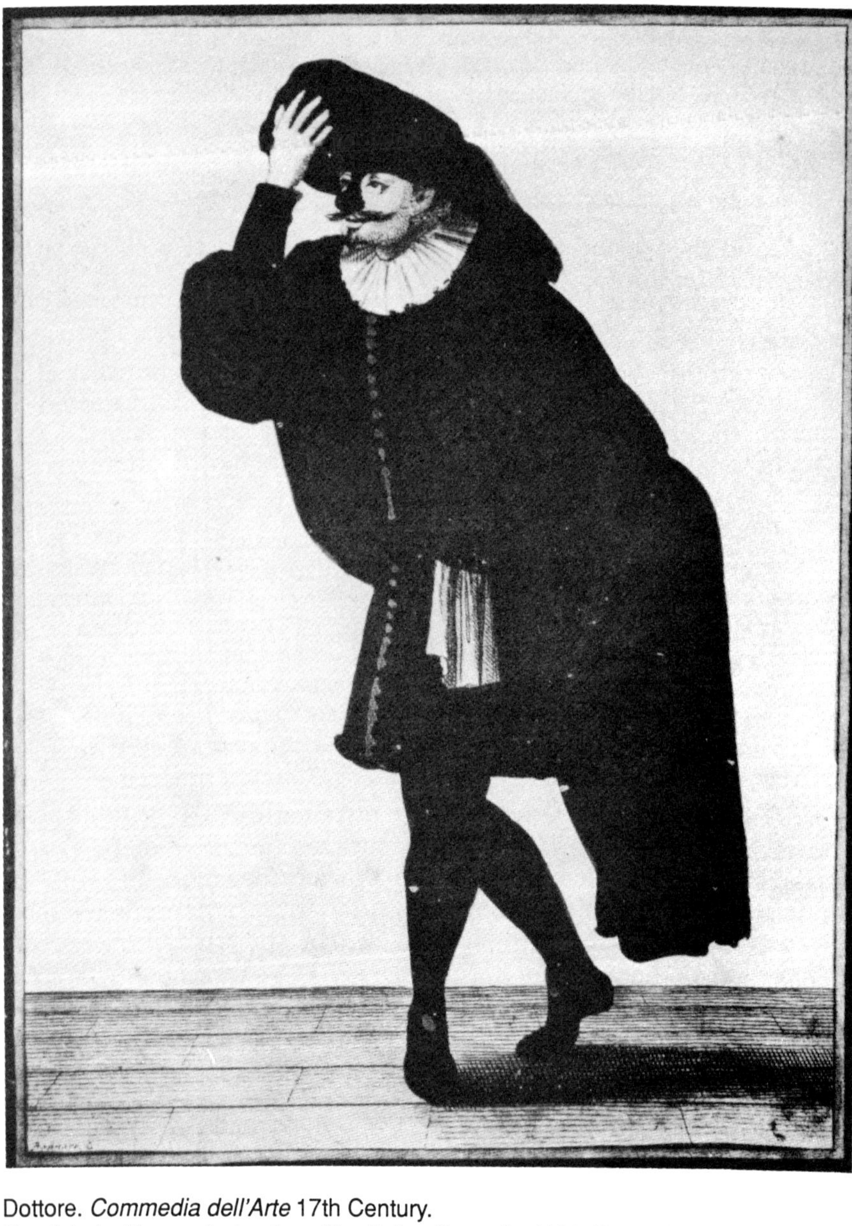

Dottore. *Commedia dell'Arte* 17th Century.
Reprinted with permission from *The Italian Comedy*, 1966. Dover Publications, New York.

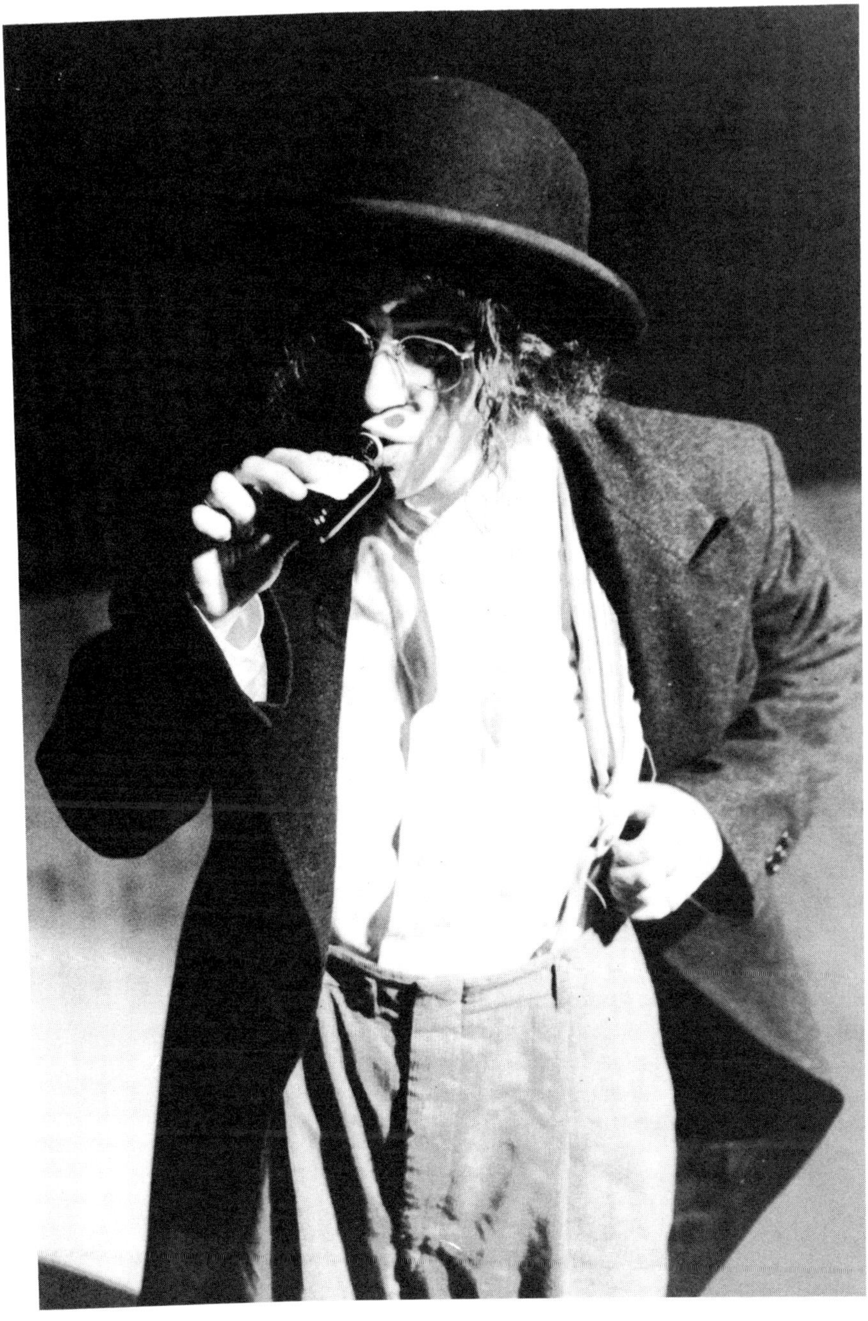

The Doctor. Sheila Zisman, Mummers Troupe 1977.
Photo: Kent Barrett.

couplet of lines. For an illiterate peasant culture, it provided a kind of "living newspaper" as well as an opportunity for satire.

> Here Comes I, Oliver Cromwell as you suppose,
> I conquered many with my copper nose....

At least one character in the Mummers Play parade, known variously as Sweep, Beelzebub, etc., also carried a club. His function, in European tradition, was to demand (or simply to take) money from the more affluent houses visited as a kind of equalization payment for the past year's profit-taking, sweeping the dirt, and the rich, from their established positions.

> In comes I, Sweep,
> All I gets, I keep.
> Money I wants,
> Money I crave,
> If you don't give us money,
> I'll sweep you all to your grave!

This tradition of "collection," finely balanced between deference and aggressive mockery— soliciting a reward as much in recognition of the potential threat of the mummers' presence as in return for their performance— survives in many solstice customs, and even in modern Halloween trick-or-treating. It is not a redistribution of wealth based upon the idea of charity (*giving* to the poor); it is the more forceful concept of restitution (the poor *taking back* what is theirs).

Fifthly, and importantly, the mummers' tradition embodied some political aspects of the old mediaeval Feast of Fools custom; that is, temporarily reversing the usual authoritarian social structures to permit a period of licensed anarchy. In the mediaeval church, the Boy Bishop was a choir-boy appointed to the temporary authority of bishop. In secular England, the King of Fools or Lord of Misrule was a local peasant who replaced the local ruling authority for the twelve days of Christmas, and had the power to decree whatever rules he wished. Lord and peasant, governor and governed— such polarities were ritually reversed. Normal order in the community was temporarily turned topsy-turvy.

> The Feast of Fools had an explicitly radical dimension. It exposed the arbitrary quality of social rank and enabled people to see that things need not always be as they are....Unmasking the pretence of the powerful always makes their power seem less irresistible (Cox 1969).

Similar customs, involving inversion of the normal social order for a short period each year, were once common throughout Europe. In sixteenth-century France, the *charivari* tradition prevailed:

> Paraders faces were tellingly disguised with mud, ashes, and flour, transforming them into devils and ghosts. Protected by the anonymity of the masquerade, the poor led the...ominous house-to-house search for alms, seeking vengeance against the municipal exploiters, usurers, bloodsuckers of the people. Each of these rituals worked on both a mythical level (calendar of feasts, ghosts) and a political level (class struggles) by means of figurative representation. Actors replaced abstract concepts (Ladurie 1979).

The Mummers Play borrowed from these customs. The players, headed by Father Christmas (in some Newfoundland communities called the King or Captain of the Play) marched into houses and took charge. Social custom dictated that they could not be refused.

> In Comes I, Old Father Christmas;
> Welcome or welcome not,
> I hope Father Christmas
> Will never be forgot....

For twelve days, from St. Stephen's Day to Epiphany, mummers represented "the law" of social inversion. They had the power to commit breaches of "normal" social decorum, and to wreak retribution upon persons who had incurred the animosity of the community during the preceding year. (In Torbay, Newfoundland, mummers are still unwelcome in many homes. The custom is well remembered as having been used years ago to "settle old scores.")

In most parts of the Canadian mainland this aspect of mummering has survived as part of Halloween: if you've incurred the dislike of your neighbourhood children during the year, or if you're too stingy in handing out Halloween candy, you may find your gate taken off its hinges or your organic humus toilet overturned. This sort of thing is not popularly considered a *crime*, exactly. On November 1st it may be a crime. On October 31st it is always a *prank*. Our society gives license once a year to the Halloween mummers to practise a little spontaneous anarchy. We allow children, who normally have no power in our society, to experience a measure of real power.

But the Canadian Halloween, which involves only children, was relatively unknown in Newfoundland before Confederation. Newfoundland had Christmas mummers. They were adults. Merely taking a gate off its hinges is child's play. Adult mummers could be capable of more violent acts.

A custom which inverts the normal social order once a year doesn't necessarily subvert the status quo; it can be a safety valve which blows off a little steam in order to ultimately reinforce it. But the effect may be less benign in times of social unrest. In mediaeval Europe, the tradition was from time to time linked with violent class struggle, leading to serious assaults on the established order. So it's perhaps not surprising to find that mummers trod the stage of Newfoundland's political history as well.

By the early nineteenth century, Newfoundland's social and political climate was changing rapidly. Settlement had finally been legalised, and with political independence in 1832 residents achieved the right to elect their own government. The large British fishing interests which had dominated the fish trade for centuries withdrew, and their places were rapidly filled by a new local bourgeois class on the rise. Succeeding decades saw tremendous jockeying for control of the new government and legal systems, and by the end of the century a homegrown aristocracy had consolidated its hold upon the new Dominion's underdeveloped economy. This was accomplished largely via the institution of the *truck* system in the fishing industry (which employed 80 per cent of the country's labour force). Under this system each fisherman went to a merchant in the spring and obtained fishing gear, food, and supplies on credit for the coming fishing season. At the end of the season the fisherman returned to the merchant with his catch to settle his account. Conveniently, the price of fish, as well as the price of provisions, was set entirely by the merchant. In good years a balance might be left, and in bad years the fisherman ran up a standing debt. No cash ever changed hands. Not surprisingly, many fishermen (most of whom were illiterate and thus unable to verify the merchants' bookkeeping) spent their lives in perpetual debt to these feudal lords of the outports. In 1841 an estimated three out of every four Newfoundland fishermen were in debt to their supplying merchant. From the merchants' point of view, it was a foolproof system for racking up profit—basically the same stacked deck that Western capitalism deals to the Third World today.

Economist Steve Antler remarks:

> It is ironic that Newfoundland's nineteenth-century economy has been described by some as a *traditional* economy....That it was favourable [to the merchants] was no accident. Every element of the system was constructed by a different decision of the Newfoundland Supreme Court....It was the [merchant controlled] court system, and not tradition, that constructed the truck system (Antler 1979).

Noting that in 1880 the per capita income of Newfoundland merchants was 439 per cent of the Canadian average income while by comparison a Newfoundland fisherman's income was only 42 per cent of the Canadian average, he points out that nineteenth-century Newfoundland remained underdeveloped not because of her geography or because adequate economic surplus was not generated, but purely because of her class structure.

> 'Tis about those cruel rogues of merchants,
> No pity nor love do they show.
> They don't pity poor weary creatures
> Or women or orphans you know.
> No they don't pity poor weary fellows
> Who are out on the ocean so grey,
> In the midst of all toils and great dangers,
> Toiling by night and by day.
> And our eyelids are closing together
> For the want of an hour's good rest,
> While those rogues are all spending our money;
> They are wearing and tasting the best...
>
> *The Merchants Song*: traditional.

In a country with no real middle class, the new electoral franchise produced two parties: the Liberals, led by intellectual democrats and radicals who initially represented the majority of the working class; and the Conservatives, led by the supplying merchants to whom the majority of the population was in debt, who enjoyed the support of the British colonial governor's institutionalised power.

The merchant classes, already monopolising the magistracy and the entire judicial system, and having secured a mandatory property-ownership qualification for elected representatives to the new Assembly "in order to discourage the nomination of ill-qualified persons," confidently expected to retain the balance of legislative power (Gunn 1966).

Soon, however, a Liberal majority in the Assembly was apparent, and could only be controlled by the obstructionary interference of the colonial governor. This so frightened the merchant classes, or as they preferred to style themselves, the "wealth and respectability," that in 1841 they desperately petitioned the British Colonial Office to rescind the Newfoundland constitution. The Colonial Office declined to do so, but agreed that most of the island's inhabitants seemed as little qualified to hold electoral franchise "as so many Malays" (*ibid.*). Presumably the merchants of Malaysia were having trouble keeping their subjects in line, too.

Political manoeuvering and violence at the polls became commonplace. With no secret ballot, and with returning officers appointed from "the respectability," open voting resulted in economic coercion by the merchants (who were almost exclusively Protestants.) This in turn prompted a pro-working-class spiritual coercion by the Catholic Church, described rather quaintly by the Governor as an attempt to "convert a naturally quiet and well-disposed people into engines of violence and disorder" (*ibid.*). The Church's intervention stressed that the Conservatives were a party of mercantile privilege, executive-level obstruction, and economic oppression. A virulently partisan press, notably the pro-merchant *Public Ledger*, tried to rally Protestant workers to the merchant side by turning class struggle into sectarian rivalry, conjuring up visions of "papist ascendency." Incidentally, the editor of this paper, Henry Winton, was one of those who drew the mummers' wrath. In 1833 a large group surrounded his house on Christmas night, and would not disperse until set upon by the troops of the St. John's garrison. Two years later, a group of masked attackers cut off his ears.

In such a charged situation, the highly popular custom of mummering threatened merchant-class security inasmuch as it represented a nonsectarian combination of the working class. Its anonymous practitioners roamed the streets disguised and armed with wooden swords, Fool's swabs and truncheons. On the one hand, its more peaceable manifestations could be described as relatively harmless:

> ...nothing so harmonises the difference between the poor and the rich as a reciprocal kindness of feeling on such occasions. The labouring classes in those days had enlarged privileges granted them, if not by positive law, at least by well-established custom. So Folly was, as it were, 'crowned, and disorder had a licence' (William Whittle, a chronicler of the time, writing of Newfoundland Christmas, *Evening Telegram* 24 December 1885).

But it was not always so genteel. Often, the wealthier and more privileged class became the target of the mummers' social retribution, and episodes like the following were not untypical. Two Harbour Grace merchant magistrates reported to the Colonial Secretary in St. John's in January 1831 that:

> ...Some persons in Carbonear have had lime or flour thrown on their clothes by such disguised persons when going to attend Divine Service. These Mummers appear in the streets with their faces blackened or covered, also men dressed in women's clothes, and of the lowest order of persons. Flour, etc. has also been thrown on the clothes of persons in the streets of Harbour Grace by such disguised characters....

> We humbly conceive that it would be much for the benefit of the public peace of...Conception Bay that the custom of mumming should not in future go unpunished.
>
> At one o'clock in the morning of the seventh instant...most daring outrage was made by persons disguised as Mummers, with their faces blackened or covered, at the house of Mr. Manuel Alcock, a respectable planter in this town....A subscription ball was given at this time by a party of respectable persons...when some of these delinquents entered the house armed with bludgeons and swabs dipped in blubber.
>
> They first beat in a most inhuman manner James K. Thompson of this town, dealer and chapman, and covered his clothes with blubber....The next attack was made on Henry Stowe of this town, master cooper, who was in the kitchen, and beat him severely and covered his clothes with blubber.
>
> These delinquents...destroyed two sets of chinaware with some dozens of glasses and earthenware, also two tables on which there were articles of food and victuals prepared for the guests. At the same time their disguised companions outside of the house broke the kitchen window and sash thereof....After the parlour windows had been so broken it is stated that three guns were presented through the windows, which so terrified the females, some fourteen in number, that some of them fainted.
>
> The number of delinquents were said to be from twenty to thirty....Nothing has transpired so as to fix by law this vile outrage on any of the perpetrators or on those who instigated them to commit the same, or in whose houses these delinquents prepared themselves for this purpose.
>
> Yet strong suspicions are entertained.... (Provincial Archives 14 January 1831.)

What is interesting about this episode is the social context in which it occurred. "Strong Suspicions" might well have been entertained, for within the year scrawled notices like the following were being tacked up all over Conception Bay:

> NOTICE:
>
> A meeting of the fishermen and shoremen of Carbonear will take place on Saddle Hill the ninth of January at half past eleven o'clock in the forenoon for the purpose of taking into consideration the best and most effectual method of getting rid of TRUCK the ensuing Spring. The fishermen of Harbour Grace are earnestly requested to cooperate with their Carbonear brethren in this truly worthy and momentous affair and show by their compliance that they are willing and able to shake off the yoke they have so long and unjustly borne! (Provincial Archives 21 January 1832).

The local "respectability" were greatly alarmed to see over 2,000 fishermen attend this meeting (the entire population of the community proper was normally only 2,500) and call for the right to be paid in cash for their share of seals in the sealing industry, plus cash wages for the cod fishery. Their alarm increased when a subsequent meeting drew even higher attendance, and when a group of fishermen chopped down the masts of a schooner belonging to one of the town's major merchants. The merchants asked the Colonial Office to issue a proclamation making such meetings illegal. The Colonial Office obligingly did so, and dispatched a special police detachment to read the riot act (injunction-bound strikers today would find the procedure familiar). The fishermen's movement was eventually suppressed, but not before they succeeded in securing half of their demands: cash payments for sealers.

The Conception Bay area continued for decades to be characterised by both hard-line mummering and class struggle. A series of sealers' strikes during the next thirty years spread to St. John's, and in retaliation some of the major merchants began to hire their sealing crews from other parts of the island.

The Harbour Grace episode is but one example of a complex tradition, and I'm not suggesting that mummering led directly to collective bargaining. But I *am* suggesting that it was far more than just a litmus paper of social unrest. As a vehicle of social change, the spontaneous anarchy of mummering was unorganised, and unlikely *in itself* to accomplish much. It was less the custom itself which the establishment considered dangerous than the encouragement which mummering contributed to working-class political organization. As class struggle in nineteenth-century Newfoundland took off the gloves, mummering represented a traditional vehicle for solidifying class consciousness, providing a cultural underpinning for primitive socialism.

> An army without culture is a dull-witted army. And a dull-witted army cannot defeat the enemy (Mao Tse-Tung 1940).

The 1840s and 1850s in Newfoundland saw increasing class and sectarian struggle and continual political manoeuvering, culminating in the events of 1860-61. The spring of 1860 produced another major sealers' strike, and during Christmas there was an upsurge of serious mummering incidents. In St. John's there were street battles involving mummers, but conditions in Conception Bay were apparently worse, as the *Public Ledger* editorialised on 4 January 1861:

> ...The condition of Harbour Grace just now is a deplorable one, the peaceful and respectable inhabitants being at the mercy of a lawless, ignorant and brutal populace....None but these ruffians dare go abroad at night. It is a raid of low, savage Roman Catholic blackguards upon the Protestants of the town. Law, order, decency, propriety, respect, and every moral and social and legal feeling is thoroughly abandoned and the Lord of Misrule reigns paramount....Martial law is an extreme measure in any community but there really does seem to be great necessity for it in Harbour Grace.

A day later Thomas Mercer, a resident of Bay Roberts, was killed by mummers. Unrest continued through the winter as the British governor summarily dismissed the Liberal government, a highly suspect gesture interpreted as a pro-Conservative attempt at political sabotage. The spring vote featured election irregularities and returned a Conservative government by a slim margin. Subsequent street demonstrations in St. John's were put down by the garrison troops, who fired into the crowds, killing three and wounding twenty. The Conservative government quickly introduced several pieces of legislation aimed at defusing future strife, including the doubling of the police detachment at Carbonear and Harbour Grace, and...*the provision for summary arrest and sentencing of all mummers*. Later, it instituted a practice of religious representation which divided up government ministries and civil service offices amongst the different religious denominations. These actions (plus the departure of many Newfoundlanders to seek work in the New England states at about this time) seemed to be effective in discouraging overt class and sectarian struggle until the turn of the century.

The *Act to Make Further Provision for the Prevention of Nuisances* which was passed on 14 June 1861 is still in effect, and states:

> Any Person who shall be found, at any Season of the Year, in any Town or Settlement in this Colony, without a written license from a magistrate, dressed as a Mummer, masked, or otherwise disguised, shall be deemed guilty of a Public Nuisance, and may be arrested by any Peace Officer, with or without a warrant, and taken before any Justice of the Peace in the District or Place where such person may be found, and on conviction, in summary manner, before such Justice, be committed to Gaol....

This suppression dealt an immediate death-blow to mummering in St. John's and Conception Bay, and within reach of official Law and Order. Outside that perimeter it quashed the more aggressive aspects of the custom, and where mummering continued, it did so meekly. The Act successfully broke the mummers and the "establishment" made sure that in future the Newfoundland theatre would stay safely behind a proscenium.

The nineteenth-century mummering tradition I've been describing involved more than just the Mummers Play itself. It was an eclectic free-for-all embracing several solstice customs. The play proper, the non-performance "guess-who-we-are" type house visitations, the throwing of flour or soot on people in the street, rigging out the Hobbyhorse to terrify passers-by, and other specific customs were as often practised together as they were separately. They were all part of "mummering," "fooling," or "janneying."

By this time the essence of the play itself lay perhaps less in its intrinsic drama than in its relationship with the audience during any particular performance. As a vehicle for "getting in the door" and performing for an upper-class audience, it could be a parade of aggressive mockery. For an audience of peers, it could be warmer and more homey.

Under suppression, mummers no longer paraded aggressively into upper-class homes, and generally abandoned overtly violent attempts at social retribution. The whole tradition became safer and more careful. And ultimately, perhaps, it became as much a victim of changing social structures as of official suppression. Within class boundaries, mummering had always nourished a collective consciousness of equality and egalitarianism. It was, as well, entertaining— a great way to have fun in small isolated communities at Christmas. These functions the custom retained after suppression. What it lost was its capacity to function as a mechanism to *enforce* such egalitarianism. As modes of production changed, Newfoundland society moved from a semifeudal structure into modern capitalism, and the "boss" became less often a resident (and therefore municipally-accessible) exploiter. Mummering was supplanted by more effective forms of social action, such as industrial unionism.

> The demise of the Feast of Fools signalled a significant change in the Western cultural mood. Its demise showed that people were beginning to see their social roles and sacred conventions through eyes that could not permit such strident social satire....Now, our feasting is sporadic or obsessive, our fantasies predictable and politically impotent. Neither provides the inspiration for genuine social transformation (Cox 1969).

As the twentieth century dawned, economic stratification in the new Dominion was secure. The control enjoyed by local capitalists over wages, working conditions, and the entire economy was ensured by the complicity of the government, which they also controlled. The gap between workers' incomes and industry profits was awesomely large. A popular resistance which had prompted demonstrations and riots for much of the earlier part of the century had been manipulated and eventually brought under control.

What was happening in the Newfoundland theatre? The suppression of mummering had successfully restricted traditional performance to outports remote from the reach of the law. In St. John's, mummers had been successfully outlawed for forty years, and the reins of Newfoundland theatre began to be taken over by the higher economic echelons of city society. Appetites were whetted by the occasional performances of British and American farces presented in the capital city by garrisoned British troops and by visiting American professional companies who sailed up from the New England states. Soon the bourgeoisie were mounting plays and operettas themselves. It was considered very chic to mount a local production of the latest Gilbert and Sullivan, or other recent hits of the London stage.

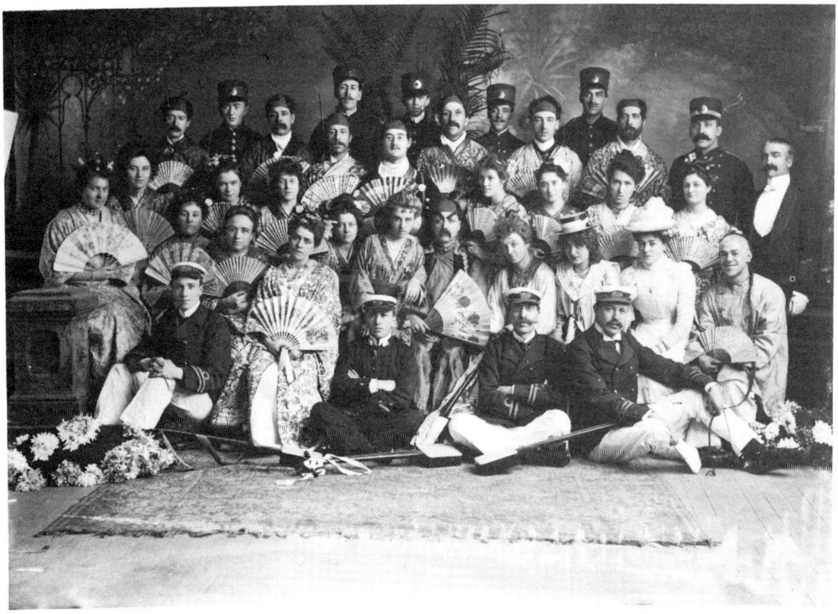

Cast of the Charles Hutton production of *The Geisha*. St. John's circa 1900. Photo: Newfoundland Archives.

After half a century of "home rule" had consolidated economic and political power in their hands, the local merchant élite now resolved to prop up their "legitimate position" with official, "legitimate" arts and culture. But as Newfoundland rounded the century, the fishocracy's right to rule was challenged on both economic and cultural fronts.

Politically, a Newfoundland labour movement was born. The working class, recognising that large economic gains had been made at its expense, and influenced by the rising tidc of North American socialism, embraced radical unionism. The movement was led by the fiery new Fishermen's Protective Union (FPU) headed by William Coaker. This, the first fishermen's organisation to be aligned along class rather than religious lines, effectively organised a large number of fishermen, challenged the entire fish marketing system, and formed a political party which nearly succeeded in gaining legislative majority.

The FPU's political tactics reinforced a *cultural* class consciousness. Elected FPU members even brought a theatrical touch to the House of Assembly. They stressed their representation of "the toilers" by sitting in the legislature wearing hand-knit fishermen's guernseys, thumbing their noses at the tie-and-tails decorum of the "merchant parties" whose MHAs they referred to as "Modified Hens' Arses."

Off the legislative stage, artistic challenges to the merchants' colonial chic proved to be as popular with working-class audiences as the union was with working-class voters. Writer James Murphy was anointed "the sealers poet" by striking FPU fishermen, who recognised in him the artistic voice of their labour struggles. And a friend of Murphy's, Johnny Burke, became a local legend in the theatre. Burke was a well-known broadside balladeer who made a precarious living by peddling songsheets of his topical and original compositions on the streets of the city. As a songwriter he was infectious, prolific, and irreverent. Many products of his satirical pen are still popular Newfoundland favourites– *The Kelligrews Soiree*, for instance, a put-down of St. John's high-society garden parties. To the casual listener today, the song may seem to be nothing more than a humorous ditty. In its own time, it was biting satire.

Burke wrote and produced many popular musicals for the St. John's stage, forming a loose semi-professional group of performers around him. Some of his favourite theatrical barbs were burlesques of the "legitimate theatre" being produced by the city's upper crust. Burke used similar (or identical) music, but replaced the original lyrics with his own, and rewrote scenes to a local setting. For example, shortly after the trendy British operetta *The Geisha* had been staged in St. John's (by Charles Hutton, later to become *Sir* Charles Hutton), Burke opened his original satire *The Topsail Geisha*. The imposition of an imported cultural model upon working-class

Newfoundland reality was clearly ridiculous, and Burke drove the point home by transforming the original Japanese chorus into Topsail fishermen. The sight of the chorus fanning themselves not with exotic oriental fans, but with dried salt fish, was the talk of the town for several years. (Seventy years later, when the Mummers Troupe restaged the scene in a musical based on Burke's life, the fish fans still raised a belly laugh of recognition from modern St. John's audiences. Proving, I suspect, that not a lot has changed about the point Burke was trying to make: culture-and-who-owns-it.)

John Burke was not what you'd call a political activist. But in the context of turn-of-the-century Newfoundland society his plays had an implicit political impact. He pricked the pretensions of the developing mercantile élite in its attempts to replace indigenous cultural expression with a highbrow "official" art. His satire was an artistic response to the tide of his times, a caricature of social and economic imbalance. Audiences loved his loaded metaphors.

Of course, as one leader of the Newfoundland Drama Festival Society sniffed half a century later: "Johnny Burke was very popular with the lower orders, but you know he was never accepted by *real* theatrical people. When visiting British and American professionals came to town they would never go to meet *him*." This may have been true. The popularity of artists like Burke and Murphy wasn't due to their ability to create paint by number copies of imported art models, but to their knack of reflecting the society in which their audiences lived, worked, and struggled. As a result, their theatre, music, and poetry weren't marginalised to "the artistic fringe." Their work was vital and direct.

Unfortunately, while they won many of their battles with ruling-class art, they eventually lost the war. The passing of the First World War sounded the death knell for the radical union movement, for the irreverent indigenous theatre championed by Burke, and seemingly for the social undercurrents which fuelled them both. The local fishocracy once again consolidated its hold. Large multinationals moved in to exploit the country's natural resources, and the new American cinema moved in to exploit the Newfoundland entertainment market. Underdevelopment remained the order of the day, both economically:

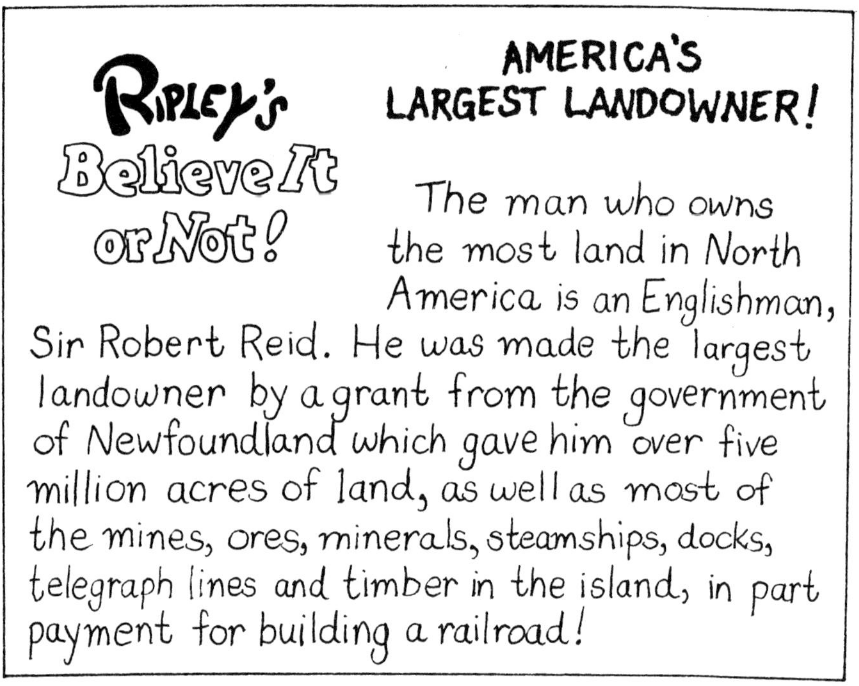

(*Ripley's Believe It or Not* 1940).

...and culturally:

AT THE POPULAR STAR TONIGHT!

Jesse Matthews in

GANGWAY.

SEE for the First Time the Big Apple Dance on the Screen by Jessie Matthews—The Dance which has Taken the USA By Storm!

Added Treats: Universal News, Cartoon.

At The Matinee Tomorrow a Picture of Charlie McCarthy Will Be Given Free to Every Child. See Him Monday in the Goldwyn Follies! (*St. John's Evening Telegram* 1938)

On the stage, Newfoundland theatre was to be dominated for over half a century by the kind of official culture which John Burke so deplored. The country's stagger into economic bankruptcy in the

1930s and the abdication of the elected government in favour of a commission of British-appointed civil servants did little to stimulate an artistic renaissance in what was, essentially, a colony once again. Newfoundland passed the next two decades under the leadership of benign bureaucrats responsible not to the Newfoundland people but to the British crown. It is hardly surprising, then, that Newfoundland entered Confederation with an (amateur) drama association interested primarily in the production of British and American plays for upper-income urban audiences. The Newfoundland Drama Festival Society found its niche as the newest member of the national Dominion Drama Festival association (DDF). Across the country the DDF with its festivals and prizes fostered a "community" amateur theatrical expression which virtually ignored Canadian history, Canadian goals, and Canadian modes of expression.

In 1951 the London Theatre Company arrived in St. John's from England for a winter stock season. This professional company, under the direction of Leslie Yeo, returned each winter to present weekly productions of imported hits ranging from *Charlie's Aunt* to *The Seven Year Itch* until the advent of local television brought about their demise in 1956. Their annual residency provided a shot in the arm for the city's flourishing amateur drama groups.

During this period amateur theatre groups per se didn't exist in outport Newfoundland, at least not in a form recognised by the Newfoundland Drama Festival Society (whose member groups represented the up-and-coming bourgeoisie of the newer industrial towns: Corner Brook, Grand Falls, and Gander, as well as St. John's). When on rare occasion a formal group sprang up outside this geography, it was generally organised by the upper strata of a community (Harbour Grace had a theatre group in the 1940s formed by the local British clergyman. In Buchans, the amateur drama group was comprised of company management personnel led by the mine manager's wife). Performance fare was chosen from standard British and American play catalogues.

Indigenous theatre survived in many smaller communities, however, via the annual Christmas Concert, although it was weakened by the proliferation of television after Confederation. The Concert, considered less pretentious than a *play*, usually involved wider community participation and featured a more original pastiche of skits and songs. One of the basic publicity lessons which the Mummers Troupe learned early on was: *never call it a play*. In many Newfoundland communities, putting up posters for a *play* will net you an audience of teachers, merchants, and the local clergyman: the community élite. A *show*, on the other hand, is considered to be quite a different matter. Miners go to see shows. Fishermen go to shows. Shows are Fun, rather than Art. You don't have to dress up in a tuxedo and gown to attend.

Throughout the 1950s and 1960s Newfoundland's registered amateur drama groups presented mostly "images of away." Tastes ranged from *Juno and the Paycock* to Broadway musicals. In 1968 *The Geisha* was staged again in St. John's. (If the ghost of Johnny Burke rolled in its grave, nobody on stage noticed.) Newfoundland writers Ted Russell and Grace Butt received occasional productions of their work, and in Corner Brook Tom Cahill successfully authored an annual "concert" type of revue. But (until the Open Group's collaboration with Michael Cook in the early '70s) Newfoundland playwrights were not the main focus of this theatre, and local plays were seen only sporadically.

The reigning stage dialect of the time was British, due perhaps to the influence of the London Players and to the expatriate Britons who dominated many of the Newfoundland Drama Society groups. At the time this didn't seem out of place. After all, it was natural for a province with an economy dominated by giant British corporations, a university dominated by British professors, and a government which had only recently emerged from the custodianship of British civil servants, to possess a drama society dominated by the British accent.

> St. Johns...is the place where Englishmen go to consolidate (Newfoundland novelist, Margaret Duley).

The situation often made peculiar demands upon local playwrights. Example: in the 1960s, Newfoundland writer Helen Porter approached the local CBC Radio drama department with an original drama script set in St. John's. The script was accepted—but on condition that the play's setting be changed to an *English* city, removing the script's immediacy for a Newfoundland audience. The reason? The local amateur actors to be employed for the production all had British accents. So deeply engrained was the colonial consciousness reigning in the Newfoundland theatre of the 1960s that the playwright obligingly altered her play.

It was a consciousness which placed no great importance upon the idea of theatre reflecting its own society. It encouraged instead a theatre aspiring to imported models of form, content and excellence; a theatre that stressed achievement, never purpose.

With so much activity in amateur theatre, one might have expected audiences to demand more homegrown material. They didn't. There were at least two reasons for this. One was the audience. The

Newfoundland Drama Society's hometown spectators were drawn, by and large, from the same social strata as the players, completing a self-sufficient charmed circle. Post-Confederation Newfoundland was awhirl with rapid social change, but it was not the newer industrial towns which were caught in the undertow. It was rural Newfoundland. The amateur groups of the 1950s and 1960s did not tour the outports, and their middle-class urban audiences, busy climbing the socioeconomic ladder, made few demands upon their theatre to address local issues. Instead they tried on plays from London and New York like the latest fall fashions, preferring a display behind the proscenium to a dialogue across the footlights. If the Newfoundland theatre was to change substantially, the pressure would have to come from a different audience.

The second reason had to do with Smallwood's Miracle.

> Miracles we saw every day—we couldn't help seeing them; they were all about us—as the benign air of Confederation breathed over us: the miracle of shopkeepers' shelves and floors filled to overcrowding with clothes and shoes and bicycles and toys, with women in tens of thousands crowding into the shops, the old men and women too, all with their Canadian cheques...coming out with armfuls of goods and happy faces....It was wonderful. It was glorious. It warmed our hearts. We felt that Newfoundland was beginning to get somewhere (Smallwood 1975).

The first twenty years of Confederation changed Newfoundland society enormously. Culturally, Newfoundlanders were bombarded by the North American media. From childrens' schoolbooks to television, a whole arsenal of cultural weaponry threw up images of North American lifestyles as romantic as Cinderella's slipper, but with a distinctly poorer fit. Newfoundland's own culture was virtually trampled to death in the stampede to create pliable consumers for the North American market. It was a kind of mass brainwashing: if they think right, they'll buy right—right?

> Confederation stopped our history dead in its tracks and set it on an altogether different course... (Smallwood 1979).

The result was confusion and insecurity. Hell, Shake and Bake didn't even work properly in a coal, oil and wood range. Newfoundlanders could see that they weren't the ideal Dick and Janes of the Pepsi generation. Why was this? The superculture told us why: because we were second best. We were second-class Canadians (which we imagined as something roughly equivalent to third-class Americans). We were a joke. It became an embarrassment to admit that your father was a fisherman, or to be caught tapping your toes to Newfoundland music. We were a textbook case: a small society being eaten by a larger one, steamrollered into compliance by a sophisticated cultural delivery system.

The Newfoundland government decided to assist this delivery system in the performing arts. Convinced by now that Real Culture was something which originated outside Newfoundland, they apparently reasoned that if Newfoundlanders could have better access to it, they would become sophisticated enough to claim their North American birthright without shuffling their feet too much. After all, a sophisticated Newf can't be a joke, right?

Anyone who has seen the old *Mondo Cane* films or has made it through an introductory anthropology course is familiar with the Cargo Cults discovered amongst certain Micronesian natives. Some isolated parts of Papua New Guinea and nearby islands had not encountered white men until the time of the Second World War. Suddenly primitive tribesmen were confronted with whites. They took them to be virtual gods, not least because these white gods were periodically visited by great roaring silver birds which landed and disgorged all sorts of great riches. The natives reasoned that if they could attract these great birds to land in their own villages,

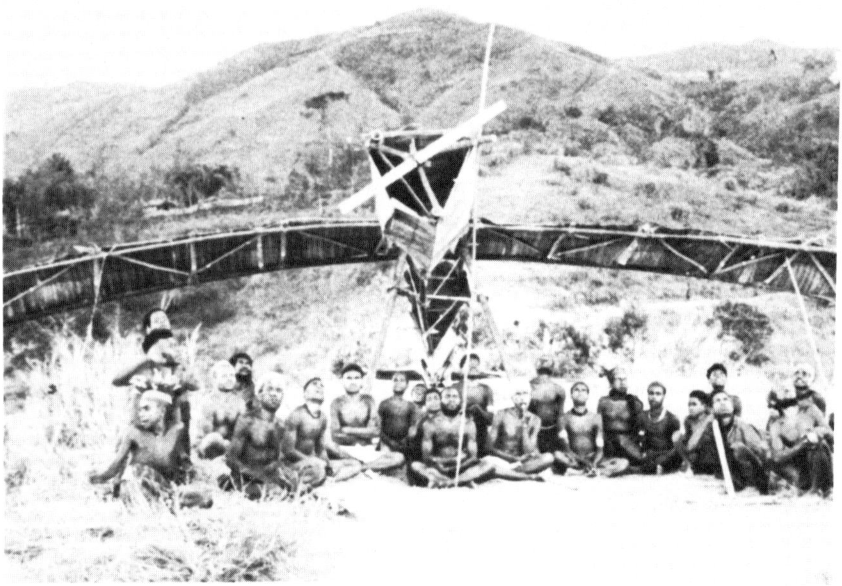

A Cargo Cult. Cult followers with model of airplane. Papua, New Guinea circa 1957.
Source unknown.

then surely all those mixmasters and toasters would be disgorged to them too. And so they cleared jungle airstrips, built big bamboo aeroplane models, and patiently waited in the bushes hoping that their models would function like duck decoys to attract the planes. Some Cargo Cults also believed that when the great silver planes landed, their own black skins would fall away and they would become white as the gods.

The Newfoundland government developed this idea into a sort of Cultural Cargo Cult. During the late 1960s they began to erect a series of Arts and Culture Centres across the island, designed less to accommodate the needs of local amateur theatre groups than to attract large touring companies from outside the province who would disgorge their artistic avoirdupois to culturally impoverished Newfoundlanders. To run these distribution outlets, the Smallwood government established a departmental Division of Cultural Affairs and endowed it with an annual operating budget of over $4 million ($9.4 million by 1988). It appointed John Perlin, scion of a mercantile family from the St. John's "family compact" to be Director of Cultural Affairs for the province. Mr. Perlin also happened to have been the treasurer of the Newfoundland Drama Festival Society. The

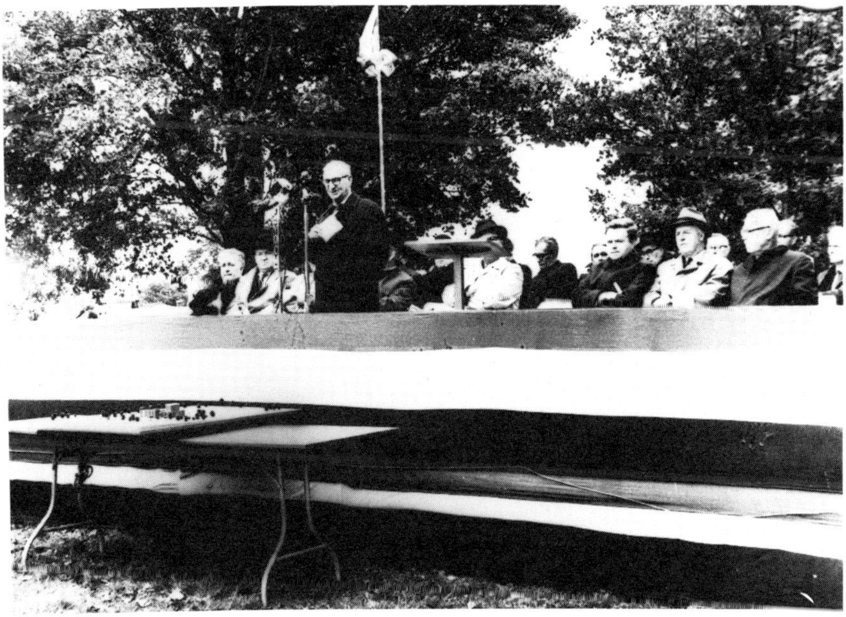

A Cargo Cult. Premier Joseph R. Smallwood with some local chiefs at sod-turning ceremony for St. John's Arts and Culture Centre, with model of Centre on table in front (1966).
Photo: *Evening Telegram.*

new director furnished his office with photographs of himself meeting Prince Philip, and began to dispense a brand of culture compatible with the decor. Under his guidance during the 1970s, Newfoundland became the only province whose government mounted, financed, produced, and toured an annual season of second-string British plays, with entire British stock company casts flown in especially from the Mother Country.

Despite the initial feasting, dancing and political speeches hailing the new cultural millennium for Newfoundland theatre, the Newfoundland Drama Festival Society itself became a casualty of this building boom. Previously member groups had performed in moderately sized, low-rent venues. Now, overextending themselves to pay a high rent, fill a sixty-foot picture frame proscenium with action and a thousand-seat auditorium with bottoms, some of the more vibrant amateur groups sickened and died. Those which survived took a decade to recover their former vitality.

The five Arts and Culture Centres exemplify a cultural superstition that permeates our society from the school system to the Stratford Festival: that *real* art, proper art, doesn't have much to do with local, regional, or national characteristics; that the best art has "universal artistic value." The classics, for example, are considered to have this pristine quality. They have it, apparently, in spite of the weather, in spite of the size, class or racial composition of their audience, the price of tickets, or even a revolution in progress outside the auditorium. Universal art is the intellectual counterpart of political tyranny: if you don't like the show then there's something wrong with *you*.

In practice, it justifies a marketing process which seeks to move the cultural information in one direction: from those who apparently have it to those poor deprived souls who apparently don't have it. Who has it? The *cognoscenti* of the entrenched social order. Who doesn't have it? The "lower classes" who are too stunned to realise that their artistic tastes are inferior.

Whose interests does this serve?

From inception, the majority of the Arts and Culture Centres were seldom well attended, and many working-class Newfoundlanders wouldn't be seen dead in the places. Not because miners, fishermen, loggers and longshoremen are uncultured dunces too boorish to properly appreciate art, but because it's perfectly obvious for whom the plays, the ballet, the opera and the symphony are primarily designed.

Who pays for these grandiose, expensive monuments? Taxpayers in 724 communities throughout Newfoundland and Labrador. What do the taxpayers in 719 of those communities get for their money? Nothing.

A people with a devalued sense of their own identity become malleable. Without a clear awareness of who they are and where they came from, they cannot know where they are going.

In the years following Confederation, Newfoundland jammed its foot into the Cinderella slipper and marched forth on the road to prosperity, North American style. Pretty soon it fell flat on its face. The new provincial government had plunged the economy into a programme of industrial development based on Upper-Canadian urban models which proved to be quite impractical for Newfoundland's resource base.

> We'll dot Conception Bay with factories. People are beginning to catch on—after all, you can't say "No" to Santa Claus! (J.R. Smallwood in Gwyn 1968).

Traditional resource industries such as the fishery were actively dismantled and over three hundred communities were erased through the now infamous Resettlement Programme (a programme which the government once boasted as "50 per cent successful"). Fishermen and their families were resettled to "Growth Centres" where they were to provide the labour pool for a smorgasbord of new industries: a chocolate factory, a shoe factory, a battery factory, a hockey stick plant, and more. The majority of the new industries failed, leaving growth centres to subsist on unemployment and welfare payments. A series of shady characters and fast-buck entrepreneurs made quick and tidy fortunes from all this and retired to condominiums in Costa Rica. The social and economic dislocation produced by these banana-republic manoeuvres was borne by the least powerful and least privileged sectors of the population. Confederation, however, had brought contact with the Canadian labour movement, and "international" (i.e. American) unions began to organise the workforce. In 1959, the first major strike in 50 years involving the island's largest industry (by now no longer fishing but pulp and paper manufacturing) became a pivotal test of labour's growing power. It was brutally broken by the intervention of the Smallwood government, which summarily decertified the striking International Woodworkers of America and set up its own pro-company union as a replacement. The warning to the rest of the Newfoundland labour movement was clear: back off. As a result, the gap between industry profits and real benefit to Newfoundland workers continued to widen for another decade.

By 1970 there was a growing feeling that reality was out of sync. Economic frustration and cultural confusion coincided. The turn of the century had spawned a radical unionism and a politicised theatre; the turn of the '70s witnessed a similar phenomenon. As the Smallwood government was toppled from its twenty-year rule, a revitalised Newfoundland labour movement began to make up for lost time. A series of bitter and violent strikes followed. A new fishermen's union, the Newfoundland Federation of Fishermen and Allied Workers, was formed and soon became one of the most powerful and progressive unions in the Atlantic area.

There was an electricity in the air. An indigenous cultural revival began to stir. And a new Newfoundland theatre movement was born.

Illegal Acts 4

> The Political potential of the arts...is the effort to find forms of communication that may break the oppressive rule of the established language and images over the mind and body of man— languages and images which have long since become a means of domination, indoctrination, and deception.
>
> Herbert Marcuse

The Mummers Troupe staggered into existence in the fall of 1972. Lynn and I spent the summer fishing out of Petty Harbour and trying to find people, money and a rehearsal space.

On the people side it was difficult. I wanted a group of actors who would be able to work together full-time (everyone trying to pay their grocery bills via part-time outside jobs would have created six tired people unable to coordinate their free time). This was impossible for most members of the Newfoundland amateur theatre community who already held full-time day jobs. There was no professional theatre in the province, and therefore no professional performers floating around. A small summer touring company, the Newfoundland Travelling Theatre, had formed two months earlier to travel British farces around Bonavista and Conception Bays, but it finished up in September and its actors, mostly students, had gone back to university. Anyone experienced was unavailable, and anyone available was inexperienced. But John Doyle, and later Kevin Pittman, agreed to join Lynn and me. We were a small group, but we started work. A few other people drifted by to watch what we were doing; most drifted away again.

We scored a little better with rehearsal space. I convinced the University Extension service to hire me as an artist in residence in the small community of Quidi Vidi, within St. John's city limits. The residency gave me the use of the tiny village church for weekday rehearsals, providing I taught community workshops on weeknights and Saturdays. It was a nice open space with lots of light— a good place to build group performance skills before heading out into the real world of audiences.

On the financial front, there was never a dull moment. From the beginning we saw that we had two choices regarding salaries. We could ask people to work on a pie-in-the-sky basis while we hoped for a government grant, or we could pool our personal finances and provide a performers' payroll from the beginning. We chose the second. Actors would be paid, establishing responsibilities for both employer and employee both. A principle which the Troupe tenaciously upheld throughout its life was that artists should not be expected to work for free.

Initially, we established a kitty and ran it according to Marx: "From each according to his abilities, to each according to his needs." I put my university salary into the pot, John Doyle contributed some of his private income, and we decided that each member of the group would take out of the kitty whatever amount he or she needed to survive on a weekly basis. What the system lacked in cash, it made up in idealism. It worked for several months, but idealism bit the dust one morning when Sandy Cantwell walked into rehearsal with a new pair of shoes. Sandy was one of the drift-in drift-out people. So was Sam Hedge. Sam challenged the purchase:

SAM: You bought new shoes!

SANDY: Yeah. Nice, eh?

SAM: So. How much did you take out of the kitty last week?

SANDY: Fifty dollars.

SAM: Fifty Dollars! Hell, I only took out twenty, and my boots are in worse shape than your old ones! If anyone around here needs new clogs, its me!

SANDY: Look. I was feeling really low last week. Buying these shoes cheered me up. I needed to buy them. It was important to me.

SAM: Bullshit! Here I was making a sacrifice, going without, taking a miserable twenty bucks while you're living high on the hog!

SANDY: The hell I am! Who are you to dictate my lifestyle?

The whole day's rehearsal was spent arguing about a pair of thirty-dollar shoes. After that, we decided that the kitty should be divided into equal weekly salaries regardless of need, ability, or Marx. What the new arrangement lacked in idealism it made up in rehearsal time.

From the beginning we set up our kitty as a nonprofit, registered charity. It seemed like a useful legal structure to have in place: in the unlikely event that some philanthropist decided to adopt us we could at least provide a tax-deductible receipt for his donation. Naturally, the legalities of registration required that we have a name.

This stopped us in our tracks at first. We didn't want a name. Names imply organisational rigidity, we thought. Someone suggested a compromise: have a name to start with, but change it every month. That seemed like a good idea. But it didn't cut any mustard with the officials at the Registry of Companies. So we gave in, and registered our little kitty as the Resource Foundation for the Arts. It sounded a little grand. Never mind, we consoled ourselves, the theatre group itself could technically be separate. And it wouldn't have to have any name. It could just be "a project" of the Foundation. For the next four years, it was the *only* project of the Foundation.

John, Lynn and I listed ourselves as corporate directors. There was a method to our madness. I very much wanted to avoid the traditional approach to theatre funding, that is: setting up a board of big businessmen, politicians and professionals who then employ their "old boy" network to raise funds. I had worked in professional theatres on the mainland long enough to see how the ideology of such an establishment board of directors ultimately dictates artistic policy. The kind of theatre I wanted to build would never survive that process. It seemed to me that those who were responsible artistically should be responsible financially and corporately. If this meant that we would be poorer, well then, we'd be poorer.

We were poorer. I don't know about others in the group, but during that first year Lynn and I lived mostly on soupbones and old leftover produce that a friendly supermarket employee gave us for free.

Since none of the people floating through the theatre company had much performance experience, all of our early activity was put into training. I was looking for an indigenous acting style. Like the Inuit approach to sculpture, which seeks less to "create" than to liberate the spirit already existing in the stone, I wanted our work to be more a matter of recovery than of invention. Whatever the Newfoundland performance style was, I felt that it was closer to recitation, song, Christmas Concert skits and mummering than to the elocution and character study of colonial melodrama.

We worked eight hours daily, and on Saturdays and weeknights I ran workshops for the village community. Things were happening in the real world outside the rehearsal hall, but as a group we felt unskilled and unable to respond to them adequately. Once, during a projectionists' strike at local cinemas, in frustration we grabbed some old puppets and improvised an agitprop we titled *The Coronation of Cecil B. DeMille* in a shopping mall. We intended it as a strike support piece, but it was a failure: sloppy, preachy and pretentious. Passers-by thought we were just another bunch of hippies doing silly street theatre. They were right. We went back to our exercises.

Our workshop needed a focus: some structure to hang the exercises on. I was curious about the old Newfoundland Mummers Play. It hadn't been performed on the island for over fifty years, and it seemed important to investigate it. Best of all, it was appropriate to a group of only four actors. Lynn, John, and Kevin agreed, and so in early November 1972 we plunged into it. It was a key decision, the starting point of what was to become our company style.

At first, we were frustrated to find that the kind of information we wanted didn't exist. Newfoundland folklorists and sociologists had paid scant attention to the Mummers Play itself, preferring to focus on some of the more accessible (non-play) aspects of mummering which survived longer into the current century. As a result, little more than written accounts of the dialogue existed. The four of us read the script, but it was like looking at a dismembered corpse: we could see arms and legs, but had no idea how it danced.

A much larger collection of folklore study existed regarding the Mummers Play as it was found in England, but it too focused on script details, and most of the published studies wound up in the same blind alley, arguing footnotes and word variations here or there. But the Mummers Play was essentially a performance tradition, not a literary one, so we began to track down anyone who could describe the actual performance.

This wasn't easy, either. In most of Newfoundland the play hadn't been seen in a hundred years. In the few communities where it did survive official suppression and twentieth century social change, it was finally finished off by the First World War.

> Most of 'em what used to do it around here went to war, my son, and never come back....

In 1972 there were less than two dozen Newfoundlanders still living who had actually seen the Mummers Play in performance.

They were hard to find, but Lynn Lunde and I managed to meet and interview several of them in Port Kirwan on the Southern Shore. We consumed dozens of cups of tea collecting every scrap of information we could. Their prodigious memories astounded me. They were part of that vanishing generation of Newfoundlanders who, unable to rely on the artificial memory of pen, paper, and tape recorder, developed their own powers of recall to a degree incredible to my generation of literate cripples. Here were men who had watched the play during only three or four Christmasses as children, yet sixty years later they could repeat (almost word-perfectly) every line of dialogue. Their recollections were invaluable, and I shall always be indebted to Messrs. Paddy Reddy, Nicks Neil, Mick Finlay and John Brothers for patiently passing on to me the last vestiges of the oral tradition. (All of our informants were men. Traditionally, the play was exclusively men's work, although in our own revivals, we dropped this principle.)

Had we started to explore the Mummers Play only a few years later, some of our most vital information would have passed forever with these fine gentlemen who had for so many years preserved it carefully in their memories. More than just reciting dialogue, they conveyed a sense of the *setting* of the play, and the ways in which the performance was sometimes changed, on the spot, in houses of particular interest. Uncle Mick Finlay, who at the age of 92 may then have been the last living Newfoundlander to have performed the role of Father Christmas in the play, was particularly helpful in recounting some of his own satirical improvisations in those houses which he felt deserved community censure. He also explained how the hobbyhorse was integrated into the Port Kirwan version of the play, and I later structured our own horse routine after his example.

The hobbyhorse was known to be one of the most fearsome of all mummers rigs. I have never been able to locate an original horse which survived the ravages of both time and firewood shortages, but I'm convinced that somewhere, in a dusty corner of some Newfoundland attic, a forgotten stallion is waiting to jump out and sink his teeth into an unsuspecting folklorist.

We carefully made our own horse, guided by a couple of models we'd seen in the University Folklore Department and by detailed verbal descriptions. Kevin chopped a junk of wood to the shape of the head, Lynn found fur and fabric for the face and body, and I set the hobnail teeth in the snapping jaw. The jaw is the most important part of the assembly: it must make the proper "snock" sound when the string is pulled. The total effect is extremely eerie. The horse's basic purpose is to chase and terrify; in close quarters it is quite effective.

It is the only traditional folk puppet to be found in Newfoundland. Similar versions can be found in many parts of the world, and it has a long history, going back to the ancient practice of dressing in the skins of animals in order to take on the power and virility associated with the animal. In some Newfoundland communities it was known as a hobby-bull, and constructed with horns. On occasion, a real animal's skull would be used for the head to make it more horrible. In the Ferryland and Tors Cove area the head was wooden, but the jaw was cut much larger than usual "so when you caught someone, you could get a man's whole shoulder into its jaws, see?"

We found that using the hobbyhorse is an art in itself. For the actor inside the puppet, the secret was to go into a neutral state and let the horse guide *him*. As the animal's personality came out in rehearsals, we were fascinated. It played well with other characters, but it constantly threatened to go out of control, balancing precariously between sly submission and manic lunges at the audience. It surprised us by showing a flair for comedy. Later, in performance, it showed a flair for passion as well. It made sexual advances to spectators. It was a remarkable sight. Even more remarkable was the discovery that spectators often made unprompted sexual advances to the horse first. We shouldn't have been surprised. Historically, such animal representations were considered to be fertility symbols. In olden times, the hobbyhorse was also used to sniff out sin in a house. The remains of this solstice custom still survive in the modern Santa's question: "...and have you been a good boy this year?" Our horse was certainly inquisitive, and could be quite vengeful if crossed.

I believe that none of these were qualities we imposed upon our hobbyhorse. They were the personality traits which the puppet already had; the sorts of things it was long ago designed to do.

We explored the whole play in similar fashion, feeling out the operational dynamics of each entrance, each encounter, each character. The process was like theatrical archaeology. We tried using the basic rhyming dialogue as a springboard for improvisation, for taking risks, with the idea that we could at any time return to the safety of the set plot action if necessary. It turned out to be a weird mix of Kabuki, Commedia, and Brecht: slapstick archetypal characters, sacred and profane at the same time. It was like watching Jesus tell dirty jokes. The theatrical style which developed out of this, over the next few years, became our company trademark. It shunned an "illusion of real life" in favour of a presentational style of acting which relied more upon gesture, action, and proximity to the audience than upon props, costumes and naturalistic detail.

After a few weeks it became obvious that there was only so much we could explore without an audience. So we decided to take our Mummers Play door-to-door in St. John's over the twelve nights of the upcoming Christmas. John was the Turkish Knight, Kevin the King George, Lynn the Doctor and I the Father Christmas (not the kindly modern Santa but the stern, older, European model. In the Newfoundland play he wore a black mask and punished people). Tom Sexton came by after school to join in rehearsals as Beelzebub. We would be the first mummers seen in the city for more than a hundred years.

Five days before Christmas I had a phone call from the Chief of Police. He had somehow heard of our intentions and was anxious to make us aware of the law prohibiting mummering. I remonstrated with him. Eventually he agreed not to hassle us as long as we only called on houses of people we knew. I lied through my teeth and assured him we wouldn't knock on any strange doors. We geared up for a Boxing Night opening.

We had absolutely no idea whether our experiment would work, whether city-dwellers in the 1970s would open their doors to us. But there were a couple of things working in our favour. Despite its slow slide into Upper-Canadian chic, St. John's was not yet Toronto, and Christmas was and is still a twelve-day affair, with rounds of partying until Epiphany. And although most twentieth-century townies had never seen a mummer in their lives, I hoped we could count on the heritage hangover: the name "mummer" was still in most people's vocabulary, and it suggested certain responsibilities. You weren't really supposed to turn mummers away at Christmas. People would feel badly if they refused us.

It worked. Scrooge and King Wenceslas had prepared the way for us. They had established the Christmas principle: that Merry Gentlemen should let nothing them dismay; their doors should be open to strangers. And strange we were, with our rude rags and bags and rigadoos and faces blackened with burnt cork. At any other time of the year people would probably have called the cops. As it was, our refusal rate that Christmas, and each following Christmas, was pretty low. Fewer than one in ten houses turned us away.

This getting-in-the-door business proved to be the crucial element of the exercise. We chose our houses by cruising the city streets and looking for telltale signs of revelry. Extra cars parked outside, lots of lights, and silhouettes fogging the window with an alcoholic haze were sure clues to a house party in progress. At first we made the mistake of all trooping up to the front step at once and knocking politely at the door.

Yes?
Any mummers allowed in?
Oh. Mummers. Oh. What do you want?
To come in and do our rhymes.

Oh. But we're having a party.
That's why we came.
Well...do we know you?
Probably not.
Oh...well...I don't know...perhaps I should ask the wife...

This was a bad idea. If we sang we were taken for carollers, given an apple and expected to go away. If we didn't sing, we appeared ominous and people said there were too many of us (five mummers?). Later we realised that this door-dealing was Father Christmas's job. The play, after all, gave him the first entrance, and people felt less threatened in dealing with one mummer at a time. The rest of us would wait in the van while he clinched the deal.

Lee Campbell, who played the role in 1974, was probably the best door-opener we ever had. He didn't smile, wheedle, waste time or drop out of character. A big, stern mountain of rags fiercely painted with burnt cork and bedecked with sleigh bells, he would pound on the door with his staff: three solid, slow, heavy knocks. It sounded like an RCMP dope bust.

Y-yes?
We're the mummers. We're coming in. Any objections?
Oh. Well...I guess not, then.

Lee then woke up the entire neighbourhood with a blast on his bugle (the signal to us, waiting), and marched in immediately to size up the situation and clear a performance space, swinging his lantern like a censer, archbishop of the secular Christmas mass. The play gave him traditional lines for the purpose:

...Room, room, gallants, room!
Room required here tonight!
For some of my bold champions
Are coming forth to fight!....

And we tumbled in the door behind him. At this point in any performance of the play, the actors already have the upper hand. By inviting strangers into the house, homeowners have accepted the mummers' active role as performers and their own comparatively passive role as audience. Everyone in the house is caught with their

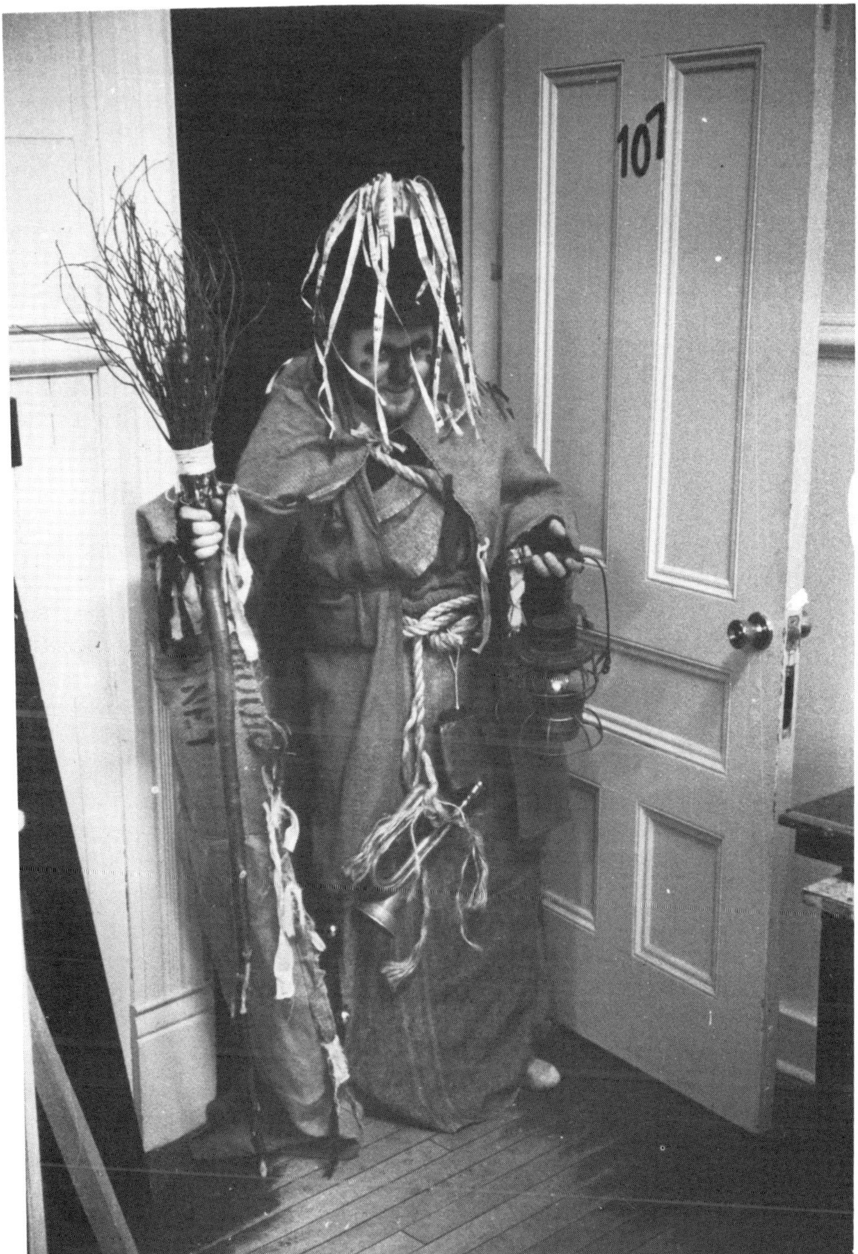

Lee J. Campbell as Father Christmas. Christmas 1974.
Photo: Chris Brookes.

mouth open, flabbergasted to find a show unfolding in the middle of their living room. It's a great opening. People rush for seats and crowd in from the kitchen to see what's happening. There's certainly no trouble holding their attention. On the other hand, the performers have to adapt immediately to a completely unknown territory: the size and shape of the room, the number, identity, and degree of sobriety of the spectators, delicate bits of furniture, the Christmas tree, the television, the stereo, the chip-dip and possibly the savage family dog. It's always instant improvisation and an acting challenge, a matter of accepting unexpected elements and *using*, not avoiding them. Example: the Turkish Knight, winding up his dying soliloquy of gurgles and groans, is startled when the telephone suddenly rings right next to him. Turk: "...and if that's my wife on the phone, tell her I won't be home tonight!" and dies.

We found that the essence of the Mummers Play lies in its proximity to the audience. It would never work on a stage. It thrives on being outrageous, on the taking of liberties, on toying with that elemental act of surrender within the actor-spectator relationship: *the audience will let you do anything if it is part of the show.* They will let you juggle their priceless collection of glassware, and the more daring and skilful you are the more they will love it. Of course, if you drop anything then you're in real trouble. Mummers are priests, not thugs. The performance is a ritual desanctifying of the house, an exorcism of the spirits of stuffiness, of sameness and safety and decorum which have accumulated in the home like dust balls all year.

We made a point of being as noisy and as boisterous as possible, improvising extra props out of whatever or whomever was lying around, taking verbal cracks at any members of the Board of Trade we thought were present, and clobbering everybody on the head with fool's bladders (pig's bladders, blown up, dried and filled with peas).

There were plenty of shows where normally docile family pets threw themselves like kamikazis at our hobbyhorse, and one where a woman actually chased it out the door and around the block for accidentally biting her breast with its hobnail teeth. There were many occasions when the call for a doctor to cure the slain warrior brought forth a lineup of real doctors who happened to be present, and who challenged our Doctor's diagnosis of "the most deadly disease known to mankind...Death!" There was a house which stalled us at the door until they could count the number of men in our group, and ultimately let us in only after making sure that their menfolk outnumbered us in case we should turn rowdy. Unbelievably tiny spaces— crowded kitchens with hot stoves— showed us that picture-frame stage conventions didn't exist for this play. When the characters had no chance to hide and make a clean surprise entrance, they could hang about in full view, fooling around and enlisting supporters so that when they finally made their entrance, they got cheered and booed like boxers entering a ring. Once a "ghost" rushed out of a back bedroom wrapped in a sheet and happily joined in the play. Occasionally the audience unexpectedly included a well-known political or economic mandarin; then our lines became *really* impromptu.

We mummered taverns and restaurants and the airport (the dead man went round and round on the luggage carousel). We mummered Portuguese fishing trawlers in the harbour, where the show worked despite the language barrier, and sat around afterwards drinking wine and singing *fado* songs with the crew. We even mummered a city bus. (There's an old Henny Youngman joke about the man who hails a New York cab and asks the driver to take him "to one of those new experimental off-off-Broadway theatres." Driver: "You're in one.") The characters each waited at different bus stops and deposited their fare as they made their entrance: "In Comes I, King George the Bold...." When the bus got stalled in traffic, some frantic improvising was required to fill the time until it finally reached the Doctor's stop.

We were a hit. We started at 8 p.m. each night and usually pulled off four to six performances before 1 a.m. Sometimes if the city was alive we "walloped 'er down" until the dawn hours. After each house show we sang and played music "for a scuff" and were pressed with drinks. We had two ways of finishing the show. In some houses we finished "straight." But in homes where we felt that a special performance magic had been achieved, we presented a small lit candle and recited an old mummers blessing:

Now may this Bless your Hearth and Fold;
Shut out the Wolf and keep out the Cold;
Take care of your Fire and Candle
And be of Good Cheer,
And may Peace and Joy be with you
Throughout the whole New Year.

Personally, I believe such blessings work, when they are properly invoked. Once I placed a mummers curse on a house which threw us out ungraciously in midperformance. I believe that worked, too.

We came to know a lot about patterns of partying in St. John's, and acquired a smorgasbord approach to choosing neighbourhoods: "What do we feel like tonight, boys—beer and cheesies, or wine and paté?" Bembo Davies, playing the Doctor in 1974, advanced the gastronomic theory of mummering, which was that the play provided his character with a late entrance purely to allow him to hide in the kitchen for a while and check out the eats in the fridge (see Appendix III).

In swanky homes we often noticed that our performances were politely tolerated rather than appreciated. We didn't match the decor. We made the hosts uneasy, as if at any moment we might steal the silverware.

> Howard, who ARE these people?
> It's all right, dear. Just give them a bottle of wine and they'll go away.

This ran to a pattern; in middle- and lower-income homes it never happened. I think it was primarily a reaction to mummering itself, rather than to our particular performance. For some Newfoundlanders, mummering still seems vaguely subversive.

For the twelve nights of our first mummering Christmas, we tried hard to blend the old magic of solstice ritual with a more contemporary magic of theatre performance. Sometimes, amongst a handful of people in a small room at Christmas, it was fine magic indeed. Thereafter, we went mummering every Christmas until the company died in 1982. What was the purpose of this exercise? There were several.

For the theatre company, it offered a challenge to the creeping careerism and mindset of the bourgeois theatre attitudes which dominate our profession. We were able to meet our audiences in their homes, on a more intimate level than was ever possible in a theatre during the rest of the year. It turned out to be a very practical public relations gesture. A chance mummering in 1975 led to the commissioning of our *Price of Fish* show; on another occasion an accountant offered to give the company's books a free annual audit. It provided excellent research opportunities, too. Often, after seeing our act, some elderly spectator in the room would talk about other paratheatrical rituals they remembered. What better way to find out that people in Bay Bulls practised the old St. Stephens Day Hunting the Wren custom with a seagull; that until the RCMP clamped down on them a few years ago, young janneys in Whitbourne used to chase each other with whips; or that one long-ago night in Pouch Cove someone's great-grandfather lost an eye while playing the part of the Doctor?

For our audiences, we offered a refreshing antidote to a Christmas and an entertainment industry ruled by cold commercialism, and a reminder of how our deeper traditions have been warped by a culture which worships consumerism. Our Christmas audiences were often astounded that house mummers had something to *give*, rather than just barging in to take a free drink. Most importantly, we allowed modern city dwellers to see where elements of their culture came from, to realise that their heritage is not dull and dusty and outclassed by "commercial entertainment" and American television programmes, but is exciting and meaningful and fun. Our house performances got Bing Crosby off the stereo and people on their feet to sing a traditional ballad or deliver a recitation.

Any political theatre which intends to really *move* its audience (I am referring to activism, not emotionalism), over the long term and on a wide social level, must seek a language not just of issues and ideology, but of ritual and ceremony rooted in a collective consciousness beyond language. It does not need to preach political awareness; it simply needs to dust off the awareness which already exists.

THE DOCTOR

(a typical traditional version)

FATHER XMAS: Doctor!

Doctor! come with speed, help me in my time of need. My time of need I do implore, I was never in such need before.

Is there never a doctor can be found to cure my son of his deadly wound?

DOCTOR: Yes, there is a doctor to be found to cure thy son of his deadly wound.

XMAS: Five pounds for a doctor!

DOCTOR: That won't do.

XMAS: Ten pounds for a doctor.

DOCTOR: Won't do.

XMAS: What *is* your fee, then?

DOCTOR: Thirty pounds is my fee, but you being a poor man, I'll throw off a farthing. That'll make it twenty-nine pounds, nineteen shillings, eleven-pence ha'penny.

THE DOCTOR

(as played by John Doyle in the 1976 Mummers Troupe production)

FATHER XMAS: Five pounds for a doctor!

DOCTOR: Won't come. Besides the pound is down lately.

XMAS: Well then, ten dollars.

DOCTOR: You realise, of course, that this is a house call.

XMAS: Fifty dollars!

DOCTOR: Saddle my horse, Jack, I'll be gone.

XMAS: Well, what *is* your fee, then?

DOCTOR: I'll tell you, if you're talking $100,000 a year plus guaranteed income supplements you wouldn't exactly be whistling in the dark.

XMAS: I suppose we don't have much choice.

In comes I, the Doctor!

XMAS: What diseases can you cure?

DOCTOR: I can cure the itch, the stitch, the palsy and the gout the raging pain within and without. If the devil's in a man I can drive him out. Why I once cured Sir Harry of the dreadful avarice....

XMAS: How come you by your knowledge?

DOCTOR: By my travels.

XMAS: Where have you travelled?

DOCTOR: Icaly, Picaly, France and Spain, around the world and back again.

I, in my time, many thousands directed, and likewise many more disected.

I'll give a coward a heart if he be willing, will make him stand without fear of killing.

Any man who's got a scolding spouse, and wearies him living in the house, I'm the one to make her civil, or else I'll send her to the devil.

XMAS: Can you cure this man?

DOCTOR: Of course I can cure him, with my ink-a-tink, wonderful white drops of life.

XMAS: Show us your medicine!

DOCTOR: I have here, in the waist-band of my breeches...a little bottle called hectum spectum high generosity, some hare's grease and mare's grease in a bird's blether, minced up with a hen's tooth and a cat's feather. the wig of a weasel, the wool of a frog, and eighteen inches of September fog.

DOCTOR: You can bet your MCP card on that, friend. In comes I, the Doctor! Hit it, Geoff!

(Accordion strikes up "Be Kind to Your Web-footed Friends")

DOCTOR: I can cure all aches and pains, cramps and sprains, hiccups, bellyaches and migraines; hipsy, pipsy, palsy, gout, raging pain within and without– if the Devil's in a man I can drive him out. And if there's any young ladies here down from Toronto would like to try a little of my inky-tinky, white drops of life...

XMAS: Wait a minute. How came you to be a doctor?

DOCTOR: By my travels, of course.

XMAS: Yeah? Where have you travelled?

DOCTOR: Oh, Icaly, Picaly, France and Spain, Saskatoon and back again. And I stayed in youth hostels the whole time and saved a bundle, too.

XMAS: Er...Doctor, there's a dead man here.

DOCTOR:

(heading over to a spectator)

Yes, so I see. Very serious case. He's gone a bit off, too. I'd say he departed about a week ago, by the smell of him. The eyes have clouded over, too...

XMAS: *Not* that man...

DOCTOR: Ah. Sorry, there. It must be the aftershave. Old-Spice, is it, sir? Really very nice. Really.

Put this into a bottomless skillet, boil it over a slow turf fire, knock it ninety-nine times against the walls of Jerusalem, first found out by old Methusalem, whose wife was sick and in great pain— I made her rise and walk again! She lived and bore children seven, and when she died she went to heaven.

Now, sir! Three drops to his temple and one to the crack-bone of his heart. I strikes a light on his whole body and he'll move one leg already!

XMAS: So he did, Doctor!

DOCTOR: Rise up, bold champion and play thy part!

XMAS:...*this* man, here, lying on the floor.

DOCTOR: Oh. *This* man. I saw him when I came in, but I thought he was just enjoying the party.

XMAS: He's passed *on*, not out.

DOCTOR: So you say. Well, obviously the first thing we have to do is confirm the diagnosis.

(pulls blanks pistol out of his pocket and shoots the body)

Yes, you were right there. He's dead, alright. Now we can get on with the treatment. Let's see...a stiff. Haven't seen one of these since medical school, you know. Quite a challenge, death. The most deadly disease known to mankind...

XMAS: What do you intend to do about it?

DOCTOR: Why, take his pulse, of course. Do you have a watch?

XMAS: Sure. A Father Christmas watch—the face is all black.

DOCTOR: Right. You time it and I'll count, ready A-one...a-two ...a-three...a-four...a-Jingle Bells, jingle bells, jingle all the way; Oh what fun it is to ride in a...

XMAS: Wait a minute. We didn't engage you for your Bing Crosby imitations.

DOCTOR: Just got a little carried away there. Well now, let's see...

(the corpse's "pulse" arm remains in the air)

...hm...Well, Father Christmas, ...I'd say...either this man wants to leave the room...or rigor mortis has set in.

XMAS: Can you cure him?

DOCTOR: Of course I can. He needs a drink, that's all.

(Takes one from some spectator, downs it himself.)

Well, is he moving yet?

XMAS: I said, can you cure *him*?

DOCTOR: Ah. Yes of course. Yes of course. I saw it on "Marcus Welby" just the other day. Or perhaps it was the late show...We have to perform an exorcism, that's all. Now...I'll take Linda Blair's part; you do Max Von Sydow, and if he turns green and throws up on the carpet, we'll know it's working. Ready? ...a-one...a-two...a-three...

BOTH: Up She *Comes*!

DOCTOR: Did it work?

XMAS: Not even a stain.

DOCTOR: Then we'll have to try electroshock. Fortunately I have my cables with me.

(pulls some dirty string out of his bag)

Canadian Tire had these on special last week.

XMAS: Really?

DOCTOR: Never would have made it here tonight without 'em. Now, I need to connect with a wet spot. Wet spot, yes...that reminds me, is there any young lady who would like a little of my inky tinky...

XMAS:

(Clobbering him with a dried pig's bladder)

That's *not* what you're here for!

DOCTOR: Ah, yes. Well,

(spying someone's drink and dropping an end of his string into it)

here's a wet spot, and here's another and, oh hell, let's connect 'em all in series and do a proper job of it.

(Droops the string from drink to drink around the room)

...Wait a minute.

XMAS: What?

DOCTOR: I wish now I'd bought the heavy-duty cables. You know how these Canadian Tire products are.

XMAS: Get *on* with it!

DOCTOR: Right. Are you ready with the switch? All right, CONTACT!

(The Doctor screams, leaps in the air, and collapses on the floor)

XMAS: Doctor, what happened?

DOCTOR: I think I forgot to ground it. Boy, do I need a drink– this medical rescue work takes it out of you, I declare. I say, do I need a *drink*. Ah, thank you very much, sir.

(Helps himself to someone's drink)

Having a little trouble with the hearing there, I see. See me after the show, sir, I have just the thing for it. Now, where were we?

XMAS: You were going to ground it.

DOCTOR: Ah, yes. Perhaps this poor deaf man here will hold one end.

Good, thank you. Now, ready again, Father Christmas. Everybody pour on the juice. A-one ...a-two...CONTACT! CONTACT! CONTACT!

(Nothing happens)

XMAS: Not enough power, perhaps.

DOCTOR: I don't understand. Didn't Frank Moores just pay $360 million of our taxes to BRINCO to make sure we all have enough power? Listen, maybe we could just sit this guy up as he is and put him in the House of Assembly as a PC backbencher, what do you think?

XMAS: Naw. There's two much dead wood there already.

DOCTOR: Well, there's only one thing for it—I'll have to get serious. You understand this could be dangerous, even boring. I have here, in the inside outside pocket of my waist-coat, a little bottle given to me by my late great-great grandfather.

(He produces a giant cake-icing syringe)

And it says here on the label, it says: Hectum, Spectum, High Generosity, Okum, Skokum, Low Viscosity; the Wig of a Weasel, the Wool of a Frog, and Twenty-Four Ounces of September Fog... Father Christmas! It's...it's the SWINE FLU VACCINE! Stand back, everybody. We wouldn't want any people paralysed at this party...at least no more than there were before we came in...

This vaccine here has, you might say, the political clout of a Don Jamieson, the negotiating finesse of a Bryce Mackasey...Why, if one drop of this spills on the carpet it could create a postal strike right here and now!

(In adjusting the syringe, the Doctor manages to squirt it all over the audience)

DOCTOR: Right. Let's inject what's left of this down his gullet, eh?...Stamp the letter, open the box and...now my good man, get up or we'll legislate you back to life, so there.

XMAS: Doctor, it's working! He's rising up!

DOCTOR: Yes, of course, but will he ever vote Liberal again? Now if he doesn't ask for back pay, maternity leave, and a cost-of-living increase, it's a miracle.

(The dead man rises and begins to dance a jig)

XMAS:...It's a miracle!

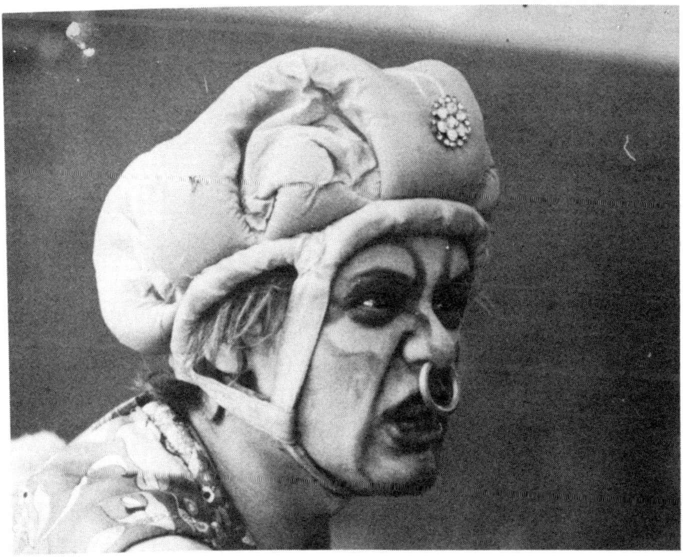

The Turkish Knight (Bembo Davies) in the 1973 Christmas Mummers Play. Photo: Chris Brookes.

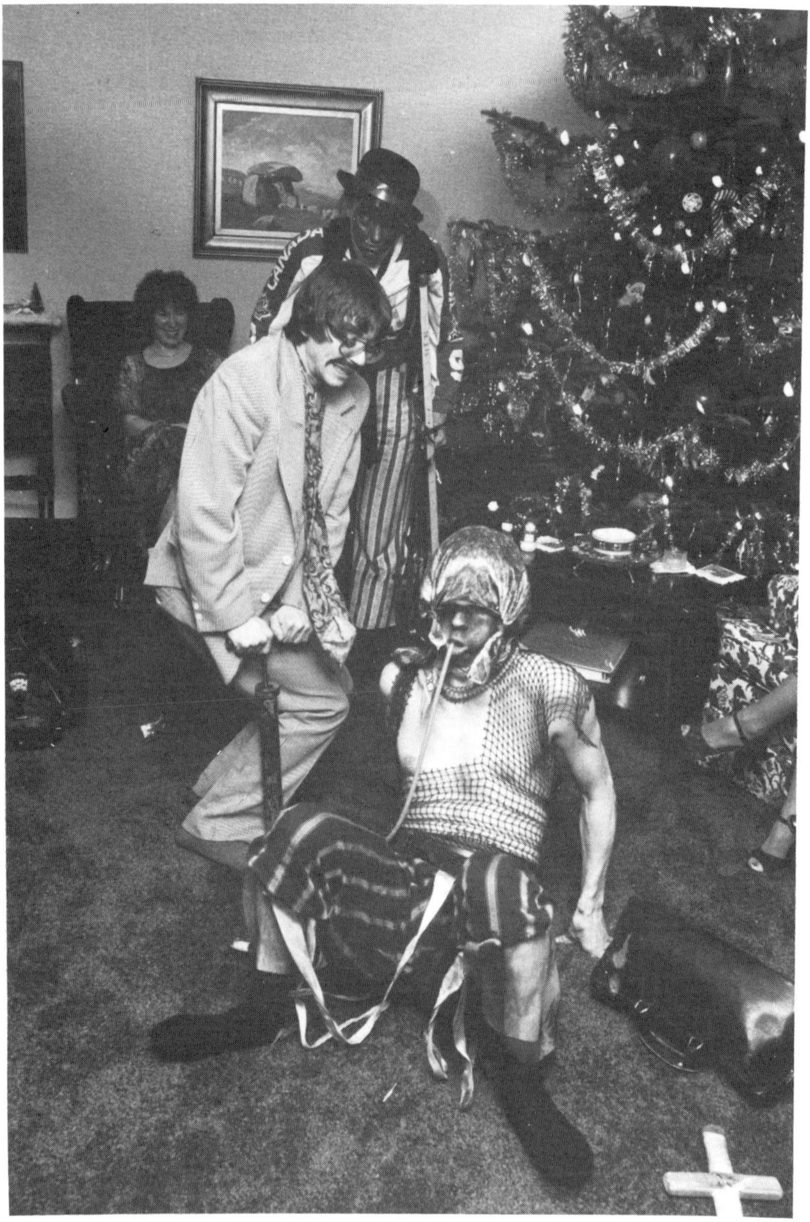

A house performance in progress, Christmas 1978. The Doctor (Kent Barrett) "revives" the dead man (Charles Tomlinson).
Photo: Ron Fitzgerald.

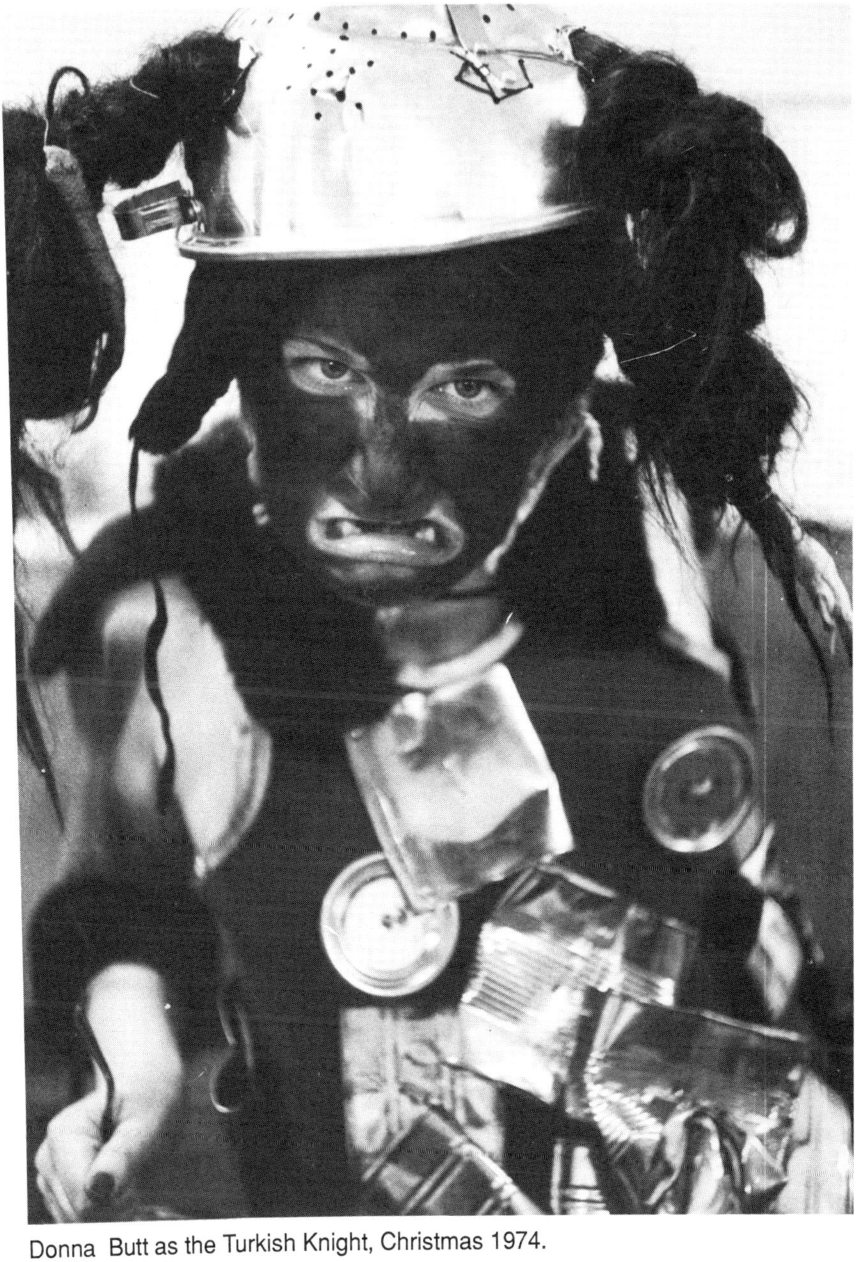

Donna Butt as the Turkish Knight, Christmas 1974.
Photo: Chris Brookes

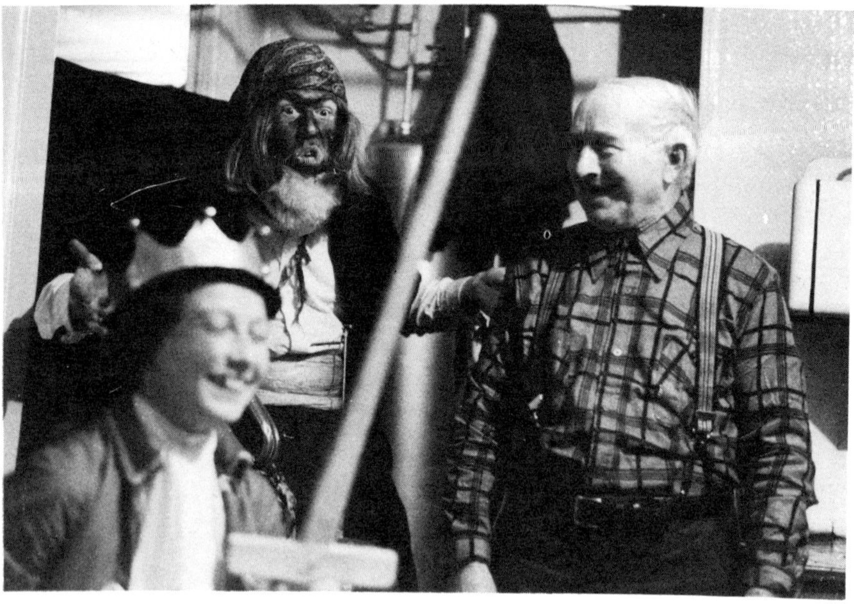

Lynn Lunde (King George), Bob Pot (Father Christmas) and Mick Finlay, the last surviving traditional Newfoundland performer of the Father Christmas role, Port Kirwan, 1973.
Photo: Chris Brookes.

Newfoundland Night 5

> Popular theatre means: intelligible to the broad masses, taking over their own forms of expression and enriching them, adopting and consolidating their standpoint, representing the most progressive section of the people in such a way that it can take over the leadership, linking with tradition and carrying it further.... We have in mind a fighting people and also a fighting conception of the word 'popularity'....
>
> Bertolt Brecht

After Christmas 1972 we continued our examination of Newfoundland's past, starting work on a dramatisation of Newfoundland working-class history. I was turned on by Leandre Bergeron's *Petite Manuel d'Histoire du Quebec* comic book series and felt there was a need for something similar in Newfoundland. Our school book histories wallowed through syrupy accounts of the glories of our colonial upbringing, and neglected even such obvious political milestones as the Fisherman's Protective Union. Otherwise the only commonly available historical overview at that time was a fat book by D.W. Prowse, a nineteenth-century judge with a distinct ruling-class bias. We wanted to create instead a clear synopsis from the working man's perspective, and to make it accessible in a popular theatre format. I hoped for a good basic history show which could be our vehicle for touring into communities around the province the following summer.

At the time I desperately wanted to work with a playwright. Previously as a director I had relied on close working relationships with writers, and my experience with collective creation was limited.

But there were no Newfoundland playwrights around with either the time or the political commitment we needed, so we began improvising dramatic material directly from research. This was a method we were to refine over the next decade.

Our first collective creation wasn't easy. We were once again a company of three: Lynn Lunde, John Doyle and myself. Kevin Pittman left after the *Mummers Play* for a radio job in Labrador, and Tom Sexton went back to high school. Occasionally someone would come around to see what we were up to, but no one stayed long enough to complete the Magical Mystery Tour.

The Magical Mystery Tour was a scheme to make our pitifully small financial kitty stretch further. Some Rochdale College types from the alternate thinktank Memo From Turner had promoted it as a neat way to turn a trick with unemployment insurance. Here's how it was supposed to work (got your pocket calculator handy?): Members of the group pair off. While both actually work, only one would be recorded on the payroll books as receiving a decent salary. The size of this official salary would normally deplete our kitty fast, so the Employee was to donate most of it back into said same kitty. It was important that our company was a registered charity. It meant that this donated amount was tax deductible so that minimal income tax would be lost on the inflated "official" salary. After eight weeks of this, the official Employee would be laid off in order to receive unemployment insurance benefits while he is replaced on the official payroll by his buddy (Employee #1 is still working, of course, though now *un*officially). His unemployment insurance benefits, naturally, would be shared into the kitty in order to help make up his buddy's "official" salary. By the time his unemployment benefit period ran out, he could change places with his buddy and "tour" through the magical mystery payroll again...and so on, *ad infinitum.* In theory the only time that this system would use up much real company money would be during the initial eight qualifying weeks. After that, the system would support itself on rotating unemployment insurance payments. Of course it was highly illegal, but we were desperate and it sounded like a fine idea.

We were snatched from the clutches of crime by transitoriness. No two people ever stayed with our group for more than eight weeks. Neophytes would drop by, give it a whirl for a week or two, and decide that theatre just wasn't for them, man. The Mystery Tour never got off the ground, and our kitty kept getting smaller.

Eventually Diane Olsen and Sandy Cantwell joined us and stuck it out until the History show previewed in late April at the university auditorium. It was still a work in progress. On most of our posters we called it *Newfoundland Night*. On others we called it *Cod on a Stick* and *Newfoundland Dressup*. I don't remember why. I think it was to avoid being pigeon-holed. It was all one show, anyway.

At the time, the provincial government's Arts and Culture palaces had a standard practice of playing a recording of the provincial anthem, the *Ode to Newfoundland*, at the beginning of all of their performing arts events. Audiences would stand in reverence to the lyrics penned by an old colonial governor, Sir Cavendish Boyle. We decided to begin our show in similar fashion, with the syrupy voices of the university choir raised in nationalistic multi-part harmony. I intercut the tape with the voice of Sam Spurrell, an elderly fisherman whom Lynn and I had interviewed during our research, and it set the general tone for what was to follow. The audience wasn't sure when it was okay to sit down:

> When sun rays crown thy pine-clad hills,
> And summer spreads her hand,
> When silver voices tune thy rills,
> We love thee, Smiling land....
>
> SAM: We had to go to the merchant in the spring to get a suit of oilskins, and a couple pairs of long rubbers, and enough to start fishin'. And then when they got their fish, in the fall, the merchant knew how much they had, and he'd put his price up if they got very much fish, he'd put his price right top high. And when they finished up in the fall they just broke even, and he had to give 'em enough food for the Winter. And in the spring they were broke again.
>
> We Love Thee,
> We Love Thee,
> We Love Thee, Smiling Land....
>
> SAM: I had a sister died, and Father bought the trimmers for the coffin. It come to six dollars. And so that fall he got so many seals and he give 'em to Uncle Bill, we used to call him, the merchant. We had fifteen seals. "Oh" he said, Uncle Bill said, "Mr. Spurrell you're just square."
>
> As Loved our Fathers so we Love....
>
> SAM: Next time he sees Father he says: "Now Thomas, when you going to pay us, pay for that bill you owes me?" Father said: "I don't owe you." "Oh yes you do," Uncle Bill said, "you owes me six dollars." Father said: "I paid you, I give you the seals!" "No" he said, "No you didn't, you didn't give me nothing." So, anyhow, Father he got some cod oil then, he sold him some cod oil. Cod oil was a good price then, you know. Same thing happened: "You're just square" he said.
>
> Where once they stood,

We Stand....

SAM: And Father could read and write a little, but not...well, in regards to figures, whoo! He couldn't do nothing with figures.

Their Prayer we raise to Heaven Above....

SAM: And the magistrate and the policeman was in the boat, and they come in, and says: "Ah...Uncle Bill come up," they said, "to straighten his accounts." And Father said: "I don't owe Uncle Bill nothing!" "Oh yes you do," he says, "you owes him six dollars." Father said: "I'm after payin' him twice!" "Don't care," policeman said, "We're goin to take that fish!" And Father said: "Over my dead body!" And the two of them grabbed Father and held him down on the flake, and said to this fella Smith, they said: "In the King's name, take that fish!" And Jack took every darn fish was on the flake and brought it down and threw it in the boat, like the dumb self. And they held Father down while they was doin it!

God guard Thee, Newfoundland....

SAM: And I took a longer off 'a the flake and hit him on the back of the neck. And he jumped up and hit me across the mouth and he split open me lip and knocked out me teeth and laid me out on the flake. Smith took every fish was there and threw it down in the boat. And we damn near *starved* that winter!

God guard Thee....

SAM: We never had a *thing*!

God guard Thee....

SAM: They treated the fishermen, those merchants, something like Hitler treated the Jews!

God guard Thee,
Newfoundland!

Our poverty-stricken set for the show consisted of two towers of borrowed scaffolding, some rope, and a few flags and puppets. Costumes were our own rehearsal clothes. Our style relied less on a literary, talking-heads approach than upon physical punctuation with sound-and-movement images. Stage images stay with an audience long after individual lines of dialogue have been forgotten, and I wanted our symbols to suggest a way of seeing the historical material.

One image was uncomfortably close to some of us in the company. We had dramatised the *Newfoundland* sealing disaster of 1914. In that tragedy over 100 men were caught out in a blizzard on the ice fields for several days and many froze to death. The blame was placed upon the owners of the *Newfoundland* who in their quest for cost efficiency had removed the ship's radio-telephone as an unnecessary luxury.

While we were working on this material in rehearsal, three Quidi Vidi fishermen we knew, who were out hunting seabirds in a small open boat, got caught in a sudden winter storm. They managed to get to land near Petty Harbour, but were soaked when the boat swamped. It was very cold, and night overtook them before they could walk to the community. One died. Another suffered severely frostbitten hands. For weeks we visited him in hospital as doctors tried to arrest the creeping spread of gangrene. Slowly, one by one, the young man lost all fingers on both hands.

Our scene of the sealing disaster echoed this terrible, impotent frustration at the inexorable approach of coldness and death. John, Lynn and Sandy performed repetitive sound- and-movement expressions under a huge white nylon dragger net while Diane and I, as the ships' captains, played cold, white flashlight beams over them and walked through the audience carrying portable tape recorders which played the voice of one of the actual survivors (Cecil Mouland, whom we had interviewed) recalling the event. Slowly and inevitably the actors' movements became hopelessly tangled in the white net, and everything wound down to a frozen, tense, absolute stillness.

Some of our St. John's preview spectators thought such scenes too avant garde and predicted that rural audiences would never understand them. There was only one way to find out, but chances of an immediate tour were slim. The four-month creation period for the show was far too long and had drained our energies. John and Sandy decided to leave the group, Diane was unsure, and Lynn wanted the summer off to finish her anthropology thesis. The kitty was empty. We had a script, but no money, no cast, and no transportation other then a decrepit Punch and Judy van.

Lynn and I had already approached the Canada Council theatre section for help. They did not come to see our work but explained the problem to us. We were, they said, clearly an "alternate" theatre. Alternate theatres were supposed to exist as an alternative to an establishment theatre, and there was, they pointed out, no establishment professional theatre in Newfoundland. Ergo, we were illegitimate. Before they could consider assisting us, they would have to create an establishment regional theatre in the province to make our existence viable. It was, I suppose, perfect bureaucratic logic, and no amount of arguing seemed to penetrate it. Reality didn't fit the rule book, so there must be something wrong with reality.

We pointed out that the structures and seasons of the establishment "regional" theatres in other provinces had absolutely nothing regional about them. They looked as if they'd all come off an assembly line in Ottawa prefabricated. Even their seasons were virtually identical. If, in a given year, the St. Lawrence Centre, say, produced *Death of a Salesman* or *Plaza Suite*, miraculously Theatre New Brunswick, the Vancouver Playhouse and a half dozen others would all be smitten by the urge to mount the very same play. It was quite remarkable.

If different regions of Canada are unique, we said, then their theatres should be unique too. Ours was not an alternative theatre, but a *real* regional theatre.

We didn't get to first base with the Canada Council theatre section.

The provincial government's cultural affairs boss regarded us with an even colder eye. We had backed into the bustle of his intergovernmental lobbying. Newfoundland was indeed the only province without an "establishment regional" theatre. The provincial government was very anxious to have such a treasure pumping out the formula one-foreign-classic-and-a-few-current-British-and-American-hits season in their new Arts and Culture centres, in order to keep up with the Joneses in the rest of the country. They encouraged the Canada Council to lay out the golden egg to set up this theatre.

Normal Council policy at the time, however, required any professional theatre to have survived for at least two seasons before being eligible for federal financial assistance. The province had been making the case that in such a cultural backwater as Newfoundland, professional regional theatre was unable to blossom spontaneously, and would therefore have to be established de facto by an up-front infusion of government cash. There were strong hints that if the Canada Council were willing to accede to this action, the province would sweeten the pot with matching finances. It was an expensive proposition.

Of course, the spontaneous appearance of a professional theatre in Newfoundland was anathema to this argument, and our fledgling company was not welcomed by the provincial footmen of official culture. In the first place, the If-You're-So-Good-Why-Are-You-In-Newfoundland syndrome ruled out the possibility of any homegrown product ever being considered more than tenth-rate. And in the second place the style and content of our work to date was clearly not what the mandarins meant by "culture." They gave us no help of any kind.

Just as the cloud cover got really black, the sky cleared. It cleared twice, in fact. My university job produced a bonus and I rushed out and bought an old school bus for touring. And a completely new branch of the Canada Council (later to become the Explorations Programme) liked the idea of a show about Newfoundland history touring small communities. They awarded us a two-month salary grant. Augmented by my university salary, the company's cash would stretch until September.

I immediately held auditions. It was summertime and a few people actually came to them: Paul Sametz, a musician and actor I'd worked with a few years before, and Mary Walsh, veteran of the Newfoundland Travelling Theatre show of the previous summer, who had just quit her winter job as a radio host. There was also a girl from a Montreal theatre school who had brought along her friend Donna Butt, a political science student, for moral support. I auditioned them both and cast the moral support. I telephoned old friends Andy Thompson and Christopher Knight on the mainland who liked the idea of a busman's holiday in Newfoundland, and the six of us sprinted through rehearsals. The new cast couldn't manage some of the sound-and-movement work which our winter ensemble had developed but they added a lot more music which filled in the gaps.

Printing posters for the tour meant once again facing the question of the company's name, or lack of it. The April preview performances had given rise to three totally different posters, all carefully avoiding tying the company down to a name. It was really confusing, but some of the audiences remembered our Christmas show, and figured it out: "Ah," they said, "You people were the mummers!" Right, I thought, why not? A name is inevitable sooner or later. We'd be the Mummers. I made it the Mummers Troupe just for style. By this time it looked as if my original plan of a permanent ensemble was a pipe dream, but the "Troupe" was a nice reminder of a good idea.

I've often wondered if this simple choice of a name helped confirm the enormous suspicion with which the provincial cultural establishment already regarded us, and whether they would have been less hostile if we'd chosen something more benign like the Royal Colonial Dramatic Corps. The question was soon to become academic anyway. Our actions over the next three months were to send half the civil service into apoplexy at the mere mention of the name Mummers Troupe.

Towards the end of June 1973, with an enthusiastic cast, six sleeping bags, a stove, borrowed scaffolding, and an eight-week supply of brown rice, the first annual Incredible Bus and Boat Tour began.

I hoped that we might be able to use the show as a springboard for discussion with our audiences. I had rewritten the final scenes of the play to bring the historical sequence up to the present, and instead of "ending" the performance, we tried to fade into the audience and ask about current issues in the local area. Depending upon how this worked out in any particular community, I thought we could use it to create extra theatrical material which would then serve as a new "final" scene. By leaving the door open for community involvement, the show could evolve.

The first leg of the tour, around Trinity and Bonavista Bays, was ragged. The cast was underrehearsed and the show was still finding its feet. I had brought the Punch and Judy puppets to give free performances for the children wherever we stopped, and St. John's newspaper columnist Ray Guy wrote it up prophetically as "*FEDERAL FUNDS USED TO MURDER MAGISTRATE!*"

Initially, we couldn't find a way to make the post- performance discussion work. I worried that the show was too arty, too city-designed, and fretted because the cast didn't have the same involvement with the show as the original winter ensemble. To most of them it was a job rather than any great underlying commitment to the Troupe or to social activism. They related to the company as a Thing, a business which employed them, and this relationship defined their approach to me and to the work. We had lost any longer-term sense of communality or responsibility. But we had gained something as well. If people now related to *It*, the institution, this was because it now *was* one. *It* had raised financing and was paying wages. If it did so once, it could do it again. It had a name, and an identity which could continue beyond the commitment of a particular cast.

Our next group of performances, in the New World Island area, were better. We found our feet in Herring Neck (so to speak). Fish plant workers generously gave us a massive bag of free mackerel for our supper, and we performed for a packed house in a beautiful old Society of United Fishermen (SUF) hall perched atop a steep hill, tying our scaffold ropes through the open windows to trees outside. This was William Coaker's old stomping ground, the community where seven decades earlier he had founded the Fishermen's Protective Union, and there was still an FPU Trading Company store down the road with old copies of the union paper, the *Fishermans Advocate* dusty under the counter. Our audience, from children to fish plant workers, were enthusiastic, and the actors took off on the energy.

The discussion afterward worked, and we were invited into people's homes for late night tea to continue talking. I found one old gentleman who remembered the Mummers Play of his youth, with a few local variations different from the Southern Shore version Lynn and I had collected.

We found a similar reception in Change Islands, a stunningly beautiful community several miles offshore. Hauling our gear off the longliner *Barbara Darlene*, we noticed the flag flying high over the SUF Hall to advertise our show, "...because we always runs 'er up when there's a Time on," the caretaker informed us. It was the first occasion in five months the flag had flown, and the hall was blocked with an excited crowd which seemed to have a wonderful time despite the temperature in the overcrowded building, which by the second act became almost unbearable. No theatre company had ever come to Change Islands before.

The next day people fed us and took us into their homes and told us about their lives. Like everywhere in this area, there were worries about resettlement, about young people leaving. One young guy I spoke with, working in the fish plant, complained that all the girls leave, and there was little for him to do in the evenings now except drink. He himself had left, worked in Toronto awhile. "But I couldn't live up there, boy. I'm a water man. That's my life, the water. And that's the way it is here— the water."

Conversations like this made me feel that the usefulness of our tour lay not just in bringing to people a show about their own history. It was important that we came at all. People leave small isolated communities for many reasons. Sometimes it is because they feel cut off, isolated from "what's happening" in a continentalism which devalues rural living and elevates urban culture, with its cinemas, theatres and nightlife, to "where it's really at." Perhaps in some small way, tours like ours help to counteract that process. Perhaps they help make it possible for people to stay. I would like to think so.

At any rate, our "avant-garde" theatrics seemed to work. People in rural communities approached our show straight on and honestly. They didn't bring expectations of naturalistic melodrama, and they didn't care whether we were avant-garde or not.

We fared less well in the few larger towns we passed through, where we made the mistake of renting the expensive government Arts and Culture Centres. In Grand Falls, the Centre is snuggled up next to the local RCMP headquarters. It was generally regarded as a Place of High Art, and most papermill workers accordingly never went near the place. Corner Brook was similar. Our appearance there attracted a small, stony-faced, upper-income audience, including a British gentleman who kept referring to our "tepid heat of youthful socialism."

The best thing, in fact, about our Corner Brook performance happened in the afternoon. Arriving on the day of the performance to find that the Arts and Culture Centre had done no advance publicity for the show, Paul Sametz and I decided that our only chance of pulling an audience on short notice would be to stage some outrageous stunt to catch the evening television news. Corner Brook is basically a one-industry town, and the Bowater Pulp and Paper Company, in an attempt to demonstrate to the town why such nice corporate citizens shouldn't have to pay any city taxes, had presented a brace of swans to the populace. They were perhaps the only swans in Newfoundland.

We decided to announce the presentation of a third swan. Accordingly we created a garbagebag and paper contraption that looked vaguely birdlike, notified the press, and paraded it solemnly through town to the swan pond near the Glyn Mill Inn (formerly Lord Bowater's guest house). It was ceremoniously launched, accompanied by Paul's saxophone playing *Way Down Upon The Swannee River* and fell over and sank. We made the television news sure enough, but the audience stayed away in droves.

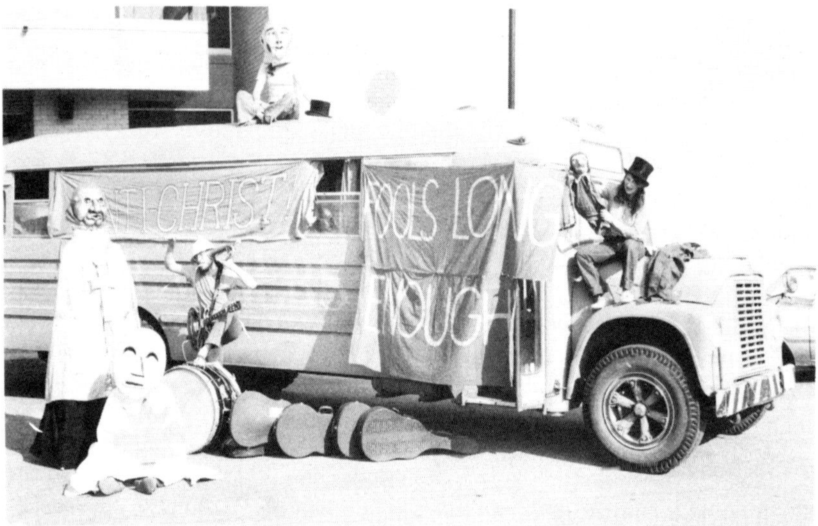

Cast members of Newfoundland Night with Uncle Bulgy, the Troupe's tour bus in Corner Brook, July 1973.
Photo: Chris Brookes.

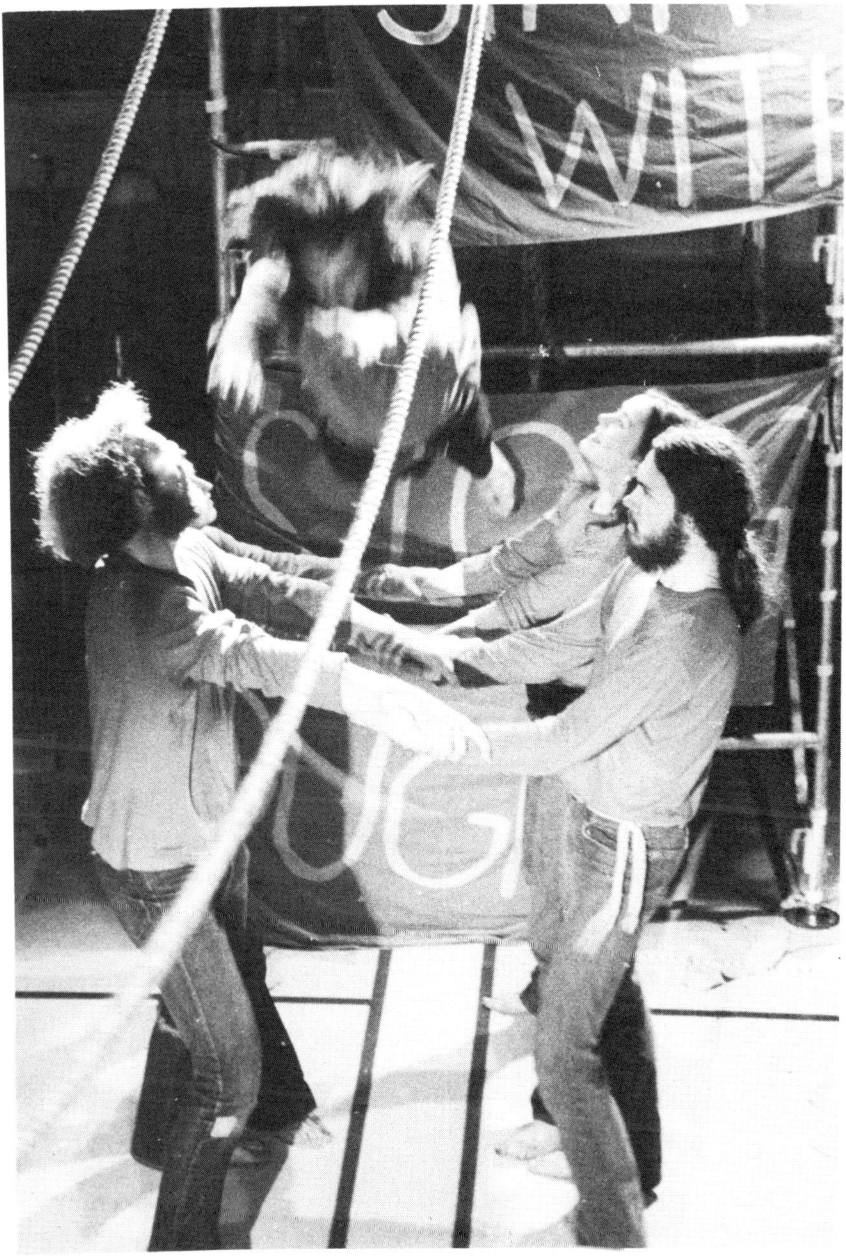

"Our style relied less on a literary, talking-heads approach than upon physical punctuation with sound-and-movement images." (The people elect a FPU member 1913.)
Photo: Chris Brookes.

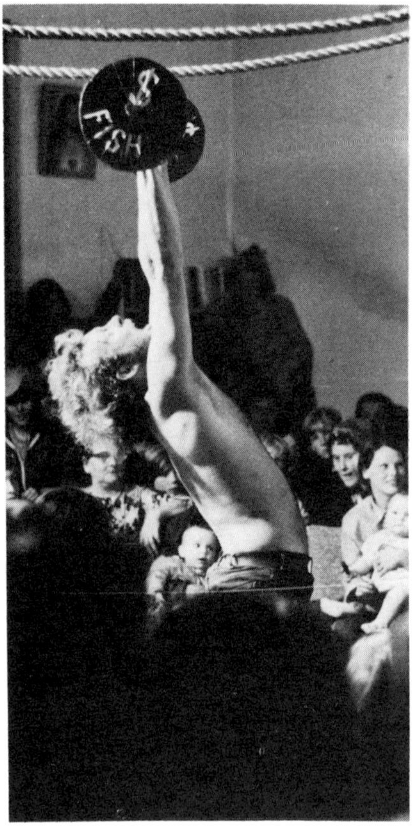

William Coaker (Andy Thompson) "raises the price of fish" to the Grey River audience in August 1973. Photo: Chris Brookes.

Most of the smaller communities we toured through had never before been played by a theatre company. Many of them rarely even had the opportunity to see films, except when some travelling movie man came through and showed an old print in the parish hall. So we were a phenomenon. This was particularly true on the South Coast of the island, where there were no roads, and even radio reception was bad.

We usually scribbled an "Age Limit 15" on our posters in a vain effort to discourage children from attending the show, which was designed for adults and tended to make children first bored, then restless, finally noisy. It was a good idea but never worked well in many communities where the kids' logic was infallible: "Why can't we come in? It's OUR hall, you know, mister!"

Along the South Coast we didn't even try to enforce it. If parents came to the show it meant that teenagers had to stay home and babysit the youngsters, and *nobody* was going to miss the only professional theatre company ever to play the community. The scene in Grey River was typical: a low sunset gilding a long winding line of people, everyone from grandmothers to babes in arms, slowly making their way up the hill to the two-room school, each person carrying a chair, stool, barrel or cushion (the little primary-grade desks were too small for sitting). Somehow the entire community, chairs, stools, barrels and all, squeezed into a schoolroom designed for thirty of their children.

We made it halfway along the South Coast by CN coastal boat, unloading our gear in each small village and humping it up to the school or parish hall. By the time we reached Burgeo, CN went on strike and we continued as best we could via a variety of small fishing boats. Sometimes we landed in a place like McCallum or Francois in rough seas and pouring rain, looking more like drowned rats then entertainers, but people took us in and treated us like royalty. We performed for donations, a gesture which people appreciated in areas where the fishing was poor. They also appreciated it in Buchans.

Buchans, built around a copper, lead and zinc mine, is an inland company town which had been the property of the American Smelting and Refining Company for five decades. At the time of our arrival, the miners were in the middle of a long, hard strike, and our performance was a morale booster. We played to a full crowd of 300 in the Union Hall. We adapted some existing scenes and wrote a couple of new ones dealing with the strike situation. When we finished, the whole audience stood and cheered and joined us singing *Solidarity Forever*. The talk and the beer continued long into the night, and we made a tentative decision to return in a few weeks and create some picket line skits with the strikers. But things didn't work out that way. During the next two weeks we toured to the Gros Morne area of the Northern Peninsula. Our plans suddenly changed.

I kept a diary of the time.

Gros Mourn—A Diary 6

So many things cry out to be done, all so urgently. The world rolls on. Time passes. Ten thousand years is too long. Seize the day.

Mao Tse-Tung

Sally's Cove, Monday 30 July 1973

This area is to be the site of the new Gros Morne National Park. Nine months ago the provincial news media carried coverage of local residents' discontent with the park's proposed community relocation policy, but later reports indicated that changes in the policy had satisfied residents, and that opposition to the park had ceased. The discussions emerging from our show's final scene here seem to contradict this media image.

Most of the talk after each performance in this area has revolved around the park, with feelings often running pretty strong. Each community reacts differently; all seem confused.

The Sally's Cove audience had the most to say: most think the park will destroy their community and they will be pushed out of their homes by a subtle but forcible relocation. They feel that outside help, particularly the news media, has deserted them. But there's a determination in these people. I am struck by a grim face which says quietly, "If they goes ahead and ruins our lives, then we got the right to spoil their dream too. If they drives me out they'll have to rename the place Charcoal Park, 'cause I'll put the torch to every tree in 'er before I goes."

We're told that the park is to be officially opened in a few weeks—no one seems to know exactly when—with a federal-provincial sign-over ceremony in Rocky Harbour, ten miles away.

There are five communities affected by the park relocation policy: Sally's Cove, Belldowns Point, Bakers Brook, Green Point and Lobster Cove. The relocation policy itself includes a scale of compensation for families who move, and has been changed several times in the past year. Originally it required residents of the five villages to move immediately; now it is tempered to allow them to remain in some cases and pass on their land to one heir. Unfortunately most resident families seem to have several heirs who want to remain in the community, but no new houses may be built, and there are other restrictions. Basically, residents see the new policy as being the same as the old, but a little slower. In five to ten years the result will be the same.

Sally's Cove is the focal point, and also the largest of the five communities. I get a curious feeling listening to these people talk about their fears. They seem desperate to talk, to have someone from "the outside" listen. Even we, young freaks from the city, are possible messengers.

Rocky Harbour, Thursday 2 August 1973

I've been thinking seriously about the possibility of staying in this area for a few weeks to create a documentary piece about the communities. If so, we can't make a show about abstract policies; we must take people as our focus, the flesh and blood individuals who live here and the things they tell us. The government's view is adequately publicised; our show will need to deal with the residents' view of their future.

At lunch we decide to do it. We're due on the South Coast with *Newfoundland Night*, but this schedule can be postponed by three weeks. We itemise resources, note pads, taperecorders (it may be important to remember precisely how people speak with us). Any props and set requirements can be improvised from available materials in the area. We will talk predominantly with residents of the five affected communities and focus on Sally's Cove (the people there have already offered the two-room schoolhouse for rehearsal space.)

Christopher Knight is afraid that our group is too diverse for any clear line of expression to emerge through the collective process, and opts for staying outside the project. He'll hitchhike up the coast to a good beach for some R & R by himself. The rest of us are eager. We discuss images that strike us as characteristic of this area: lobster pots, contrasts, the optimism of government publications and the pessimism of the residents who read them. Andy suggests a final image for the piece: a champagne christening which breaks the communities instead of the bottle. We decide to leave such ideas hanging while we get out and talk to as many people as possible.

The official park opening is rumoured to have been rescheduled for August 13.

Rocky Harbour, Friday 3 August 1973

Two days into research. Friends have arrived from the city; I worry that our energies will be seduced away.

This community is an "enclave" in park lingo: i.e. it is not a part of the park but is enclosed by the park's boundary. It is also the site of park headquarters. Donna and I have spoken to the park supervisor, young and friendly—fresh from Nova Scotia. He explained wilderness park philosophy. It doesn't include people at all but it makes sense: parks mean conservation; and people living in a wilderness park are an inconvenience sooner or later. Four-footed residents are fine. Two-footed ones are trouble. Is it true that the park won't provide as many permanent jobs as originally touted by provincial politicians? Yes, less then half as many, and most will require special skills. Few area residents will qualify.

We also talk with the provincial government's coordination office. These are the people who deal most directly with community residents, and they give us a whole different story from what the residents have been telling us. There's a pretty big information gap here somewhere. Yes, they have held public meetings to disseminate information and listen to the feelings of residents, but these have been very few, and only when requested by the residents. In the meantime they continue to implement policies which they know are unpopular. Do they think the people are really informed about the regulations and policies under which they will soon have to live? "The trouble is, the people are too well informed.... They're just looking for something to fight about."

Feelings of Rocky Harbour residents are mixed. As an enclave, there will be no pressure on them to relocate, and they expect to make money on the park's tourist business. We learn that Sally's Cove people have a reputation for "stubbornness" at public meetings.

Sally's Cove, Sunday 5 August 1973

Collecting data in this place is saddening and frustrating. We all feel it. People here generally fear their community is doomed, and feel powerless to make their voices heard. They say that their opinions were never solicited by the officials, that their homes will be "signed away" by government bureaucrats, and that even the new park relocation policy will simply be a "slow freeze-out," forcing them out over a period of a few years while making the government look good.

There's suspicion and distrust. No one is sure of what is happening, which families have already agreed to move, how much money, how large a plum the government is offering to those who do leave, etc. All the classic subtle workings of the archetypal resettlement policy. People are divided, nervous of confronting each other. "Is it true Phil is going to move?" "I heard they're going to close the school." Rumours abound. Why don't the government people realise what is going on? It all looks so clear in their office memos.

Last evening the company attended the regular Saturday night slide lecture for tourists at the Park Interpretation Center in Rocky Harbour. An impeccably nice young biologist from the mainland showed impeccably nice colour slides and explained marshland plants. The mosquitoes were thick. No one asked him to explain the new park's human fauna, whose roots cling as tenaciously to the same rocks. This morning he came to find us in the bus and presented a sample handful of bakeapples to Andy, who had never before tasted them. These Parks people are so *nice*. It would be easier if they looked like villains.

Conversation with a child from Green Point:

I: Well, is your family moving out?
He: Yup.
I: Are you glad?
He: Yup.
I: Why?
He: Because when we moves, I gets a bike! Me father's gettin' me one.
I: But wouldn't he buy you one anyway, if you were staying here?
He: No. 'Cause when we moves, see, the government gives us lots of money, and I gets a bike. We don't get no money if we stays.

Sally's Cove, Monday 6 August 1973

People here are kind to us. This is a small community (fifty families) but no one seems to mind that we, young strangers, are inquiring about their affairs. It's probably presumptuous of us to expect people to talk and trust us. Why should they care about the creation of a play? Perhaps they feel that we can be their voice? I'm not sure. At any rate, the community has embraced us with gifts of fresh fish (West Coast cod tastes different from East Coast cod), homemade bread and beer, invitations to dinner. Everyone in the community seems interested, even the kids.

Coyley Endicott and his wife live close to the schoolhouse. They are militant about their situation but think that we should have the answer to their problems. I try to explain that we're simply a group of actors, at best able to give Sally's Cove a reflection of itself. We can only re-express the questions— the people themselves must find their answers. They press us to finish the piece in time to perform it before the official park sign-over ceremony next Monday. My God, we can't make anything respectable in six days! Our last show required four months of work. Yet we have a responsibility to these people, the subjects of our creation. We can't simply use them in the name of art. If they are willing to take us into their homes and their confidences we can at least try to do what they ask. But can we make it in six days? Andy has the flu. I pray it doesn't spread to the rest of our company. We've spent all our time so far in research— first rehearsal is not in sight yet. With so little time we won't be able to get far enough with character studies to portray local individuals recognizably, and will have to rely on signs, nameplates instead.

Images of flames, of burning, keep cropping up. Clarence Lang, talking to me over coffee in his small house on the beach, explains how the Parks Canada people will dispose of vacant houses as residents leave. He's heard how it was done in the Gaspé park, while neighbouring houses were still occupied.

> Accordin' as they shifts the people out, they'll burn 'em. Thats what they says they're gonna do. Tractor come, crawl over'er, flatten 'er out, then they'll burn 'er. Bulldozer come then, cover 'er over, just nice, and a land-mark'll be gone. Then the people gonna start realisin'. Boy, it's gonna be 'ard.

He doesn't know what to do. They sent a petition to the provincial government a while ago— no result.

Cow Head, Tuesday 7 August 1973

I'm speedy— full of static sparks. The drive up here was beautiful; it's no wonder they want this scenery for a park. It is ironic that the people who live in the most beautiful parts of the coast are the ones to be relocated. Those who chose to live closest to beauty will be punished for their sensibility. Example: Cow Head has been allowed to remain. It's a nice place, nothing special. Belldown's Point, however, a mile away, is slated for relocation. The reason? Belldown's has the most breathtaking sweep of white sand beach to be seen anywhere in Newfoundland.

A long, gentle talk with the local minister; he feels deeply concerned about the changes the park will bring to this area, and doesn't see any easy answers. It was he who helped arrange the first public meeting between Sally's Cove and provincial politicians two years ago. Before that, most Sally's Cove residents didn't know that their community was slated for resettlement. Although the federal and provincial bureaucrats signed the initial park memorandum in 1969 providing for the resettlement of the five villages, apparently no one had thought to inform the residents. This kind of information lag isn't helped by the non-availability of newspapers on this coast.

Jane Hutchings is a retired nurse who has lived on this coast, and kept it healthy, for twenty years. She feeds us, stomach and spirit, while digging out a wealth of information on the park which she has collected over the years. Reading it, I am constantly assailed by the dichotomies of Parks Canada studies which carefully explain how animals and birds are to be treated with care and respect and left undisturbed in their traditional habitats, but make no mention of policies toward people.

It's enlightening to read biologists' reports which underline the importance of preserving, via the park, a particular stand of virgin forest which is crucial to the survival of the park's primary threatened species (and the official symbol of Gros Morne National Park): *lepus arcticus bangsi*– the Arctic Hare. Enlightening because this crucial piece of forest will not be included in the new park. It belongs to the Bowater Pulp and Paper Company which is keeping it for future pulp wood cutting, thus ensuring the downfall of *lepus arcticus bangsi*. The official park symbol assumes a curious touch of irony.

Jane agrees that big business rarely loses. The new park's tourist attractions may line the pockets of a few motel owners and ski lift concessionaires, but for many people the rewards will be negative. How is it that a giant paper company is permitted to hold on to an apparently vital piece of land while Dawson Roberts will be squeezed off his?

Sally's Cove Schoolhouse, Wednesday 8 August 1973

The first day of real work on the show itself! Creative juices loosened up around five o'clock and we have some good images and directions to work with. There's still some research to be collected, and endless amounts of transcription to be typed from audio cassettes, but we've started putting it together. Things are clipping along so much more quickly than they did during last winter's creation of *Newfoundland Night*. I'm ironing the bugs out of this group writing process, and can now see one of the undeniable virtues of playwriting by collective creation: it's fast. For the immediate response required by this situation, it is ideal. A single playwright could never manage this pace alone.

Christopher Knight's back. Six days of sandflies finally got to him.

The Sally's Cove kids, who've been hanging around the school all day watching us (see the actors eat their sandwich, see them use a typewriter, see them drink coffee), ultimately prove invaluable. We have decided to use a mask in the final scene, but have no clay to model one. The kids triumphantly tell us of a natural clay deposit by Big Brook, only 100 yards away, and lead Christopher up there to prove it. It's true! Now he and the kids are fussing about in the back room with it.

We are becoming a spontaneous workshop for these kids. Half a dozen are involved with the mask work, another dozen are trooping down the road with Mary Walsh, videotaping everything in sight with our borrowed portapak camera. Oscar and Otto are our chief helpers, organizing their friends into work crews and cannibalising their fathers' junk piles to construct a giant lobster pot for our set. The lobster pot won't be just for rustic background—it will be a human-size working model, symbolising the relocation programme: once residents allow themselves to be baited by the relocation monies, they will be trapped in the enclave of Rocky Harbour. And like the lobsters they used to fish for, they will never be able to return to the place from whence they came.

In the local bar last night we found solitude impossible. Everyone wants to find out how our work is progressing, if we need help, if we've heard the latest news: that the government is laying on a special free bus service next Monday to give all residents a free ride to the park sign-over celebrations. "A big haw," Clarence says. We are feeling very close to the people here. Their hopes and fears are becoming ours. It would probably have happened in any case, but this kind of working process accelerates empathy. When I'm talking with someone here I'm trying to get inside his skin, to see things with his eyes, because I may be portraying him on Sunday night, speaking his words, using his inflections, believing his beliefs.

Sally's Cove, Thursday 9 August 1973

Andy, still feeling quite ill, went to Norris Point hospital today, where the doctor encouraged him by saying he didn't know what the disease was, but his staff had it too. Andy came back and composed some music for the show.

The regular Thursday evening community card game took place in schoolroom No. 1 tonight while we continued in room No. 2. We're still spending most of our time transcribing and arranging material.

At this rate there will be little time to improvise and play around with themes. We're working long hours, sleeping little.

The sea tonight is regular and strong, a slow rhythm on the beach. The all-day mist cleared up in time for a brilliant sunset of watercolour clouds. I am an East Coast person, unused to the sun setting into the ocean like this. It's like standing on the other edge of the world.

Donna came back from a day at Bakers Brook with a storybook scene from the Decker family. As one of their children was hustled off to bed, his elders reminded him: "...and don't forget to say your prayers: God Bless Mommy, God Bless Daddy, and God Damn the National Park...." I make a note to remind myself to visit the Deckers next time I'm on this coast, and suddenly realise that next time Bakers Brook and the Deckers may not be there.

Today I heard men in the bar counting the days until Monday: "Well, boys, Sally's Cove got four days to live." Later, pausing in the tiny village graveyard trying to piece together the family bloodlines, I notice the relatively short history of this community. The oldest stone still standing is *JUCIAM CHIMERY, D. 1848*. He was a former pantry boy from a French fishing ship who deserted to hide out and make his home here. He took to wife *REBECCA, D. 1856*. There are flowers at the foot of some small wooden grave-markers. What will become of these stones when all the people have moved out? How will the nice young men of the Park Interpretation Centre reconcile a small human graveyard with their National Wilderness Preserve?

I am in emergency working moods, wrapped in my caffeine tenseness like a ball of Christmas styrofoam, brittle and non-biodegradable. Time is the missing factor in this show's creation. We need time to walk the beaches and deserted fishing stages, to kick the lobster pots and listen. Time to stop knowing the answers, time to stop chasing the rainbow and climbing the mountain. Time to slide out the pores of our skins and let the fog finger our souls. We don't have much time, but neither do the people who live here.

Sally's Cove, Saturday 11 August 1973

A drain day. Interpersonal frictions blew most of it, petty things we are all prey to. Well, what can anyone expect from six people living in a cramped schoolbus, throwing a play together in a week flat? I worry that the show may be like a campus revue. Is it worth all this for a bad show? Are we doing anything more than scratching the surface of this community's reality? Will the residents be offended by our version of their voices, their lives? Most important, will there be truth in what we do? At this point I can't hope to see this show objectively. There is so much still unfinished; we'll be lucky to have time for a complete run-through before tomorrow evening's performance.

Dawson and Edith Roberts, who live next door to the school, watch over us and are kind. Last night I accepted their offer of a bath and even read a *Macleans* magazine— the outside world is still there! Homemade bread, rhubarb jam and pie: what luxuries!

Most of our lives we don't really listen to the words around us. Working like this, hanging on every syllable of conversation, memorizing or taping, one begins to notice the poetry in the speech of ordinary people. This play will at least have some beautiful lines, not from poets cloistered in attic rooms, but from lobster fishermen over a kitchen table. The whole myth of Art is autocratic nonsense. Everyone, not merely the artist, speaks poetry, breathes music. It is simply a matter of listening, not just in the art galleries and concert halls but out in the dust of the street. Shakespeare would have us believe that only noblemen speak in poetry, while the common people speak prose. Yet listen:

> 'Tis not me home they're takin' away from me. I can get another one someplace else— good as this one, p'raps better. But 'tis everything else they're takin' away: me freedom.
>
> Look out there now— I got me few vegetables sot. Sot the spring. I can catch me few fish for the winter. I can pick me few berries. I can go up to Corner Brook. I used to go up twice a week and load the truck and bear 'er down and sell 'er out. And when I strikes, comin' down that arm, I can smell the fresh air. And that's true. I think you'll take notice o' that. There's a different air down here.... (Coyley Endicott).

Sitting in the bar at 4 a.m., Harold Payne sings some of the most delicate and lovely folksongs I've ever heard. Shy and self-conscious, he says he learned them as a child from his grandfather, and that he doesn't sing them often now since the jukebox has been installed. Tonight it's unplugged. He lofts a high, soaring accapella: "Rise up, William Reilly...."

Three years ago I saw a series of skits performed during a university student/faculty strike in Vancouver. The scenes about the strike were quite funny. The audience laughed a lot. But somehow when people walked out of the auditorium they knew the strike was over. They had lost. The performance had robbed their energy and sapped their will to continue, despite its heroic plot line. It had punctured their balloon with a *stage* catharsis, allowing the audience to feel that it no longer needed to achieve climax in the *real* struggle outside the theatre's doors. The play was well-intentioned but badly crafted, a pre-ejaculation. I do not want our show to be like that.

It has something to do with finishing things. A play which is designed to animate will not finish off its line of energy. It will pass the ball to the audience. The next scene, whatever it is to be, must be theirs.

> If you draw a series of parallel lines closely together, and then another series across them at an angle, you have the simplest visual example of the dialectical process. Cross-hatching, as they call it. You have the first series of line, then you have the second series in opposition to the first. But out of the two you get a series of diamonds.
>
> Now, if you look at these diamonds, remembering that every one has to be drawn, you are overwhelmed by the length and complexity of the task. Yet, courage. The first series of lines is there. All we have to do is to cross them (Berger 1959).

My theatre is not just the sum of all the disparate elements: music, visuals, dance, etc. It is an unique and individual essence resulting from the intersection of those elements with the *presence of the audience*, in order to create the dialectic of action. Hush. The audience is already there.

Sally's Cove, Sunday Evening 12 August 1973

We made it. And we couldn't have wished for a more enthusiastic audience: 200 people of all ages and sizes squeezed into the tiny schoolroom watching our vision of them. They heard their own words and those of their friends, their stories, their fears, their frustrations, their jokes and their rage. Many of the things people said to us strangers would not have been said as openly and candidly to their neighbours. It is similar, surely, with one's personal relationships—often deep truths can be shared more easily with strangers, while they are still simple revelations unsullied by the leaden shoes of need. So it is that ours is an intimate show for this audience, and this has made for a rare sense of closeness. The play manifests their identity as a community rather than as isolated individuals.

Our performance was speedy and jittery, but scruffy as it was, it seemed to have substance. None of us has ever before felt this kind of intimacy between performer and audience. Acting out these people's visions and feelings is akin to an act of love. It won't be the same for any other audience. Of course we received a standing ovation.

After the performance the room is busy with small knots of people discussing the show. Jane and her husband Roland drove down from Cow Head to be present. She looks us over with her practised nurse's eye and pronounces us pale, tired, and undernourished. Yes, but we are ecstatic too.

Eventually most of the discussion adjourns to the bar, retelling the show's jokes and images. Do I imagine that there is a pride in all this talk, a pride that they and their community have been the fabric of a good piece of theatre? More to the point, I hope, is that they recognized a reflection of themselves, and saw some truth in it. Everyone is in high spirits, particularly our company of six. The community's response has even won over Christopher Knight's skepticism: he step-dances for the first time in his life.

Coyley, Eric, and some others sit together talking quietly and intensely. Later we hear that an ad hoc community meeting has been called for tomorrow morning.

Rocky Harbour, Monday 13 August 1973

Official Park Signing Day. The morning's community meeting decided to protest the signing ceremony, scheduled for 3 p.m. in Rocky Harbour. We were asked to come along and perform the show (now dubbed *Gros Mourn*) before the ceremony. I was cautious, fearing that we might take the focus away from the residents of the area, but Coyley put it to us straight: don't we empathise with them, share their concerns about the whole affair? Yes, of course. "Well then, you gotta come. You fellas helped us by what ye done." He won't feel right about it if we're not included. As it developed later, the park officials refused permission for a performance.

Most of the community turned out to dampen what was obviously planned by both governments to be a gala occasion: a multicoloured bandstand, bunting flapping gaily in the wind, a Canadian Forces Sea Cadet band from St. John's, refreshment tables, lots of speeches. The Sally's Cove protesters made a point of not taking the special government bus—they all drove here in their own cars.

The Minister of Indian Affairs and Northern Development, Jean Chretien, is stopped as he tries to walk through the crowd of demonstrators. He is the federal minister responsible for National Parks, and Sally's Cove is pinning its hopes on him. Many hope that Chretien is simply unaware of the depth of their objections, and that by speaking with him they can convince him not to sign the Park agreement today. As they talk, I notice a curious phenomenon: our show has crystallised a terminology for many of the demonstrators. They use metaphors drawn from the play's imagery as they present their case. The play has clarified the Sally's Cove reality: it has given people a "handle" on it. Like any work of art, our show represents a way of seeing. It is not neutral; it does not simply uplift people in some nebulous way. *Which* people does it uplift? Whom does it serve?

Chretien says he is sorry, his planners tell him it must be done this way, because "...it is the most striking piece of land we have in Eastern Canada." Tempers flare. Bud threatens: "If you goes ahead and signs it, I'd say there'll be fifty miles of park burned within a week!" Eric quiets him and tries to reason with Chretien: "We're not asking you to give up your park. Just let us stay in our homes, give us a two-mile boundary around Sally's Cove, and give our children the freedom to build homes on our own land...."

The federal Minister is adamant. He pushes through the crowd. I notice Milton cursing and breaking his picket sign over his knee again and again, until it is in tiny ragged pieces. He looks around helplessly. No one affected by it even knows the exact terms of the agreement which is to be signed. It has been kept secret and will only be made public after all the signatures are on.

Ed Maynard, the provincial member for this riding arrives and is cornered by his Sally's Cove voters, but he demurs, saying it is not his responsibility. It is his signature which will go on the agreement as representative of the provincial government. In the background the implacable Sea Cadets thump out:

> This Land is Your Land,
> This Land is My Land....

The ceremony begins, by now an hour late. Most speeches hailing the popularity of the new park are squelched by the grim Sally's Cove contingent. As Chretien and Maynard move to the table to sign the agreement, there is an agonized mass wail from Sally's Cove. Jane (who has travelled up here from Cow Head with a picket sign taped to her walking stick) and Edith begin a chorus of *O God Our Help in Ages Past*. The agreement is signed. The band loudly strikes up *O Canada*. No one cheers.

Sally's Cove, Thursday 16 August 1973

It is hard for us to leave this place. Last night was official goodbye time; we were treated to a big bash, with beer and songs and special sandwiches. There's a deep sadness in the air which everyone tries hard not to recognize. Our company is leaving for the South Coast, and those who live here avoid speaking of their future now.

Our Sally's Cove friends asked us to perform *Gros Mourn* in other communities in the park area, and so we have spent the past two

The Western Star

Vol. 21 No. 274 Corner Brook, Newfoundland, Tuesday, August 14, 1973 16 pages 12 cents

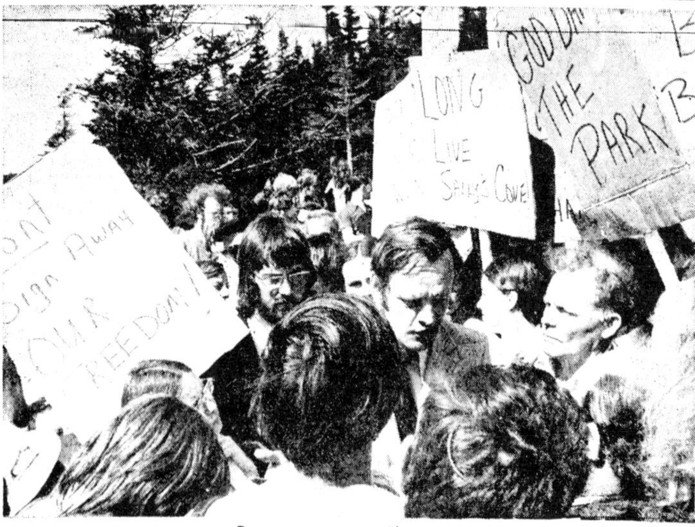

Protesters meet Chretien

Jean Chretien, Minister of Indian Affairs and Northern Development, was met by a group of about 30 protesters from the community of Sally's Cove, who were demonstrating against the placing of restrictions on property rights in communities inside the boundaries of the Gros Morne National Park. Mr. Chretien told the demonstrators that he could have had a policeman escort him past the mob, but he wanted to talk to them. (Star photo)

Demonstrators' threats fail to stop Gros Morne signing

ROCKY HARBOUR (Staff) – A group of about 30 demonstrators from Sally's Cove protesting restrictions placed on property rights in communities inside the boundaries of the Gros Morne National Park delayed ceremonies here yesterday which officially transferred the park to federal jurisdiction.

The small but vocal group, organized by a travelling theatre group from St. John's named The Mummers blocked the road way to the Park Interpretation Center where the formal agreement providing for the transfer was to be signed by Indian and Northern Affairs Minister Jean Chretien and Forestry and Agriculture Minister Ed Maynard.

They carried signs reading "We love Sally's Cove", "We want outside the park boundaries" and "God Damn the Park".

One demonstrator told Mr. Chretien that 50 miles of timber land inside the park would be burned if the agreement was signed.

The Sally's Cove demonstrators are particularly annoyed with the regulations demonstration grew out of this.

Other members of the group are: Paul Sametz, Mary Walsh, Chris Knight, Chris Brooks and Andy Thompson.

The Mummers even made the signs—hastily drawn lettering on cardboard nailed to wooden slats.

They trotted out a chant of the mid 1960's variety "Hell no, we won't go, 'Help us save Sally's Cove.'"

The chant by the six member group was rather desultory with none of the assembled people joining in.

The Mummers had also carefully orchestrated "booing" sessions prepared whenever park officials their wives and guests arrived. People hurried through the waving signs to the accompaniment of boos and sneers from the Mummers.

However, the moment of truth came when Mr. Chretien and Mr. Maynard arrived around 3 p.m. Mr. Chretien was surrounded by the park demonstrators who demanded to know why the agreement for the park had been kept secret.

Most of the demonstrators' throughts and beliefs were articulated by the Mummers and Eric Norman, a school teacher who has relatives in the area.

Mr. Norman wanted to know why the people were not consulted about the land question. He also pressed Mr. Chretien to answer why the agreement over the park was kept secret up to Monday.

Mr. Chretien, still surrounded by the demonstrators pointed out the federal government had relaxed its policy and allowed people to stay within the communities. He said this was done after representations from the people in the area, the provincial government, Mr. Maynard and Jack Marshall, the member of parliament for Humber-St. George's-St. Barbe.

He also said he had answered numerous questions in parliament on the park and replied to letters.

"I am very suprised at this," he said referring to the demonstration.

Other people asked Mr. Chretien the same question. At one point, Mr. Chretien said he could not understand the accents of the people because they spoke so fast. He then jokingly told the people perhaps they had trouble understanding his French accent. However, he said the matter may be looked at again though he made no firm committment on this point.

Clarence Roberts remained unimpressed.

"What you are doing is telling us that this place is too good for us," he told Mr. Chretien.

'You're telling us that we can't live here."

Several other people, including Mr. Norman and the

Gros Morne park has final signing

Front page of the Western Star, 14 August 1973.

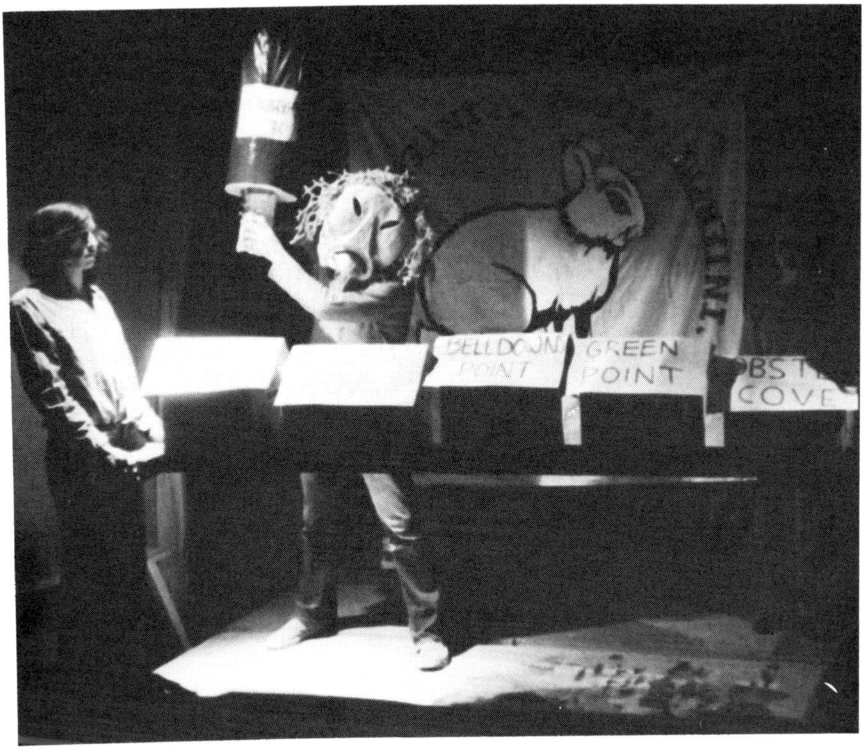

The champagne christening scene from *Gros Mourn*. Paul Sametz, Andy Thompson (with champagne bottle.)
Photo: Chris Brookes.

days playing St. Paul's, Cow Head and Rocky Harbour. We were accompanied to each performance by an escort group from Sally's Cove who helped us set up and talked with spectators after each show. Perhaps the play expresses a part of themselves which they normally find hard to explain to neighbouring communities. They sat amongst the audience of their peers, assessing responses.

Each of us in our own separate way has come to feel a part of this place. As artists we have actually done something useful. We have given birth to a work of theatre which is also a real and tangible tool for social action. We have put our shoulders to the wheel.

It is strange for me now to think about the popular conception of the Great Artist. It seems to be common in our society to consider some of the "important" artists of the past to have been mad and/or romantic and/or alienated from their contemporary society. The idea appears to be that we of later generations are more intelligent and sensitive than the uncaring slobs the Great Artist had to tolerate for an audience in his own time. We are better able to appreciate His work because it expounds universal notions about Beauty, Truth, and the tortured inner Nature of Man—which is what Real Art is supposed to be about: standing the test of time. These Great Ones would have perished from neglect at the hands of boorish simpletons had they not been magnanimously taken in by rich and refined patrons from the nobility—the wider working-class audience being presumably too preoccupied with such petty concerns as food, work, oppression, or revolution to have time for Great Art. Between the Goldberg Variations and *Gros Mourn*: a thousand miles of deaf ears.

> There are artists who demand the privilege of irresponsibility, as if the function of culture could be separated from history and from social struggle. As if books and paintings happened through this chosen élite, whispered into their ear by fairies, or demons, or private visions; these artists are supposed to have been born with the seal of impunity. I do not share the view of those who claim for the artist a kind of privileged freedom, a sacred status in society unconnected with the freedom of other workers (Galeano 1981).

Coyley came by the bus this morning with a copy of the *Western Star*. He was upset. I was, too, after I'd read it. Their coverage of the demonstration is a real hatchet job. The front page headlines a photo of the demonstration: *DEMONSTRATORS THREATS FAIL TO STOP PARK*, and goes on the describe a "mob" of residents "organised by a travelling theatre group called The Mummers."

Great. The old red scare. Outside agitators stirring up the otherwise peaceful peasantry. We are described as having "made the picket signs," "organized the booing sessions," and having staged the "contrived demonstration" as a piece of street theatre with the residents of Sally's Cove cast as spear carriers. Sally's Covers are presented as avaricious real estate speculators, hanging onto their land as an "investment!" The writer quotes Donna Butt extensively: it turns out that they were old enemies from alternate-press days. Apparently at the demonstration she laid into the guy for selling out to the establishment press. She thinks it may have got under his skin, but it's hard to believe such a vitriolic and biased piece of journalism can be motivated just by personal vindictiveness. It not only smears the Mummers Troupe, but discredits the people of Sally's Cove and taints their whole cause with illegitimacy. A couple of pages further on we find the clincher: a big half-page article eulogising the new park and its natural beauty. It's all taken from the official Parks Canada information releases, and it is by the same writer.

Coyley left to drive the 120 miles to Corner Brook and demand a retraction from the editor. It never appeared. A week later there was a flurry of letters from area residents decrying the original reportage and explaining their opposition to the relocation policy, but lucid letters on page four hardly offset the effect of front-page headlines.

Postscript

We played *Gros Mourn* briefly in St. John's to interested audiences and good reviews. If nothing else, this seemed to make people outside the immediate park area aware of the issue. We finished each performance by playing a tape recording of the real park signing ceremony as we slowly set fire to a row of smashed cardboard houses onstage.

Later we toured the show to communities in the other three Atlantic provinces where three new national parks were being instituted, and where similar relocation policies were being proposed. In one case, Kouchibouguac Park in New Brunswick, the policy had already been implemented, and some residents had been forcibly moved. Those remaining were becoming increasingly militant. Jackie Vautour, one of the leaders of the citizen's group sponsoring our performance in Richibucto, was one of them. Lynn accidentally sat on a rifle in the back of his car. "Is it loaded?" "No," said Jackie, pulling a handful of shells from his pocket, "but it wouldn't take long. We never know when we may need it. You see, you Newfoundlanders have a lot to learn yet about fighting national parks." The years since then have proved Jackie Vautour to be a remarkably determined man. Attempts to get him off his land have many times resulted in armed shoot-outs. When authorities finally burned his house down, he returned with other resettled residents, some tents, and lots of ammunition. Twelve years later he is still there.

Residents of all three other park areas who saw *Gros Mourn* found remarkable similarities between the Gros Morne situation and their own, and confirmed the mutual interdependence of the four park schemes. Community opposition to a particular aspect of National Park Policy in one province seemingly produced a corresponding change of that policy later in other provinces. All the separate communities were facing the same national policies, and our tour helped establish the need for information exchange between the different areas.

This led to the first People's Conference on National Parks in Halifax in December 1973. Delegates attended from all four of the in-progress Atlantic parks, including two delegates from Sally's

Cove. Three weeks later the much-disputed Ship Harbour National Park in Nova Scotia was cancelled in favour of a series of provincial recreation areas which allow residents to remain in their homes. National Park policy went under official review.

For eight years the Gros Morne Park authorities stuck to their guns. Half of Sally's Cove was resettled. The remaining residents continued to fight. Finally, in 1980, Parks Canada said it would be willing to negotiate enclave status for the broken community. Some of those who had already left under duress talked of suing the government for damages. One of them was Coyley, quoted in 1981 by newspaper and magazine articles:

> I never intended to leave. I lived there eight years with the park, but it came down to either move and get my life straightened out or keep fighting, and there didn't seem much point in that anymore. If they turn it into an enclave now, I'm going to get a lawyer and push it right to the bitter end. They put us through hell, and 'twas no need of it! (*Atlantic Insight* June 1981).

And in the song *The Government Game* there is this echo:

> Come all you young fellows and list while I tell;
> Of the terrible misfortunes that upon me fell.
> Centralisation they say was the name;
> But me I just calls it the Government Game.
>
> My name it don't matter; I'm not young anymore;
> But in all of my days I've never been poor.
> I'd lived a right good life and not felt no shame
> 'Til they made me take part in the Government Game.
>
> Sure the government paid us for moving away
> And leaving our birthplace for a better day's pay;
> They said that our poor lives would ne'er be the same
> Once we took part in the Government Game.
>
> It's surely a sad sight our moving around;
> Wishing we still lived near the cod fishing ground;
> But there's no going back now there's nothing to gain;
> Now that we've played in the Government Game.
>
> (Pat Byrne and Al Pittman)

How did the Mummers Troupe come out of this experience? Well, we learned some practical lessons about technique, for one thing. We learned that a specific show built for a specific community can be valuable not only to the original target audience, but to wider audiences. Of course this may not always be the case; a show's primary function and responsibility must always be to serve the community from which and for which it was built. Such a show will always be seen differently by outside audiences, and its function will then be different (communication rather than animation).

We certainly learned the importance of stage-managing the press. Thereafter we became much more careful about what company spokespeople said to the media.

Most importantly, we learned to respect the dangers of parachuting into a community by ourselves. We were a theatre company. Theatre artists do not generally have the commitment to stay in a community for years if necessary, organizing and providing lead-in and follow-up to a project like *Gros Mourn*. Their job, the one that they do best, is to be off and doing again. The danger is that this can merely raise unfulfillable expectations if the community is left high and dry without the skills (organisational, not theatrical) to continue their fight. In the case of Sally's Cove, despite the dedication and determination of many residents, half of the community relocated over the next decade. This might not have happened had there been an organisation on the spot with the ability to tackle the park bureaucracy and the long-term commitment to see it through. A play like *Gros Mourn* can be a useful and valuable step in a process, but it must not be the only step.

We saw two possible directions for the company in future.

One would have been to style ourselves less as a theatre and more as a community development agency, and to attract staff with the organisational skills and ability to commit themselves to an area for the long term. It would be unusual for such staff to have professional theatre skills or the need to employ them very often. There were agencies in the province already doing this job. They were experts in rural development. Our expertise was in theatre.

The other alternative was the one we adopted. We resolved to go into future projects wherever possible in conjunction with a rural development association, union, or other local planning organization with the experience and expertise to follow through. Our shows, instead of becoming a one-shot shoot-out, could highlight continuing development programmes, with a greater chance of ultimate success.

We examined the values of *Gros Mourn* as a community development tool. Memorial University's Extension service had experience in the use of film for community animation, and they made a comparative analysis. They noted that theatre is a much "hotter" medium than film or videotape, moving an audience more powerfully through involvement with live performers rather than with an unresponsive piece of celluloid. Theatre tailors its dynamics to its particular audience; film does not. Actors can answer questions;

film cannot. Theatre is flesh and blood and belief and support; by comparison film is cold and mechanical. On the other hand, film is permanent and travels far more easily. The *Gros Mourn* experience doesn't necessarily mean that plays about communities have to be overtly political. The explicit politics of *Gros Mourn* were mainly a result of our timing. We arrived in Sally's Cove at a time of crisis. Had we arrived and created the play six months earlier, all the rest might have happened differently. We might not have catalysed a demonstration. We might have catalysed something better, something ultimately more effective. Why *didn't* we get there six months earlier? We didn't know about it. Why not? We didn't have the contacts. Yet.

After *Gros Mourn*, development organisations in Newfoundland began to take an interest in our work. As our experience grew over the next few years, our work became more useful to those organisations, and the Mummers Troupe established fruitful working relationships with many of them.

There was one more lesson we learned, by now a familiar one: that the collective "we" ultimately boiled down to Lynn and myself. In the fall of 1973 Donna Butt went back to university; everyone else in the summer cast went upalong to Toronto. Who could blame them? We had no money left. Lynn and I went back to Maddox Cove to discover that *Gros Mourn* had not endeared us to government officialdom. They were out for blood.

7

Anarchist, Agit-Prop, Political Warfare...

> The function of the artist is to disturb. His duty is to arouse the sleepers, to shake the complacent pillars of the world.... In a world terrified of change, he preaches revolution...he is an agitator, a disturber of the peace.
>
> Norman Bethune

The sleepers were aroused, all right, but they didn't favour Bethune's point of view. They saw our show as an act of political sedition, especially offensive because politicians had been confronted at the demonstration. Blood pressure in the Arts and Culture Centre's throne room was, as they say in the stock market, limit up. The provincial government's cultural officials now had proof of what they had been saying all along: that the Mummers were not artists, they were political rabble-rousers. Their plays were not culture but an incitement to riot and civil disobedience. They would have to be put down. A flurry of letters and phone calls passed between provincial civil servants and Ottawa underlining our treasonous disrespect for both Art and Canada. One, which I have always treasured, derided our work to the Canada Council as "anarchist...agit-prop, political warfare type productions...."

I liked the ring of that. Perhaps some day we'd be able to live up to it.

At the time, I was amazed at the energy and vehemence of the official reaction. They seemed to think we were *so* dangerous. They were bursting a blood vessel to discredit us. In retrospect I realize what it was. We had exposed their stranglehold on art. We had broken their carefully constructed illusion. The ruling class had spent a century safely enshrining Newfoundland theatre in a gilded proscenium. Now a bunch of pinko mummers had torn it down again. Off with their heads!

Well, we thought, if our work is giving *these* guys apoplexy, we must be doing something right.

As we passed through the valley of the shadow of government censure, we looked about anxiously for rods and staffs to comfort the company's empty bank account. Many standard approaches to professional theatre funding weren't applicable to a politically active theatre. We made a list of them.

Rod #1: Box Office. There was only one professional company in Canada which managed to survive from box office alone: a dinner theatre in Alberta. Faded American stars shuffling through faded American sex comedies; audiences of faded city-dwellers shuffling through plates of faded food; tickets $32.50. We couldn't go that route. High ticket prices and no touring would render our work pointless.

Rod #2: Corporate Sponsorship. We tried to imagine IBM sponsoring shows like *Gros Mourn*, but there was a limit even to our crazed imaginations. And business would not be likely to support any project which challenged capitalist hegemony.

Rod #3: Contract Jobs. We *could* imagine working with labour unions and rural development agencies, although we knew of no successful collaboration since the Canadian Workers Theatre groups of the 1930s. Certainly we couldn't come on to them as "artistes." We'd have to prove the practical usefulness of our work first. For this we needed more experience.

Rod #4: Government Funding. Well, why not? There were several reasons "why not." Most federal arts programmes thought we were too socially-oriented, while federal social programmes considered us too arts-oriented. On the surface of it, we were too artistic for LIP, too healthy for LEAP, too old for OFY, and too permanent for another injection from the Canada Council's Explorations programme.

Certainly the provincial government wasn't about to help put our finances in the black. As far as they were concerned, we were already black. Black as sin. We had refused to genuflect at the altar of Official Culture, a grave heresy, and our financial excommunication was assured. Still, we felt morally entitled to some provincial support. It was public monies that filled the Newfoundland government's cultural affairs war chest, and it didn't seem unreasonable to expect that Newfoundland professional theatre artists should see a few pennies of it. But expectations weren't going to pay our grocery bill.

We thought we'd have better luck with the Canada Council's Theatre Section. Why them? Their programmes were designed to provide theatres with a continuing lifeline on a yearly basis, not just per show assistance. We needed a measure of stability to get out of a hand-to-mouth existence and into longer-range planning. And unlike the Newfoundland government's Cultural Affairs Division, the Canada Council is intended to be an arms length funding agency, insulated from political influence. Artistic quality, not ideology, is supposed to be its criterion. Fine. Who wants to bore the audience? (The converse is also true, although less often remarked upon. Just as commitment is no excuse for lack of quality, so quality is no excuse for lack of commitment.)

We had few illusions about the basic contradiction involved in seeking government funding for plays intended, on occasion, to nip the hand that fed them. Would we be coopted? We worried. The Perfect Revolution, as they used to remark in Rochdale's Seventh Floor Ashram, will never be won with guns, man. Sure. But the Practical Revolution isn't just a matter of macrobiotic diets, either. Shortchanging effectiveness for the sake of ideological purity is pretty useless, especially when the other side has most of the heavy artillery. One has to learn to live in the dialectic. We were going to try.

It wasn't going to be easy to get the opportunity. The province's cultural mandarins were heading us off at the pass, urging Ottawa to reject the upstarts who embarrassed the politicians in Rocky Harbour. And in the nation's capital, many of the bankers of official art already shared the opinion of Hamilton Southam, then director of the National Arts Centre:

> I don't believe that artists have anything to do with politics; the artists who get mixed up in politics are usually secondclass artists...the great ones have nothing to do with politics, nothing to do with unions, nothing to do with campaigns.

Canada Council officials gave us a tepid reception, explaining that "as soon as you use real names your theatre becomes political rather than creative." Their Newfoundland counterparts had told them that *Gros Mourn* described Jean Chretien as a "fucking frog bastard." The play contained no such line, and I righteously produced the script to prove that even anarchist agit-prop political warfare didn't have to stoop to racism. I shouldn't have done that. After reading the script, Council found even greater reason to be appalled. They declared frostily that we should have exercised a better sense of responsibility than to incite audiences to burn federal forests.

Hold on a minute. *Gros Mourn* didn't try to incite arson, although there were references to burning in the script. But that was not the point. The point was, Lynn and I argued, to whom did we owe this sense of responsibility?

We rejected the Council's implication that an artist's responsibility was to uphold bourgeois values. We asserted that an artist who creates a documentary mirror of a community must acknowledge a primary responsibility to the community. The work belongs morally to them; it is their reflection. If people are talking about burning down a park, then it would be irresponsible to deny this observation simply because it doesn't conform to Ottawa's sensibilities. An artist's job, we said, is to be faithful to his subject— not to protect bourgeois values.

In this way our work differed from the approach to theatre documentary then becoming popular in Toronto. That approach placed relatively more emphasis on the entertainment potential of the play for audiences outside the original community, "bringing 'em back alive" as pieces of rural exotica for the Toronto theatre season. We were more concerned with community development, and we would never, for example, perform a documentary anywhere outside the target area without the permission of the original community itself. Our primary allegiance was not to art, to entertainment, to Canadian theatre or to the audiences back home. It was to the target community. Slowly we began to suspect that this principle might be at odds with the underlying aesthetics of official art funding.

The Canada Council wasn't really on our wave length. Under the then Secretary of State Gerrard Pelletier, Ottawa was beginning to talk about "access" and "democratisation of the arts." But in practice this seemed to boil down to touring the Stratford Festival through the boondocks so that rural taxpayers could feel they were getting their money's worth and presumably vote Liberal. It was still the Arts and Culture Centre approach: a merchandising of culture, the misguided extension of the same ethic which wants to provide every North American town with a Colonel Sanders takeout. It doesn't answer the real questions about democratisation and access.

But the winds of change were blowing through Ottawa, and we hoped they would eventually blow the Canada Council in our direction.

Meanwhile, we were between times. We had been lucky to get through our first year. Now how to continue? The arts establishment thought we were social workers, the rural development establishment thought we were artists. Most people thought we were crazy. And those who appeared to value our work—rural fishermen, miners, families in Sally's Cove—were not those in power. Officialdom scoffed at us. *Gros Mourn* had blown any possibility of credibility, they said. Give up.

We did not intend to give up. But we had to force the arts establishment to accept the validity of *Gros Mourn*; the future of our company rested upon it. We had made a crack in the wall. Now to widen it, before the wall fell on top of us. We began the long and difficult transformation from unknown guerrilla theatre group to established political performance company. It was a rocky road.

Lynn and I worked our asses off. I wrote an article for *This Magazine* describing the Sally's Cove project, hoping to give us wider credibility. It worked. Publication feedback was very positive, and gave our energies a boost—we weren't alone in left field!

We were living on borrowed time and borrowed money, but went ahead with shows anyway. Fund raising was mostly hit-and-run. We scored a once-only award from the Secretary of State Multiculturalism programme (provincial civil servants later "advised" them not to renew it), and the University Extension Service extended my salary for another year. We scraped together a few other crumbs and between the jigs and the reels managed to pull off two more projects during the winter of '74.

In November, we held auditions in St. John's again, with little success. Almost no one showed up. The few local performers who were emerging had either gone to Toronto like 50,000 other Newfoundlanders to seek their fortunes, or were back in university. Then a man from Parks Canada walked in. Uh-oh, I thought, he's come to argue about last summer. He hadn't. It was Bob Pot, with a wonderful clown physicality and a background in classical trombone. The first virtue made him a strong Father Christmas for our 1973 *Mummers Play* production, while the second came in very handy for blowing up the pigs' bladders needed to hit spectators over the head with. Lynn was King George. Bembo Davies and Jan Henderson came down from Upalong, Jan full of Richard Pochinko's clown techniques to be the Doctor and Bem full of Peking Opera ideas to play the Turkish Knight. It was a very good show, and after mummering the twelve nights of Christmas we toured through schools in January.

School touring was important to us. At that time indigenous Newfoundland material was almost totally absent from the school curriculum. Students had virtually no exposure to Newfoundland literature, poetry, plays, visual art or folklore, and only minimal acquaintance with Newfoundland history.

This was 1973. In 1973, only 3 per cent of the educational book market in Canada featured Canadian-authored books published by Canadian publishers. A national survey of high school students revealed: 89 per cent could not identify Gabréal Dumont; 69 per cent, René Levesque; 92 per cent, Norman Bethune. Fifty-nine per cent could not say into which ocean the Mackenzie River flows. Given a list of 8 names and asked to circle the Canadians, 78 per cent did not recognise E.J. Pratt; 69 per cent, Margaret Atwood; 79 per cent, Al Purdy; 70 per cent, Margaret Lawrence.

We became the first theatre company to play Newfoundland schools, and it was an uphill grind all the way. Newfoundland Department of Education authorities held the view that the 3 R's came from books, thank you very much, not from theatre. But the close-quarters dynamics of the *Mummers Play* transferred easily from living rooms to school rooms, making it a fine classroom performance piece, and students and staff were very enthusiastic. They lobbied their superiors, and slowly the Department of Education's attitude began to thaw. The following year we outflanked them for good by getting our Mummers Play script safely included in a curriculum anthology. They responded right on cue: if it was a book, it must be all right.

That January we also played to some very warm and ingenuous audiences at the Newfoundland Penitentiary, a custom we continued for years whenever the authorities allowed.

In February 1974 we mounted a production of Steven Bush's fairytale play about U.S. foreign policy and Canadian resource development, *Once a Giant*, with giant puppets. It toured to schools in March and to the Nova Scotia Puppet Festival in October. The chief protagonist, operated from inside by Bob Pot and Judy Marshak, stood twelve feet high and was covered with 178 dried pigs bladders. The audience smelled him long before they saw him. By the time we finished blowing up the 178th bladder we all could have gone on to a career in classical trombone.

In May, we took *Gros Mourn* to high schools across the island. If students and teachers related to the subject matter as positively as we thought they would, it would make our detractors in the cultural ministry look foolish. The tour came off well. We developed a follow-up classroom study kit on the larger question of resettlement, and in resettled areas it had particularly strong impact. I remember one student who talked with us after our performance in a Marystown High School. His family had been resettled from Bruit but he went back alone each summer to tent out for two months where the community had been. He described the original move, the insidious pressures. One man, who opposed the move, stalled his own family's departure until the very last barge trip. While his wife and children watched the vessel pull into the wharf, he went downstairs and shot himself. The boy's story came out through clenched teeth. The man was his uncle.

Meanwhile, back on the Troupe's financial front, there was a whole lot of fancy footwork going on. The Burmese Dosshouse Meeting, for instance. The BDH was a meeting between playwright Michael Cook, myself, and the artistic director of the Newfoundland Travelling Theatre, Dudley Cox. (Dudley's company was a seasonal operation which had toured light British comedies through outport communities for the past two summers.) It was held at the request of the Canada Council, which was now dangling the carrot of federal funding a little closer to everyone's noses. The donkeys gathered, accordingly.

The meeting got its name because Michael had suggested that we talk over a beer at the United Nail and Foundry Club, a tiny tavern off Patrick Street. When I got there Dudley was stalking up and down outside, muttering to himself. He didn't like the look of Mike's meeting place. "This place," he harrumphed, "looks like a Burmese doss-house!" I'd never seen a Burmese doss or her house, but loved the description. We went in and found Michael. There were no dosses, just a bunch of guys playing darts, but the beer was cheap. So was the talk, as it turned out.

Word was out that the Canada Council Theatre Section had finally decided to invest in a Newfoundland regional theatre. A brand new one. Ottawa had suggested that the Newfoundland Travelling Theatre, the Mummers Troupe, and Mike Cook all band together to make One Big Company for administrative convenience. Some mainland director was to be hired (at three times the actors' salary levels) to come down and run it. Newfoundlanders were to be the cheap labour, just like in the province's other industries. The new theatre would tour British and American hits, foreign classics, and the occasional Newfoundland play— a strangely familiar formula. It would base itself in the five government Arts and Culture palaces. Above all, it would not be controversial. Michael and Dudley supported this plan. They felt it was the best we could get.

All that was required of me was not to contaminate the One Big Company with politics. The plan required me to stop creating embarrassing plays like *Gros Mourn*, and settle down to a comfortable career as director of a make-no-waves school touring unit. After all,

Mike and Dudley explained, no one could seriously expect to get financial support for a *political* theatre. I didn't go for it, and the meeting dissolved into shouts and curses. It was the first of many donkey fights that winter.

Financial feuds are one of the most unfortunate recurring features of the Newfoundland theatre scene. This one was typical. Before the appearance of the Canada Council carrot, the province's practising professional theatre artists were quite friendly to each other. A spirit of chivalrous camaraderie suffused the theatre community. Yet as soon as the federal greenback appeared on the horizon, we were at each other's throats, each faction desperately discrediting the other to get their paws on the loot. A decade later, federal and provincial arts funding bodies continued to exploit this lamentable phenomenon to the detriment of the province's unorganised cultural workers.

> The arts scene in Newfoundland is like a cageful of starving animals. Throw in a dollar bill and watch the artists tear each other apart (Newfoundland visual artist Peter Walker).

The Canada Council forged ahead anyway, and presented the holy grant grail to the as yet non-existent Newfoundland Theatre Company under Dudley Cox's care in April 1974, on condition that he hire "a professional artistic adviser" to chieftain it. But at the eleventh hour the Mummers' lobbying began to bear fruit. By now, our Troupe could claim to be the only professional theatre in the province which had been producing more-or-less continuously for eighteen months. And we had mustered considerable support for the concept of theatre as a community development vehicle. Scenes from *Gros Mourn* appeared on CBC television's national *Take 30* programme. The Mummers were becoming credible. The feds began to look confused.

The provincial government's culture mandarins rattled their sabres: unless they got what they wanted, they'd take their ball and go home. There would be no provincial money, so there. In June, hoping to head off an increasingly embarrassing situation, the Council resorted to that old federal standby: a commission. They appointed Keith Turnbull, a theatre director from Toronto, to tell them just what the hell was going on in the Newfoundland theatre scene. And they gave him three whole days in the province to find out.

By now the situation was even more complicated. Some of the Newfoundland performers who had been seeking their fortunes in Toronto had formed themselves into a group called Codco (the Cod Company), and returned to take St. John's by storm with their first show *Cod On A Stick*. They didn't look any more like the Canada Council's formula favourite than the Mummers did. Turnbull had a brave try anyway, recommending that Council set up a non-formula-fare company based on outport touring, under the thumb of the provincial Director of Cultural Affairs and under the aegis of a mainland director, because "there is no one in Newfoundland with the talent and professional expertise to run a company of this nature." We all wondered who this poor unnamed mainland director was that everyone was trying so desperately to find a job for. Some Canadian, disqualified from running the Stratford Festival or Citadel Theatre because he wasn't British?

Codco thought the whole idea of rolling a brand-new theatre off the Ottawa assembly line and into Newfoundland stank. Lynn and I certainly thought so. Together we eventually convinced Dudley Cox that valour would be the better part of discretion. All three companies rejected the Turnbull report and struck a heroic posture of solidarity together. We were Newfoundlanders, we said, wrapping ourselves in the rhetoric of righteous regionalism. We were different. We remembered the Terms of Confederation. We remembered Term 29. Hell, if it could have helped our case any, we would have remembered the Alamo.

Our theatre battle was part of a wider war taking place on other fronts. In February 1974, over 150 representatives of the province's amateur and professional artists and organizations from all fields—film, literature, crafts, visual arts, folk arts, dance, theatre and music—met together in two giant conferences and agreed upon a workable structure for a provincial Arts Council to supplant the dictatorship of the Director of Cultural Affairs (the guy with Prince Philip on his wall.) Such an arts council would be made up of elected members of the arts community instead of a single civil service appointee, and would direct arts funding more towards cultural *activity* than towards polishing the bricks and mortar of the Arts and Culture Centres. The province's artists petitioned the government to recognise such an arts council, believing that the tide was turning away from élitism towards democracy in the arts. All this added ammunition to our demand that the Canada Council recognize the province's indigenous professional theatres in their own right.

Finally, in the fall of 1974, the Canada Council Theatre Section gave in. Despite the objections of the provincial government, it agreed to support the work of the three existing companies: The Newfoundland Travelling Theatre under Dudley Cox's direction, the Mummers Troupe under mine and Lynn's, and Codco under its six actor-shareholders. As long as we formed a holding company representing all three theatres to receive the grant, they said, we could split up the cash later.

If you're confused reading this you can imagine what it was like to live through. But the unwieldy arrangement had its advantages. As only one-third of a triumvirate, the Mummers Troupe's politics were proportionately less threatening to the Council. Codco, with only one show under its belt, benefitted from the older two thirds of the triumvirate which had demonstrated their stability by completing Canada Council's requisite two years of production. And Dudley Cox, who had perhaps the least to gain, vastly improved his personal chances for sainthood.

In October 1974, the members of all three companies got together in Bob Joy's (of Codco) house for the big moment: choosing a name for the Canada Council's holding company. "Whatever we do," someone emphasized at the outset, "we will *not* call it something mundane like 'Newfoundland Theatre Limited,' right?" Yes, yes. Five hours of wine and dope later, in grandiloquent testimony to the collective process, we had decided to call it Newfoundland Theatre Limited. Just in time for Christmas, the Canada Council got to play Santa Claus. The Newfoundland Cultural Affairs Division shrieked, but instead of turning into a puddle of Perrier water as we'd hoped, they played Scrooge. They refused to sponsor Newfoundland Theatre Limited productions, withheld financial support, and played divide-and-conquer strategies with one or another of the three member companies whenever they thought any of us were financially desperate enough to fall for it.

Later, with a flurry of bureaucratic footwork, a three-man committee of civil servants headed (naturally) by Cultural Affairs Director John Perlin advised the government to turn thumbs down on the elected provincial arts council, affirming (naturally) that Perlin himself provided an "adequate vehicle for the initiative and development of the arts." Naturally.

> The government (has) placed all the arts under state control with one director acting as generalissimo. Premier Moores probably doesn't realise that outside the dictatorships Newfoundland will be the only place where arts come under such rigid state control (*St. John's Evening Telegram* 1 December 1975).

But we had ensured that for at least the rest of the decade, Newfoundland's professional theatre would not be beaten into the standard "regional" model with which other provinces were afflicted.

Meanwhile, six months before the funding breakthrough, Lynn and I— broke again— had put our Maddox Cove house and hens up for collateral, borrowed money, and taken the Mummers to Buchans.

Flying

Company Town—The Story of Buchans 8

It would turn your stomach to see what American Smelting and Refining took out of Buchans in the years they have operated there, without paying to this province hardly anything in taxes and employing people there at miserable wages in a company town with miserable housing. It would really cause you to become a savage—you know, Marxist.

John C. Crosbie, MP

The summer of 1974 was immortalized by the Newfoundland government's decision to celebrate the glories of our twenty-five years of Confederation with Canada: Jubilee Year. It would be a big celebration: fireworks, films, music, shows, CULTURE! The gleeful announcements were met with a certain amount of cynicism. Confederation is not all it's cracked up to be, baby bonuses notwithstanding, some said. Amongst the more visible naysayers was the April Fools Society (so called because Newfoundlanders woke up to their first day of Confederation on 1 April 1949). The Fools ran up pink white and green nationalist flags on public flagpoles and circulated statements like the following:

> WHY ARE WE CELEBRATING?
>
> BECAUSE major decisions affecting Newfoundland's development are being made in Ottawa?
>
> BECAUSE key positions in Newfoundland have been consistently given to outsiders rather than to Newfoundlanders of equal ability?
>
> BECAUSE Newfoundland society is being steadily absorbed into North American mediocrity?

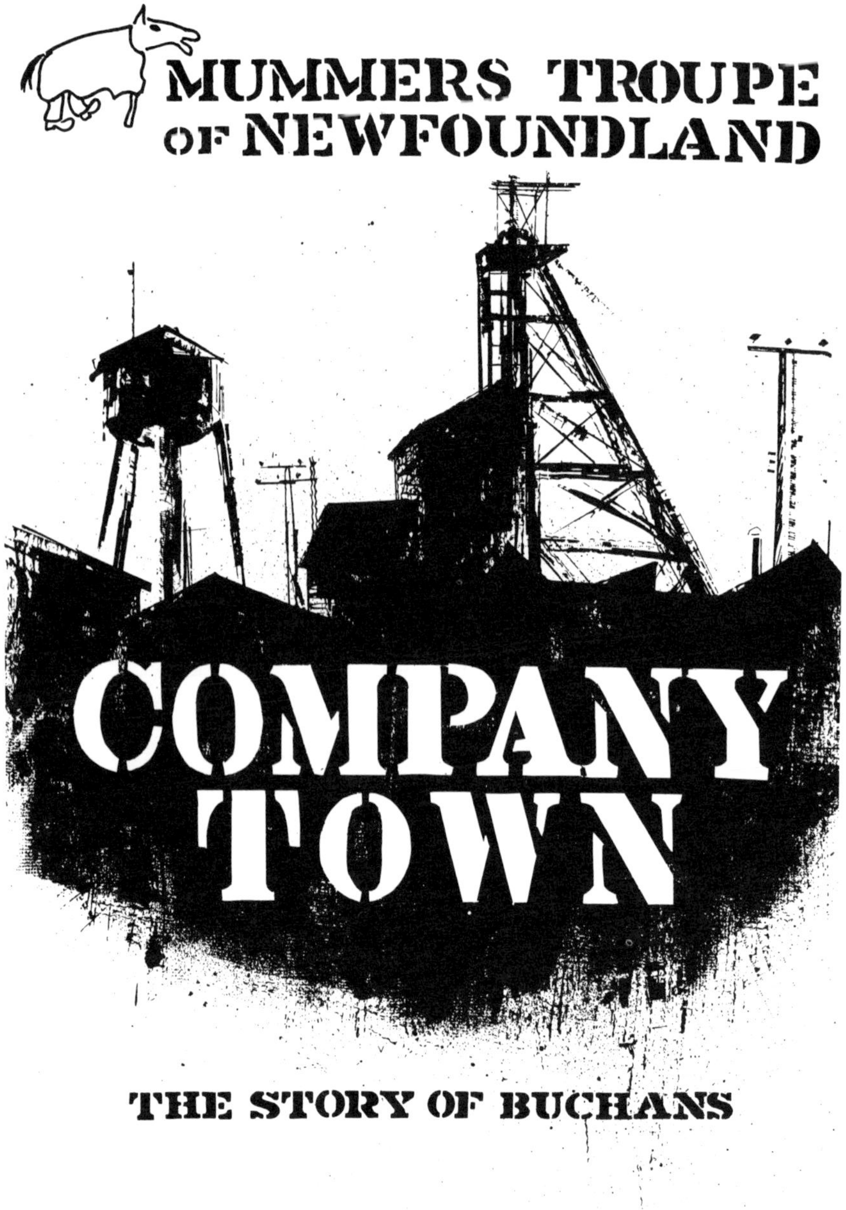

Poster by Don Wright based on a painting by Max Walsh of Buchans.

BECAUSE our resources have been sold out to foreign and mainland interests?

BECAUSE our people are forced to emigrate through a failure to develop local opportunities?

BECAUSE our fisheries are dying?

Signed: THE APRIL FOOLS.

The provincial government, perhaps fearing that Newfoundland artists would find too little in the past quarter century to celebrate about, hired out-of-province artists to show us how to do it. It blew most of its entertainment bankroll on a flock of tired music hall comedians who were flown all the way over from Britain to be toured through the province all summer at taxpayers' expense. Nobody is quite as good as the Mother Country when it comes to celebrating the joys of colonialism.

The province also commissioned a homegrown historical pageant (a kind of official antidote to *Newfoundland Night*) which toured the island.

For Lynn and me it was frustrating to have to borrow the money for a sandwich while watching steak dinners being given away in front of our noses, but we figured those government grapes were sour, anyway. We had our commitment to keep us warm, right?

Our conception of celebration was somewhat different. We wanted to make a show about Buchans. Buchans didn't offer the kind of picturesque sleepiness that the government liked to show off to the tourist trade (the Department of Tourism's official promotion film was titled *Come Paint and Photograph Us*). It was a grey, scruffy mining town owned lock, stock and barrel by the American Smelting and Refining Company (ASARCO). In Buchans, for example, company cars drove around without provincial license plates. They didn't need them because the company, not the province, was the law in Buchans. The town's 2,000 residents were no-nonsense militant trade unionists who in the previous three years had been responsible for two of the province's longest and most bitter strikes. People there remembered us kindly from our free performance during their previous summer's strike, and the union local, Steelworkers 5457, encouraged our new project.

We calculated that our borrowed money would pay for a cast of six, as long as I didn't take a salary. But finding performers proved to be as difficult as finding their salaries. Lynn was due to leave for an eight-month arts administration apprenticeship with the Manitoba Theatre Centre, and most other luminaries of the local theatre scene were already contracted to the big cast, better-paying Government Pageant. After much cajoling, I convinced Donna Butt, now on her university summer holidays, to join the company for a second summer. Bembo Davies, who'd gone back to Ontario after the Christmas Mummers Play, agreed to fly down, as did a zany actor-musician I'd once worked with on a puppet project in Toronto, Allen Booth. I didn't really want to overweight our group with non-Newfoundlanders who wouldn't be able to handle the Buchans dialects, but there was no choice. Other mainlanders completed the rest of the cast: Connie Kaldor, a fine singer from Saskatchewan; Howie Cooper, who'd just completed a community documentary with Toronto's Theatre Passe-Muraille; and Lee Campbell. Lee was big, down-to-earth, and fresh out of a woods camp somewhere in northern Ontario: the antithesis of a middle-class sophisticate. If anyone would be able to relate to hard-rock miners, he would. It was an exciting cast, but anyone with half an ear could notice that Donna and I were the only Newfoundlanders in the lot. Accents, however, were only the tip of the iceberg. It was as much a question of dialectics as dialect.

Newfoundlanders have keen ears for accents, and for many, the whiff of a mainland accent can cause a whole set of preconceptions to snap into place. A lot of Come-From-Aways interpret this as spurious xenophobia. Xenophobic it may be, but spurious it is not. It's the result of long-term regional economic disparity. Meet a Newfoundlander in Toronto and chances are that he'll turn out to be a labourer or industrial worker; meet a mainlander in Newfoundland and ten to one he's a boss, a manager, a professional who's running things. Here, a central Canadian accent is a symbol; in general it denotes a member of a dominant class. What is resented is not the pronunciation, but the power.

In our cast, the noticeable differences in accent echoed the obvious: as middle-class urbanites, most of the actors did not share the working-class Newfoundland background of the Buchans miners who would be the subjects of their research. But with luck, I thought pragmatically, we might be able to make our "outsiderness" work like Brecht's *verfremdungseffekt*: the "alienation effect." Placed in the right context, the cast's accents would distance Buchaneers from their reflected portraits onstage. This could encourage the audience to analyse what the play was saying about their community's history, instead of getting sucked into sentimental identification with character.

This meant challenging the actors' pride: the professional ability to *be* anyone— Othello, John Proctor, Don Head. We must be careful here. Othello and Proctor are fictional characters; Don Head is a real one, and what's more, he'd be sitting in our opening night audience. How would a Buchans miner act in a given situation? We could not be sure. We could only be sure of how a middle-class actor from outside would *imagine* acting in that situation. We must not muddy class realities.

> By not pretending to become the people of Buchans, but merely "indicating" the audience to themselves, the company committed itself to a style which reveals the idea of theatre itself while it plays. Any artifice was immediately broken. The actors made the sound effects in front of the audience. They wore no costume more elaborate than a hat or an apron. They indicated "This is a bunk now, this is a movie theatre now, now it's a house, now a mine-shaft." Even the lighting switches were fully visible, so that any manipulation of objects was stripped of mystery. This made it possible to show patterns, to be analytical without objectifying, to be informative. At the same time, because the characters were copied or made by composite from actual members of the community—the original audience—and because the bulk of the play was accurate narration, there was more reality in this verbatim accuracy than in the more slippery technique of fiction (Sandra Heindsmann, *Mayday* No. 1 1975).

It was a question of our attitude, as artists, towards the material. The trick was, I felt, to encourage this attitude in our research and creation process as well as in performance. So before we began, I suggested a few rules to pre-structure the experience:

1. We would rely on taped narrative. I borrowed six tape recorders and insisted that everyone use them. We would avoid inventing people's speech or lives—where invention was necessary we'd find ways to let the audience know that we were inventing on our terms, not on theirs.
2. We would create a *people's* history of Buchans. To my mind the most glaring evidence of the union-company standoff lay in the way the two parties viewed the community. To the company, Buchans was a temporary mining camp, a statistic in their annual corporate report. To the residents, it was a home with a forty year-old history, a history which demanded an equivalent corporate responsibility.

   I felt that a dramatisation of oral history could emphasise the existence of Buchans as a place where people *lived*. It would document the long and tangled roots of the struggle which had recently surfaced in strike violence, and which bound the community and its union so tightly together.

3. We would be extremely careful about our image as researchers in the community. Engineering chemistry calls this the Heisenberg Uncertainty Principle: the presence of the observer always influences the reality which is being observed.
4. We would be in a total-immersion research situation. The mine manager had given us permission to live in the bunkhouse and eat at the messhall alongside miners and kitchen staff. He was kind enough to extend to us the "bunkhouse rate," the full-board miners' rate which would make the actors' paltry $65/week salaries a liveable allowance. We would be permitted to accompany underground work shifts. The principal of the Catholic school allowed us to use the school's gymnasium for rehearsal. It even had a piano.

We arrived in early July. The six-week creation period fell into the more-or-less typical collective creation pattern for documentaries:

Week One—Immediate Impressions

We mostly watched and listened. All of us were impressed immediately by the community's vitality, a liveliness which seemed perhaps to be a survival mechanism, developed in reaction to the company's dry balance-sheet mentality. Our habits changed: the first mineshift went on at 7:30 a.m., meaning that anyone who got to the messhall later than 7:15 (usually Howie Cooper) got cold fried eggs.

Each morning we met at the school for a show-and-tell session: that is, we acted out the material we'd gathered, rather than just talking about it. I kept notes but made little attempt to edit any of the presented "scenes" at this point— that would come weeks later when we would have a large body of theatrical material from which to choose. In this initial phase I pushed purely for quantity. Not surprisingly, much of this early material was facile, but our sharing of first impressions helped establish a collective working pattern and a "group language" which was vital for our politically and theatrically disparate group.

We began each morning's sessions around the school piano, warming up with some of the original songs which Buchaneer Angus Lane had written as morale boosters during the 1971 and 1973 strikes. *All Because of ASARCO* was set to the well-known tune of *Surrounded by Water*:

> 5457 is now out on strike;
> We seek from ASARCO what we deem is right;

'Til Hell freezes over, we'll continue to fight;
We won't beg or plead from ASARCO.

The Company makes millions on concentrate tons,
While miners wind up with lead on their lungs;
Mining makes old men out of our young sons,
Producing ore for ASARCO.

Stick to your guns boys and never relent,
Don't go back for a few paltry cents
To boost the wages of those New York gents
Who get damn well paid by ASARCO.

Our plea, our plea, is for You and for Me
To demand what we want from this company.
And no one here will go down on their knee
To beg or to plead from ASARCO....

For most of the cast, this project was their first contact with labour militancy. Three days earlier, no-one had even known the words to *Solidarity Forever.*

Week Two: Up to the Elbows in Research

First impressions quickly deepened. (Example: We discovered the difficulties of doing our laundry. There *is* a laundromat in Buchans, but its use is restricted to management personnel.) Buchaneers generally viewed our group as a curiosity, and were warm and friendly. The union executive, in particular, took an active interest in our research. We began asking more intelligent questions.

We encountered Buchans' unique blend of humour. The two-man "buddy" system underground gave rise to some wonderful comic/straightman routines oriented around work. Howie and Lee spent a whole nightshift underground with miners and were able to recreate some excellent observed comedy. Bembo, meanwhile, encountered the supernatural:

> Sure, there's ghosts down in the mine. That's right. I sees 'em every day. There's three or four are my personal friends. Now these ghosts, when I go down there if I don't see, well, on the average of six or seven ghosts every fortnight, well...I'm lonesome. That's right.
>
> Now there is this one ghost down there, well, it's just a pair o' legs. That's right. Just a pair o' legs stickin' out of the side o' the drift, from the knees down. That's right. Well, he's very good, he comes by and has a smoke, watches me work, you know.
>
> There's a couple of others. There's a big tall one and a short one and they come by regular too, you know. You see 'em down the drift and, well, you hear the feet, eh? And eh...the tall one whistles. And

> you look down the drift and you see their lights. From their hats. And ya holler out to 'em but they don't make no answer. Ya start down towards 'em and they disappears. And ya goes down to where they disappears to, and there is nothin'. Just nothin'. Just rock. That's right. And eh, the tall fella, his name's Alvin. And the short fella, he's Jack. And eh, the legs? Well, they got no name.
>
> You believe that?

The tag line was a trick that Allan Booth had picked up from conversations with Charlie Perrier, an old trapper living up the road in Buchans Junction who had helped discover the mine forty-odd years ago. Charlie was a great storyteller with a penchant for tall tales. After earnestly relating some piece of local history he would pause to see how the listener digested the story, then ask elfishly: "You believe dat?" It was a nice snap back to reality, a reminder that his tale was open to analysis. This was exactly what we wanted our audience to remember, and so we adopted the "Perrier Technique" widely throughout the show.

Week Three: Up to the Armpits in Research

This week a remarkable thing occurred. I had become quite close to Peter Noftle, a retired driller with a photographic memory and an endless collection of recitations. Several years earlier Peter had been a recipient of the ASARCO 25-year watch. The annual watch presentation was one of those typical obsequious ceremonies by which companies commemorate long-term employee service. The spectacle of a rich multinational company attempting to compensate victims of industrial disease with cheap jewellery was too bitter an irony for Peter, and he had refused to attend the ceremony to receive his own watch. It seemed to me that he now regretted missing that opportunity to speak publicly his mind to his employers.

One morning I switched rehearsal from the school to the Union Club where I knew Peter could usually be found, in the hope that he might be able to help us with an improvised scene. I brought my tape recorder, just in case.

I asked the actors to improvise a scene in which a miner goes to the watch presentation ceremony and raises hell. One by one the actors of our group entered the scene, refused to accept their watch, and demanded to speak. The scene was not working. The improvised speeches sounded false, unlike what a real miner would say. Peter, sitting in the back of the bar, suddenly came forward, entered the scene, accepted the watch, and politely asked the "company manager" for permission to speak. I switched on my tape recorder, and

I suspect the remarkable speech which followed had already had years of rehearsals in Peter's mind.

> Friends and fellow-workers of Buchans, ladies and gentlemen. As I gaze around the audience tonight, I miss quite a few familiar faces. Men with whom I worked over the past twenty-five years. Today they are dead and gone, which brings sadness to one's heart. Those men, as you know, gave twenty-five years and more of hard, faithful and honest work to the American Smelting and Refining Company. Today they are no longer with us. WHY? Because of that dread disease that every miner fears: the disease called silicosis. What, today, did these men, or their families, receive from Buchans? From the American Smelting and Refining Company?
>
> I came here when I was thirty-three and in the prime of life. I gave the best years of my life to the American Smelting and Refining Company. After twenty-five years, I am given a watch.
>
> Now, it is not my intention, ladies and gentlemen, to criticize or to ridicule the mining company. Many will say: you made your living here, you raised your family here. I grant you that. But in over twenty-five years of hard and honest service, American Smelting and Refining Company never gave me anything I never worked for.
>
> Today, many of us are just about worn out. When we're finished, if we live until we're sixty-five and retire or if we are disabled, what do we have to look forward to? We will not be allowed to stay in a company house. We will have to leave Buchans. As you know, my pension after twenty-nine years and ten months is $63.40 a month from the company. Not very much to look forward to in the later years. But I thank God I am one of the lucky ones: I came up out of the mine and took early retirement without a trace of silicosis.
>
> However, I did lose my hearing while working underground. Now, I did not try to get any compensation for my loss of hearing. But I know of one miner who went to St. John's to the Compensation Board, and what they told him was, they said: "you can get deaf anywhere."
>
> I grant you that. There's fellows today suffered loss of hearing who have never worked underground. But why is it that so many who HAVE worked underground have suffered loss of hearing? Would they have lost their hearing if they had worked on the surface? How many that worked on the surface have ever suffered loss of hearing? I cannot name one man.
>
> Now, that miner got no hearing aid, no compensation from the company nor from the Compensation Board. I did not try. What I wear here on my head today cost me $740.00 out of my own pocket. And today I am offered...a watch...which I am fully prepared to say cost no more than $40.00!

> Does this compensate me after more than twenty-five years of service to this company? NO! Definitely NOT! I will not, I never intend, EVER to put it on my arm and I never will.
>
> Thank you.

We placed Peter's speech in the play exactly as he delivered it that day.

Week Four: Lost in the Woods

By this time we had accumulated masses of material and individual scenes, but had not yet edited, nor structured any long sequences. I sensed that we had a handle on the show, but some of the cast were losing faith, unsure whether any structure was possible from the material. As we began piecing together segments, frustrations surfaced. There was a showdown over working method: the question of improvisations.

The sequences must be made "more dramatic," some said, and more character invention would help. I disagreed. It was essential not to take Buchaneers' lives away from them, give them mainland accents, graceful movements, and more dramatic actions. The operative dynamic of this whole project was in the first place social. Fictionalising Buchaneers' lives in order to spice up the entertainment value could increase the *theatrical* dynamic of our play at the expense of the *social* dynamic of their community. In any case the two shouldn't be mutually exclusive. The objective was to pass the ball to the audience. This didn't mean that we were restricted to being theatrically dull; it meant that we had to find new ways of being theatrically interesting. We must not take the easy way out. The play belonged to our audience. It was to be their history, their lives onstage. As actors, we needed a style which only *borrowed* characters and incidents in order to describe or represent patterns to the audience. The point was to borrow, not to co-opt.

Eventually we worked out a good compromise. We would stick faithfully to actual documentary monologue and dialogue. Our own comments on this material would be made through staging (using puppets, etc.) and by the editing process itself. When we introduced scenes entirely of our own invention, we would do so in an obviously different presentational style, using a kind of agit-prop shorthand.

For some episodes we developed a diagrammatic style of presentation for added emphasis. The intention was to place a border around important elements of the historic sequence, to frame them in bold face with repetition and rhythm.

The Les Forward Scene:

MINER: Les Forward. That's the name of the fella that won the strike battle for us in '41, was Les Forward. Yup. He took on the whole thing and done a wonderful job. He got us a seven-and-a-half-cent-an-hour increase and a lot of fringe benefits that were never heard of in any other mine in Newfoundland. Well, after that, see, the company bought he over. They offered he a job, see. Foreman up to the mill. He had to leave the union. And after he was on the job a very short time they turned around and fired him. The union couldn't do a thing. That's a fact.

VOICE: The Les Forward Story!

(Shift whistle blows a short blast, like a "starting lineup.")

MINER: Les Forward joins the union and gets his union card!

LES: Thank you.

MINER: Les Forward is elected president of the union!

(Much clapping)

LES: Thank you.

MINER: Les Forward wins the 1941 strike almost single-handedly!

(More clapping, cheers.)

LES: Thank you.

BOSS: Les Forward is offered a job as mill foreman.

(voices: "ooooooh!")

LES: Thank you!

BOSS: Les Forward passes over his union card! Uh...Les?

LES: Oh...uh....Thank you....

BOSS: Foreman do this! (stands militarily at ease. Les obeys.)

Foreman do this! (stands to attention. Les obeys.)

Foreman do this! (salutes with hand to temple. Les obeys).

Foreman do this! (slowly waves goodbye with salute hand)

EVERYONE: 'Bye, Les....

(The shift whistle blows for a long slow time. Les is left waving sadly.)

By now most of the actors were finding it difficult to see the woods for the trees. This stage of a collective creation period, before the show's structure is finalised, is always characterised by restlessness. It is a luxury to still have time for arguing. With impeccable timing, a theatre student from York University, Alan Filewod, showed up in Buchans to research the methodology of collective creations, and we were able to yell much of our frustration into his tape recorder instead of at each other.

Weeks Five and Six: The Home Stretch

In most collective creations this is the time when stark panic hits the participants, and most of the work gets done. Chaff is sorted out, the more important material is developed further, and over two thirds of the show-and-tell scenes are usually trashed. We rolled up our sleeves and sweated, and watched our play's structure emerge more clearly day by day. Our set, a huge 2,000-pound timber "square-set" from the mine lashed to our ubiquitous scaffold, was now erected in the school gymnasium. It brought a reassuring unity to rehearsals. We knew we must have a show— because the set was ready.

Structural gaps in the show became apparent. Earlier, Donna Butt and Connie Kaldor had problems interviewing miners' wives. As a result we had lots of scenes about men working, but very little about women's work. We wanted to show that women at home worked shifts which complemented those of their husbands in the mine. A song (*Who Says We don't Work by the Whistle?*) and two good scenes eventually emerged. One of these we inserted into the middle of our underground work sequence, during a scene about the men's lunchbreak. As the miners joked over their lunchboxes, the action froze, and underneath them, at breakneck pace, Donna performed the following:

> I can't let the poor man starve to death, you know. Every Monday morning I gets up and makes him chicken sandwiches. Then every Tuesday morning I gets up and makes him cheese sandwiches. And every Wednesday I give him leftovers and if we got no leftovers I give him a big tin of meatballs. Every Thursday I gives him a bit of raw bologna, because he LOVES raw bologna and every Friday I give him fish. He has fish for lunch and fish for dinner.
>
> Now let me see...that's three times a week I make sandwiches and I make two sets for him every time so that's 3 times 2, that's 6, and I makes 'em 52 weeks a year...that's 312 sandwiches I makes for him every year. And most of the time I does that I uses homemade bread, except on Mondays, 'cause Mondays I got to do the wash and I don't have time to make bread. Usually I got enough to do me for the rest of the week unless of course the youngsters gets at it just when it comes outa the oven and then I got nothin', but other than that I got enough to do until Tuesday morning. I uses 4 slices on Tuesdays and I uses 4 slices on Thursdays to make sandwiches.

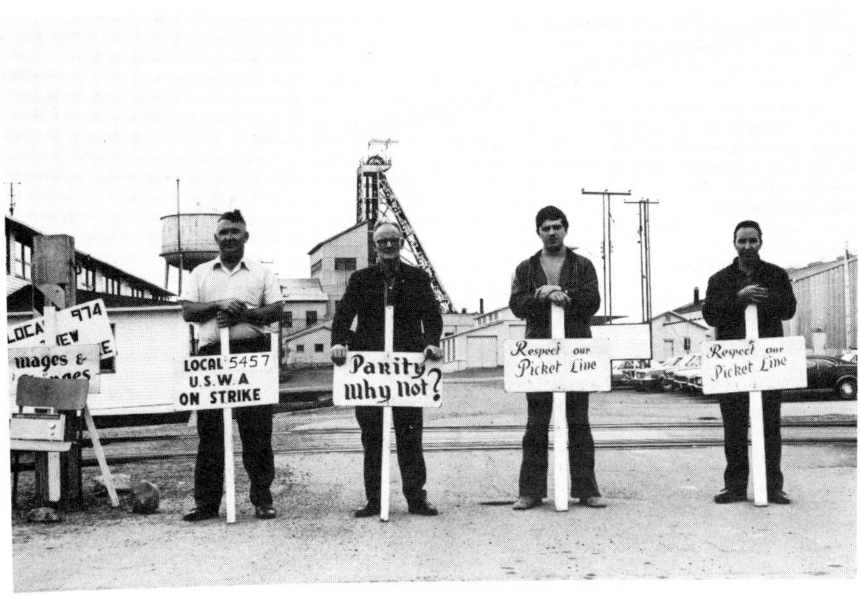

Picket line, Buchans 1973.
Source unknown.

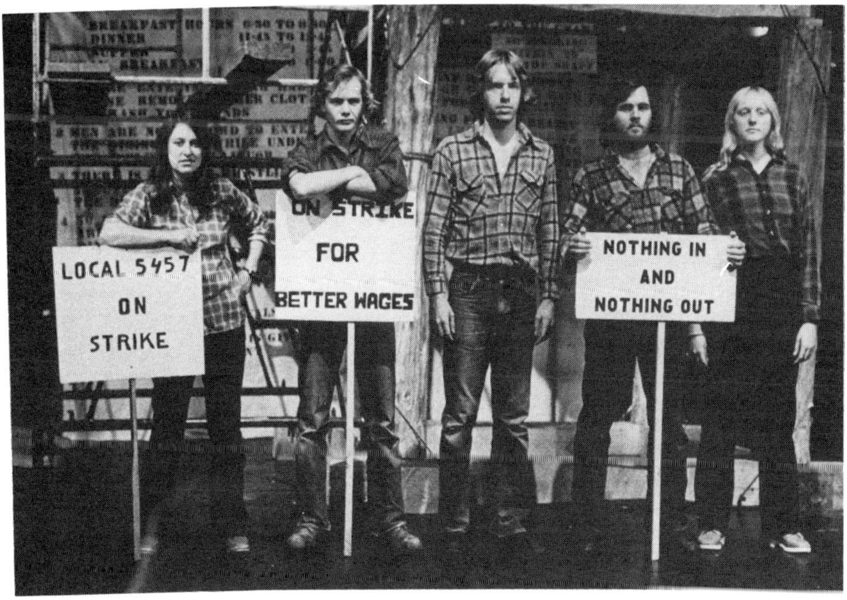

Picket line, *Buchans a Mining Town/Company Town,* 1974.
Left to right: Donna Butt, Bembo Davies, Allan Booth, Lee J. Campbell, Connie Kaldor.
Photo: Michael Schmidt.

4 and 4 is 8. I uses 3 slices with the meatballs, that's 12, and I uses 4 slices with the biscuits, that's 16. That's 52 times...that's 677 slices of homemade bread. Now I only uses 'bought bread' on Mondays. Mondays I uses 4 slices. That's 52 fours...that's 208 slices plus the 30 or 40 I uses when the youngsters gets at the homemade when it comes outa the oven...that's...328 slices of Mammy's bread!

Now cake. Every Monday morning I gets up and I makes nut-bread cake. He loves it. He eats so much I haven't got enough to put on the table for supper. Then every Tuesday I makes orange-bread cake. He can't stand that, but I makes it every Tuesday anyway. Then every Wednesday I makes date-bread cake, and what he don't like about that, well, he brings home again. Now that's 3 lots of cake I makes, that's 3 two's...56...257!

Cookies! You wouldn't believe the cookies I makes for that man in the run of a week! I got to give him 10 cookies on Mondays, and 12 when he don't like the cakes and 4 for when he takes the orange-bread cake...that's 26. I give him 3 on Wednesdays and 4 on Thursdays. That's 26 and 3 and 4 that's 32...52 times 32, that must be about 66,000 COOKIES I MAKES IN THE RUN OF A YEAR! AND 257 CAKES AND 1100 SLICES OF BREAD AND 312 SANDWICHES AND...AND...AND I'LL TELLYOUSOMETHING I'M NEVERGETTINGMARRIEDAGAIN!

Work responsibilities always stratify in the home stretch. The actors focus on their roles and the director worries about piecing everything together. As Bembo put it: "Well, I hope you know where this show is heading because I'm going to get into my characters now. Goodbye." The time for discussion was past. We all pulled together to make the best show of what we had.

At the eleventh hour of a collective creation, the rehearsals draw on the lengthy immersion which by this time each member of the creative team has had in the subject. As a result, scenes take shape and polish rapidly. This is different from a scripted play, where rehearsal dwells not upon shaping the show out of the actors' experience but more upon shaping the actors' experience to fit the requirements of the show. Script actors must spend a lot of rehearsal time exploring their roles, trying to piece together a background, a past, and an environment for their characters. The advantage of collective creation is that when it comes close to actual performance, the collective actor often needs far less rehearsal than the script actor, simply because he can draw upon his weeks of immersion in the community. His conversations with residents, the time spent accompanying underground work shifts, and all the dozens of improvised scenes which didn't make it into the final show structure now make him intimately familiar with his subject matter, and provide a secure performance base.

When our show opened, the school gymnasium was packed solid for three nights and matinees. Every man, woman, and child in Buchans must have seen it at least twice, and we got the community seal of approval. Management had some serious misgivings, but Local 5457 certified that the play told it like it was in Buchans. They encouraged us to show it to other areas of the province.

In 1974 touring Newfoundland was neither easy nor cheap, especially with a cast and crew of nine and a ton of mine timber for a set. The provincial government, flush with their Jubilee Year funds and a $300,000 Touring Subsidy programme, considered *Company Town* too hot to touch. (This was difficult to justify to our bank manager, who already frowned at us so hard he looked like John L. Lewis with indigestion.) But Steelworkers union locals in Baie Verte and Labrador City came through in the crunch to help out with travel costs. The eventual tour was able to link up the province's mining areas and draw attention to some common problems (particularly industrial disease). As a propaganda exercise, it acquainted spectators in St. John's and other centres with the reasons behind Buchans' recent strikes, and helped shed light on some of the problems in Newfoundland's mining industry. A Royal Commission was set up to enquire into the future of the Buchans mine (ASARCO had threatened to close the operation after the last strike because of dwindling ore deposits), and the play generated additional public interest to help prod government action.

> With each audience we have to come out and say: this is what we found. It may not be important. It may be. But here it is. And the audience goes: okay. And they get interested. It leaves a space for them to fill. It's an attitude you have to have along with the material onstage.... The question is, how much power does theatre have? About all you can do, is make people aware. And if they're concerned, it will move them. If not, it won't.
>
> One of the things that happened to me is, one night, one of the first shows, we played [the town of] Baie Verte, and I could FEEL everybody absorbing. And the next year they had a strike. Now, you can't know. But, like, I feel somewhat responsible for that (Howie Cooper and Bembo Davies from *Mayday* No 1 1975).

The success of *Company Town—the Story of Buchans* knitted our own company closely together. It was our "shared language." Had the play been bad, I think we might have torn each other limb from limb. As it was, the tour together was a joy; our commitment to the show overcame many potential obstacles. When, for instance, our wheezing old tour bus wasn't able to reach the mining community of Tilt Cove because of impassable road conditions, Allen Booth walked and hitchhiked into the town alone and improvised a one-man performance of the show with the school piano.

We also brought *Company Town* to mining areas in Nova Scotia, where the national theatre critic for Southam News, Dave Billington, unexpectedly turned up and gave our company's fortunes a crucial shot in the arm:

> GLACE BAY, N.S.—When the Newfoundland group called the Mummers Troupe staged their play *Company Town* here at the miner's museum the result was as exciting as Michel Tremblay's opening night in New York City.
>
> The excitement was generated not just because this struggling group of theatre people were so talented and professional in their work, but because their play spoke so eloquently to the audience which was comprised of local miners and descendants of miners....One of the most moving moments came during a sketch about the 25-year watch....When the speech ended, the audience broke into long, heartfelt applause. But the clincher came when, at the play's end, the real miner himself, Peter Noftle, stood.... Miners are tough people, but there was a catch in Noftle's voice as he spoke and thanked the actors for telling his and others' stories so accurately and so well.
>
> And there, in that museum with the walls hung with the picks and hammers of soft-coal miners long gone, with a real miner giving a short impromptu speech, theatre ceased to be an imitation of life and became life itself.
>
> It was a moment rarely experienced and never to be forgotten.

Billington's review was a godsend. Previous to this, our fundraising efforts had been handicapped by a peculiar Catch-22 unknown to Toronto theatres, but familiar to many groups working in "the sticks." The catch was this: many agencies (such as the Canada Council), required evaluations of our work from recognised critics before they could consider investing in us. This was a reasonable request in areas where such recognised theatre critics tend to live and work. The problem was, Canadian critics at that time didn't travel much, and they never, ever, came to Newfoundland. The Toronto critics association met annually to award the Floyd Chalmers Award to the "Best Canadian Play of the Year" based exclusively on Toronto productions, in the pompous assumption that any play worth producing would be produced in Toronto. Our references from anthropologists, development educators and hometown theatre reviewers did not cut any critical mustard at all in big-time artsy circles. There simply was not, we were told, anybody in Newfoundland sufficiently qualified to assess us.

Billington's review was carried in Southam Press newspapers across the country, and helped free us from the hammer lock of regional obscurity.

Ultimately, of course, to prove that we *really* existed, it was necessary to go to Toronto itself. In the spring of 1975 Rick Salutin and Toronto's Theatre Passe-Muraille won a Chalmers award, and with great fanfare gave it to us as a solidarity gesture. George and Mona Luscombe and June Faulkner of Toronto Workshop Productions offered us free use of their theatre for a two-week run, and thanks to both of these kind gestures we were able to bring *Company Town* successfully to Toronto in June of 1975.

With that, the goat was fed: the Canada Council was finally impressed.

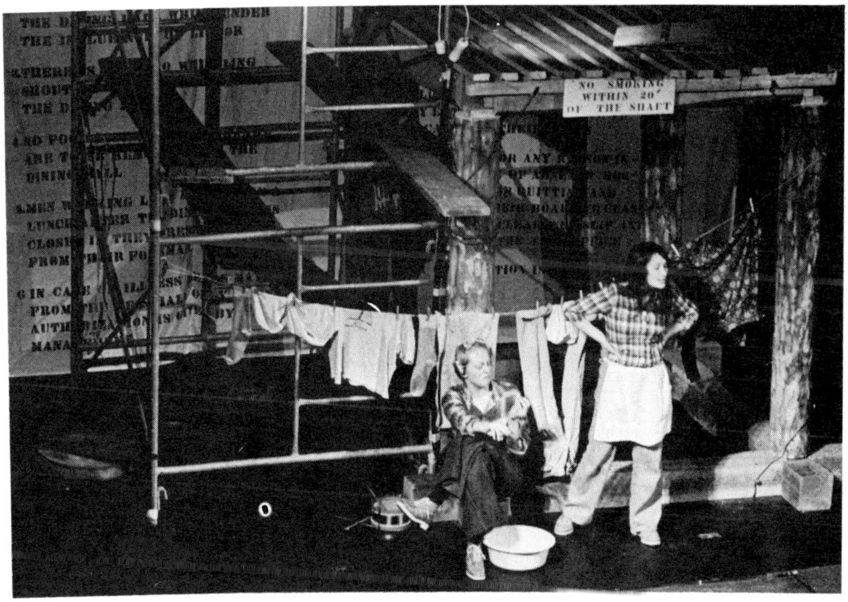

Women's work scene, *Buchan's A Mining Town/Company Town,* 1975.
Left to right: Connie Kaldor, Donna Butt.
Photo: Denys Short.

You Should See the Picture 9

> Neighbour: "What a beautiful baby you have."
>
> Mother: "That's nothing. You should see his picture!"

In 1975 we had our first taste of working hand in hand with an agency that didn't give a damn about art. It was an intoxicating experience. The St. John's branch of the Community Planning Association of Canada (CPAC) commissioned us to produce a play about neighbourhood development in the downtown East End of the city. They provided us with research, guidance, long-term organisational follow-up, and funding. This was a precedent for Canadian theatre at the time.

The commission meant we could keep our eye fixed solidly on the target: community development. But the experience also taught us something: don't let obsession with the target cause you to forget how to get there. In particular, don't mix media and expect the results, in development terms, to be equally successful.

The CPAC wanted to sensitise the downtown's predominately working-class population to a problem: the erosion of residential priorities in the city core. Urban development policies were increasingly favouring high-rise office and hotel construction at the expense of the people who lived there. The historic family housing in the area was falling prey to absentee slum landlords and real estate speculators. Neighbourhood pride was almost a thing of the past. Working against this trend were two new federal programmes, the Neighbourhood Improvement Programme (NIP) and Residential Rehabilitation and Planning (RRAP). NIP and RRAP stressed the heritage of the East End as a place for people to live, rather than as an office-tower ghetto. The programmes encouraged citizen participation in urban planning, provided grants to establish neighbourhood facilities such as playgrounds and green spaces, and made available low-interest loans for residential repairs.

The problem was that downtown residents didn't know or didn't care. CPAC's job was to inform residents about the programmes, and organize a neighbourhood improvement group which could formally participate in the planning process. Instead of producing pamphlets and literature which might not reach or might not interest lower-income residents, they decided to use theatre. They hired Codco (who produced a series of sketches titled *What do Ya Want to See the Harbour for, Anyway?*) and us.

> We hired the Mummers because their technique was going to draw on the information we thought was the most important: what people said about where they lived and how people acted where they lived. We weren't interested in demography, we weren't interested in structural quality analysis, we weren't interested in statistics. We were interested in that qualitative information that professional planners shy away from so often.
>
> One of the objectives in commissioning the play was that we would experiment with a technique that would have immediate payoffs for the people who were the subjects of the research. If it created a neighbourhood awareness and stimulated somebody to some kind of social action then it would be a success (Roger Bill, CPAC St. John's Executive Director).

For St. John's in 1975 this was a new approach to urban planning: an attempt to revitalise the downtown core through the participation of an animated citizenry rather than upon governmental dictum from City Hall.

It was clear that the play would have to be performed in the downtown area, something that had hardly been done since the early 1950s. Downtown residents who wanted to go to the theatre these days had to drive or take a bus all the way uptown to the higher-income residential areas which housed the university, the public art gallery, and the Arts and Culture Centre. Most didn't or couldn't. The downtown East End had once been at the heart of the city's arts and cultural activity. Now even the nearest cinema was ten miles away.

> The houses in downtown are like teeth biting into the side of the hill and holding on for dear life. And when you talk about down town, you don't talk about the heart and the guts, you talk about the teeth. Because that's the only reason that St. John's survived, because it hung in there by the skin of its teeth. Downtown is where the teeth's at (Resident's speech, *East End Story*).

I searched the neighbourhood for a likely performance space, and encountered the Longshoremen's Protective Union (LSPU) Hall. Belonging to the oldest surviving union in Newfoundland (once large and powerful but with their considerable membership now decimated by container-loading facilities at harbourfront), the Hall in 1975 housed only occasional union meetings and the LSPU office. It was a beautiful little theatre space, centrally located, acoustically excellent and seating about 150. Best of all, as a union hall, it had none of the sanctimoniousness associated with church and school auditoria downtown. I immediately fell in love with it. The union allowed us to rent the upstairs space for rehearsals and performance for five dollars a day. We started rehearsals in early June while *Company Town* was still playing in Toronto.

The cast of what came to be titled *East End Story* was made up of Maddy Williams, Rick Boland, Rhonda Payne, Wayne McNiven, Steven Bush, Jane Foster and Ron Hynes. Alan Filewod, who had documented our previous year's experience in Buchans, was dramaturge for this show (thanks to Alan's dedication, commitment and low grocery bills, the Troupe enjoyed the luxury of his dramaturgic presence for over eight months.)

We tried to balance our participant-observer style of research with census maps, city plans, and socioeconomic data. Each morning we would meet at the Hall and compare notes in a show-and-tell session, where Alan and I prompted the actors for scenes on specific themes. Afternoons were spent in the streets, the stores, the bars and the bingo halls getting the feel of the neighbourhood and sharpening our powers of observation. We tried to pin down what made the downtown unique, different from anywhere else. We developed scenes from childrens' street games, wall graffitti, and neighbourhood characters. Jane Foster spent an evening on the neighbourhood beat with two of the local cops; Alan Filewod got up early one morning and accompanied the garbagemen on their collection run. I spent an afternoon hanging around a corner "Groc. & Conf." and discovered that the small downtown corner stores sell over a ton of bologna each week. That's a hell of a lot of bologna. It was a symptom of the downtown disease. All the larger food supermarkets had moved to suburbia. Finding nutritious food at affordable prices in the East End was as difficult as finding a concert or a play.

We tried to phrase issues in the way that local residents felt and understood them, rather than in the vocabulary of professional urban planning. It was ineffective and alienating to talk about "urban blight" or "residential priorities in urban core planning" when issues could be presented in more recognisable ways.

EXECUTIVE: Well, what happened was, I was going down to the museum and I went up to park on Gower Street, just at the edge of Masonic Terrace, and I hauled into a parking spot just clear of something, and this buddy came up and says:

RESIDENT: Do you live here?

EXECUTIVE: And I says no. Then he says:

RESIDENT: Well, what are ya doin' parkin' here?

EXECUTIVE: I said well, there was no other place to park. He said:

RESIDENT: Well, I live here.

EXECUTIVE: I said well, you know, there's not much that I can do about that. And...and then he started to get nasty.

RESIDENT: (rolling up his sleeves) Jesus CHRIST!

EXECUTIVE: Look here. I don't give a particular fuck. I'm parked here and that's that!

RESIDENT: Well, what are people like us supposed to do around here anyway? I mean, we come home from work, we got nowhere to park, what are we supposed to do? Eh?

EXECUTIVE: Well...okay. I see you got a reasonable point there. But what...what can I do? There's no parking meters here, there's nothing like that here....

RESIDENT: (Glares fixedly at executive)

EXECUTIVE: So anyway, eventually I said I'd give the space up to him and go find somewhere else to park. All right?

RESIDENT: (walking away) Naw. I just wanted to make my point.

CHILDREN: (in background, skipping)

had a little car, nineteen sixty-four
Drove it...
Round the...
Cor...ner!
Slammed on the brakes...
Policeman came and put me in jail;
All I had to drink was gingerale;
How many bottles did I drink?
...one...two...three...four...

After four weeks of rehearsal (too short—some organic mystery of our creations seemed to prescribe six weeks as the optimum research/creation time for most plays) we opened the show nervously at the LSPU Hall. No one had mounted a live show downtown in decades, and we weren't sure whether we would be able to draw audiences to an unknown theatre space. Another worry was my decision to drop our previous practice of "pay-what-you-can" ticket prices for the target audience. That policy had backfired more often than it had worked. The North American mind set ("if they're giving it away, there must be something wrong with it") usually meant that adult audiences assumed free shows would be either dull or intended for children. I hoped that affordable admission prices would lend the show legitimacy without restricting accessibility too much.

I needn't have worried. The show was a smash. It quickly sold out for two weeks and had to be extended for a third. It was well attended by neighbourhood residents and by uptowners as well, for whom the themes of the show: ugly architectural renovations (the "Lockwood window syndrome"), lack of parking , etc., were visually underscored as they walked uphill to their cars after the performance humming Ron Hynes' tunes:

Give us a place we can play
So we're not in the streets every day
The sidewalks are dirty, the glass is too sharp,
There's too many sailors in Bannerman Park,
They're waiting to grab us as soon as it's dark
Give us a place we can PLAY!

One big plus in working with community action groups is that they are usually in a much better position than the theatre troupe to judge the effectiveness of a show. In this case the CPAC was pleased—the show seemed to do the job in the neighbourhood, and its high profile focused wider public attention on the needs of the East End. Downtowners were proud of their reflections in the play; during the entire run of the play our standing-ovation audiences had nothing but praise for the show.

All the more curious, then, that a television version of the project had the opposite effect. CPAC hired John, Kate and Bill Doyle to shoot a film documentary of our show, mixing clips from the performance with on-the-street interviews and contrasting the reality with the theatrical images. The idea was to translate the play into film so it could reach a wider audience as a community development vehicle. We all thought it was a pretty good film. It was screened on the local CTV affiliate on Easter Sunday, 1976.

The morning after, John decided to test viewer reaction with an old Mummers media-manipulation trick which we used often over the years. It's useful for instant research. In an emergency it's useful for advertising shows, too, and I recommend it to any theatre company. Simply phone up the radio openline shows with a phoney voice (it's good practice in characterization) and offer some outrageously praiseworthy or damning remark about a show (or if you're desperate to sell tickets, try something like: "Bas, I hear that new Mummers show got nudity in it!"). Then sit back with your radio on to see what happens. John phoned in anonymously saying that he thought the television screening was very nice. It got the ball rolling....

HOST: And we have Mary on the line here. Good morning.

MARY: Good morning, Bob. I want to speak about the show that was on yesterday?. I was out around the Bay for the weekend and of course there was a group of people knew of it and they all gathered together where there was a television just to see the Uptown Downtown show. They were horrified. Mortified....

HOST: Is that right?

MARY:...at the thought of puttin' that on, not only on Easter Sunday, but on any other day. The first thing they all agreed that they hoped it would NEVER be shown ANYWHERE in public again. Because they think it would downgrade Newfoundland so badly that we'd never rise no more.

HOST: Well, we tend to criticise, but do you have any constructive criticism about it...why was it so bad?

MARY: Well, it showed the very worst of everything. The way the girl that took part spoke, the way she acted, the whole thing, it was ridiculous. I often hear of Newfie jokes and so on and so forth, which you know, you put over, but if this ever went out of St. John's I think it would be a disgrace. I think it would be our last push off, goin' underneath as far as we could go. And there was a group of about twenty people in the room, and they all came to the same conclusion, it was horrible, they just...you could see the horror in their faces, you know.

HOST: Well, thank you for calling. And we have George on the line. Good morning George.

GEORGE: Yes, boy. You know that programme that was on yesterday? Well, boy, everyone is knockin' it but there was one good thing I see on it, and that was our fine policeman we got on the foot of Prescott Street there. He's doin' quite a job. But regards to the rest of it, complete garbage. Its a real disgrace to Newfoundlanders, as far as I'm concerned, anyway....

HOST: Its strange, you know, that a bunch of Newfoundlanders should be complaining about something Newfoundland. So you don't think it should be shown again?

GEORGE: And that's what I don't.

HOST: Well, thanks for calling. Good morning to Marie. What's on your mind today?

MARIE: I'd like to comment on the East End Story on the downtown. I thought it was a disgrace to Newfoundland, Newfoundlanders and the Catholic Church.

HOST: Well, what are your big objections?

MARIE: Well, you know, we got such beautiful buildings and everything, and they always show the worst.

HOST: You felt it showed the...seamy side of St. John's, shall we say?

MARIE: To show men sittin' on the War Memorial, drinkin', you know....

HOST: Well, I'm hoping that one of the members of the Troupe who filmed it will call us sometime this morning, and we can perhaps get some comments from them. Thank you for calling. And now we have Rose on the line, good morning.

ROSE: Mr. Lewis? Chris Brookes was responsible for that show yesterday.

HOST: Chris Brookes, eh?

ROSE: Outrageous.

HOST: Was it?

ROSE: It was silly and foolish and no sense to it.

HOST: I see. Why do you think they made it?

ROSE: I'm sure I don't know. I'm some glad I didn't PAY to go see it! Oh, my. It was disgusting. Popeye the Sailor would'a done better!

HOST: Well, I'm sorry that everyone seems to feel that way. We've only had one person, our first caller, who's called in this morning who thought it was great.

ROSE: Well, I'd like to see what was so great about it. It was degrading to Newfoundlanders. Oh, the IDEA! Really and truly.

(Eventually even the Deputy Mayor, John Murphy, got into the act)

MURPHY: It's a bit of a slap in the face to the fine people of St. John's East. I'm sure that those people who saw that programme would agree that the actors— and they were pretty good as actors— but certainly they were not typical of the old East End people of St. John's who are very conservative, both politically and otherwise, they're very solid people in the East End, most of them, many of them are older people who were born there....

HOST: Well, its obvious when you look at some of the HOUSES! Let's take another caller. Good morning Emma....

EMMA: Mr. Lewis. I notice people with townie accents were very hurt this morning over that production on TV yesterday. Because while these Mummers people may be trying to do something they think is good, the reaction from everyone that saw it is the reverse. People just don't like it. As I see it, these young people are presenting our city in the wrong light. I further wish to state that the fellow who was, you know, on the show, wishing he was sorry about the old city and that, came to my door one time with a salt-and-pepper cap on, you know, like the movie, with a pronounced MAINLAND accent! (This was Rick Boland, born and raised in Curling, Newfoundland.)

I think that the Mummers are subsidized heavily, somehow, by us, by the federal government. I don't know about anybody in Newfoundland. Is that so, Mr. Murphy?

MURPHY: Oh, yes, they have gotten federal grants. I don't know how much, but they have gotten money.

EMMA: And somebody tells me they're all shackin' up somewhere, all of 'em in the one house, you know. I'm not tryin' to put them down, but I think....

HOST: Then what ARE you trying to do?

EMMA: Pardon?

HOST: What ARE you trying to do?

EMMA: Who's this? Bob, is it?

HOST: Yeup.

EMMA: Ahem. May I talk to the Deputy Mayor, please?

And so on. Even the few positive callers who phoned in qualified their remarks.

...Well, I'm in favour of the programme being televised, because I mean it was a...it makes people aware of what's going on in their community, and a lot of it is fact, it's the truth, and it makes people more aware.... But now, I'm not in favour of it being broadcast on a CANADIAN network, up in Canada!

Common to all the responses was insecurity, a sense of "what will *other* people, up on the mainland, think?" Callers' objections seemed to revolve less around the accuracy of the community image shown in the film, than around the shame and disgrace that it would bring to Newfoundlanders when outsiders saw it. As an experiment in community development, the television screening failed.

So why did people accept the play but not the film? The answer probably had more to do with the comparative natures of the theatre and television media than with the East End show itself. The theatrical experience is a communal one. Each spectator can see who the

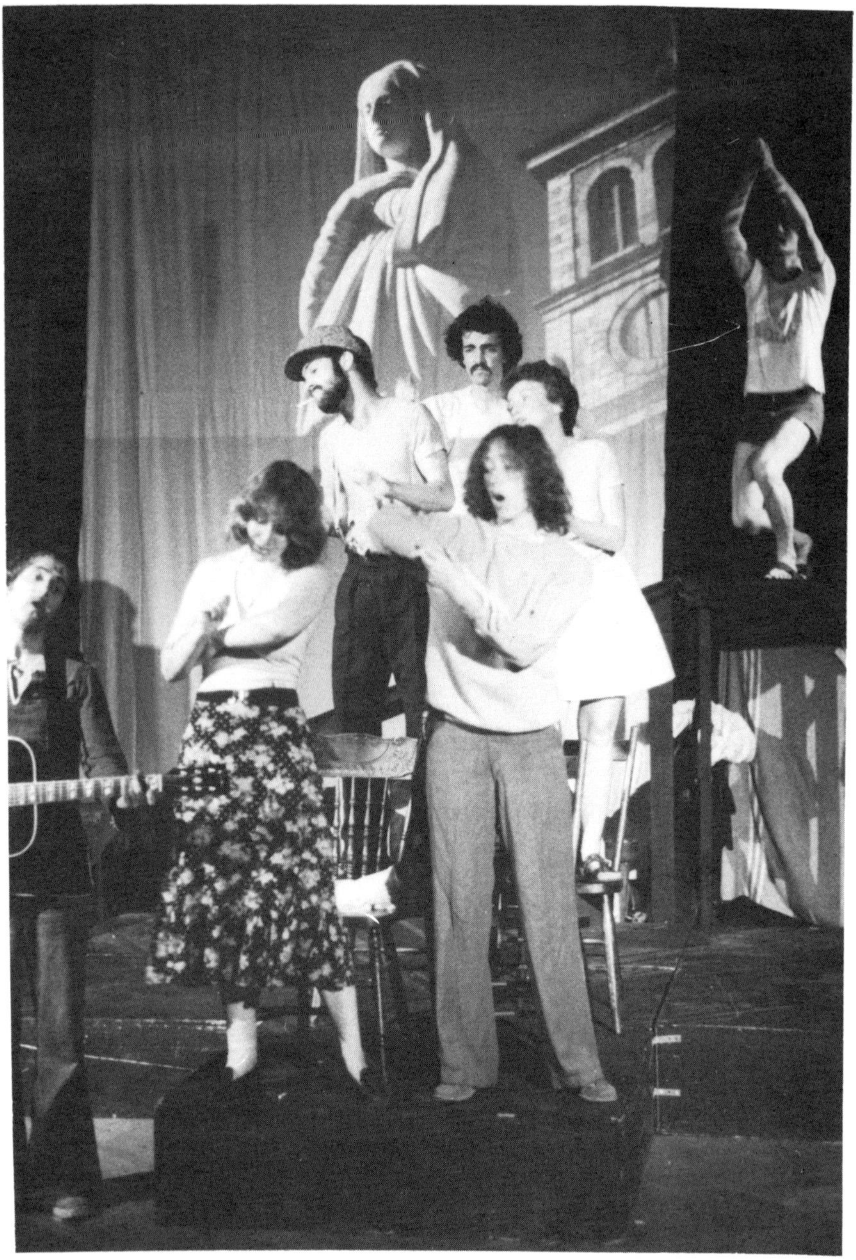

Church bingo scene, *East End Story* 1975.
Left to right: Ron Hynes, Rhonda Payne, Rick Boland, Steven Bush, Jane Foster, Maddy Williams, Wayne McNiven.
Photo: Chris Brookes.

other spectators are, and how they are responding to the show. If they like it, they can laugh and clap. If they don't like it, they can boo and throw rotten vegetables. The medium is *within their control*. Their experience is contained within the theatre space, manageable, so that each spectator can see and feel consensus. It is the consensus of a community.

Television is quite different. It is not a bringing together of people for shared dialogue. It is a delivery system, beamed from a distant transmitting point to the home receiver. The audience is fragmented. The experience is not one of active communal participation but of passive individual consumption. The spectator has no control over the television medium. If he smashes his set, no one else knows or cares. Who are the other watchers and what do they think of the programme? Are they friends or enemies, Canadians or Townies? Are they sneering at the television image of Newfoundlanders? The spectator doesn't know. The spectator is alone. Alone with the knowledge that the broadcast is not confined to his or her living room, but is being transmitted far and wide. Perhaps even to Toronto. Whether you like it or not, there's nothing you can do about it. The medium is in someone else's control.

The paranoia which swallowed up the East End film was not new. For two years, local playwright Michael Cook had been carrying on running battles in the local press about whether or not he (a British-born playwright resident in the province for seven years) was transgressing local cultural mores by writing plays about Newfoundlanders. Many Newfoundlanders resented Cook's characterizations of their culture. Most of them, however, first saw his plays not in their community halls, but beamed down from a Toronto television studio. Michael interpreted their response as regional racism. But their rage was prompted less by the playwright's birthplace than by the indignity of seeing Newfoundland culture served up by the same massive media delivery system which had spent much of the past twenty-five years paving over the province's indigenous identity.

> What disturbed [native people in America] most was the feeling that when their dances and tales were filmed, taped, and written down, they were stolen away from them as surely as their lands and furs were taken away. When they saw their sacred treasures under glass, heard their songs on the radio, watched their dances on TV, they not only objected to errors they spotted, they felt robbed. None of this had anything to do with them. They felt used. And they were...Throughout many cultures it's commonly feared that if one's name or image falls into the hands of an enemy, he may use it mis-

> chievously. A sorcerer who possesses any part of his victim...has him at his mercy (Carpenter 1972).

The public debate focused on Mike Cook, on Chris Brookes. But the real sorcerer was television.

Not the House of Assembly 10

> If you want to see the best theatre in town, go to the House of Assembly; if you want the best politics, catch the Mummers' latest show.
>
> CBC Radio commentator Rex Murphy

1975 was a productive year. Our reputation was growing. With the success of the CPAC project we attracted another commission, from Oxfam. The Canada Council decided that their previous insistence on a financial "holding company" to amalgamate all three provincial theatres was unwieldy and unrealistic. They began funding each company individually. Suddenly we had money to work with.

Steven Bush stayed after *East End Story* to direct a new show, *Dying Hard*. Company meetings during the previous winter had been lukewarm to this idea, and I'd pushed it onto our production schedule. The subject matter was intimidating: industrial disease.

While we had been in Buchans in 1974, Memorial University anthropologist Elliott Leyton had been interviewing miners, wives and widows in St. Lawrence, a community crippled by respiratory disease resulting from working conditions in the nearby fluorspar mine. During the winter Elliott showed me his manuscript edited from those interviews (since published as *Dying Hard, The Ravages of Industrial Carnage*, McLelland & Stewart, 1976). Poetically, courageously, and with great dignity, the transcripts spoke of rich, valuable lives sentenced to an early and agonizing death. It was shockingly powerful material. In North America, occupational disease killed 110,000 workers every year. In Buchans, silicosis and pneumoconiosis had struck down many miners. But in St. Lawrence the extent of the carnage—the sheer size of the graveyard in one small town—was horrifying. In most cases, dying miners were ignored by the company and refused Workmens Compensation benefits. Elliott felt that a dramatisation of these testimonies would help to alert workers in other mining areas to possible dangers in their own working environment. It seemed the logical extension of our work in Buchans.

Steven and the cast developed Elliott's manuscript into mostly straight-on monologues, and worked hard with characterisation. The audience was confronted with carefully understated portrayals of severely ill miners and their wives quietly describing their lives, their work, and their approaching death. It was hardly a show to send spectators whistling and dancing out of the theatre. We had established a mining town tour circuit the previous year with our *Company Town* tour. Now we contacted the various mining union locals across the island, and they encouraged their members to see the show. Elliott prepared an information sheet advising miners of action they could take to protect themselves. It was enclosed in every programme.

On tour in Baie Verte, the show addressed an audience with particular reason to be concerned. Miners there were already beginning to fear asbestosis, and within a year after *Dying Hard's* visit, the Steelworkers' local brought in medical expert Dr. Irving Silicoff and a team of researchers to check asbestos fibre levels. They found intolerably high levels in work areas, homes and even drinking water, and the company was pressured to bring in better control measures.

The worry with such pulmonary diseases as silicosis and asbestosis is that noticeable symptoms may not appear for years after exposure. In 1981 the Johns Manville Company, operators of the Baie Verte mine, closed it for an indefinite period due to falling market prices. It was later sold and reopened as a more limited operation by another company. Who will pay if workers suffer aftereffects of asbestos exposure twenty years later?

There is a postscript to the St. Lawrence story. A few years after our *Dying Hard* tour, in abrupt response to several hard-fought strikes in which working conditions were a central issue, ALCAN permanently closed the St. Lawrence mine, announcing that they were opening a similar fluorspar mine in Mexico (where workers were cheaper and more cooperative.) ALCAN president David Culver said: "I admire the way those Newfoundlanders hang in there, but the world doesn't owe you a job where you happen to want to live." A new joke made the rounds:

> What's the Newfie definition of manual labour?
>
> Newf: Manuel Labor? Some Mexican who's got my job....

Dying Hard left its mark on us, too. After the tour Lynn Lunde dickered with the Newfoundland Workmens Compensation Board and in 1976 the Mummers Troupe became the only theatre in the country to have its performers covered by Workmens Compensation.

I'd pushed hard for us to do this show partly in order to stretch our actors. Steven was a very good actor's director, and his careful character work in *Dying Hard* was excellent training for the under-experienced cast. The kinds of people who were attracted to the Mummers over the years came from a variety of backgrounds, but they seldom possessed extensive theatre experience, and even less often possessed formal acting training. For most of the "family" of performers who circulated through the various local companies and independent productions, the developing Newfoundland theatre scene was their first and only exposure to theatre. They were growing up with it.

For the most part, that "scene" focused on collective creation. On the mainland, the collective method of play-writing often represented a change and a challenge for actors used to traditional script work, but in Newfoundland some performers had never acted in a scripted play at all. This did not always work to their advantage. The rapid show-and-tell improvisation of the collective creation process thrives on an actor's ability for quick character "phrasing" on the rehearsal floor, and it can encourage the careless to dwell in shallow characterisations. Some younger actors were already in danger of getting stuck, capitalizing only upon what they could do most easily.

Part of our function as a Newfoundland theatre was to train young Newfoundland performers (later the Mummers established a formal theatre apprenticeship programme). Hiring actors from the mainland as I had done for *Company Town* only made sense as an emergency measure. We really needed skilled performers who had a good grasp on the social, cultural, political and linguistic idiosyncracies of the province. Year by year, the pool of local actors was slowly growing as it became increasingly possible to make a living from the province's professional theatre. At this time, most of them jobbed around between the Newfoundland Travelling Theatre, The Mummers, and Unemployment Insurance (Codco, with its seven actor-owners, was closed to outsiders).

The problem we faced with trying to upgrade skills in any organised fashion was that the membership of the Troupe still changed show by show. After *East End Story* some local artists began to return more often, edging us slowly closer to a small permanent core of performers which could be supplemented by transients. But we never did seem to mount two consecutive productions with the same cast. It didn't help that we were never in a financial position to be able to provide an entire company of actors with permanent work, but there was more to it than simple poverty.

The Mummers Troupe did not look like the typical Canadian professional theatre, and young actors were attracted to it for a variety of non-typical reasons. Sometimes those reasons had little to do with theatre. In general, performers fell into one of several categories:

1. Those who came from a straight theatre background, out of the National Theatre School or some other formal training course. Acting was their established profession, and a small touring company like ours offered a change-of-pace, an interesting item for their résumé, and another stepping stone en route eventually to the mainstream Stratford Festival/Citadel Theatre circuit. They had the necessary theatre skills, but little interest in research and politics. Usually after a couple of shows they would leave, alienated by our political slant.
2. Neophytes unsettled in either career or psyche for whom theatre was primarily a psychological attraction; that is, it offered a certain group camaraderie and an ego boost with every curtain call.
3. Those who were attracted primarily by our internal group politics, getting turned on by the opportunity to experiment with collective work relationships. For them the perfection of an internal socialist utopia became paramount; engagement with an audience became a secondary concern.
4. Serious students of theatre and/or politics. For some reason, those with the greatest theatrical talent and skill most often tended to be politically naive, while those with the most political sophistication were generally lousy performers. So that it was never very easy to marry political understanding with theatrical ability in creative rehearsals. Part of the group was usually in the dark about either the objective or the means.

The membership of the Mummers was constantly shifting amongst all of these types, and much of the time if we weren't suffering a financial crisis we were flirting with an artistic or political one. It made working for the Mummers a particularly intense experience.

So why didn't we insist on a permanent group for all shows, a balanced ensemble with a range of performance skills? It didn't seem to be possible. People had to survive, and many just couldn't take it all the time either financially or psychologically. As a result the organisational and emotional makeup of the company threatened to become unstable at any time. Trying to maintain both a consistent political stance and a consistent quality and style of performance over the long haul was bloody hard work. Shows like *Dying Hard* were a training opportunity as well as a performance exercise for the actors, but I had no idea whether as a company we'd be able to cash in on the experience for future productions.

The Troupe's growing involvement with labour issues led us to examine the most significant event of Newfoundland's post-Confederation labour history: the International Woodworkers of America strike. It was our province's equivalent of the 1919 Winnipeg general strike. By the time it ended, its many casualties included a policeman's life and a federal justice minister's political career. It permanently affected the lives of thousands of Newfoundland workers.

The IWA began its organizing drive in Newfoundland shortly after Confederation. They signed up the majority of loggers and in 1959 led them out on strike against the province's huge multinational pulp and paper industry. Premier J.R. Smallwood was less than pleased.

> It is not a strike they have started; it is a civil war!...How DARE these outsiders come into this decent Christian province and by such desperate, such terrible methods, try to seize control of our province's main industry!
>
> As long as I live on this earth, as long as God gives me breath, I will denounce this vile outfit for what they have done to our decent Newfoundland people....We will save the loggers, we will save Newfoundland from this terrible scourge that has come upon her these past few weeks (J.R. Smallwood, Radio address to the people of Newfoundland).

In a step unprecedented in Canadian history, Smallwood's government decertified the union. The resulting battle broke lives and careers, and virtually stopped the province's labour movement dead in its tracks for the next decade. For many Newfoundlanders it was the turning point in their love affair with Smallwood and his populist politics.

Strangely, sixteen years after the event, no retrospective examination of the affair had been published. The strike was virtually a forbidden subject. School history textbooks omitted any mention of it. The sole analysis available in print was contained in one chapter of Richard Gwyn's book *Smallwood the Unlikely Revolutionary*.

So in the fall of 1975, when we announced our intention to create a play about the strike, it produced quite a stir.

We started work on the show in September. Donna Butt, Alan Filewod, Rhonda Payne, Rick Boland and I had already compiled some firsthand research and interviews during the previous winter. This gave us a base to work from. Playwright Rick Salutin, who had become interested in our work in Buchans, came down from Toronto to work within our collective creation process as writer. Salutin had recently been involved with a strike in Ontario (the Artistic Woodwork strike), and the experience had given him structural ideas which he wanted to work out in the IWA show. As director, I was fascinated by the materials and technology of the pulp and paper industry in 1959. It had been the end of the hand bucksaw era; gasoline-powered chain saws were revolutionising woods work. I wanted to contrast the fragile tissue of newsprint paper with the snarl and stench of chain saws to symbolize vicious union-busting.

All in all, there was a lot of great stuff cooking in the creative stewpot.

I was lucky to be able to include in the cast Pam Morgan and Jeff Pitcher, whose parents had been pulp and paper millworkers in Grand Falls at the time of the strike. Ron Hynes, our musician from *East End Story* and *Dying Hard*, had a particular interest in collecting loggers' songs. The old woods camps had brought together men from isolated fishing communities with different musical traditions, and the long bunkhouse evenings were always an opportunity to exchange old folk tunes and write new ones. The wealth of loggers' ballads and bunkhouse games from the 1950s era furnished the show with a rich texture.

We spent early rehearsals in the woods of Central Newfoundland, watching modern loggers work, getting the feel of the environment. For Rick Boland the feel of the woods environment was almost disaster. He got his boot caught in a bear trap. We toured the paper mills, borrowed chain saws, and scrounged scrap rolls of newsprint for the set. For this show we had for the first time been able to afford to hire a set designer, and local artist Frank LaPointe (who once spent his summers logging on the Exploits River) produced a wonderful construction centring around a huge and seemingly endless roll of newsprint mounted horizontally like the delivery end of a papermaking machine. It was like a paper doorway. We scrolled it up and down, used it for sound effects and entrances, wrote on it, tore it, cut shapes out of it, cast shadows on it, and finally ripped it apart with a chain saw. By the end of the show the stage was filled with torn, crushed newsprint which a defeated striker (played by Pam Morgan) pushed through. She scrawled on the tattered paper doorway the dates of the province's major industrial strikes of the seventies, finishing with the words, "until next time."

I.W.A. opened in late October at the LSPU Hall. The opening night audience included some former labour leaders and politicians of the time. The programmes were simulations of 1959-era newspapers, filled with actual 1959 press clippings. Old vacuum tube radios scattered through the seats played period music and newscasts. It was a strong show and it was hot. The St. John's morning paper for the first time front-paged a theatre review as a top news story. It was headlined: *I.W.A.—Reopening the Wounds*! Our box office was immediately swamped.

Two days later, our phone rang. It was a tipoff: the mayor of St. John's wanted the show closed. Three hours before curtain time two City Hall employees walked in with a closure order. Our lawyer said there was little we could do. The order cited "violation of fire regulations." For over seventy years community groups, unions, and other organisations had used the LSPU Hall for public and private meetings, and for the past five months both the Mummers and the Newfoundland Travelling Theatre had used it for theatre performances. The building, built long before modern building codes, didn't have a sprinkler system. Neither, of course, did any of the schools, churches, meeting halls and auditoria downtown but the mayor was not alarmed about them. She was alarmed about the building where the *I.W.A.* show was playing.

Technically, City Hall was simply enforcing their 1975 building code, but they enforced it with such speed and selectivity that some observers suggested more devious political motives were involved. The Mummers were known shit disturbers. Mayor Dorothy Wyatt ("Vote for Wyatt; She won't be Quiet") did not appreciate our criticism of her city planning policies in *East End Story* three months earlier. Perhaps she saw *I.W.A.* as another red flag. No one really knew. Speculation ran wild.

The city's labour unions smelled a rat. Many offered us their support. The longshoremen offered to call a snap membership meeting to fill their own hall and defy the closure order. Ultimately, however, under legal advice we moved *I.W.A.* uptown to a university hall. The substitute space was poor, available only for a limited run, and the move cost us time and box office.

Finally the show went on tour around the island. Because of the play's relevance to the Newfoundland union movement as a whole, we toured it to our established mining town tour circuit as well as

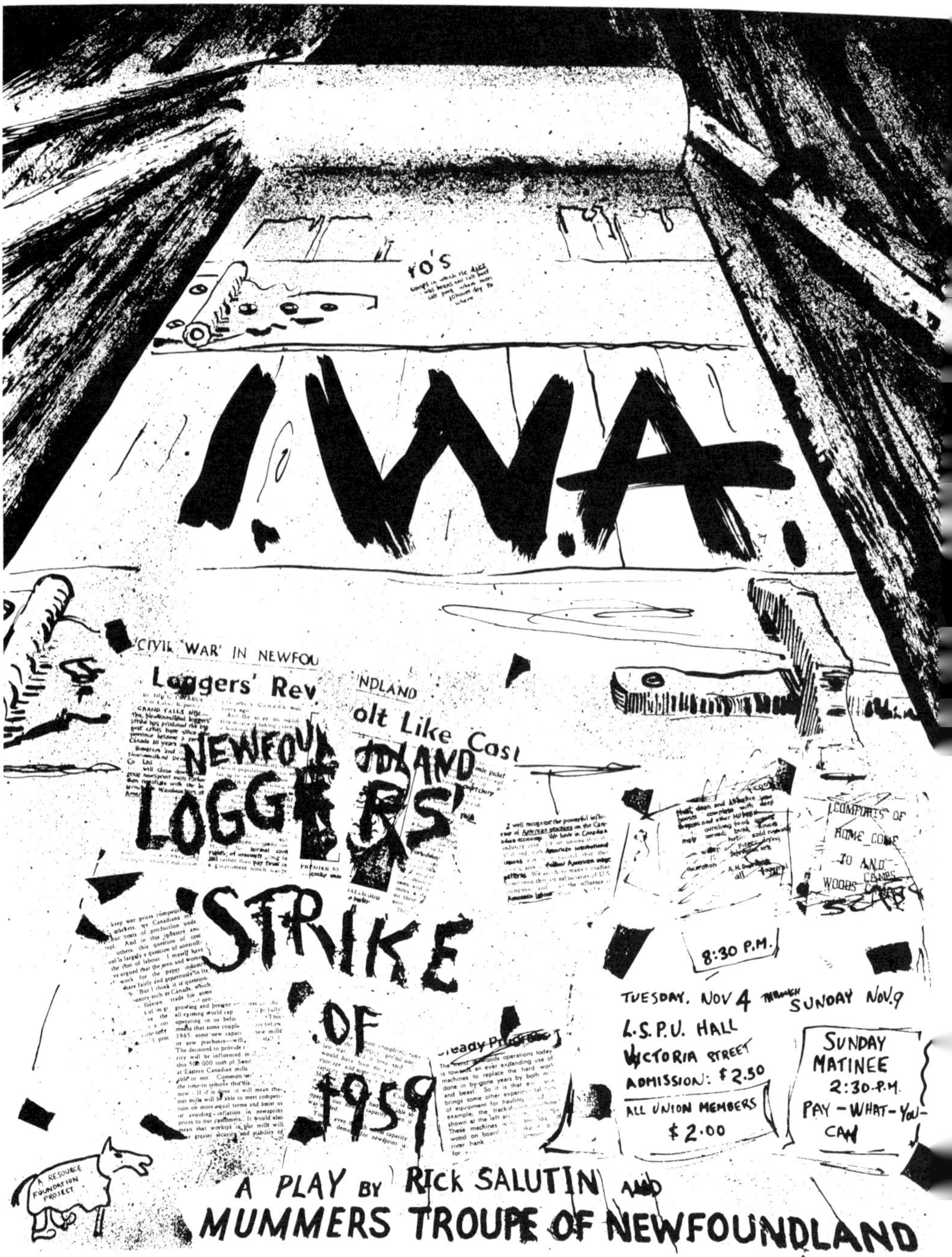

I.W.A. poster by Frank Lapointe, 1975.

to logging areas. It attracted a wide popular audience. Our opening in the paper town of Grand Falls coincided with the eve of a millworkers' strike. As Pam Morgan scrawled the post-1959 strike dates at the end of the performance, a millworker in the packed audience shouted "Tomorrow morning—GRAND FALLS!" and a huge cheer went up. In Buchans, a large crowd turned out. Even the Peace Riders Motorcycle Club rode in, freaking out our ticket taker. In Badger, a former IWA stronghold, the Central Newfoundland Bikers came, opened beer bottles with their teeth, and freaked us all out. Despite that, the Badger audience impressed a visiting *Saturday Night* magazine writer, Sandra Gwyn:

> I.W.A. broke through to its audience here like nothing I've seen before in theatre. An intense psychological experience that moved me profoundly and gave the women sitting next to me a sense, possibly for the first time in their lives, of having been important.

The experience of working collectively with an outside playwright on the script of this play opened up a new can of worms for us: in terms of copyright, who *owned* the final dramatic work, Salutin or the cast?

In 1975, Canadian theatres addressed the issue of copyright in various ways. The traditional situation, in which a playwright writes a script alone and then approaches a theatre for production of it, was a standard contractual arrangement. Actors flesh out the playwright's written script in production. But a collective creation process, where the actors create their own script from scratch, is quite different. Although the collective process was popular in the Canadian theatre of the 1970s, many theatres flagrantly abused the actor-authors of the plays. Managements commonly demanded at least 50 per cent of copyright ownership and royalties on the finished script; many totally disenfranchised the real authors by retaining 100 per cent.

The Mummers Troupe had always been idealistic about copyright ownership. The final play resulting from any of our collective creations was legally registered as belonging jointly to all those who created it (usually the original actor-authors plus the director). Any reincarnation of the work after its original Mummers production run, whether for stage, print, film, radio or television, had to be approved by each and every one of the authors.

Salutin argued that this egalitarianism was unworkable in practice, and that a single owner of the copyright (in this case, himself) could more easily facilitate future productions. With regard to *I.W.A.*, the question was complicated by the fact that as "writer," Salutin had not technically *written* anything. His approach was to mould the rehearsal improvisations, nudging the actors towards themes he wanted to explore. Asking "would the real playwright please stand up..." was no solution here. Nine of us were already on our feet.

The dispute seesawed back and forth. At least, Salutin offered, if ownership of the play had to be jointly shared, decisions about what to do in case of future productions should be made by majority rule. But majority rule, we argued, never solves the problem of minority alienation. Eventually it was agreed that *I.W.A.* would be owned 50 per cent by Salutin, and 50 per cent jointly by the actor-authors and director.

In retrospect, Salutin's point was well taken. *I.W.A.* was never remounted. Very seldom were any of the Mummers' plays revived in any medium, a result of the inability of all authors to agree. The process of reaching consensus can be very trying for anyone used to getting their own way, and in later years political infighting within the Troupe often made unanimous agreement impossible. Television adaptations, publication of scripts, and even stage remounts of many plays were vetoed by individual members of the joint authorship, often as revenge for petty jealousies.

In theory, this was entirely fair and equitable. In practice, as Salutin pointed out, it often condemned perfectly good plays to an everlasting limbo.

The Marvellously Ridiculous Building

11

A marvellously ridiculous building with good space.

John Fraser, *Toronto Globe & Mail*

Back in St. John's, thanks to City Hall's closure order, the Mummers and the LSPU Hall were a *cause célèbre*. Up to this point we had simply rented space from the Longshoremen's Union, but now Lynn and I began to consider the company's residency there in a more permanent light.

We had been yearning for a permanent home for ages, with rehearsal, performance, storage, and office space under one roof. The Mummers, along with the Newfoundland Symphony Orchestra, the Newfoundland Travelling Theatre, and Codco, had in 1974 considered buying an old congregational church on Queens Road in St. John's and turning it into an all-purpose space for the four groups. The purchase price was well beyond our combined reach, and the deal fell through in the spring of 1975, but not before we received encouraging noises from the federal government's Secretary of State Department. They administered a funding programme designed to assist homeless performing arts companies to acquire resident work spaces.

So when I found the LSPU Hall a few months later, the three theatre companies (the hall was too small to house the symphony as well) agreed to apply for federal assistance, mount a fund-raising campaign, and jointly purchase the building. The Longshoremen's Union was willing to sell at a reasonable price, especially if they could continue to use it as an office and occasional meeting space. We talked to the lawyers, filed the applications, and settled back with fingers crossed to await the verdict of the federal bureaucrats.

By early fall, Codco decided to focus on national and international touring, and withdrew from the partnership. Since they didn't tour rural Newfoundland they had less need for a permanent home base in the province than did the other two theatres. And they felt that the LSPU Hall would be too small a house for their periodic St. John's performances. By November, the Newfoundland Travelling Theatre found itself in financial difficulty, and feared that the administrative strain of fund-raising, buying, and renovating the Hall would precipitate their downfall. They also withdrew. We were left holding the bag. Some members of our company, Rick Boland and Donna Butt in particular, opposed plunging ahead on our own, fearing that the increased financial responsibility, mortgages, etc., would make the Mummers more administratively rigid.

Lynn and I wanted to go ahead anyway. She now had the administrative training to handle the logistical problems involved. And our chances for federal funding assistance looked good. For some reason, "Newfcult" (as *Saturday Night Magazine* anointed it) had suddenly become the latest "in" thing for mainland sophisticates transfixed, like bunnies in the headlights, with cultural fascination.

> [They are] Newfoundland's death-watch beetles...they have discovered what they believe to be the last agonised writhings, the final death-rattles, of a poor, doomed race. "This primitive, unspoiled Newfoundland culture...," a pure, simple, unspoiled, ecological race now on its last legs (St. John's *Evening Telegram* columnist Ray Guy).

There was no denying it. On the mainland, Newfoundland had the sympathy vote, and as a result the Mummers' star was rising high in the heavens of Ottawa's civil service. We knew it would be a temporary romance. Whatever trendy popularity our theatre had attained long-distance, it had to be mistaken. Only a year earlier, after all, we were considered a pinko threat. Sooner or later the upalong crowd would discover we didn't live up to the image they'd created for us, and would drop us in favour of some more titillating manifestation of grassroots Canadiana. I felt that we might as well grab the brass ring while we could; it might not come round again. Besides, if we didn't buy the LSPU Hall, it was quite likely to become a parking lot for the Bank of Montreal, and the city's arts community would lose a potentially valuable resource.

Once it looked as if the Hall might be owned by just one, and not three theatres, we realised that the Mummers alone wouldn't be able to fill it with a year-round city production season. Our finances weren't up to it. Besides, we certainly didn't want to acquire a home at the expense of our touring activity. Lynn and I thought that a "downtown cultural centre" concept would be preferable to styling the Hall as "The Mummers Theatre." It could be the resident home for the Troupe but still open for use by other groups on a rental basis. *East End Story* had already shown the need for a downtown cultural focus in St. John's. We approached the Community Planning Association to join us in financing and operating the Hall. They agreed. This was a real plus: not only would it ease the day-to-day burden of running a cultural centre, but such a permanent liaison with a community development agency could be a terrific influence upon our future work.

Unfortunately it didn't work out. The Secretary of State Department's renovation assistance turned out to have strings attached. The Hall must be owned solely by a performing arts company, it said, not by a community organisation. Shortly afterward, CPAC's own federal funding was cut back, and the St. John's branch, the most progressive in the country, faced financial starvation. It died. It was a harbinger of things to come for many arts and community organisations. During the next five years, as the country swung politically towards the right, federal funding priorities would align themselves accordingly.

The Mummers barrelled on with the Hall alone. To no one's great surprise, neither the municipal nor the provincial governments helped us out with renovation costs. And most of the local arts groups who promised to help by giving benefits, etc., never got around to actually doing it. But the closure of our *I.W.A.* show had given us a high profile, and we used the publicity to kick off a fund-raising drive.

We found a lot of community support. Individuals and private business responded, and labour unions (many of whom viewed City Hall's closure order as a politically-motivated response to a play about a labour issue) provided invaluable help. The International Brotherhood of Electrical Workers and the Sheetmetal Workers Union gave advice and assistance with renovations, while the Longshoremen themselves went out of their way to accommodate our poverty-stricken financial situation. We hoped it would be the beginning of a closer relationship with organised labour. They were the kind of audience we primarily wanted to serve at the Hall.

The building was an exciting theatre space to work in. It provided a chance to break out of the restrictions of our touring set designs. Touring sets always seem to come down to something-to-hide-behind-between-scenes. Now, at least for our city productions, we could explore more environmentally adventurous set concepts. We kept the Hall's seating plan flexible so that different shows could configure the layout of the audience differently.

Best of all, the LSPU kept their office in the building, and occasionally longshoremen on their way there would walk in on our rehearsals and stay to watch awhile. Their presence was a reminder for us not to get too artsy-fartsy. The LSPU flagpole was the only one in the city to sport the pink, white and green nationalist flag instead of the British Jack or Pearson's Leaf.

Buying into the LSPU Hall gave us, for better or worse, increased legitimacy in the St. John's establishment. No longer could we be dismissed as itinerant hippies. We had a physical plant. We were visibly a force to be reckoned with.

As Rick and Donna had predicted, once we had a mortgage to meet, the company's internal structure became more rigid. Management of the building demanded at least one full-time administrator and a stage technician (both of whom doubled as janitors, watchmen, electricians, plumbers and cleaning staff). In theory, our legal incarnation Resource Foundation for the Arts now had two independent projects: the LSPU Hall and the Mummers Troupe. In practice, however, the two overlapped constantly as necessity shuffled people and cash back and forth. We had limited resources, and we were trying to support a downtown cultural centre within a more-than-usually-impoverished arts community.

On any comparative basis, the local arts scene was cruelly disadvantaged. Per capita, the Canada Council invested far fewer arts dollars in Newfoundland than in any other province. The provincial government, although spending millions annually on their official Arts and Culture palaces, invested virtually nothing in working Newfoundland and Labrador artists. And the municipal government of St. Johns won national notoriety through a survey which rated it the worst major city in Canada for its support to the arts. There was no provincial arts council, and private sector fund raising was unknown to most of the province's arts groups at this time.

By the time the newly renovated LSPU Hall opened in the fall of 1976, the situation had been worsened by the death of the Newfoundland Travelling Theatre. There was even less money and fewer jobs to go around the province's professional theatre community than before.

A downtown cultural centre was useless if local arts groups couldn't afford to use it. In an attempt to keep rental rates down to a level affordable by the city's financially destitute arts community, we siphoned off about $10,000 of the Mummers' finances annually to subsidise rents at the Hall. Lynn and I devised a scale which we hoped would give the building the tone we wanted: 50 per cent rent subsidy for "arts" groups using the building, 30 per cent for "community," "leftist," or "small" groups, and a flat fee for union meetings (the Hall was a traditional meeting place for several city unions). The completely destitute, the Figgy Duff band and others, usually managed to get space for free. In theory, everyone else was to ride full fare. In practice, we saw fewer than half a dozen full fare riders annually.

Prior to 1976 the provincial government with their Arts and Culture Centres held a virtual monopoly on performing arts auditoria. With the LSPU Hall we set out to prove that an independent professional arts organisation could build and run a cultural centre, sponsor projects, lobby arts policy-makers, and provide a more nourishing transfusion to the indigenous performing arts scene than could the Division of Cultural Affairs with 200 times our budget. We were regarded with admiration by some, jealousy by others, and resentment by a few, but despite limited cash and human resources we were flexible, fast, and effective. Administratively we simply outdistanced other professional arts organisations in the province at the time.

Lynn Lunde, the company's administrator, was determined that professional artists should be paid professional fees for their work at the Hall, whether as performers, technicians, or box office ticket takers. Cultural workers deserved to be paid for their jobs, she felt, just as the longshoremen, sheetmetal workers and postal workers who used the Hall for meetings were paid for theirs. Accordingly, we didn't solicit volunteer labour from the arts community. If a project couldn't afford to pay salaries, then it didn't happen. (Years later this policy of ours became controversial, but it initially sprang from a desire to establish certain basic rights for artists.) The concept hinged on successful fund raising, so we hustled our buns off to raise the cash. We managed to get a small basic annual operating grant from City Hall, and we scored supplementary cash from sources no one in Newfoundland had thought of before, to finance theatre conferences, neighbourhood arts festivals, street shows, actors workshops, and concert series by local pop musicians.

One of our projects established a kind of "mini-arts council" to provide financing for the development of independent experimental performance events. We called it the *FISH Fund*: the Fund To Initiate Stage Happenings. The idea was to make small grants available locally to anyone who wanted to mount an innovative performance project. Dudley Cox (of Newfoundland Travelling Theatre), Andy Jones (of Codco) and myself comprised an instant, on-the-spot jury to evaluate applications and hand out cash. FISH avoided the bureaucracy of application forms and six-month waiting periods which discouraged many younger artists from connecting with Ottawa-administered arts funding. It filled the hole which had appeared as Codco and the Mummers (and Newfoundland Travelling Theatre before it died) became more professionally established. Audiences demanded consistency of quality, and accordingly the three theatres took fewer chances with shows and personnel. FISH was supposed to provide opportunities for performers, writers, directors, etc., to develop ideas outside the constrictions of the established companies' production seasons.

Almost as soon as the LSPU Hall opened, it became the focal point of the city's indigenous performing arts scene. Despite its rickety low-budget seating, poor lighting (the Mummers' stage lights were only available in between tours), and generally primitive facilities, over 25,000 people passed through its doors annually.

Great. But who were these 25,000 people? We had hoped they would be predominately working class, and that many would be downtown area residents.

The majority of spectators for the Hall's theatre performances seemed to be young, middle class, middle- and low-income people. Some of them lived downtown, but there were a lot of arts buffs and university intellectuals from the suburbs. The older working-class residents of the neighbourhood seemed more interested in community events such as our Sunday flea markets, while longshoremen, sheetmetalworkers, posties and others came on weeknights for union meetings.

Despite our efforts, we were never very successful at integrating the different types of clientele. Although, for example, we offered theatre ticket discounts to members of the Longshoremen's Union, and although many longshoremen attended union meetings in the building, few came to any theatre performances. It was hard to attract a working-class audience without concentrating on the kinds of shows which that audience wanted to see. And it was hard to do *that* without imposing a blanket artistic policy on all groups using the Hall. Some of the outside arts groups renting the Hall specifically wanted a bourgeois audience; others didn't care as long as the seats were full. We hoped that our rental subsidies would encourage users more in line with the kind of audience base we were trying to build. I think it worked to some extent, but building that base turned out to be a much longer process than we'd expected. Meanwhile some users resented what they considered were unfairly selective rental subsidies.

By 1979, the Mummers Troupe was finding it increasingly difficult to support the Hall financially. During the winter of 1980 we approached several organisations who we hoped might be interested in taking it over. None were. But some members of Codco (now disenchanted with national touring) got together with other interested artists and audience members and, after several months of complicated negotiations, took over ownership of the building in September, 1980.

It sounds simple, but it was fact an extraordinarily byzantine political dogfight. Everybody was paranoid. We suggested giving the Hall over to the new group. Not on your life, they said, fearing that the Mummers would waltz off with the seats and the floorpolisher. They proposed taking over the Mummers instead. Not on your life, we said, fearing that they'd waltz off with our tour bus and lighting equipment.

At stake, in technical terms, was how to divide the Resource Foundation for the Arts. Until now, the charitable "Foundation" had been a legal phantom, a small group of friends who rarely had meetings and never bothered to make it a very open public institution. The original purpose was to avoid having the Mummers Troupe artistic policy dictated by a middle-of-the-road community board. And years before, when Resource Foundation had no assets, nobody wanted it anyway. Now that it owned a successful theatre company and a valuable piece of real estate, it was coveted. And in the heat of argument, the fact that operation of the LSPU Hall was a heavy fiscal burden tended to get forgotten. Some believed it was a golden goose rather than a financial albatross.

After a lot of name-calling, dirty looks, and letters to the newspapers, it got sorted out. The Mummers Troupe legally became a separate entity (with the bus and the lights), and the community group legally voted themselves into control of Resource Foundation for the Arts (with the seats and the polisher). The Foundation's name was symbolically changed to Resource Centre for the Arts to cleanse it of the sins of the previous regime.

Programming and fund raising suffered for a while after the changeover, but volunteers were located, and after a couple of years the LSPU Hall found its feet financially. It changed its character a little. Neighbourhood events and union meetings were discouraged in favour of an exclusively "artistic" orientation. In 1983 the Longshoremen's Union moved out, and a year later demanded that its name be removed from the Hall. But today the building is an established resource centre for the city's cultural community. The most vital and innovative original theatre produced in Newfoundland invariably premières within its walls.

The Price War 12

> Bertold Brecht remarked that 'the proof of the pudding is in the eating,' a comment that might appear blindingly obvious until one observes that the major preoccupations of many socialist theatre workers are with the origins of the recipe, the cleanliness of the spoons, the decision-making process employed by the chefs, and the address of the restaurant .
>
> British playwright David Edgar

The nature of the collective creation process seems to precipitate internal structural crisis for many theatres sooner or later. This is especially true for politically oriented theatres.

1976 was the year of reckoning for the Mummers Troupe. We had more production work than we could comfortably handle; we were growing fast, and our reputation was mushrooming. Yet limited time, limited money, and limited resources, inexperience, and low salaries intensified our struggle for survival. We seesawed between idealism and necessity. Artistic, organisational, and personal pressures converged. It was like living in the middle of a juggling act.

You are what you eat, they say. With us it worked artistically as well as nutritionally. Company self-image tended to be shaped both by the *way* we worked on shows, and by the particular *subject matter* of each show. It also depended, of course, upon which side of the administrative fence one was on.

The way we worked on shows— at least in the rehearsal room— was by collective consensus (although a play's director or writer might predominate in decisions about style and shape). Company management, on the other hand, generally rested with an administrator (until 1976, Lynn Lunde) and an artistic director (until 1980, myself). This was in line with the sort of traditional management structure which most of our funding sources (such as the Canada Council) expected. It worked quite well, patrolling the border between the Troupe and its official support systems efficiently and economically. When necessary, it cut its hair and carried a briefcase.

This kind of church/state separation allowed performers and directors the space to breathe, to think, and to create in any way they wished. The administration could be relied upon to screen out most of the everyday flak and interface with the world of the grocery bill.

Like non-holistic medicine, it worked...but it had its side effects. By making the rehearsal hall sacrosanct, for instance, a caste system was created. Actors sometimes viewed non-performance personnel as less important "untouchables." Administrators, technicians, and designers often complained that although they were excluded from performers' decisions about scenes in the rehearsal room, actors often didn't return the favour. Some actors resented administrative decisions being made (regarding an in-rehearsal production) without their collective participation in the office. What the rehearsal-room collective seldom realised was that the making of administrative magic with severely limited resources is in its own way as much of a creative process as the improvising of scenes. At issue was not simply the impossibility of collective participation on every single task. It was a matter of respecting each worker's integrity, leaving them sufficient room to move, and not barging needlessly onto their turf. If you want a job done creatively, treat the creator accordingly; if you just want someone to carry out orders, then lower your expectations of what can be accomplished.

Originally, when the Mummers began in 1972, all performance and non-performance work was shared (in theory if not in practice). Very soon it developed that no one wanted the burden of bookkeeping. This responsibility eventually devolved onto Lynn Lunde (who initially didn't want it either but eventually became inured to it). Administrative complexities grew along with the company and ultimately required the attention of a full-time non-performing administrator. Similar specialisation occurred with the company's technical requirements. At first, every Mummer carried props, erected sets and put up lights. But later, as the company's technical equipment became more complex (and heavier) a non-performing permanent technician position (filled by Derek Butt) became necessary. Had more of the company's members in 1976 been around to participate in the earlier evolutions, they might have found the company structure more acceptable. Or their participation might have long ago shaped a different evolution. Perhaps, too, if more of our cast members had had experience in "traditional" professional theatre, role-division by function would have seemed axiomatic. But as it was, the rehearsal room's participatory democracy often challenged work-function specialisation. At best, we made headway in only one direction: that is, we involved actors in office decisions, but never managed to integrate non-actors into rehearsal-room decisions.

It was more difficult to get a handle on the way the *subject* matter of particular shows influenced the way we saw one another within the group. It sometimes changed from show to show. Acting seems to be the craft of autosuggestion. It is useless to *pretend* to be Hamlet; you must *become* Hamlet. During weeks of rehearsals and performances, the line between onstage and offstage realities can sometimes become muddied.

I was often intrigued by the way a political show would galvanize strident politics in a cast of individuals who often showed no perceptibly strong political beliefs either before or after the project. This was particularly noticeable when we would go into a community to develop a project. Everyone became fiercely committed to the community issue which we were dramatising, yet after the production was over, few ever returned either to the community or to the political issue again. It was, of course, our job to identify with the community issue, in the same way as the classical actor's job is to identify with Hamlet. This in no way denigrates the artist's morals or intelligence; no actor would choose to take part in a production about either Hamlet or a community issue if he or she were not interested in the "role" in the first place. But once committed to the role, autosuggestion—the professional ability to *believe*—becomes part of the job. It was for this reason, I suspect, that the subject matter of Mummers' shows often seemed to exert their own peculiar tidal pulls on the evolution of group process.

To no one's great surprise, for instance, after *Company Town* we began to question the labour-management relationship within the Troupe, and to see each other in traditional worker-boss terms. *Company Town* was a pro-union show produced by a non-union company; an interesting dichotomy. (We had our political differences with Actors Equity Association, as did they with us. We balked at their Americanised rulebook catering to the needs of big mainland theatres, dictating unequal salaries for stage managers, actors and directors. Equity balked at our regionalism. In the early 1970s their only small-company contract applied to so-called "studio" theatres. Because we weren't based in a large metropolitan area, we didn't qualify.)

In an attempt to structure the company more formally along labour-management lines, the cast of *Company Town* produced the first "Mummers Manifesto" in the fall of 1974. It declared the artistic director to be part of management, with primary say in major decisions like choice of the production season. But it insisted that the same individual should not be company administrator. The company administrator should be a separate, salaried, non-performing position. The Manifesto called for a minimum wage (at that time $70 per week—it was always a basic tenet of the Troupe that everyone was paid equally), basic working conditions, open-to-inspection budgets and books, a kind of shop-steward position playfully titled *The Master of Pretense* and periodic company meetings to be known as *vichychoises*. Except for one clause which suggested that "management" should hold 100 per cent copyright ownership of collectively-created scripts ("management" rejected that proposal, in favour of joint ownership by all authors) the Manifesto was accepted all around, and we slurped our way through several vichychoises during that winter.

The vichychoise was watered down considerably when only half of the *Company Town* cast came back to the Troupe for our 1974 Christmas mummering, and still further when, after the Toronto run of *Company Town* in June 1975, only one cast member and Manifesto author (Donna Butt) returned to Newfoundland. Without a stable group membership, responsibilities came down to the same old management leadership. Long-term membership suffered not only from the pressures of individual careerism and burnout, but also from the fact that at no time during the decade could the company count on sufficient financing to be able to guarantee a whole year's employment to actors. Usually the best we could manage was "Well, we can definitely hire you for the next two shows, but after that it all depends on how our fund-raising turns out." During the winter of 1975 the vichychoise constantly fell victim to poverty, geography, and membership turnover.

> Donna Butt:...that whole grant-giving system, I don't know. I'm really suspicious of what it does to people, especially people who want to keep an ongoing concern. It forces you to hoard, to hold back money, to keep the group going. But if you don't get to choose to take lower wages...then you're a worker who's exploited.

> Lee Campbell: I don't think, personally, that actors should be involved in the negotiations, the administration of grants. But it's a

> matter of integrity involved.... I don't think it's a good thing to have animosity to the director. It interferes with the work....
>
> Howie Cooper: But I think it's necessary to have a director. You need an outside observer who understands the process. And usually it's the director who has a vision. They see something; they have an overview. That's what Chris did.... So he should be called the director. I think the idea of someone like Chris is: someone who was in on the company before any of us were. A director who appreciates the collective process and can function with it can be very useful. The problem that evolved with this company is that the head of the company is also the head of the management end (*Mayday* No. 1 1975).

After mounting *East End Story* and *Dying Hard* in 1975 with entirely local casts, we felt that there was more hope for carry-over, and the vichychoise evolved into the "core group" structure. We considered inviting people into the core group after they had worked in at least three Mummers' shows. Size of the core and balance of ability within it were screening factors. The idea was an expansion of the Master of Pretense shop-steward position into a small group which would consult with management on long-range planning. In general, production casting would use core members supplemented by transient performers. Rhonda Payne and Donna Butt were the initial core members, joined in November 1975 by Rick Boland.

Collectives are very good at having meetings. We certainly were, initially at least. The problem was that we came to precious few decisions. An example: the core group discussed plans for our forthcoming 1976 season interminably, yet by the time rehearsals for a new production began early in the New Year, we had only managed to plan out the first half of the season. Despite a rapidly approaching application deadline for Canada Council season funding, it proved to be impossible to get the group together for scheduled meetings once rehearsals had started. Someone was always tired, had a date, or had to wash their hair. After eight hours of hard work in daily rehearsal, most people had had enough, and the prospect of a long evening meeting in the office was decidedly unattractive. No one was prepared to put in fourteen-hour days. No one except Lynn and me. Eventually the two of us decided the remainder of the season unilaterally, in order to get the funding application in under the wire. It was discouraging. It looked as if we could be either a group that made meetings or a group that made theatre. But not both.

It was our version of the syndrome which afflicted many of the Back-to-the-Land agricultural communes that dropped out of the sixties. After the founding collective thinned out, members came and went, and it was often left to the same few old hands to plant the potatoes each year. Ultimately, in many rural communes, those old hands demanded a share of the decision-making power proportionate to their burden of responsibility. Traditional social values, of course, reinforced such thinking.

If the Mummers Troupe had remained a permanent collective with a stable membership since 1972, it would undoubtedly have developed a more collective sharing of responsibility. As it was, by 1976 it was the product of a different evolution. Lynn and I felt we'd carried the company on our backs for four years, and the tree had grown as the twig bent. We defended our control. It was difficult for new members to appreciate past company experiences without having gone through them first-hand, and older hands were loathe to repeat previously learned mistakes with each new production and each change in the collective *status quo*. The core group system was an attempt to maintain a dependable administrative through-line while initiating others into the mechanics of the Troupe's survival skills. But it didn't work fast enough to meet the demands for democratic control. Within three months the structure was challenged.

Meanwhile, our winter 1976 production was in rehearsal, and it tinted our perception with its own colours. We started to see internal company structure as a reflection of the dramatic material we were improvising. That material was a show commissioned by Oxfam with Canadian International Development Agency backing. It was supposed to explain the concept of a New International Economic Order being lobbied at the time in the United Nations. It would tour the country to help make Canadians aware of the issues involved in Third World disparity. The play was scheduled to kick off our first-ever national tour in late March without ever being audience-tested. Audience-tested, hell. As it turned out, we didn't even get a proper dress rehearsal.

Up to this point, we had created what Oxfam called "development-education plays" made exclusively for Newfoundland audiences. At least we had had a few clues as to what made our target audience tick. Now our primary audience was to be mainland Canadians. We had far less understanding of what brought them into the theatre. They looked like a pretty bland lot to us. Their interest in international relations amounted to rah-rahing at the Canada-Russia hockey games (which, incidentally, are still far better propaganda shows than any theatre the Canadian Left has come up with to date). They were as excited about the Third World as they were about the laundry list, the dishes, and the kitty litter. Action on any of them was prompted only by proximity or when things just piled up *beyond* the beyond. The popular solution to world economic injustice was the care package. Oxfam wanted us to break through that attitude. We had to demonstrate that the roots of Third World poverty are not thousands of miles distant, but right here, now. On the doorstep. In us.

Oxfam sent me off to New York to watch the preliminaries for the Fourth United Nations Conference on Trade and Development (UNCTAD) and hopefully develop a show concept. I returned convinced that it would be extremely difficult for our cast to play Nicaraguan campesinos, SWAPO guerrillas or Peruvian peasants in a convincing way. To the extent that it could be possible, it would be offensive. So I opted for a more familiar focus. I asked the cast to consider Newfoundland as a Third World entity within Canada. We would root the show's concepts in a deeply personal awareness of the muzzle end of imperialism which, as Newfoundlanders, each of us shared. I did not want a preachy show which wheedled with its audience for social justice; I wanted an angry show, demanding it.

The difficulty was going to be getting our mainland audiences to take us seriously. North American society in general is very adept at defusing potential hostility by absorption: giving it a full-colour glossy in the "People" section of *Macleans* or *Time* magazine. Even dissent is featured as radical chic. And as a Newfoundland theatre in 1976 we had an additional problem: Newfcult. The latest taste sensation. Another Newfoundland theatre, Codco, had already been swept off its feet by mainland adoration. Their comedic caricatures of rustic Newfoundlanders were the talk of the town in Toronto, Ottawa, Vancouver and Philadelphia. (Those same Codco caricatures were practically booed off the stage when they toured rural Newfoundland. Codco soon stopped touring the island altogether — outside of St. John's— and tailored their material for the mainland entertainment market. I didn't want the Mummers to follow that route.)

Mainland audiences seemed to miss the darker side of Codco's satire. They preferred to see Newfoundland as a kind of Atlantic Disneyland, a rugged and rubber-booted Elizabethan garden of ethnicity created for the holiday recreation of central Canadians. In this romanticized vision, regional disparity is applauded: isn't poverty wonderful, to make Newfoundlanders create such appealing survival techniques? "They think we are cute. They think we all got rhythm. And we has, yassuh, we has."

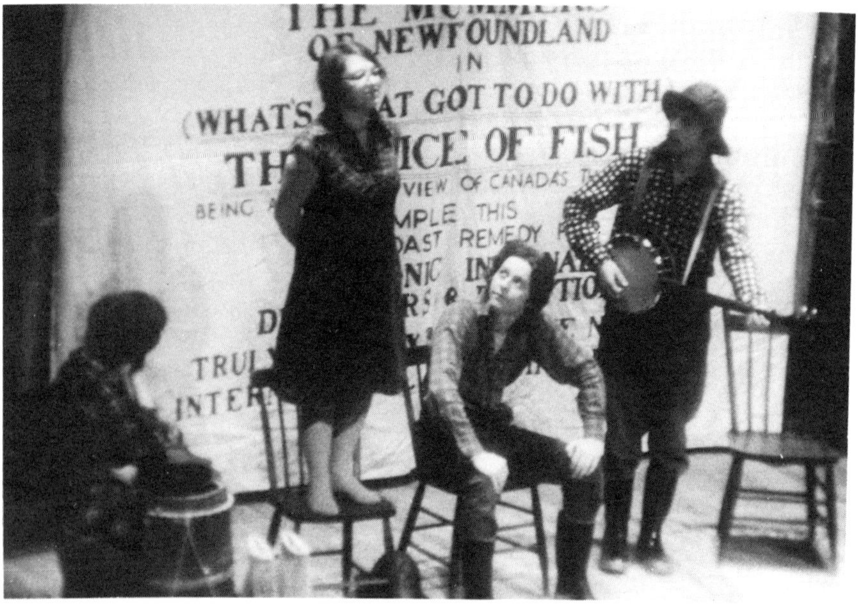

Above: opening minstrel song, *What's That Got To Do With The Price of Fish*? national tour 1976.
Left to right: Maddy Williams, Donna Butt, Jeff Pitcher, Ron Hynes.
Below: Skipper Eph and Skipper George (Maddy Williams and Rick Boland) tell Newfie jokes with the heehaw chorus.
Photos: Derek Butt.

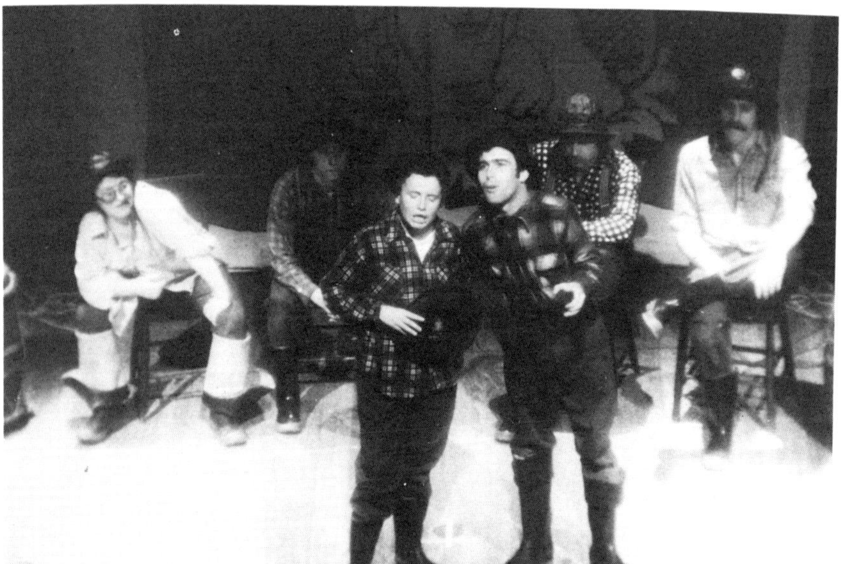

I proposed a model for our production: an old-time black minstrel show, with Newfie jokes and rubber boots instead of nigger jokes and Jim Crow. The opening number, sung by the whole cast to the tune of *Camptown Races*, tried to set the tone in the worst possible taste:

NEWFIES: Newfoundlanders sing and dance,

Do Da, Do Da,
Inshore fishery got no chance,
Oh Do Da day.
Who do we have to thank?
Romeo LeBlanc!
Wherefore art Thou, Romeo...?

FISHERMAN: Over in New York at the Law of the Sea Conference screwing the Newfoundland fishermen, and if I could get my hands on him, I'd....

NEWFIES: We all have to say Amen,

Do Da, Do Da,
To Ottawa's regimen,
Oh Do Da day.
Amen to the offshore limit;
Amen to the no fish in it;
Amen to Canadian welfare cheques....

WELFARE RECIPIENT: Which we wouldn't be needin' if Upper Canadian businessmen stopped fattening their pockets at our expense....

FISHERMAN: Amen to that, sister!

NEWFIES: Aaaaa...MEN!

It seemed appropriate to use the Newfoundland fishery as a motif for many of the economic issues Oxfam wanted to examine. As an independent country, Newfoundland once had the greatest fishery in the world. Now no more. Under federal Canadian fisheries policy, the Newfoundland saltfish industry had gone steadily downhill. In 1976 the federal government had not yet introduced the 200-mile offshore fishing limit, and fishermen had spent most of their twenty-seven years of Canadian confederation competing with hordes of foreign fishing trawlers under a three-mile, and later a seven-mile, offshore limit. The title for our show was obvious: *What's That Got to Do with the Price of Fish?*

Making abstract theory come alive theatrically is tough slogging at the best of times, and most of this cast lacked a highly developed political consciousness. Our previous community documentaries had reflected an audience to themselves, "pulling zooms" out of an observed fabric of community life. An inductive process. This time, we would have to work in reverse, hanging improvisations on a purely theoretical framework, fleshing out abstractions. Such a deductive process presents the danger of creating stereotyped stock Newfoundlanders who serve the play's purpose, but may not exist anywhere in reality. I wondered whether we had bitten off more than we could chew with this project.

Oxfam brought in the development-education team GATT-FLY from Toronto to conduct seminars for our rehearsals. The Fishermen's union, Oxfam, and Memorial University's Extension Service also participated. The seminar translated national and international economic relationships into blackboard cartoon diagrams. We studied this as we screened faded minstrel-show films from the twenties. Eventually we came up with a sleuth scene based on a vaudeville blackboard routine, which ostensibly unravelled the mysteries of fish pricing:

SLEUTH: So after I went through the plant I thought I'd go down to the grocery store and see how much fish costs there. It was $2.80. That's a lot to pay when you can buy it from the fisherman on the wharf for only eleven cents a pound. Processing costs in the plant were $1.50. What happened to the other $1.30?

ALL: That's the profit!

SLEUTH: Profit! $1.30 a pound is a hell of a markup on a pound of fish! Just a minute, sir.

PLANT OWNER: Yes?

SLEUTH: You are making an enormous profit on a pound of fish. While the fisherman is hard put to make ends meet, you are making more than 90 percent profit!

OWNER: I beg your pardon, my man. I am merely making one seventh of the total price of the fish. Are you seriously suggesting this is too much for the processor to make? I have overhead...

SLEUTH: It seems to me you're making a hell of a lot more than that!

OWNER: You have the figures?

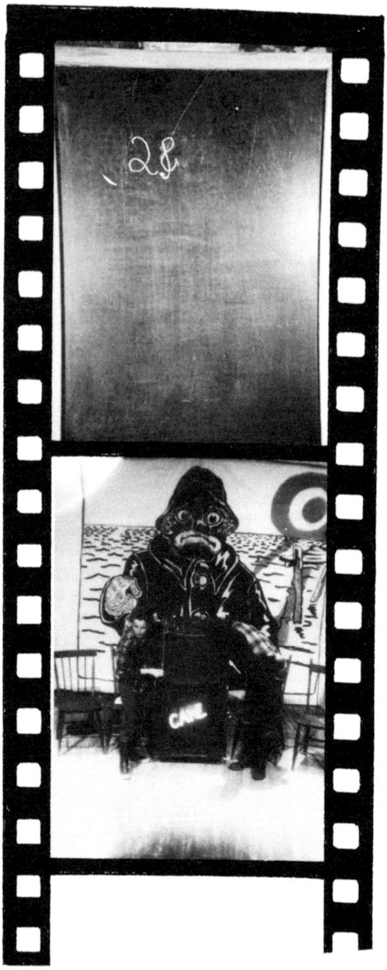

SLEUTH: I certainly do.

OWNER: And you're calling me a liar.

SLEUTH: I'm saying that your precious profit of $1.30 is practically half of the $2.80 selling price. That's elementary mathematics.

OWNER: Indeed it is elementary mathematics, but my paltry $1.30 profit, sir, is a mere one-seventh of that $2.80.

SLEUTH: What? One seventh?!!!

OWNER: I'll prove it to you. Bring out my visual aids, boys. You see you can't just ream off all these figures and expect ordinary lay spectators to understand the intricacies of fish processing. It's a complicated business, demanding skill and expertise from those of us who monop...I mean, manage it. So let's take a good hard look at it in black and white, here.

First I put down the total cost of the fish that you bought in the store, which is $2.80.

SLEUTH: Just a minute. What is that figure there?

OWNER: Like a fish standing on end? That is a capital eight. We are dealing with capitalism here, you know. Now I put down my divisor, which is the one-seventh, right?...

SLEUTH: What is that!?

OWNER: That, sir, is a period. It shows that this is as far as I am going to go with this seven. Now. Seven will not go into two, even you know that. But seven will go into my capital eight and it will go one time and I have one left over. Seven goes into twenty-one three times and I bring down my zero. A dollar thirty!

SLEUTH: Ah...Just a minute. I want to see you multiply that dollar thirty profit by seven.

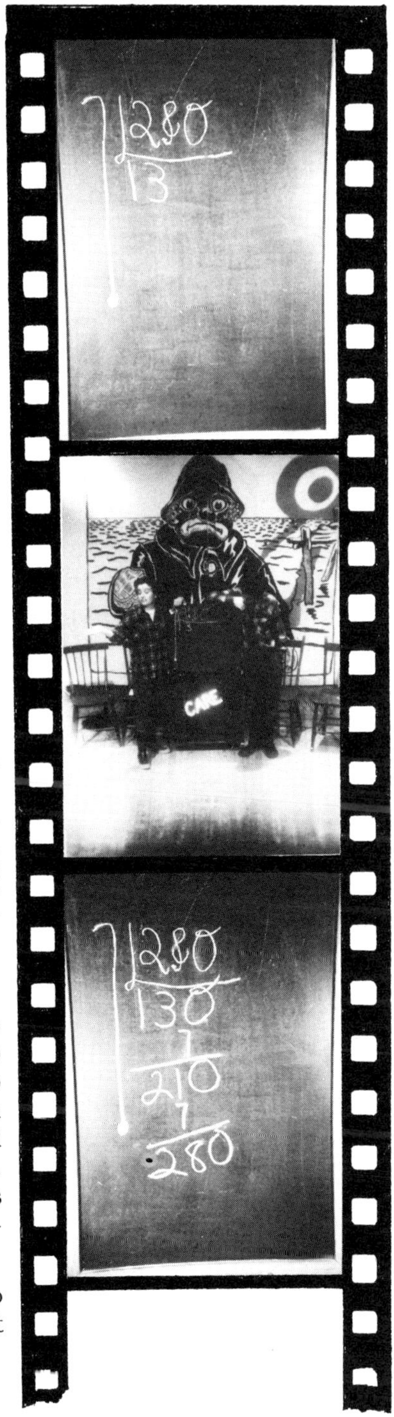

OWNER: I see. You question my figures. Well then, 7 times zero is zero— which is what your investigative journalism will be worth when this demonstration is over...

And 7 times 3 is 21...

And 7 times 1 is 7.

$2.80! There you have it, sir.

(By now our detective is totally confused but hangs on desperately)

SLEUTH: Wait, now. Hold it....I am going to mark down $1.30 seven times and add it up. And I bet it won't be $2.80...! Three, six, nine, twelve, fifteen, eighteen, twenty-one...

OWNER:...twenty-two, twenty-three, twenty-four, twenty-five, twenty-six, twenty-seven, Twenty-EIGHT!

There you have it, sir. Two dollars and eighty cents!

There was only so far we could go with blackboards and statistics. When the pace flagged, we threw in a few commercials with familiar Canadian faces:

ANNOUNCER: And now, the makers of Imperialist Margarine present...

MADAME BENOIT: (daintily lifting off the top of a Newfoundlander's head as if preparing a pudding bowl) Good evening Ladies and Gentlemens. Dis evening's recipe is what to do wit dem leftovers— de regional disparities of de many kitchens of Maple Leaf. Dis recipe 'ere calls for changing de dumpy little Newfie pudding into de great Canadian torte.

First of all we have to get dis bread pudding to become more fluffy; we want it to be as light as de Canadian dollar. Just be careful it doesn't fall. Now what I suggest is a cupful of university professors.

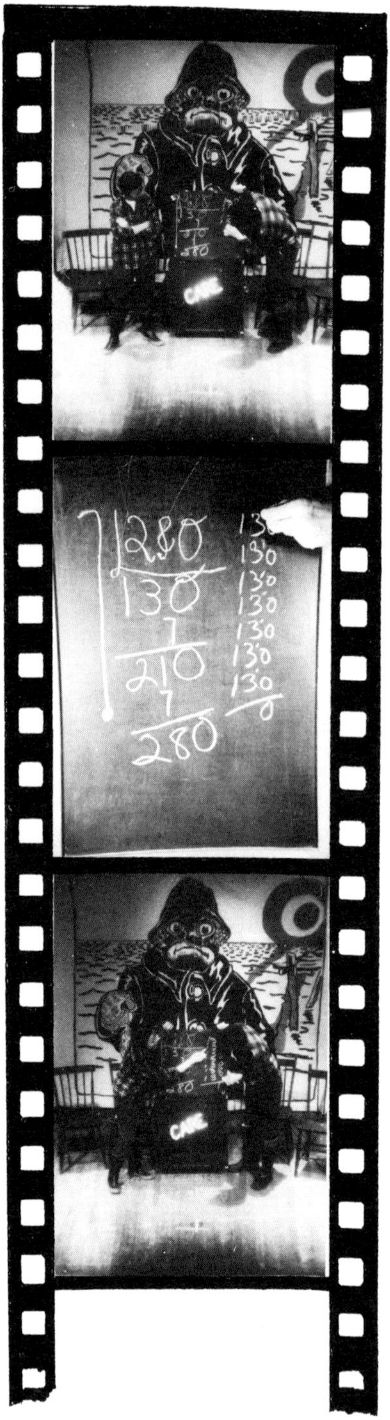

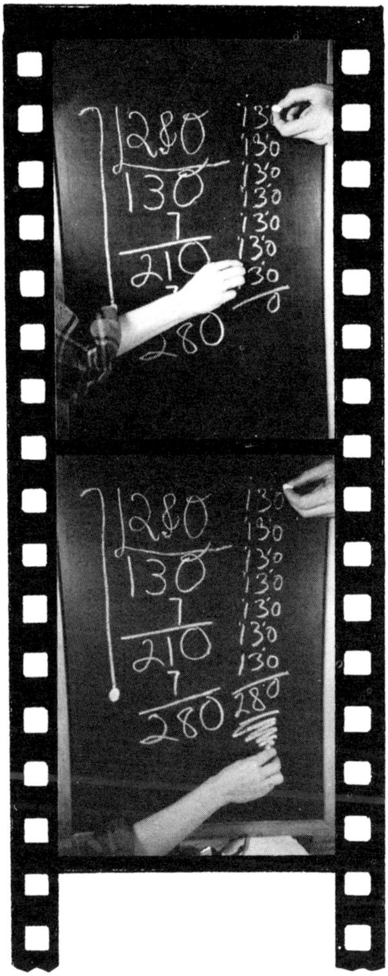

I like de American professors, dey always get de job done best— but you can use British instead if you like, there's always plenty of dem around, dat's for sure. Never use Canadian— at least not at de head of de department... Now ...(stirring the head vigorously)...beat dat around good...

Now once everything is all mixed up in dere, de torte will start to rise. But you still need to get rid of de rather bland taste of de Newfie pudding. What I suggest for dis is national radio and television flavouring. If you like Canadian flavour you can use CBC; if you are used to American flavour den use CTV— dey're pretty well de same 'ting anyway....Now you put de whole mess in de oven for two-and-a-half decades.

While it's in dere you make de topping to cover up de torte wit after. I usually use an American base for de topping— now whether dat be an army base, an airforce base, or a naval base it don't really matter...de Americans are always very good at cover up.... On top of dat we sprinkle a little bit of Woolco, a pinch of Zellers, some MacDonalds, a couple of famous authors who don't know what dey are talking about, and finally a mother country up a gum tree. Beat dat!

Take de torte out of de oven...y voila:

NEWF: A Canadian Tart!!

BENOIT: No, dear, dat's something else...

In case anyone found the show insubstantial, we loaded our programmes with take-home statistical data, such as:

A Breakdown of Household Cash Income in Rural Newfoundland

(percent)	1953	1967
Fishing	63.6	36.9
Other Work	18.2	18.2
Federal Transfer Payment (UIC, Welfare, etc)	18.2	45.5

We didn't know what a mainland audience would think about any of this stuff, but it certainly touched our own nerve ends in rehearsal. The Mummers became what we ate. Doctrinaire xenophobia ran rampant in the cast. Mainlanders were the enemy. Lynn Lunde became "the mainlander in the office." Rhonda Payne was asked not to join the cast for the show because, as one member of the core group proposed, she was not a "proper" Newfoundlander. (Despite having been born and raised in the province, her "formative high school years," it was argued, had been spent upalong.) Nova Scotian Susan Perly, who had come over from Halifax to work as co-writer on the show, was only accepted in the rehearsal room after winning a long ideological arm wrestle.

In 1976 Newfoundland nationalism seemed a necessary evil, in the short run at least, a handy and available weapon for a province battling its way out of a cultural insecurity complex. But it left part of the Newfoundland theatre with a legacy of simplistic political analysis for the rest of the decade.

We had given ourselves a dangerously tight rehearsal schedule. I pushed the actors hard. *The Price of Fish* was to open in Sydney, Nova Scotia, immediately following a short run of *I.W.A.* at Centaur Theatre in Montreal. As the final rehearsal count-down began, we were almost two weeks behind schedule. It became increasingly apparent that we would not be able to make our dress rehearsal deadline in St. John's. We were all a bundle of nerves. My six-year personal relationship with Lynn Lunde had just gone on the rocks, and I was going none-too-daintily round the bend. At home in Maddox Cove, one of my goats broke its leg in the barn and three new born kids died from neglect. Steven Bush wrote from Toronto saying that the earth had tilted another fraction of a degree on its axis and that Rochdale's 3HO (Happy, Healthy, Holy) Yogis were predicting dire consequences: wars, pestilences, strife.

It was a hell of a winter.

Finally everything ground to a halt. We all screamed, cancelled the dress rehearsal and sat down together for five days to figure things out. It was a major company crisis. Central to the debate was the question of the core group—whether everybody should be in it, and whether it should continue its consultative function or instead supplant the administrator and artistic director.

A variety of related issues presented themselves. Some were easily seen. The question of company style, for instance. Donna Butt was unhappy with *The Price of Fish*'s theatrical style. To her, vaudeville was trite; naturalism was more appropriate to political theatre. I feared that sentimental excess too often led us into maudlin self- indulgence. (The kind of thing that usually began: "I minds the time when....") She wanted audiences to have an emotional catharsis; I wanted them to be analytical.

For most of the cast, this issue came to be more about personal allegiances within the group than about effective animation of an audience. The solution seemed simple: there should be room within the company for individual growth and for a variety of theatrical attitudes. I should direct fewer shows. Rick Boland had already directed his first show, our traditional Mummers Play, last Christmas. Donna should boss some productions herself. It was planned that she would direct our upcoming summer show on the inshore fishery. Ah, some questioned, but should future shows *have directors at all*? Didn't any director represent artistic authoritarianism?

Issues having to do with group dynamics were more murky. There were battles of personalities and of egos (the theatrical profession rarely attracts self-effacing wallflowers) and much of the egalitarian rhetoric being trotted out neglected to deal with the obvious presence of two powerful leadership personalities (Donna and me) within the group. We were a young company (average age in the cast was about 20.) As director, I had unwittingly become a father /guru figure for some members, with all the attraction-repulsion and incipient revolution implied in such a relationship. It was all as clear as mud. On the one hand, there was a tendency to portray problems which arose from personal hang ups as problems of group structure. On the other hand, structural problems of the collective tended to be portrayed in terms of personality deficiencies— someone was a "good person" or a "bad person."

All of the issues wove themselves through our *Price of Fish* rehearsals. Many of us declared that we weren't willing to continue working together in the future without a larger measure of personal and artistic autonomy. We each needed room to move. Wayne McNiven and Donna Butt felt it was essential to abolish such roles as director, administrator, designer, etc., since they represented artistic hierarchy. Divisions of labour should be replaced by a participatory democracy that included everyone in the company. I opposed this. The size and make up of the company still changed from show to show, and I didn't want anyone showing up for auditions to automatically get the part and become a lifetime Mummer. I feared we would wind up with a congratulatory participation, more likely to lead to middle-of-the-road artistic and political choices than to effective social intervention. Successful collective effort has focus. I proposed that work functions be rotated so that different individuals would get a chance to be director, designer, administrator, actor, etc., on different shows. The idea did not fly.

Passions burned high. During the first day, we argued, cried, paced the floor. Some left. Rick Boland got the flu. The second day was even worse. Lynn Lunde resigned, effective at the end of the national tour. At lunchtime, Donna and Wayne quit too; later in the afternoon, they changed their minds.

Amongst the various dynamics in the group, an emotional hierarchy reigned supreme. To the extent that the proponent of an argument could pull off a greater display of emotion he or she got support. Points could be scored either by staging a wounded withdrawal— in which case no one wished to inflict further pain upon such demonstrably enormous suffering— or by histrionics, in which case no one dared suggest that anyone who cared so passionately (and yelled so loud) could possibly be wrong.

In the middle of the mess, Pam Morgan (an ex-company member from our previous *I.W.A.* cast) walked through the door with a rose, placed it silently in the centre of the floor, looked at us sternly and left again. It was like a moment of prayer. But after a brief hush, the marathon continued. "You know what you've done?" Donna confided to me over a beer, "You've created a bunch of little Frankensteins!"

On the third day I brought in a quote by Sandy Archer of the San Francisco Mime Troupe, relating that company's experience four years earlier:

> When you attempt to break out of the divisions of labor, you also begin to break down the trust and respect that was associated with those divisions. And when those divisions were in terms of skill (or who could do that part of the common goal best) you open the doors to those areas to skilled and unskilled alike, to the experienced and inexperienced. While this can bring out innovative ideas or techniques, it primarily focuses on breaking down identities built upon what we would call experienced or professional wisdom. In this way, anyone's opinions become as valid as anyone else's. The extreme result of this would be individualism, i.e. total expression of each in all areas. A true collective action, on the other hand, would be based upon emotional and political peers using their specific experience and skills for a common goal (Davis 1975).

To the extent that this axiom is not observed, I urged, we will drive skilled professionals from the Troupe.

I felt we had to get our priorities straight. The Mummers had a mandate to animate an audience and a society. If a participatory-democratic internal structure was the best way to implement that mandate, then okay. But we should not reverse the order of priorities. Methodology should be at the service of the objective.

In general terms, of course, it is important to change the traditional means of production in the theatre. Greater equality in relationships between workers in theatre production can often be the first step towards getting socialist ideas across the footlights in performance. But it is also true that within a capitalist society, theatre has to be sold in the market place. There is a big investment in getting opening night on. On schedule, on budget.

Successfully forging egalitarian socialism amongst even a small group of individuals (each of whom lives in a society based upon quite different principles) requires great care, energy and time. The reward is that if successful, the achievement can stand as a shining example of the possible. But (and this is something our Troupe never seriously addressed) how does such a group evolve into a healthy collective without ultimately tackling the question of the personal hang ups of its members, each a product of the society he or she lives in: individualistic, egocentric, and neurotic enough to choose the theatre as a profession in the first place?

There are a host of obstacles strewing any theatre collective's path between professional survival on the one hand and an ideal group *gestalt* on the other. The problem is that in practice, most groups who opt to follow the path to structural enlightenment generally get so bound up in it that they have little time or energy left to push and shove for change in the larger society. And a theatre which neglects to wrestle with its audience is a dull theatre. I had seen too many theatres turn in on themselves, perfecting their internal structure to the detriment of their social effectiveness, to assume that the Mummers Troupe was immune to the same fate. Psychological health is better sought through therapy than theatre groups.

On the other hand, a purely pragmatic attitude isn't very satisfactory either. But it often gets the job done quickly. Sticking your finger in the dike may not be the perfect solution in the long run, but it does stop the leak. In the early 1970s some of us thought we were watching Newfoundland's identity being led to the precipice. The babies being thrown out with the bath water included much of our culture, our heritage, our language and our future. We lacked the luxury of time— our job was to head 'em off at the pass, quickly. As a consequence I believed the company had to learn to live with its finger in the dike.

To some extent it's a numbers game, and I believe it is vital to get to Pretoria even if one's march is a little ragged. Most members of the cast which put together *Gros Mourn* were politically reactionary and personally ill-motivated, fought pitched battles over breakfast and never worked together again. That was all relatively unimportant. What was relatively important was that those imperfect artists inspired a whole community to stand up and take action. Audiences in Sally's Cove or anywhere else don't usually give much of a damn about group infighting in the dressing room; they come to see the performance. Effective theatre, like revolution, can be made by less than perfect people if necessary.

The Mummers' marathon meeting lasted for four days. After nearly eighty hours of weeping, yelling, table- thumping and hair-tearing, the fever of our conflict abated. As we assembled for the fifth day, the atmosphere was noticeably different. Nothing had really changed (other than a general blood-letting and clarification of positions), but instead of sitting against the far corners of the room warily eyeing each other as on previous days, we all grouped exhaustedly in a close circle on the floor and talked quietly. The tour would go on. Some of us were due to leave for Montreal in two days with our remount of the *I.W.A.* play, and our structural standoff would be postponed until we regrouped in June for rehearsals of Donna's Fishery show.

The *Price of Fish* tour went amazingly well under the circumstances. We squeezed in extra daytime rehearsals in Montreal while running *I.W.A.* at night with a partially- overlapping cast. *Fish* was a flawed play, but it worked with our audiences. Critics across the country were divided in their opinion. In Halifax they loved it:

> A small masterpiece...in the best tradition of black humour (John Howitt, *Halifax Chronicle-Herald* 7 April 1976).

In Ottawa thay hated it:

> Why don't the Mummers give up their pretence at theatre and settle for a straightforward political lecture.... Even the program looks like a political tract! (Audrey Ashley, Ottawa Citizen, 30 April 1976).

In Winnipeg they were suspicious of our sponsors:

> I'm not certain what international development groups are, or who is involved in them. As for the UN, spare me. This new economic order seems to consist chiefly of giving the go-ahead to terrorist activities! (Lee Schacter, *Winnipeg Free Press* 4 May 1976).

In Vancouver they were suspicious of our audience:

> The audience, knowing cheap and nasty theatre manipulation when it sees it, and loving every minute of it— hit us again! again!— gives it a standing ovation.... (Max Wyman, *Vancouver Sun* 20 May 1976).

But Toronto *Globe and Mail* (20 April 1976) critic John Fraser was probably closest to the mark:

> The show...takes dramatic and emotional aim at the broad side of a very large barn. To be fair, I would have to admit that quite often it hits that barn....

The kind of direct style that disappointed Fraser was a reflection of the entertainment tastes of our usual home audience. Rural working-class Newfoundlanders like to know exactly what you are trying to do or say to them. They don't much like plays that try to impress by purposefully obscuring something that could be presented in a perfectly straightforward way. By comparison, middle-class urban audiences tend to prefer a certain intellectual obliqueness. They like to feel that they are deciphering some secret code of the author so that they can leave the theatre with a sense that their university educations were not acquired in vain.

The Canada Council seemed flabbergasted that we could pull off a national tour without either government or corporate assistance. Development-education groups across the country brought out their supporters to fill houses for us, and they seemed pleased with the result. Oxfam's project evaluation concluded that the show had achieved its goals, although they would have preferred the dramatic references to have been more internationalist. I suspected that the show preached mainly to the already converted. While the tour finished up in Western Canada, I went to Cuba on a package vacation to lie on the beach and let the breeze blow through my brains, rustle my soul around some, and hopefully tell me what to do next. For the first time in a long while I felt the billow of my own life as something apart from the Mummers Troupe. Quitting the company would have been easy. I tossed a coin.

It came up heads. I went back to Newfoundland, got a tattoo and a motorcycle, and began renovation work on the LSPU Hall. The 3HO Yogis be damned; I was high. It was spring inside and out, the end of a phase for the company and for me. Whatever the outcome of the Troupe's structural crisis, the four-year body of work behind us had at least accomplished something for the record: a political theatre could survive in Newfoundland. It could be effective at home, and it could hold its own on foreign territory. Now would it self-destruct?

Losing Altitude

Revolution Shoots Itself in the Foot

13

Discontent is the mother of progress.

J. R. Smallwood

The *Price of Fish* national tour finished up in Vancouver in early May 1976, and after a month's holiday the cast returned to St. John's to begin work on our scheduled show about the Newfoundland inshore fishery. I was to be in charge of the LSPU Hall renovations during the summer; Donna Butt was to be in charge of the show. February's marathon meeting had worked out this plan to calm the battle of wills shaping up between Donna and myself.

We hoped to develop a working relationship with the Newfoundland Federation of Fishermen and Allied Workers Union in creating the new show. It was a promising project, and we were aiming for a late summer tour during the inshore fishing season.

Everyone showed up for opening rehearsal except the director. The second and third day the same thing happened. Donna had disappeared. Friends said she wasn't in the province. Unfortunately, the research and planning for the show had disappeared with her. Other members of the cast weren't prepared to step in and plunge ahead on their own. Most were pissed off. Some had cut their holidays short; all needed the rehearsal pay. Finally rehearsals were postponed. The cast received two weeks salary for the inconvenience, the standard Actor's Equity compensation, but it wasn't much. Some of the actors went home. Others signed on as painters and carpenters with the federally-funded Hall renovation project to fill their employment gap.

Ten days later Donna showed up. She wasn't ready to face rehearsals yet. This didn't do much for group self-confidence.

Fishery Show rehearsals were rescheduled for September. We held meetings instead. Long, interminable meetings, chewing over the same basic questions that had surfaced during the previous winter. By now we'd all had more time to think about them and to make up our minds. Some of the faces around the table had changed. Lynn Lunde had left the company. Ann Narvaez had replaced her as administrator. Jeff Pitcher was leaving temporarily to work with the Newfoundland Travelling Theatre, and musician Ron Hynes would be gigging in Toronto until Christmas. This shifted the balance of argument somewhat, and the tone of our debate became more strident. Positions had solidified. Discussion turned into grandstanding, proposals into ultimatums, and patience into despair. The Machiavellian atmosphere of power politics now pervading our meetings admitted only monotheism: Us or Them. Soon Donna and I represented unalterably opposed camps. We recessed for a couple of weeks to consider the irresolvables. Things looked dismal.

More letters from Steven Bush arrived, advising that the 3HO Yogis had now declared 21 June to be the most critical day of the Aquarian Age, "a time of great dissolutions and rampant negativity." Attendance at our twice-weekly mime classes dwindled to just Jeff Pitcher and myself. There were murmurings that training reinforced artistic hierarchy, a reactionary ideology. By mid-July rumours down the street at the Terra Nova Lounge said that the Mummers had already broken up. In St. John's, tavern gossip is given great credence.

Eventually Donna Butt, Rick Boland, Wayne McNiven and Maddy Williams presented a manifesto. It stated that they still recognized former working comrades as personal friends, but they now saw "no alternative to an open struggle that could threaten the company's credibility and hurt the quality and success of the political theatre we try to create." They felt that the lack of a collective administrative structure within the Troupe was unfair and exploitative, and that "we have in many respects become victims of a (government grant) handout programme and a push for success. The scramble to stretch the money has caused serious damage to the Mummers Troupe.... The basis of this company has always been trust.... Now that trust has been betrayed." They announced their intention to leave and form a separate theatre company: Community Stage.

> My major argument with the Mummers as a group– and this is quite apart from the shows we created– my major complaint then, and I'll tell anyone who asks me, was that I felt that the Mummers were a collective unit, not only in that they created plays collectively but that they were owned collectively, so that we were all in it together.... So when we left the company, that was the major reason

we left. Because when the Mummers purchased the LSPU Hall we ceased to be a collective....

See, when you start off a company, okay, you have a vision— this is the way I see it— you have a vision of what you want to do. You don't have very much money. So in any capitalist system what will happen in a case like that is that people will exploit the workers to get what they want. The workers won't own it in the end, but they will be the ones that are exploited to build it up, as with ASARCO when they went into Buchans.... That was how I felt the Mummers had turned out. They had started out with very little money. We all worked for practically nothing, you know, the salaries were very low, the actors were not paid in between shows...and I'm not bitter about any of that, about putting the time into it and doing the work, because we were politically motivated, very sincerely motivated. I think you were also sincerely motivated. But somewhere along the line I think you exploited us, you know, because you needed our labour and our dedication. The Mummers couldn't pay us for all of that, so it told us we were a collective company building the dream together. We built the dream together and then you said: "Wait a minute, this is not everybody's; this is mine!" (Donna Butt, interview with author, 1982).

There was the thought that we could do it ourselves, and that it might be an easier route, or a cleaner route, starting off from a fresh start rather than breaking down the already-existing structure of the Mummers. But it was all wrapped up in a lot of emotional things, and alliances and mini-alliances and alignments and mini-alignments and coalitions. I've thought, in retrospect I mean, how much of Donna's relationship to you was really a love-hate sort of thing, and how much was it the other way around? It was just so incredibly bound up with the interpersonal relationships. And I don't know, everything got so wrapped up in the end, it's really hard for me to pick out of it what was truth and what was personality and what was just the fiction of the moment. It would be hard to judge what was the Mob and what was the Revolution.

And you know, even if we hadn't left, if instead the structure of the Mummers had changed the way we wanted it, I don't think we were ready for it. It would have been quite anarchic. It might have been the demise of the Mummers. Because we didn't know what we were doing, basically. I mean we had some aspirations and some idea of what we'd like to do. But nobody knew anything, actually, about what it took to keep a theatre going administratively. I don't know, for example, how prepared I was at that time for a weekly meeting of the company, discussing business and getting it out of the way efficiently enough so that the company could function. I don't know how prepared I was for that— or if what I was prepared for was ideological and artistic arguments about what we were doing. I could have handled those a lot better than sitting down day to day

> and working out the practical decisions that any company has to make.
>
> I think, in retrospect, it was all a process of growth for everybody involved. In some cases it was, you know, growth inside of a shoe that's too small for you and in some cases it was rampant cancerous growth bubbling all over the place.... (Rick Boland, interview with the author, 1982).
>
> The Mummers was the first professional theatre group I was ever in. And the first show I did, *East End Story*, was a really enjoyable creative experience for me. I mean it was gay and happy, right? The second one, *Price of Fish*, with most of the same people, was really grim, arguing and quarrelling. The creative experience wasn't fun.... I think if Donna had been in *East End Story* the same thing might have happened then.
>
> It was a power struggle between two people, really. A vicious power struggle. And a lot of people caught in the middle, you know? And a lot of bitter feeling. As simple as that (Maddy Williams, interview with the author, 1982).

I tried to see the split as a learning process for us all. Once faced with the problem of survival, Community Stage would either make the same kinds of organizational compromises Lynn and I had made and wind up looking structurally similar to the Mummers, or they would discover new solutions and we could all learn from their example.

With the declaration of the manifesto, dialogue between the two factions effectively ceased. But the official parting of the ways didn't take place for another six weeks. At the request of the sponsor, Oxfam, we toured *The Price of Fish* by bus and boat around Central Newfoundland and the South Coast, and gave it a short run in St. John's. The tour was an horrendous personal experience for all of us, particularly for those members of the cast and crew who tried to stay neutral. You couldn't. You were either part of the problem or part of the solution. (The line was drawn somewhere in the middle of the tour bus. Anyone who sat up front with me was ostracised when they went to the back with Donna.)

The mechanical state of the old school bus was as ragged as the mental state of those riding in it. I found great consolation in automotive repair. It was comforting to be able to tinker with the air pump without having half the spark plugs, the connecting rods and the timing chain throw brick bats at me. Inside the vehicle it was wartime, full of suspicion, innuendo, emotional violence and verbal assault. We took ourselves very seriously, to the detriment of our work, our audiences, and ourselves. Close friendships were manipulated or terminated, and working relationships degenerated from strained tolerance into veiled hatred. We were more like a troupe of travelling psychopaths than a touring theatre. I found myself farting a lot and dreaming about animals chewing my hands off. By the end of the tour all of us desperately wanted out.

The four founders of Community Stage left the Mummers in September 1976 with a *FISH fund* grant and plans to create the long-awaited play about the Newfoundland Fisheries. The play never came about.

To fill the gap in the Mummers' own season I began work on a new show about a major Newfoundland addiction—bingo. Notice that it is not a ruling-class pastime. It is the opiate of the near-poor. Its "winner take all" ideology epitomises a social system which declares that it is right and proper to offer one winner for every thousand losers. David Ross, John Doyle, Judy Parsons, Jeannie Becker, Brenda Devine, musician Terry Reilly and I plunged into rehearsals, determined to build a show which would work as a game. I thought we might be able to offer a social critique by way of bingo. Besides, we fantasised, if it were successful it might actually make money on box office like the real bingos. It could run forever, a whole new approach to theatre funding which would free the Troupe from bondage to any granting agency. Nice idea. Five weeks later we had *Irregular Entertainment*, a tepid show which pleased audiences and the critics, and even drew some bingo buffs who would otherwise never have darkened the door of a live theatre. We peddled bingo cards to the spectators for each scene as it came along, and left the financial and dramatic outcome of each section to chance. It was fun, but it ultimately said nothing, and as a fund-raising scheme it was a total bust. The experienced bingo sharpies who came took us to the cleaners.

As autumn wore on, the 3HO Yogis' predictions of gloom and doom seemed to catch up with all of the province's professional theatres. The members of *Codco* decided to split up and suspend operations entirely. They said they were creatively exhausted. The Newfoundland Travelling Theatre, after a year of artistic and financial troubles, finally packed it in for good just before Christmas. Effectively this meant the combined loss to the province's professional theatre scene of about 14 jobs and $50,000 in federal funds. When 2,000 trade union members paraded through St. John's streets in October in the Canadian Labour Congress's anti-wage controls protest, the Mummers' giant puppets were conspicuously the only theatrical marchers in the parade. Now we weren't just the only established left theatre in the province. We were the only established theatre left in the province.

Up in the plush of the St. John's Arts and Culture Centre, the government's Cultural Affairs Division spent a reported $45,000 on its annual Thanksgiving production of a tired Broadway musical. The retread for 1976 was *Brigadoon*. Five thousand miles away, at another highly subsidised opening in Milan, 4,000 demonstrators threw rotten eggs at La Scala opera patrons and heaved firebombs at 2,500 police in protest against an exclusive $160 per ticket premiere of *Otello*. Newspaper reports described disgruntled gold lamé and black-tie spectators being escorted through roadblocks by riot squads.

Meanwhile, Community Stage was being ripped by its own internal power struggles. Its production plans were soon cancelled in favour of a campaign to lobby the Mummers Troupe's funding agencies. The pitch was that the Mummers funding should be withdrawn and given to Community Stage instead. Rumours began to flow thick and fast through the city's tavern circuit. Some said that the Mummers management had stolen copyright ownership of all the Troupe's collective creations from the real authors. Others said Chris Brookes had paid himself three times the standard company salary and was preparing to abscond with more; and so on. Any actor who continued to work for the Mummers was threatened.

Reputations weren't the only casualties. Soon there were defections from Community Stage, performers who couldn't take the hassle of the new party line, now drifting alienated out of the Newfoundland arts scene back to university, straight jobs, or the mainland. Already bystanders were eager to dismiss the whole idea of politically relevant theatre as unworkable in practice.

By December, the gloves came off. I was acting King George in our annual Christmas Mummers Play. After a house performance at a Boxing Day party one of the partygoers dragged me into an alley to defend Donna Butt's honour by beating me up. In the process he broke glass into my left eye and left me for blind. Fortunately it happened only two blocks away from a hospital, and my sight was saved.

It was a colourful Yuletide scene: a fake mummer doctor delivering a fake king to a real Emergency Ward. Lying on the operating table while a real doctor picked the shards of glass out, a blood-spattered Union Jack on my chest, sleigh bells around my torso flinching and jingling with every stitch of the surgeon's needle, I remembered the old man in Pouch Cove who once told me that his own grandfather had lost an eye whilst acting in the Mummers Play. No wonder they carried clubs in the old days. Mummers feuds are no joke, as I was learning. I consoled myself with the thought that I had just survived a modern-day research opportunity which any folklorist might have given his eyeteeth for. And I still had the teeth part, ha ha.

Heritage. Tradition. Cold comfort in St. Clare's Mercy Hospital, twenty stitches in my eye, Boxing Night 1976.

So it was with considerable relief that in mid-January I joined Jeff Pitcher, Judy Parsons, Jane Dingle, and Terry Reilly to spend the entire winter in the remote northernmost communities of Labrador, two thousand miles away from St. John's. In Nain, nobody had ever heard of Chris Brookes or Donna Butt. In Inuktitut, in fact, there isn't even a word for "theatre."

Going Towards the Day 14

In six days, God made the world. Then on the seventh day he sailed inshore and threw rocks at Labrador.

Labrador coast saying

On March 22, 1977, the temperature outside the Nain community hall was minus 28 degrees Fahrenheit. Inside the building, the Pinguatet Mummers Troupenut opened their play about Labrador: *Silakepat Kissiane (Weather Permitting)*, and temperatures were soaring. Most of the southern whites in the predominately Inuit town hated it. The school principal said it would stir up trouble in the educational system; the local RCMP constables warned that it was in contempt of court. But most of the community's Inuit and white settler residents raved about the show. The critical moment in the performance came as we mimed a scene about violence and alcoholism (chronic in Nain), linking it to the government's forced resettlement of the Inuit years earlier. It was an extremely touchy subject. The audience went dead silent, and for an instant we feared we were about to be run out of town. Instead, most spectators were staring malevolently at the town's two Mounties (noted for intolerance toward Inuit), daring them to react to the scene. The community thought we were telling it like it was.

The three-month lead up to that evening was a very delicate undertaking. The procedure of creating a community documentary was familiar enough, but this time we had been in an environment which climatically and linguistically was very foreign to us. The problem was not simply our inability to speak Inuktitut, the language which 30 per cent of northern coastal residents spoke, but the lack of common cultural reference points with a people whose background was totally different from our European Anglo-Saxon cultural heritage.

The Labrador Inuit saw the world in a very different way than we did. And they viewed the *kablunaat,* southern whites, with justifiable suspicion.

The original impetus for the project had come from the head of the Royal Commission on Labrador, Don Snowden, who suggested two years earlier that the Mummers undertake it. I had worked to set it up with the utmost care, spending three weeks in Nain in 1975, developing liaisons and raising sufficient funds to allow us to spend three full months on the coast. Ultimately we were sponsored by the Labrador Inuit Association (LIA) and the Labrador Resources Advisory Council (LRAC). The contract provided that we would have complete artistic freedom in the creation of the show, but that our sponsors would have the right to vet the final content in dress rehearsals. Without their approval it wouldn't be performed.

The fact that the show was commissioned by the two most powerful representative organisations in the region was crucial to its success. They provided guidance, invaluable research, and arranged for our integration into the communities in a way which would otherwise have been impossible. They set our terms of reference: the play would focus attention on the salient social issues in Nain, Hopedale, and Makkovik, the three mixed Inuit and white settler communities of the northern Labrador coast which came under the federal/provincial native peoples' agreement. The goal was to raise awareness of the issues both in the communities concerned and in the southern white world of Newfoundland and Ottawa, where most of the major decisions about Labrador were usually made.

Leo Barry (the provincial Minister of Mines and Energy, speaking to an audience in Nain about Labrador resource development):

> ...and what this kind of development will mean is jobs! Right here in Nain....
>
> Nain resident: Excuse me....
>
> Barry:...Yes?
>
> Resident: We don't want jobs.
>
> Barry: I beg your pardon?
>
> Resident: We don't want jobs.
>
> Barry: You don't...you don't want JOBS?
>
> Resident: We are hunters.
>
> Barry:...oh.

When we first stepped off a single-engined Otter aircraft onto Makkovik's small iced-over harbour in January 1977, all togged out in army surplus mitts, huge foam-insulated boots and the kind of down-filled clothing we assumed was *de rigeur* for the sub-arctic, we must have looked like an advance party for the Michelin Man. I have no idea what residents thought of us; they were polite enough not to giggle, and we were naive enough not to realise how out-of-place we appeared. The process was only apparent to us in reverse, four months later, when we recrossed the cultural frontier in the other direction. As we disembarked at the St. John's airport in mid-April, dressed in fuzzy seal skinboots, bright fur-trimmed Inuit-style *silapok* and caribou mitts, holding an overgrown husky puppy and hunting for our *komatik* sled on the luggage carousel, the bystanders were in stitches. Working on the project had been a humbling and fascinating journey for us, as the people of northern Labrador slowly taught us a different way of seeing the world, their world. Thrust back into our once-familiar world again, we were in culture shock.

But we brought back with us a strong show which had worked well in communities all along the Labrador coast (we had travelled over a thousand miles by skidoo and bush plane) and which soon proved successful in St. John's as well. Many of the techniques which we used to make the English-language sections of the play understandable to Inuktitut-speaking audiences in Nain now worked to clarify the Inuktitut scenes for white city dwellers (the play included one scene entirely in Inuktitut). The performance stressed visual symbolism. We relied on broad mime, puppets, string games and masks to portray the traditional legends and lifestyles of Labradorians as well as the present-day policies imposed upon them by the equally ritualistic bureaucracy of southern white society. Throughout the play we used a white pair of fishermen's gloves, mime-like, to draw attention to the traditional manual skills of a people who lived off the land: setting traps, plucking partridge, cleaning rifles, skinning caribou. Later, after the white-masked forces of *kablunaat* government, *kablunaat* religion, *kablunaat* education and *kablunaat* medicine forcibly resettled entire northern communities further south, the gloves were hung up, empty and useless.

In a gesture which Bertold Brecht might have liked, we introduced each scene by setting out a placard with a quote in both English and Inuktitut which announced the basic issue to be featured in the scene. The dramatic action then elaborated upon the placard. Throughout, the placard remained on the set in full view, to remind spectators to think about the scene's political ramifications.

Most scenes took as their premise a Labrador setting. But one scene, *St. John'sime Sanajusemajuk (Urban Improvement)*, usually brought the house down by reversing that premise. It was about native land claims, traditional land-use patterns threatened by the provincial government's resource development plans for the northern coast. Instead of dramatising the reactions of Labrador residents, we set the scene in downtown St. John's and inverted the normal political power relationship. In our scene, the inherited "commercial land-use pattern" and traditional lifestyle of Newfoundland corporate mogul Andrew Crosbie was wiped out by a Labrador-dominated government which was razing the entire downtown business section to create a caribou breeding ground. It sounds hokey, but it was hilarious and brought the point home nicely to city audiences.

> We are not trying to preserve the past. We are trying to preserve the future (Labrador Inuit leader Bill Edmunds).

We finished the play by pulling together the main visual symbols which we had established throughout the performance. Three large bolts of coloured cloth (white, blue, and green) which we had used in various scenes to invoke snowstorms, sea, land, and legend— and later to represent the encroachment upon that natural environment by mineral exploitation— came together to suggest a result: the politicisation of Labrador people. Against the white, blue, and green cloth now forming the Labrador nationalist flag, Jeff Pitcher played Innu [Naskapi Indian] leader Bart Jack:

> We say this to the government in St. John's: we are different. We are not like you. What we want to do with our lives is different from what you want. What we want for our land is different from what you want to do with it. What Labrador people— Indians, Inuit, and Settlers— want is control! Why are we all so scared to say this? It should be plain to anybody who's been in Labrador any length of time that the people feel they are governed by a government which is not theirs. We have no power to say what will happen to our lives or our land.
>
> We do not want to be looked after; we do not want other people to decide what is best for us; we do not want to be owned.... We want the ultimate authority over what happens in our own country!

When most island Newfoundlanders think of Labradorians they don't think of Innu like Bart Jack. Nor of Inuit and white settler people, of subsistence hunters, of native land claims, of different languages and cultures. They think of the iron mining towns of

Labrador City and Wabush, inhabited by southern white industrial workers. They view Labrador as Joe Smallwood did, as a "great storehouse of wealth," to be developed for the benefit of island Newfoundlanders. They see Churchill Falls as "our" great hydro resource which is being ripped off by Quebec through an infamously rotten contract deal, not as a monstrously destructive power dam which expropriated and flooded hundreds of acres of native hunting and trapping ground without permission. To Newfoundlanders, Labrador is simply a vast, exploitable piece of real estate.

This ignorance worked to our disadvantage when we toured *Silakepat Kissiane* around the island in the fall of 1977. Our sponsors, LIA and LRAC, wanted to use the play to make Newfoundlanders more aware of Labrador issues. This it seemed to accomplish in the capital city. The St. John's performances attracted sold-out crowds, including high-ranking civil servants and politicians. But outside the capital, attendance was generally poor. People expected the play to be about real estate, and real estate is boring. In too many communities our audience stayed home to watch American sitcoms on TV.

> I will walk with leg muscles
> Which are strong
> As the sinews
> Of the skins of the little caribou calf;
> I will walk with leg muscles
> Which are strong
> As the sinews of the skins of the little hare.
> I will take care not to go towards the dark.
> I will go towards the day.
>
> (Traditional Inuit poem)

On the home front, things slowly seemed to be going toward the day also. By the summer of 1977, the theatre battles of the previous year had cooled. Community Stage had disbanded. The whirlwind war had permanently affected the Mummers. We certainly weren't in Kansas anymore. The Troupe had lost two of its most talented artists, Rick Boland and Donna Butt. This was quite a loss, but the old atmosphere of suspicion and distrust had departed with them. Some former performers and Lynn Lunde had returned. The company, once burned and twice shy, was even less open to structural experiment then before, but it was more stable and a great deal more efficient. The previous year had been characterised by a collective helplessness in the face of administrative decisions (the Labrador project itself almost fell prey to collective inaction. The old core group had been unable to agree about whether or not we should proceed with it. Meetings had dragged on interminably while members read up on northern affairs and pondered the idea of spending four months freezing their buns in forty-below weather. No collective decision was ever made). Planning was now less democratic but immeasurably quicker and simpler.

Ron Hynes returned to the company, and in late summer starred in a collectively created musical about the life and times of the Newfoundland balladeer Johnny Burke. The cast was one of the finest the Troupe ever assembled: Bob Joy and Mary Walsh (formerly of Codco), Jane Dingle, David Ross, Janet Michael, and Brian Hennessey. The resultant play reflected their varied talents; dramatically speaking it was one of the best-crafted scripts the Mummers created. It was also an opportunity to experiment with an environmental set. For years our touring sets had been limited by having to fit into a wide variety of small halls throughout the province; they were basically something to change your costume behind. For *The Bard of Prescott Street*, we tried to turn the auditorium into a turn-of-the-century experience for the audience. Backdrops were painted, two-dimensional roll-ups. Houselights were mock gaslamp streetlights. Spectators entering the theatre had to find their way to their seats by stepping along old wooden sidewalks and clambering through mud puddles. They were assailed all the way by real East End kids trying to sell them show programmes (written as a ballad) for a dime each. The kids were selling on commission, so they got nice and pushy about it. Acting spaces were scattered through the auditorium, so that performers climbed through the spectators, shouted across them, and flew over their heads on a giant swing.

Burke died in 1930, and a few elderly St. John's residents still personally remembered the Chaplinesque little man in the bowler hat. Some remembered scenes from his stage shows. We even managed to track down one actress, then in a senior citizens' home, who had performed with him in his later productions. But despite this, detailed information about his lifestyle and work methods was pretty scant. Of his many original plays, only one script survived and of his hundreds of topical ballads, only a couple of dozen remained. Rebuilding the story of his personal life was largely a matter of educated guessing. So we tried some experiments with our research.

Burke was known as an "East End" poet—he lived on Prescott Street, just two blocks away from the LSPU Hall (he once wrote a song about the building, *Teapots at the Fire*) and he sold his songs on street corners throughout the area. He was often helped by local East End kids, whom he enlisted as commission salesmen of his

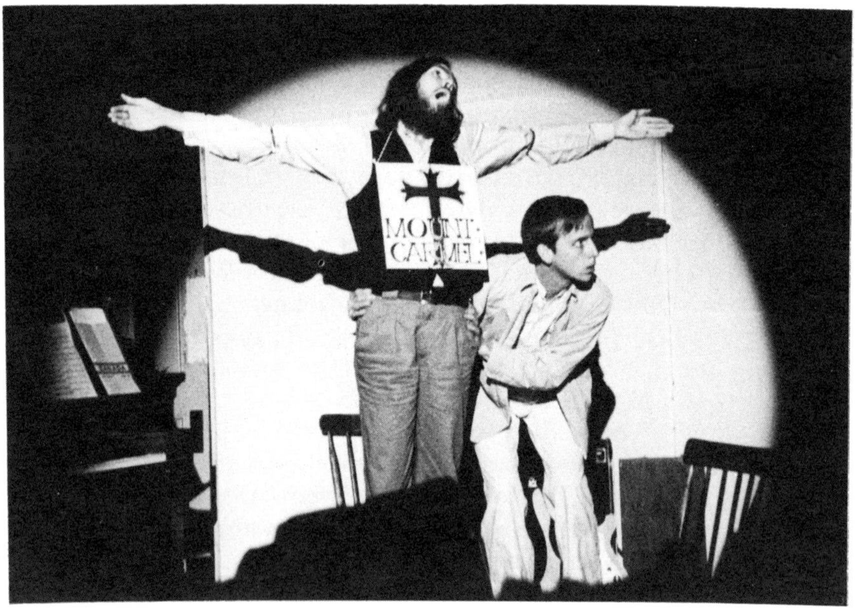

From *The Bard of Prescott Street,* 1977. Escaped convict Phil Brady hides out in Mount Carmel cemetery. Bob Joy as Brady, Brian Hennessey as the cemetery. Photo: Kent Barrett.

five cent broadsides. Chronically broke, Burke was hopeless at managing his "salesmen." I decided to find out how his commission system might have broken down. We wrote our own topical ballads about local current events of 1977 and tried selling them on the streets for nickels and dimes. Amazingly, they sold well. Then we enlisted local kids as our "commission salesmen." It was fascinating. They would cart away piles of broadside sheets—but seldom returned with much cash. Their mind-boggling alibis and excuses were always amazing, and supplied us with a gold-mine of ideas for our period scenes.

The Bard of Prescott Street wasn't a political show (although in a country awash with foreign culture, the mere production of a Canadian play by a Canadian theatre still seemed to be a political statement in 1977). As a flavourful reincarnation of the life and times of a colourful Newfoundland hero, it was motherhood. Audiences had fun. The play was a hit, and the entire run quickly sold out.

There are virtually no full-length Newfoundland stage musicals. It had cost us $23,000 to research, write, and mount an original one—less than half the amount shelled out each fall by the St.

John's Arts and Culture to remount an out-of-date American musical.

Because of its production design, the Burke show was physically too unwieldy to tour through the kind of small community halls our provincial tours usually played. It needed a full stage. So we offered it to the government's Arts and Culture Centre circuit for the fall of 1978. They turned it down because, they said, its subject matter was "too local." (The official 1978 government musical was the fifteen-year-old American hit *A Funny Thing Happened on the Way to the Forum.*) Determined not to let a fine show die, we tried to sell a tour to sponsors in the Atlantic provinces, and found ourselves competing head-on with the provincial government itself. While we stayed home and contacted potential sponsors by phone and mail, the Division of Cultural Affairs flew a civil servant to the Maritimes to woo the same sponsors with a personal sales pitch for its subsidised tour of a British stock company. As a small independent theatre receiving no provincial subsidy, our promotional budget was too limited for jet-set public relations. For comparable services, on a dollar-for-dollar basis, we couldn't compete with the provincial government.

In most aspects of the provincial economy, we pointed out in a submission to the province, government scrupulously avoids driving private companies out of business by directly competing with them (in 1977/78 there was not yet an arms-length provincial arts council). If government is going to spend taxpayers dollars on cultural projects, we asked, why not treat theatre like highways, construction, or any other industry: put out a call for tenders and let independent Newfoundland companies bid on the contracts?

The province never replied.

The Bard of Prescott Street was never performed outside St. John's. When plans for the tour fell through, musical director and cast member Bob Joy left Newfoundland for a successful stage and film career in Edmonton, New York, and Hollywood. Meanwhile, the Newfoundland government flew in British actors Ralph Bates, Richard Todd, and Hildegard Neil to tour its own production of the British murder-mystery *Double Edge* to sparse houses in Gander, Grand Falls, Corner Brook, Stephenville, and the Maritime provinces.

Double Edge was not a box office success, but the foreign performers were no doubt as delighted to collect their Equity touring salaries as the foreign playwrights must have been to receive their royalty cheques. Payable in Canadian dollars, of course.

David Defying Goliath 15

Distinguished American voices boom through the auditorium. One threatened species has rallied to the aid of another: the ancient great of Hollywood—Walter Pidgeon, Henry Fonda, Gregory Peck—are on record deploring the annual hunt of the harp seal over the Newfoundland floes. Their challenge sounded, lights rake the stage for takers. Like so many Davids defying Goliath, seven tatterdemalion youngsters wearing fishermen's sweaters, granny glasses and funny hats swarm into a tiny, sawdust-strewn arena. Newfoundland's answer to Greenpeace is on the road.

Maclean's

In 1977 Newfoundland was the only province in the nation which still refused financial aid to indigenous professional theatre companies. The situation meant that it was harder to make a living in the theatre here than anywhere else in Canada. Over the years, the Mummers had tried time and again to loosen the provincial purse strings. We had exhausted most standard approaches, and even some of the offbeat. Once, in desperation, we challenged the Division of Cultural Affairs to an "arts race" at the annual St. John's Regatta, on the offchance that maybe if we rammed the bastards in the middle of the lake we could sink the province's whole arse-backwards arts policy at one blow. The Division didn't take up the challenge. Up until now, all our efforts had been in vain. But in the fall of 1977 we were able to make the government an offer it couldn't refuse.

Outside the province, the annual Newfoundland seal hunt had been the subject of growing controversy for the past decade. Year by year, the International Fund for Animal Welfare (IFAW) revved up its anti-hunt campaign another notch. Year after year, Newfoundlanders watched the airlift of Hollywood starlets and American airline stewardesses to the icefloes in order to be photographed cuddling seal pups. The sealers were stoic. The protesters were just another bunch of crazies from upalong. "Just ignore 'em, my son. They'll go away."

Lynn Lunde had suggested a couple of years earlier that the Mummers should produce a show on the seal hunt. The fact that we'd never followed up on the idea had as much to do with my own ignorance of hard scientific data on the hunt as with the feeling that the company's primary mandate was to address Newfoundland, not mainland audiences. But the issue was becoming unavoidable.

In 1976 the Greenpeace Foundation joined the IFAW's anti-hunt crusade, and the heat really began to build up. "Save the Seals" was now a massive national and international campaign. In 1976, Canada's embassy in Washington received 40,000 letters decrying the "barbarism" practised off its Atlantic coast. Newfoundlanders began to realise that those crazies from upalong might, just might, be able to lobby enough support to stop the hunt.

On their side, the anti-hunt lobby had Brigitte Bardot, full-page newspaper ads, petitions from schoolchildren, glossy brochures and lurid film footage of grim-faced sealers beating cuddly seal pups on the head. Strong stuff. Opposing them, the seal hunters had history, logic, economics, and government licences. Unquestionably dull stuff. It wasn't a fair fight. One side had all the theatre.

When we first announced a forthcoming Mummers show on the seal hunt, our mainland fan club applauded happily. Community action groups and development-education organisations across the country which had sponsored our *Price of Fish* tour offered to bring us in to their cities. They assumed that a political theatre like the Mummers Troupe would naturally line up with the protesters and against the government. Isn't that what we did on every issue? Weren't we social activists, progressives like them?

After we explained that our show would actually *support* the Newfoundland seal hunt, most of our *Price of Fish* sponsors rolled up their welcome mats. Some wrote us letters suggesting that we had flushed our politics down the drain in favour of blind parochialism.

> It's a sad day for art and theatre in this country....(Greenpeace Foundation).

It was a rather odd position for us to be in. The government's official seal hunt apologists seemed outraged by the protesters' tactics: media-grabbing stunts and petitions. When they muttered darkly about "damn rabble-rousers" and "unwashed hippies" I felt like LeRoy Jones in a Ku Klux Klan meeting. These guys were on *my* side? On the surface, the other team looked more like my colour. Although I'd never warmed to the opportunistic IFAW, I'd always vaguely assumed that I belonged to the same crunchy granola generation as Greenpeace. Saving whales sounded all right to me. I supported their stand against nuclear testing. But after a month's research on the seal issue, I began to have doubts about the integrity of the anti-sealers. It seemed to me that they were deliberately misrepresenting the facts—facts which anybody with a public library card could research as easily as I had.

The IFAW contended that the seal hunt is inhumane. It was not. Clubbing a seal pup on the head may not look pretty, but scientific studies have proven it to be the most humane way of killing a seal. It is quick, and the animal suffers little psychological stress. This is more than can be said for the way most Canadian pigs are turned into pork chops. Take a tour of a commercial slaughterhouse (or an *abattoir* as such institutions are euphemistically known in English Canada) some day and see. You may also notice that the slaughterhouse sends little lambs off to Lambchop Heaven in the same way as a sealer performs the *coup de grâce* on other little white mammals: with a club.

Twenty years ago, there was nothing much known about whether the Newfoundland seal hunt employed humane killing methods or not. The annual harvest went largely unmonitored. By 1977, (thanks, in fact, largely to the IFAW's efforts, and for this—and this alone—they deserve credit) the Newfoundland whitecoat seal hunt was probably the most monitored slaughterhouse in the world, monitored not only by federal government inspectors, but by independent humane organisations such as the Canadian and Ontario Humane Societies, the Canadian Council on Animal Care, and the International Society for the Prevention of Cruelty to Animals, all of which endorsed the seal killing methods used in the Newfoundland hunt as humane. But despite all the evidence to the contrary, the IFAW continued to insist that the hunt was inhumane. According to my research, the IFAW was dead wrong.

But the International Fund for Animal Welfare was careful not to say that the harp seal herds were in any way *endangered* by the annual hunt. It was the Greenpeace Foundation which said that.

Greenpeace jumped on the seal bandwagon in 1976. They were triggered by the 1975 report of a Canadian scientist which suggested that the size of the North Atlantic harp seal herd may be substantially smaller than anyone had previously thought. Greenpeace's alarm was understandable, and presumably motivated by a sincere concern for adequate marine resource management (although it is unfortunate that their concern had never been aroused by long-standing reports of the North Atlantic herring and salmon stocks becoming endangered. I'm sure this had nothing to do with how hard it is to make fish faces look cuddly in poster campaigns).

The report which alarmed Greenpeace was contradicted by four other seal population surveys, each conducted by different methods, which indicated that the population was much higher and that the federal government's annual harvest quota was allowing the herd to grow by an acceptable 2 per cent per year. The dissenting report was based on a brand new ultra violet aerial survey method, which was later found to contain some errors. By 1977, the ultra violet method had been improved, and it then indicated a herd population 60 per cent larger than its original 1975 figure, which correlated with the more traditional surveys. The author of the ultra violet survey notified Greenpeace accordingly. But by this time, the Greenpeace publicity machine was in high gear, and it paid no heed. There are almost a thousand endangered species in the world, according to the most respected international conservation agency, the World Wildlife Fund. But the harp seal is not amongst these. So why didn't Greenpeace admit that it was wrong, and make a gentlemanly retreat? I was never able to get a very straight answer from Greenpeace spokespeople, although one confided to me that if they admitted to being wrong on such a high-profile issue as the seal hunt, "...it would destroy our credibility on other issues." As surely as the Argus Corporation, Greenpeace seemed to have been swallowed up by its own expansionist momentum.

For both Greenpeace and the IFAW, Saving the Seals provided their single greatest source of income, representing well over $5 million in donations annually.

On the other side of the coin, no one questioned that if the hunt were stopped, 4,200 persons would lose employment and $5.5 million would be lost to the Atlantic economy. The average Newfoundland fisherman/sealer, with his seasonally diversified livelihood (in late spring he may hunt lobster and salmon; in summer, codfish; in fall, herring, and March, seals) would lose $800/year; some would lose as much as $2,400. Piffle, said the middle-class opposers of the hunt. And indeed, to anyone pulling in $30,000 a year, the amount might seem insignificant. Yet the average Newfoundland fisherman in 1978 supported a wife and three children on an annual income of just $7,500, an amount which placed him below the Canadian poverty line. To a family in such economic circumstances, $800 was important.

Relatively unorganised, with no experience in media manipulation or public relations, the sealers were sitting ducks for the protesters. The humane and ecologically sound harvest of a thriving renewable marine resource had been emotionalised to a point where intelligent examination of the issue by the general public was virtually impossible. Anonymous hate mail poured in to individual sealers.

> You dirty rotten son of a bitch. If I could get to you I'd beat you senseless and then I'd skin your hide like you do to the seals. You're a mean bastard. You'll pay for your sins. You're lucky I don't go up there now and do it. I hope you die. Don't be surprised if you hear or see me because I'd pay anything to have you for five minutes.... (Letter to a St. Anthony family, quoted in the play *They Club Seals, Don't They?*)

Newfoundland fishermen, already suffering economic discrimination, were now being slandered and vilified from London to Los Angeles, and a significant part of their livelihoods was going to be needlessly destroyed. The lie was halfway around the world before the truth had its boots laced up.

We decided to go for broke in their defence. We planned a show which would grab as much media attention as possible. I put together the strongest cast I could find, and invited Donna Butt back to join us (seeing this, some said I had an organisational death-wish. But it was a pragmatic decision. The show must go on. I needed a good cast.) I asked Chris Pratt, Newfoundland's best known visual artist, to design our poster. Chris tried, but he just couldn't find a way to make the image anything but what it was, he said. White seal, white ice, black sealer's club, red blood—the symbolism is loaded. As the IFAW had already discovered. Chris threw up his hands. I contacted Terry Mosher, the Montreal artist who, under his pen-name Aislin, is Canada's finest political cartoonist. We knew each other through mutual friends, and he liked the idea behind our show. He produced a monochrome cartoon which made a terrific poster.

The protest itself was commonly described as a media circus. For three weeks every March, the ice floes off Newfoundland were crawling with camera crews from all over Europe and North America, pointing their lenses at the glamour girls and stunt men who

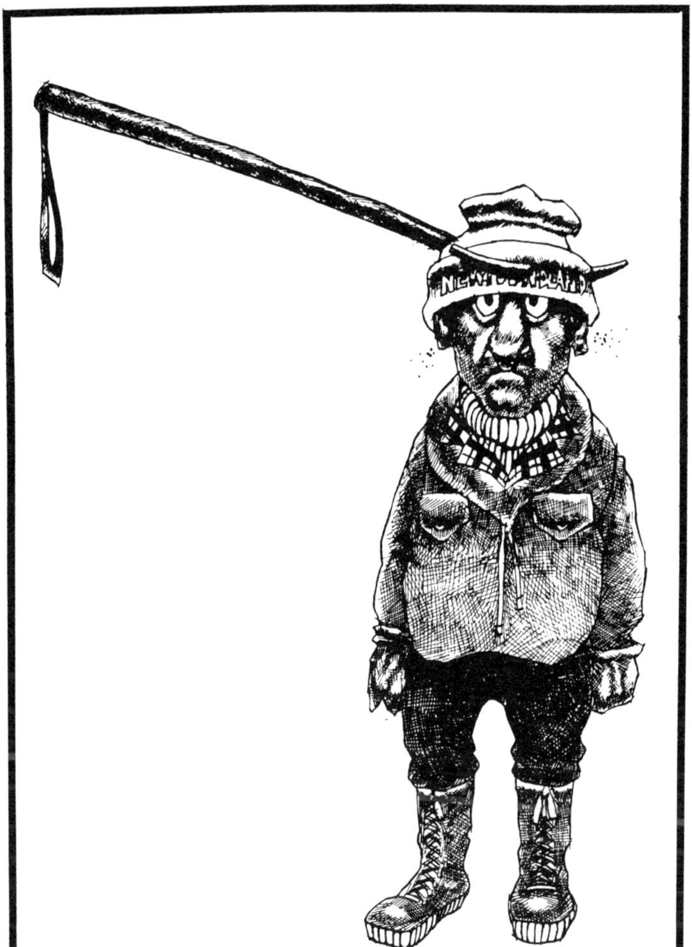

They Club Seals, Don't They?

an other perspective on the Nfld seal hunt

by the

Mummers Troupe of Newfoundland

helicoptered in to kiss, paint, fondle and chain themselves to the nearest whitecoat seal pup. I wanted to use the circus metaphor as a show motif. In September I went off to work for a few weeks with the Moscow Circus (then on a Canadian tour), and came back with a bagful of ideas. In November we brought in ex-Mummer Jan Henderson and Ian Wallace from Toronto to conduct a three-week workshop in clown techniques, and most of the cast participated in it.

We booked our tour into mainstream theatres in nine major centres across the country (arranging a full week in most cities) and planned our dates for maximum publicity impact. We would preview in Petrolia and Kitchener, Ontario, in early March to work the bugs out of the show. Then we would open at Tarragon Theatre in Toronto. A week later we'd play St. Anthony, Newfoundland, the day before the seal hunt opened. We'd open at Ottawa's National Arts Centre two days after that, play Vancouver the following week, etc. The only way to keep such a hectic schedule was to travel by air with everything. Expensive. The entire set (a circus ring and trapeze platforms, with huge banners suggesting a ship's rigging), all props, costumes, sound equipment and musical instruments had to pack into suitcases and fly with us as excess baggage.

Raising the funds to pay for all this was a monstrous task, but it actually came together. Although the $70,000 rehearsal and touring budget was three times the cost of our usual shows, it was still a drop in the bucket compared to our opposition's finances (In February, Greenpeace announced receipt of a major donation for the anti-hunt campaign from Baron de Rothschild). Box office, of course, covered a substantial part of our outlay, and in the end, the show's net loss was underwritten by a whole gaggle of agencies from a sealer's rights organization to the Canada Council Touring Office (which received letters accusing it of "involving itself in the promotion of killing"). In Newfoundland, the seal hunt was motherhood, and I knew it gave us leverage with the provincial government. Their Cultural Affairs Division turned us down as usual, but after another department, Rural Development, underwrote 20 per cent of our production costs, we went back and challenged their Arts and Culture Centres to book the show. This time they didn't complain it was "too local." They booked it. The issue had become so political, they couldn't be seen to refuse us.

Rehearsals, during January and February, 1978, went well. Originally we'd planned to work with playwright Michael Cook on the show, but this fell through. Instead, it was a collective creation like most of our plays. As director, I introduced certain broad ideas

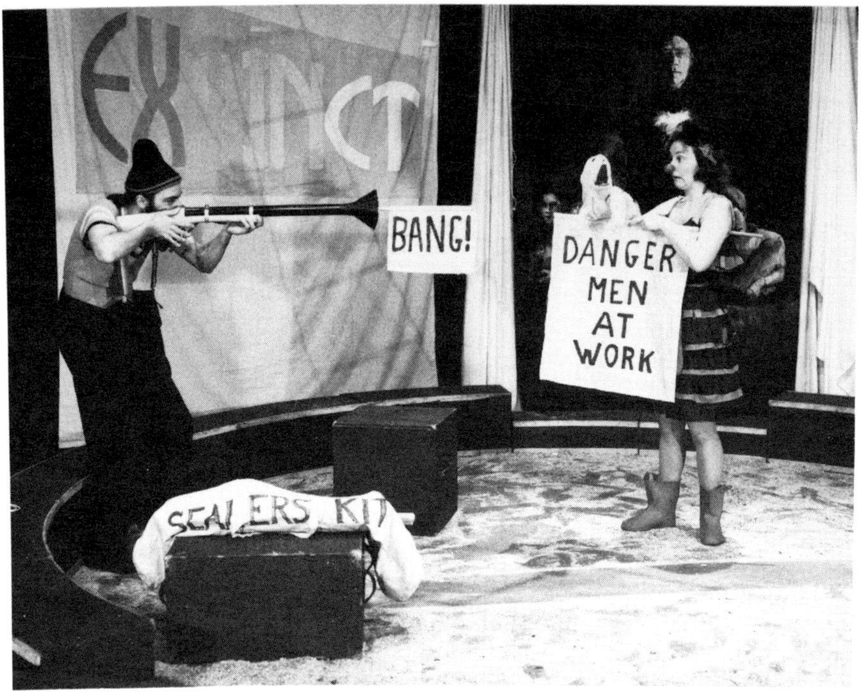

How to Kill a Seal clown routine, *They Club Seals, Don't They?* 1978. Pierre Beaupre and Rhonda Payne.
Photo: Mannie Buchheit.

about content. Improvisations fleshed these out and took them further. Despite the difficulty in getting across to the audience a certain amount of statistical information, the actors came up with some wonderfully evocative material. We had humour, pathos, and good music. Michael Cook sent in a moving historical monologue. Pierre Beaupre and Rhonda Payne created a series of nice clown turns, including one hilarious routine in the finest tradition of black humour, demonstrating why a club was more effective than a rifle for killing a little hand puppet seal.

Attitudes toward the Newfoundland seal hunt are generally determined by demographics. Most opposition to the hunt comes from middle-class urbanites, whose lifestyle is quite different from that of rural primary producers. Fishermen and farmers know what happens to the creatures they handle daily in their nets and pastures. For most city dwellers, on the other hand, contact with live animals comes primarily from pets. The plastic-wrapped steak they buy on a styrofoam tray at Sobeys' meat counter does not gaze up at them with big, soft, watery eyes. It is acceptably inanimate. Even some of the names on the packages protect consumer innocence: dead calves become veal, dead sheep become mutton, and ground up pigs are wieners. But the language of the anti-sealers is more anthropomorphic: it is "baby seals" that those fiendish fishermen hit on the head. They're not "harvested," they're "beaten to death." To many urbanites, harvesting seals is like murdering Spot and Puff. To Newfoundland fishermen, it's like catching lobster, netting cod, or seining caplin.

Accordingly, we developed our show by contrasts. The basic dramatic throughline of the play paralleled the lives of a Newfoundland sealer's family and an urban mainland family. The link between the two was the seal hunt protest. We hoped it would provide food for thought. The whole performance built up to a four-minute film finale which we'd shot at the St. John's slaughterhouse with local cinematographer Mike Jones. In a series of quick colour cuts, the film traced a pig's path from hoof to hotdog, while onstage in the circus ring Terry Reilly, David Ross, Pierre Beaupre and Glen Tilley accompanied it with a lusty Country-and-Western ditty:

> To see animals killed; you say you can't stand;
> But you're eatin' your porkchop with your other hand;
> It's easy to judge when you're one step removed
> And you don't have to walk in another man's shoes.
> Who pays the price? Do you know who pays
> For your comfortable cushions and affluent ways?
> Who pays the piper who's singing your song?
> And who owns the hog that you're livin' high on?

Subtle, it was not. But effective? Absolutely.

By the time we hit the road in March, *They Club Seals, Don't They?* was more than a show; it was an event. At the same time as sealers and protesters were confronting each other on the ice off Newfoundland, we were confronting audiences in major urban centres across the country. As a result, our publicity ran itself. Normally, you have to work to get media coverage for theatre productions; with this one we practically had to fight off the television cameras. We were instant celebrities, hitting every major current affairs show in the country at least once, and the national news several times. Our performances played to packed (if not always supportive) houses.

I've always considered that any theatre event begins not when the curtain goes up, but at the moment the audience enters the auditorium. Because of this, programmes to previous Mummers shows were often a bit weird. They set the scene, conceptually, for the play. It seemed to me a wasted opportunity for a programme to merely list the names of the cast and advertise gasoline and cigarettes. With this show, the event usually began before the audience even reached the theatre. The IFAW set up picket lines outside our box office in some cities, so that by the time spectators got into the theatre, they already had pamphlets in their hands. When they entered the auditorium they got more of the same. On each seat, we left a small envelope with a bunch of cards inside. One side of each card had pro-hunt information; the other side contained anti-hunt information. Spectators could shuffle them as they chose. Meanwhile, over the theatre's sound system, we played the IFAW's "Every Letter Counts" radio campaign:

> People are ztarting to realise zat ze destruction of our wildlife for luxury and novelty fur products ees a cruel and brutal travesty. Hello. Zees ees Zsa Zsa Gabor for ze Internazional Fund for Animal Velfare...ze senseless keeling of 170,000 baby harp seals off ze coast of Labrador steel conteenues. Ze remaining market for zese fur treenklets like bookmarkers and ztuffed animals ees mynyoot. Ze zealing industry only zupports 195 zo-called hunters. Ees time zat zis zlaughter was ztopped. Zees ees Zsa Zsa Gabor urging you to write to ze Canadian guberment weeth your feelings. Every letter countz!... (sound effect of seal pup bark sounding almost like "Please!")

The commercials had been sent to radio stations across North America with a request to play one or two during the broadcast day. We all played 25 of them, back to back. Our audiences got to hear Jimmy Stewart, Beatrice Arthur, Burgess Meredith, Gregory Peck, Mary Tyler Moore, and dozens more American movie stars reading exactly the same script. So many familiar voices one after another, each reading identical scripts with identical sincerity, slowly became a self-parody. Waiting in our dressing room, we learned to gauge the mood of our audiences in advance by this pre-show tape. If they laughed at number eighteen, Donny Osmond, then we knew they were a live bunch. If not, we knew the performance would be uphill most of the way.

At the end of each performance, we invited the audience to stay, and turned the auditorium over to anybody who wanted to discuss the issues. Many spectators seemed to be won over by our play, but there was usually a strong anti-hunt faction. These debates often went on into the night. It was quite an experience.

In Toronto, a week before the hunt began, the influential *Toronto Star* critic gave us a quarter-page review entitled *Baby Seals Don't Club People, Do They?* which we interpreted as a sign that we were definitely getting somewhere. The review hardly mentioned the show. Instead, it critiqued the issue. Gina Mallet was outraged:

> ...the only number that meant much to me was that the average seal hunter earns $7,500 annually. Can it be true that better paying jobs can't be found? If it isn't, and the fishermen refuse other jobs, then thumbs down on them! (*Toronto Star* 2 March 1978).

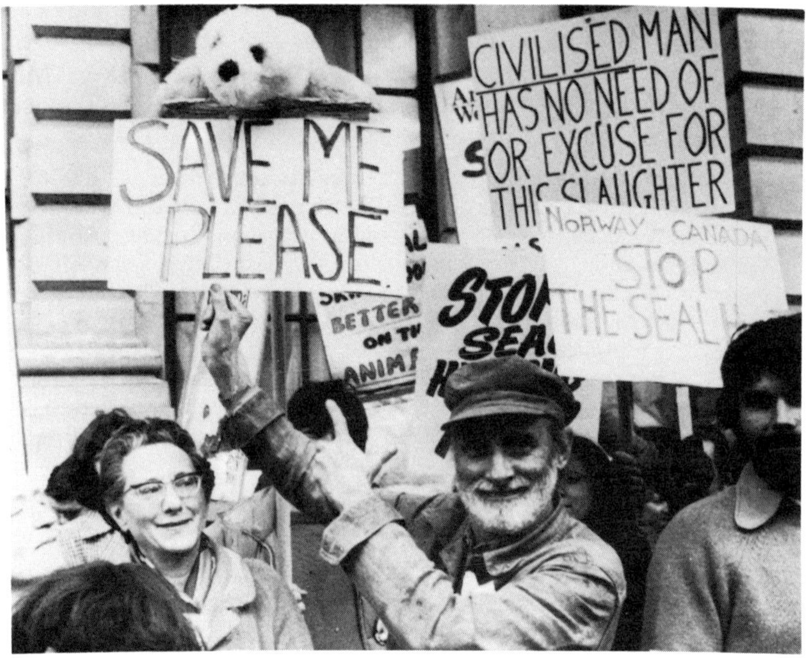

How to Save a Seal. Actor Spike Milligan at a seal hunt protest demonstration in London, England, 1977.
Photo: Wide World Photos.

It was shortly after our Toronto opening that hate mail started to arrive at our office back home. The nicer ones expressed the hope that our show would drop dead. The not-so-nice expressed the hope that *we* would drop dead. And the nasty ones assured us that they would personally ensure that we did so. Some even cared enough to outline the method they would employ. Skinning alive was a favourite.

We played St. Anthony, Newfoundland, on the eve of the hunt. Afterward we holed up in the Viking Motel drinking beer along with scores of reporters and television crews who were waiting for the annual circus to start. The Greenpeace helicopter hadn't shown up yet, and everyone was desperate for a story, any story. In the middle of this, the National Arts Centre telephoned me from Ottawa to talk about the reception they were planning for our opening night there in two days' time.

We had never before performed at the National Arts Centre. It was the pinnacle of official art in Canada, and opening night receptions, apparently, were *de rigueur*. Many Ottawa dignitaries would attend, they assured me. Since we were a Newfoundland theatre company, it had been decided to serve a selection of seafood. What did I think? I replied that a seafood reception was very thoughtful of them, and reminded them that in Newfoundland at this time of year, seal meat was considered the prime seafood. Would they include seal meat in their buffet? They decided they'd have to caucus to discuss that. Later they called back to say they were terribly sorry, but we had to realise that important people would be at the reception, and serving seal might offend some of them. I reminded them that this was the whole point of our play. We would be offended if it wasn't served. They said they'd have to caucus again on that. Later still, they called back to say they'd decided to scrap the whole seafood idea and just serve cheese instead. We could take it or leave it.

The next day, 10 March, we made it into *Hansard*.

Mr. John Crosbie (St. John's West):

> Mr. Speaker, I rise on a matter of urgent and pressing necessity, under the provisions of standing order 43. In view of the fact that the Mummers Troupe of Newfoundland are to open their production *They Club Seals, Don't They?* at the National Arts Centre on March 13th, with a reception after to be given by the management of the Centre, in view of the fact that...the Mummers have arranged for three dozen flippers to be consumed at the reception, and in view of the fact that the National Arts Centre has now advised the Mummers that they will not serve the flippers, thereby causing a crisis in that without the flippers there will be no Mummers...I move, seconded by the honourable member for Don Valley, that this House direct the National Arts Centre to reverse their anti-flipper decision...so that they be open to all the people of Canada no matter what their tastes or habits....

Et cetera. Later in the day the Minister of Fisheries told Parliament that "to prevent a story in the media," the Arts Centre would indeed serve flippers after all. And so they did. They were served in delicate little French pastry puffs. The Centre's chefs did a masterful job of making them taste like beef bourguignon.

A week later still, we were in Vancouver. This was Greenpeace's home turf, and we arranged a private meeting with part of their directorship. I naively thought that we might be able to come to some understanding. We didn't. But they were a great bunch. One of them actually threw the I Ching to determine the size of the seal herd. During the day, we fielded callers on Sandy Webster's radio phone-in show, reminding them that each year 500,000 dogs and puppies were euphemistically "put to sleep" in the greater Vancouver mainland area by urbanites who didn't want them any more. Surely, we said, such a pointless waste of animal life overshadowed the economically useful harvest of 180,000 seals by Canadians on the other side of the country? Callers said we were murderers and hoped that we'd die. Later, several Greenpeace directors came to our opening night.

> ...The troupe reappeared on stage and almost dared the audience to debate their creation. This in front of television news cameras which were present in hopes the play would strike sparks. And sparks there were, lots of them.
>
> There was a heated exchange between actress Donna Butt and Paul Watson, with Butt the apparent winner as members of the audience accorded her applause and a few even came out of their seats to kiss her.
>
> Life imitates art and art imitates life. All in all, a strange and entertaining evening (*The Vancouver Sun* 22 March 1978).

Meanwhile, on the ice floes off Newfoundland, other television news cameras recorded the arrest of Greenpeace president Patrick Moore and the cuddling of seals by actress Pamela Sue Martin, star of NBC's *Nancy Drew* series. It was theatre versus theatre.

On the Prairies, as we expected, most of our audiences didn't see what the fuss was all about. They shipped their cattle off to market every year.

Somewhere along the line, David Ross was asked on national television to justify why seals should be hunted merely to satisfy the fashion fur industry. David replied that 45 per cent of a sealer's income comes from the sale of seal oil and meat. He thoughtfully pointed out that seal oil is used in such things as industrial lubricants and margarine, and went on to name the major Canadian chocolate company which, he idly remarked, uses it in their product, too. The chairman of the chocolate company's board (who, we learned, lived in the United States), got on the phone at five o'clock in the morning to threaten legal action.

And so it went.

By this time, back in Newfoundland, we were local heroes. The show was a huge and very visible success on the mainland. Everybody knew about it. The Mummers were defending Motherhood.

Once a theatre, we were now an institution. I decided to capitalise on our new-found image. I flew home ahead of the tour to whip up a big publicity splash for the play's return. Shag the province's Arts and Culture Centres, I thought, with their monopoly on government arts funding and their penchant for colonialism. We'll mount a flank attack on their official arts policy. If we couldn't budge it now, we'd never be able to. The policy was dictated from the throne room of the St. John's Arts and Culture Centre. By striking while our show was hot, I thought we could bypass it.

I printed up a theatre funding booklet and sent copies to every member of the provincial House of Assembly. It quoted national critics testifying that our show had "significantly affected public opinion" on the seal hunt, and made it clear that we'd busted our arses all across the country in order to defend the livelihood of Newfoundland fishermen. The average fisherman, as we had told Canadians, has a sub-poverty-level annual income of only $7,500. But, I asked the MHAs, were they aware of the irony? Did they know that Newfoundland professional actors, *our* arse-busting actors, earned far less than the fishermen they were defending?

Politicians are not generally noted for the length of their attention spans. Getting them to listen to a pitch on culture, I figured, would be like talking to the hearing impaired. So I worked out an information pamphlet with lots of bells and whistles, something like this:

> Look here.
>
> Our theatre company is committed to producing 100 per cent Newfoundland material, and touring it to communities all over the province.
>
> Hooray. Whoopee.
>
> But commitment will not pay the grocery bill. Professional theatre companies in other provinces receive, on average, 30 per cent of their income from their provincial government. We do not.
>
> Lights. Action. Bar graphs. Razzamatazz. Lots of black colour for average mainland theatre. Lots of red colour for us.
>
> So we have 30 per cent less money to spend.
>
> No Hooray. No Whoopee. No Razzamatazz.
>
> Professional sealers don't kill seals just for fun. Professional actors don't do what they do just for fun either.
>
> Right? Right.
>
> Actors have to eat and support a family like everyone else.
>
> So?

So if this situation doesn't soon change, the better professional theatre artists will leave the province. And then who'll defend yer seal hunt?

This is not our fault. It is yours. Do something about it!

Beep. Flash. Tilt.

In fine print, the details looked like this. The Troupe's total yearly operating revenue at this time was $140,000. Of this, one third came from box office income. The average Canadian theatre pulled in one third of its income from ticket sales, too.

For each dollar of federal support the Mummers received, we fund raised another 41 cents from the private sector. The average Canadian theatre raised 40 cents.

But for every dollar of federal support to the Mummers, our provincial government contributed nothing. The average Canadian theatre, on the other hand, received another 65 cents from their provincial government.

Two thirds of the average Canadian theatre's spending was on personnel. By comparison, we spent 80 per cent on personnel, but

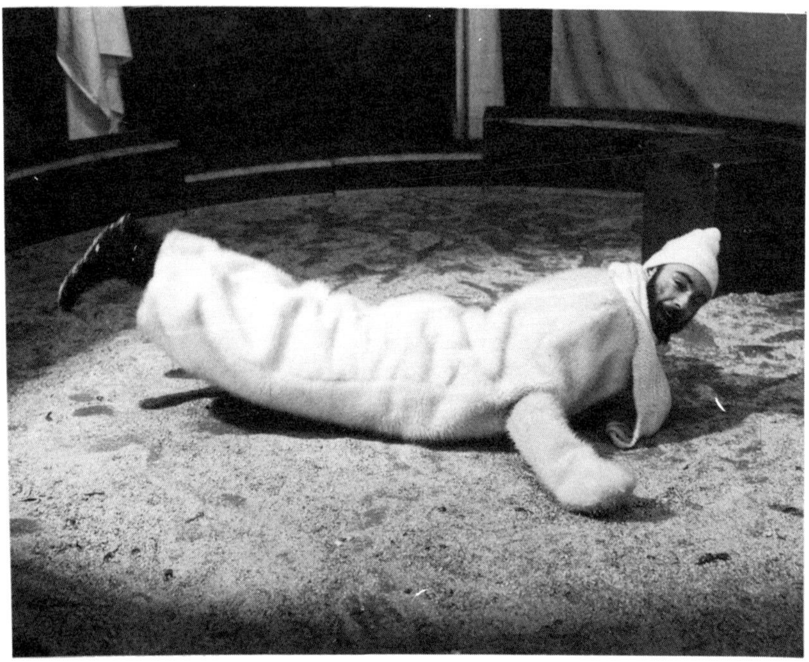

Pierre Beaupre as The Baby Seal. *They Club Seals, Don't They?* 1978.
Photo: Mannie Buchheit.

this still didn't eliminate the income gap between our actors and their mainland counterparts. We simply had less cash coming in.

In 1972, actors in Mummers Troupe productions were young, single, and able to survive on salaries of $40 per week. Now the Newfoundland theatre community was six years older. Some actors had families to support. And it wasn't always easy on $225 per week, the standard Mummers non-touring salary in 1978. (Everyone, no matter what their job with the Troupe, still received the same salary. But performers worked on a per-production basis, never for 52 consecutive weeks.) Our actors could command better-paying jobs at any comparable professional theatre on the mainland. There wasn't much we could do about it. Unless we could break the Arts and Culture Centres' dollar dictatorship.

Most MHAs read the pamphlet politely enough. One who seemed particularly interested was the Minister of Mines and Energy. The former principal of a high school in Springdale that took our school tours. A hungry-looking guy by the name of Peckford. He talked about wanting to make "a revolution between the ears" in Newfoundland.

The Great Spur to Artistic Endeavour 16

It is money that sacks cities, and drives men forth from hearth and home; warps and seduces native innocence, and breeds a habit of dishonesty.

Sophocles

Our financial situation cast its shadow over plans for the 1979 season. I hoped to arrange a British tour for *They Club Seals* during the 1979 seal hunt. Under the company's copyright contract, this could only take place with the agreement of all the play's author-actors. Most of the cast was interested, but only if they could expect a hefty hike in salary. Donna Butt's bottom line was a little heftier: a restructuring of the Troupe into a collective. For her, many of the issues of 1976 were still very much alive.

Discussions about the show's revival stalled, while we waited for our flank attack on the provincial government to bear fruit. Meanwhile, in May 1978, I went to England to talk up the tour idea.

I returned to Newfoundland in August to find news waiting. The director of the province's Cultural Affairs Division had approached part of the cast of *They Club Seals, Don't They?* and asked for a written letter which would suggest that the Troupe was not a legitimate entity. Shortly thereafter, the Troupe's lobby for tour funding was deep-sixed within the bowels of the Confederation Building. Suddenly the Division of Cultural Affairs began to hand out production financing for Newfoundland professional theatre. They backed *They Club Seals* cast members who produced plays independently of the Mummers. Donna Butt and David Ross had decided to found a new theatre company, *Rising Tide*, and Rhonda Payne formed *Mollygrub Productions*. *They Club Seals* was dead.

At a gala occasion at Toronto's Park Plaza Hotel in October, someone dressed up as a cook slipped past security and hit Newfoundland's Director of Cultural Affairs in the face with a cream pie, just as he was about to be presented with a citation for his contribution to the arts in Canada. Some said it was not a pie, it was a peach cake. According to media reports, the inscription on the pie/cake read: "From the folks back home...." The thrower made a clean getaway, and a culprit was never found. But you can guess who got blamed for the deed.

The defeat of the Mummers' funding initiative meant trouble for our provincial touring. The economy was moving into recession, and costs were increasing: transportation, accommodation, wages. The Troupe's salaries had increased 30 per cent in the past three years, an amount which merely kept pace with inflation; the support it received from the Canada Council, its main benefactor, had meanwhile increased by only 10 per cent during the same period. Now the Canada Council's own budget was being cut back by the federal government for the coming year. Assistance for performing arts tours would be particularly affected. The Council, ostensibly an "arms-length" operation immune to political pressure, is nonetheless dependent upon the federal government for 90 per cent of its funding.

> Our grants cannot even keep pace with inflation, while the operating costs of our arts organisations exceed it...We cannot escape the brutal fact that even our best established orchestras, publishing houses, theatres, and other basic institutions are at this moment in mortal danger...the loss will be for all of us—across the board. And we may never repair the divisive effects of what must appear to the disadvantaged as regional and artistic discrimination (Canada Council 1979-80).

Federal policy was swinging to the right in non-cultural areas as well, a shift which also boded ill for the Mummers Troupe. Over the previous six years we had built up a relationship with a network of development organisations across the province. Many of our projects relied upon them both for guidance and for partial funding. But there was a catch: groups like the Labrador Resources Advisory Council, the Progressive Rights Organisation, Oxfam, and the Community Planning Association of Canada had in turn tapped third-party assistance from federal funding agencies for those projects. Now, with federal agencies cutting back (the Secretary of State announced a cut of $60 million) many local development organisations were watching their own funding dry up. The prospects for future theatrical collaborations looked slim.

The writing was on the wall. It meant, in effect, that it would be impossible, in 1978-79, for us to produce a season equivalent to the one we produced three years earlier in 1975-76. Our options were limited. We could:

1. Reduce touring.
2. Produce fewer plays with smaller casts.
3. Produce non-original plays.

We didn't like any of the above. In terms of our company's mandate, option number three was unthinkable. But it was a choice which some other Canadian theatres were forced to make. Other factors being equal, it is always more expensive to create an original play than it is to reproduce one which has already proven to be a hit in New York, London, or elsewhere, and for which the "research and development" costs have effectively already been taken care of. Producing "classics" is even cheaper, as in this country, anyway, no royalties need be paid to the dead authors.

We considered upping our ticket prices. But there was a limit to this solution. In 1978 few Newfoundlanders, however nationalistic, would on a regular basis pay $10 to see a play about Newfoundland when it cost only $3.50 to see a play or movie about the United States. In the absence of protectionist tariffs on foreign cultural goods, our work would be restricted to a small, well-heeled audience. No touring would restrict it further— to urbanites.

There was one other alternative. It was costing the Mummers $10,000 a year to keep the LSPU Hall afloat as a downtown St. Johns cultural centre, a subsidy which, increasingly, we could ill afford. This precipitated the decision to give the Hall to a community group.

In October 1978, all across the country the Canadian arts community staged a big "Support the Arts" campaign: letters to Members of Parliament, appeals to the public, press conferences and demonstrations. Dour predictions were sounded: unless the federal government recanted on its arts funding freeze, financially undernourished theatres, symphonies and art galleries would start dropping like flies. It was no joke. In their financial affairs, most arts organisations had already been in a holding pattern for the past several years, and many were now so close to the wire that cuts in federal support could push them under.

The federal government responded by encouraging arts groups to get out and raise extra support from the private sector. Private business had already been touted as the force that would save Canada from the recession, and it was now recommended as a saviour for the arts as well. Politicians pointed with pride to the corporate art collection assembled by the makers of Rothman cigarettes, and to IBM's backing of the National Ballet Company.

Corporate sponsorship as a replacement for public funding of the arts seemed as if it might indeed be possible for the National Ballet or the Stratford Festival. It is in the best interests of IBM to protect Official Art. But smaller arts organisations found it rather difficult to attract substantially greater private-sector backing than they already did. And any groups which addressed political subjects in their work were crazy to think that the private sector was going to get behind *them*.

We gave it a try, anyway. A local television station donated advertising spots, and we saturated prime time with a series of "Support the Arts" commercials. I dressed up Babbitt-like and addressed Rotary Club meetings. We put on skates and hockey uniforms to demonstrate at St. John's City Hall when councillors cut municipal arts support by 24 per cent (and simultaneously boosted assistance to sports groups by an astonishing 937 per cent).

We made a lot of noise, but in retrospect it was a bizarre exercise. The Mummers Troupe was exactly the kind of arts organisation disqualified by the federal government's deferral to the private sector. Imagine asking your local corporate giant to underwrite your future theatre work after you've just produced a show about, for example, industrial disease in their mining operation. It was ludicrous. In all my corporate fund raising efforts, the most progressive response I got was: "Look, we admire your company's work, and we'd like to contribute. But we just couldn't be involved with anything controversial." Surprisingly though, our effort had one payoff. We snagged an important corporate sponsorship for the annual school tour of our only non-controversial production: the traditional Christmas Mummers Play.

As the country's political climate became more conservative, the Canada Council's Theatre Section aligned itself accordingly. They diverted some theatre subsidies into an "investment" scheme which would finance large productions which promised "commercial potential." Free enterprise would save the day.

> Chutzpa, that's what we're trying to develop! The great spur to artistic endeavour is the profit motive! (Walter Learning, Theatre Officer of the Canada Council).

The arts were going to be business, all right. And the bigger the better. Consolidation was in order. This was good news for the country's large "regional" theatres, who already ate up the lion's share of federal theatre subsidy and spewed out predominantly foreign plays. Cash bonuses were now introduced to induce these behemoths to produce Canadian plays. (Smaller Canadian theatres, already producing Canadian work, were not eligible to apply for the bonuses.) The National Arts Centre received a special grant of $1 million to establish two resident companies and travel the country. They toured *Hamlet*.

During the winter of 1979 it became obvious that the Mummers Troupe wasn't on the Canada Council's best seller list. At first, no one said so directly. Their Theatre Section sent up smoke signals in other languages, flying down from Ottawa to see our shows and muttering darkly into their beer.

The mutters hit the fan in April 1979, when we opened a new collective creation: *Some Slick*. It was a play we were particularly proud of, and it owed a lot to an Ontario actor, William Roberts, who wasn't even in it. William had showed up a year earlier, on sabbatical from the Kam Lab Theatre of Thunder Bay, along with fellow Labber Pierre Beaupre. Kam Lab's work was supposedly similar to the Mummers', and they'd decided to come down East and see how similar it really was. They both got involved with a couple of our shows and went back home in the summer of 1978, but not before making some astute observations. William pointed out that the Mummers often latched onto an issue after it was too late for our efforts to make a substantial difference. Our play about industrial disease, for example, occurred after many miners in the province had already contracted silicosis. "How much more effective it would be," William remarked, "if you could create shows about social issues *before* they became crises. Then a play might be able to inform public awareness from the beginning, and help *avoid* the crisis."

Aha!

We had originally planned to spend the winter of 1979 creating a community documentary on the Southern Shore of the Avalon Peninsula, focusing perhaps on the fishery. But just before Christmas, the multinational oil industry announced plans for a massive step up in their exploration efforts off Newfoundland the following summer. For the past several years there had been only minor offshore exploration activity, and the multinationals seemed to have lost interest. Suddenly they were talking about spending over $100 million next summer. Clearly they smelled a major find. If they found anything, rapid development of the resource could begin almost immediately, on a scale never before seen in Newfoundland. The social impact would be enormous. We decided to cancel our community show and take a chance on the William Roberts theory. Our winter show would address the "what if?" scenario, predicated on the possibility of a major offshore oil find.

The target audience for such a show would be the potential offshore workforce. Roughnecks, roustabouts, deck hands. The problem was, I figured, they'd be the hardest kind of spectators to get into the theatre. Generally speaking, those guys preferred to head down to the local tavern for a beer and a game of darts rather than hike up to the community hall for a dose of theatre. So I got together with a local blues band and we worked up a rock musical that could play bars.

The show was written in consultation with a local sociologist and offshore expert, Dr. Doug House of Memorial University's Institute for Social and Economic Research. He had carefully examined the Norwegian and Scottish North Sea oilfield developments. Offshore oil was not necessarily good news. Elsewhere in the world, the enormity of offshore development had steam rollered local decision-making and had torn large holes in the onshore social fabric. It had sabotaged traditional industries like the fishery, greatly inflated the cost of living, and seriously threatened the environment. It had made a few rich; it had made the average man-on-the street poorer. There was every reason to fear the worst.

Some Slick was not a pro-business show. Its message was that the pace of any offshore development must not be at the mercy of the profit motive. What's good for the Seven Sisters would not necessarily be good for the people of the province. Decisions on the offshore must be made by *Newfoundlanders*, not by Mobil Oil.

No one had ever created a rock and roll cabaret show in Newfoundland before. Ours included all the requisite special effects, from dry ice to live video cameras. And it sold beer, too. At its opening run we turned the LSPU Hall into a beer hall and sold out every performance. The local reviews were raves.

The Canada Council, however, was very displeased. This was not the sort of show we should have produced, they said. It was not proper art, it was not even a proper Mummers show, they insisted. Eighteen months previously we had told them we were planning a community documentary; to substitute a different play reflected poor planning, they said. We replied that such might be the case, were we a theatre whose season consisted of *Hamlet, Equus* and *The Odd Couple*. But we were a company whose mandate obliged us to respond to events in our society. And events had shifted. They accused us of deliberately pulling the wool over their eyes by changing plans; they wouldn't have funded our season if they'd known it included *Some Slick*.

At this point, we had been receiving season funding from the Canada Council for five years. Now their Theatre Section had new staff and a pro-business philosophy. To them, changing plays in mid-season reflected administrative incompetence and bad business management. I think they also had problems accepting the concept of a rock and roll bar show as proper art. The Canada Council traditionally backs "artistic," not "commercial" music. "Highbrow" symphony orchestras get Council's support. "Lowbrow" bar bands do not. For the record, I felt that lowbrow art was exactly what *Some Slick* was *not*. Lowbrow art, supposedly exemplified by television soap operas, Harlequin romances, and *Emmanuelle II* at the local drive-in, is no more a product of working-class culture than are the Coca-Colas and Fords produced in Oshawa and Detroit factories. It is a mass-produced manipulation of the fantasy life of North American capitalism, part of a marketing strategy designed to mould passive consumers, reflecting the effects of The System on the lives of "ordinary people" in such a way as to discourage them from altering the status quo.

Our show also differed from the standard stage musical form (that is, a play with brief musical interludes). *Some Slick* was the reverse: music with brief dramatic interludes. It relied primarily on amplified music and lyrics to advance the thesis of the show. This worked well for its intended audience: noisy, beer-drinking, working-class Newfoundlanders who *liked* AM radio rock and roll and who considered "drama" to be for the stuffed-shirts and the bosses. It expressly didn't work for the Canada Council Theatre Section.

I believe that we looked unacceptable to the Theatre Section not because of our work per se but because of their particular ideology of art. They were redefining artistic acceptability in a way that automatically disenfranchised the basis of our work. To us it was a question of censorship—not an overt political censorship, but an implicit structural censorship.

In late 1979 the Canada Council pulled the plug on our season funding. From now on, they said, they would consider assisting Mummers Troupe productions only on a per-play basis. If they approved of the idea of a particular show, they'd support part of the costs. Otherwise, freeze in the dark.

The frost spread. Apparently concerned about the Mummers' transgressions in Newfoundland, the Theatre Section introduced a new "collective policy," intended to apply to Canadian theatres from coast to coast which produced plays by the collective creation method. In the Council's opinion, all such theatres were "inherently unstable," and were to be disqualified from season funding as we had been. The policy was not made public.

Meanwhile, as Herman Melville once observed, "Reality has a habit of outracing apprehension." In July, 1979, 200 miles off Newfoundland's Avalon Peninsula, Mobil Oil struck an oil deposit which they announced was the largest offshore oilfield in the world. In Toronto, the stock market leaped. In St. John's, real estate values skyrocketed. Land speculators jetted in from Alberta. Oil fever had arrived, and was spreading fast. Suddenly, many of the problems which *Some Slick* examined were hypothetical no longer.

Development associations around Newfoundland began asking for the show. There was little time to lose. We made plans for an extensive fall tour to taverns and halls all over the province, focusing particularly on areas likely to be hit hardest by offshore impact. We scored an $18,000 tour sponsorship from PetroCanada, by far the largest private-sector donation any Newfoundland arts group had ever received up to that date. But...corporate sponsorship from the oil industry? Marx would roll in his grave. We searched our souls. What would Groucho say about this? We told ourselves he'd pat us on the back and say there, there. He'd tell us that PetroCanada wasn't the same as Exxon, that it was nationalism and National Energy Policy and Canadian ownership and so forth. He'd remind us that they only gave us the cash because their corporate arm was twisted anyway. (Under the government's offshore regulations, oil companies were required to spend a percentage of their offshore expenditure on in-province training and development. I managed to get *Some Slick* certified as "training" for the general public.) The Canada Council's theatre section was having a kitten. They would definitely absolutely positively not support the tour, they said. It was our mistake to have produced the play in the first place, they emphasised. If we would like to tour a different show in its place now, on a less controversial topic, well then, they'd consider funding it instead.

The idea of doing something like *Plaza Suite* at a time like this seemed to us ridiculous. For us, the fall tour of *Some Slick* represented everything the Troupe stood for. We decided to go down in a blaze of glory. We didn't have a lot more to lose in the long term, anyway. Short of outright excommunication, there wasn't much more the Canada Council could do to punish us. But thanks to PetroCanada, in the short term our finances were surprisingly solvent, and on the strength of that we took out sizeable loans. We had a hit show which could count on doing well at the box office.

I informed the Canada Council that we would mount a kamikaze run, touring the show to communities throughout the province, then onto the mainland and eventually up to Ottawa, going completely and gloriously bankrupt and closing the company right on their doorstep, screaming loudly all the while. The Council was unmoved.

Some Slick toured for almost four months, and had a noticeable impact on public awareness of the offshore issue throughout the province. It was an immensely popular show. We adapted it for the provincial CTV-affiliate and it was later broadcast as a 90-minute television special. It sold out at the Neptune Theatre in Halifax, bombed at Toronto Free Theatre, and was a hit at Ottawa's Beacon Arms bar.

In January, 1980, just before the show opened in Ottawa, the Mummers Troupe and the Canada Council Theatre Section struck a deal. Council agreed to reinstate our season funding and convene a national meeting of all theatres affected by their "collective policy;" we agreed not to commit suicide on their doorstep.

Neither party completely lived up to its side of the bargain. That is, the Canada Council did not reinstate the Troupe's season funding, and the Mummers did die, two years later. But the national theatre meeting took place, and the discriminatory national "collective policy" was dropped.

I finished out the company's 1979-80 season, and quit. It was pretty clear which way the wind was blowing. As a theatre, I felt we were fighting a losing battle. As an individual, I felt that I had explored most of what I set out to do when I founded the company eight years earlier. I no longer woke up in the middle of the night sweating about whether I'd be able to pull off whatever the show of the moment was. I missed the challenge, I guess.

Rhonda Payne took over as the Troupe's artistic director and bravely piloted the company through the next two years, producing collective creations like *Makin' Time with the Yanks* (a play about St. John's during the Second World War) and scripts like Al Pittman's *West Moon.* I left Newfoundland to learn Spanish and wander around Latin America. Eventually I worked for a while in the Nicaraguan theatre.

Crash Landing

No Firepower

17

> We must consider theatre as a gun, as a weapon to free ourselves from imperialism. I think any weapon is good for defending oneself. But between a .45 and an M-50 I prefer the M-50. The problem consists in how to make our theatre a weapon potent and effective, with great firepower.
>
> Nicaraguan playwright Alan Bolt

In Newfoundland in 1981 the theatre wasn't an M-50. Perhaps it was because there was now less need of defence. Perhaps it was because ammunition was so scarce. Perhaps our aim was shot.

Ammunition was certainly as scarce as it had ever been. Across the country, Canada's professional theatres had seen a 100 per cent increase in their accumulated deficits during the previous three years, with an average deficit of $70,000. Newfoundland, already suffering the effects of regional disparity in most areas of its economy, found its arts activities similarly blighted.

Although there were now four professional theatre companies trying to make a living in the province, Newfoundland was still in last place on the Canada Council's gravy train. While other provinces received between $0.29 and $2.42 per capita from the Council for theatre activities, Newfoundland and Labrador received a grand total of only $0.12. A Newfoundland Arts Council had finally been set up, but it was too underfunded to be able to provide sustaining grants to professional theatres. Offshore development had bogged down in federal-provincial wrangling, and the slowdown in the province's general economy discouraged much private-sector arts support.

The aim had also shifted. Newfoundland's professional theatre was now facing a different audience. Tight money (and to a lesser extent, dwindling interest from Newfoundland theatre artists) had virtually eliminated any theatre touring in the province outside of the Arts and Culture Centre five-town circuit. The adult target audience for the Newfoundland theatre had become exclusively urban middle-class. This influenced both the theme and the style of presentations. Critics began to remark that local plays relied too much on cheap caricature. It was no accident that these were not caricatures of the urban middle-class, but of the rural working class; that is, the kind of spectators who were no longer included in the theatre audience. It is not so easy to get away with cheap caricatures of fishermen when your primary audience is full of the real thing.

As well, the whole battle had cooled. The need for cultural defence was now felt less strongly by the artistic community. The expression of the Newfoundland identity had been to a great extent taken over by the partisan political arena. The new premier, Brian Peckford, brought to provincial politics a strident sense of nationalism which linked cultural integrity with territorial identity and resource ownership (although the answer to the question of *ownership by whom* was a little too simple: by Newfoundlanders, of course. The question of *which* Newfoundlanders would benefit by such ownership— the richer minority or the poorer majority— was less frequently addressed.) Local radio and television stations produced commercials and bumperstickers by the thousands declaring: *I BELIEVE in Newfoundland!*

We had always intended the Mummers' brand of theatre-for-development to be a vehicle, a means to an end rather than an end in itself. We did not want to create art for art's sake. Our objective was to "throw the ball" to the audience. That the ball would be used to score political touchdowns for the Progressive Conservative party was not quite what we had envisioned. Nevertheless, the ball was in play and this may have been a sign that it was now time for us to let go of it. In 1970, the province's artists had been challenged by Newfoundland's need to hold a mirror up to its own nature. During the following decade, the relationship between the society and its art had been extraordinarily vibrant and dynamic. But by 1982, it seemed to have become relatively static. The romance had cooled.

By May, 1982, the Mummers Troupe was in serious trouble. Administrative hassles were sapping creative energy. Financial difficulties forced the cancellation of the final production of the 1981-82 season. The company was owed thousands of dollars in unpaid bills by other local arts groups. Its urban productions were still popular (10 per cent of the population of St. John's came to see *Makin' Time with the Yanks*, a fairly impressive figure.) But it hadn't been able to mount a tour outside the province's five major urban centres in over two years. By comparison, in its 1979-80 season the Troupe travelled over 20,000 miles by bus, boat and bushplane, giving 312 performances from St. John's to Nain to Vancouver. It was suffering a crisis of spirit as well, the result of a deteriorated relationship with part of St. John's professional theatre community. The bad vibes had begun with the first *Community Stage* split in 1976, had revived with the formation of *Rising Tide* in 1979, and were exacerbated by the financial hardships which the entire Newfoundland theatre community endured. Some members of the local theatre community believed the Canada Council's Theatre Section had signalled that if and when the Mummers Troupe died, the Council grant thus freed up would go to them. (In the end, this didn't happen. But if wishes were horses, the Mummers Troupe would have been trampled to death.)

Many Newfoundland actors were no longer interested in the kind of theatre which the Mummers Troupe represented. They'd cut their teeth on original political plays. Now they wanted to try their hand at other things: Joe Orton, Arthur Miller, Shakespeare. It was the eighties. The Mummers Troupe looked like an anachronism.

> ...It's not really that chic to be writing political poems, political plays, in the 1980s, is it? (Robert Enright, CBC Radio "Stereo Morning").

In September, rather than make the compromises necessary for survival and face a future of foreign plays and city audiences, the Mummers Troupe held its breath and died. It became the fifth Canadian theatre to close its doors in 1982.

> OPTING FOR AN HONOURABLE DEATH.
>
> For the past year government freezes on arts spending have been taking a visible toll. Last week in Newfoundland, the province's oldest theatre company, the Mummers Troupe, joined Quebec's Festival Lennoxville, Toronto's Open Circle Theatre, and the NDWT Company among the ranks of the defunct. Mummers co-founder Chris Brookes, whose militant socialism set the tone for the company's "community documentaries" on such volatile issues as the seal hunt and the Hibernia oilfields, laid the blame squarely on Canada Council policies, not lack of popular support: "Funding bodies believe art occupies one pole and politics another," says Brookes. "But often the more controversial a show, the greater its public appeal."

> The Mummers have been in decline for several years, however. In 1976 the company acquired a longshoremen's union hall but begrudgingly relinquished control in 1980 to a community arts committee which claimed that the Mummers were excluding other artistic groups from using it to best advantage. Recently, under artistic director Rhonda Payne, the troupe slimmed down to a production company that sponsored less controversial shows, such as *Makin Time with the Yanks*, set in wartime St. John's. But extra money for future projects was not forthcoming. Says Brookes: "Rather than produce middle-of-the-road shows with limited social relevance, we opted for an honourable death." Whatever the post-mortem, Newfoundland has lost a major theatrical resource (*Maclean's* 22 November 1982).

Six years later, as this book is published, I feel it would be nice to be able to succinctly sum up what it all meant. This is difficult for me, but I encourage you, the reader, to do so.

SKILL TESTING QUESTIONS

(Answer any five of the following.)

1. Was the Mummers Troupe an anomaly in the Newfoundland theatre?
2. In the Canadian theatre?
3. If the Mummers Troupe had stuck around, today it would look like:
   (a) Rising Tide Theatre.
   (b) The Stratford Festival.
   (c) The P.L.O.
   (d) Opus Dei.
4. What is the Mummers' legacy? (15 words max.)
5. Whatever happened to Chris Brookes anyway?
   (a) Became famous Latin American dictator.
   (b) Sold out.
   (c) Works in a bank.
   (d) Married Donna Butt.
6. Whatever happened to Donna Butt anyway?
   (a) Became famous Latin American dictator.
   (b) Sold out.
   (c) Works in a bank.
   (d) Married Brian Peckford.
7. Can art change anything?
8. Did the Mummers change anything?

9. Were they a public nuisance?
10. What's for lunch?

Appendix 1: Chronology

WHAT HAPPENED (More or Less)

May 1967

Newfoundland government opens Arts and Culture Centre in St. John's. Cost $7 million.

March 1968

Newfoundland government opens Arts and Culture Centre in Corner Brook.

31 March 1970

Newfoundland government ends First Resettlement Programme, having moved residents from 371 outports.

1 April 1970

Newfoundland government announces beginning of Second Resettlement Programme.

5 October 1970

In Quebec, the FLQ kidnaps British diplomat James Cross.

16 October 1970

Canadian government imposes War Measures Act in response to FLQ "insurrection."

October 1970

The NFFAWU is founded as a union to represent Newfoundland fishermen.

January 1971

Miners in St. Lawrence go on strike.

4 June 1971

NFFAWU begins landmark strike against Newfoundland fish merchant Spencer Lake.

21 June 1971

Miners in Buchans begin six-month strike.

July 1971

Newfoundland government opens Arts and Culture Centres in Gander and Grand Falls.

22 September 1971

Newfoundland fish merchant Spencer Lake states: "You haven't got the local leadership to run [a fishermen's union] intelligently, with all due respect to the people—I'm very fond of them."

18 January 1972

Joseph R. Smallwood steps down as Premier of Newfoundland after 23 years. Progressive Conservative Frank Moores sworn in as new Premier.

17 March 1972

NFFAWU wins strike in Burgeo.

July 1972

First performance by Newfoundland Travelling Theatre Company.

September 1972

Mummers Troupe/Resource Foundation for the Arts founded.

26 December 1972

First performance of *Traditional Newfoundland Christmas Mummers Play* by Mummers Troupe.

15 March 1973

Miners in Buchans begin eight-month strike.

May 1973

Mummers Troupe opens *Newfoundland Night* in St. John's.

12 August 1973

First performance of Mummers Troupe production *Gros Mourn*, in Sally's Cove, Newfoundland.

13 August 1973

Federal-provincial signing of the Gros Morne National Park agreement, in Rocky Harbour, Newfoundland.

11 September 1973

In Chile, CIA-orchestrated coup topples elected president Salvador Allende, installing military dictatorship.

26 December 1973

Mummers Troupe opens second production of the *Traditional Newfoundland Christmas Mummers Play.*

27 December 1973

First barrel of oil produced by J.R. Smallwood's economic development showpiece, the Come-By-Chance oil refinery.

1 January 1974

Newfoundland government proclaims Jubilee Year to celebrate 25 years of Confederation.

8 January 1974

First Mummers Troupe school tour.

February 1974

Codco opens first production *Cod on a Stick* at St. John's Arts and Culture Centre.

March 1974

Mummers Troupe opens *Once a Giant* in St. John's.

August 1974

Mummers Troupe opens *Buchans a Mining Town* in Buchans, Newfoundland.

26 December 1974

Mummers Troupe opens third production of the *Traditional Newfoundland Christmas Mummers Play.*

April 1975

Newfoundland government opens Arts and Culture Centre in Stephenville.

30 April 1975

"The biggest peacetime movement of people in North America" Newfoundland's Resettlement Programme, finally ends, having erased almost 1/3 of the province's fishing outports.

May 1975

Mummers Troupe opens *Company Town* at TWP Theatre, Toronto.

9 June 1975

Miners in St. Lawrence begin eight-month strike against ALCAN.

July 1975

Mummers Troupe opens *East End Story* at LSPU Hall in St. John's, Newfoundland.

August 1975

Mummers Troupe begins provincial tour of *Dying Hard.*

November 1975

Mummers Troupe opens *I.W.A.* at LSPU Hall in St. John's.

15 December 1975

Memorial University Art Gallery opens "Black Exhibition" to protest control exercised by Province's Director of Cultural Affairs over visual arts policy.

26 December 1975

Mummers Troupe opens fourth production of the *Traditional Newfoundland Christmas Mummers Play.*

February 1976

Come-By-Chance oil refinery is declared bankrupt.

March 1976

Mummers Troupe opens at Centaur Theatre, Montreal with *I.W.A.*

April 1976

Mummers Troupe opens national tour of *What's That Got to do with the Price of Fish?* in Sydney, Nova Scotia.

September 1976

Mummers Troupe open LSPU Hall in St. John's as downtown cultural centre.

September 1976

Community Stage Theatre formed by disaffected members of Mummers Troupe.

20 October 1976

Direct from England, the play "Shakespeare's People" opens at St. John's Arts and Culture Centre, beginning a decade of Newfoundland government-sponsored British theatre productions.

November 1976

Mummers Troupe opens *Irregular Entertainment* at LSPU Hall, St. John's.

4 December 1976

Codco closes *The Tale Ends* in St. John's, the company's last performance with its original seven members.

26 December 1976

Mummers Troupe opens fifth production of the *Traditional Newfoundland Christmas Mummers Play.*

31 December 1976

Newfoundland Travelling Theatre Company ceases operations.

1 January 1977

Canada declares 200-mile offshore fishing limit.

April 1977

Mummers Troupe opens *Silakepat Kissiane/Weather Permitting* in Nain, Labrador.

June 1977

Joseph R. Smallwood retires from political life in Newfoundland.

19 August 1977

Groucho Marx dies.

September 1977

Mummers Troupe opens *The Bard of Prescott Street* at LSPU Hall in St. John's.

26 December 1977

Mummers Troupe opens sixth production of the *Traditional Newfoundland Christmas Mummers Play*.

1 February 1978

ALCAN closes mine in St. Lawrence.

March 1978

Mummers Troupe opens national tour of *They Club Seals, Don't They?* in Petrolia, Ontario.

26 July 1978

The Queen and Prince Phillip begin 1978 Royal Tour in Newfoundland.

September 1978

Rising Tide Theatre founded by Donna Butt and David Ross.

Ooctober 1978

Mummers Troupe and Mollygrub Productions begin provincial tour of *Stars in the Sky Morning.*

December 1978

Mummers Troupe sponsors *Bread and Circuses*, first conference of Canadian political theatre artists with international popular theatre practitioners, in St. John's.

26 December 1978

Mummers Troupe opens seventh production of the *Traditional Newfoundland Christmas Mummers Play.*

26 March 1979

Brian Peckford sworn in as Premier of Newfoundland.

April 1979

Mummers Troupe opens *Some Slick* at LSPU Hall in St. John's.

July 1979

Hibernia, world's largest offshore oilfield, is discovered off Newfoundland.

19 July 1979

Revolution in Nicaragua. FSLN guerillas topple despot Anastasio Somozoa.

September 1979

In St. John's, LSPU Hall Downtown Cultural Centre taken over by wide-based community group, adopting a new name: Resource Centre for the Arts.

October 1979

Mummers Troupe begins provincial tour of *Some Slick.*

14 December 1979

Province of Newfoundland and Labrador establishes a provincial Arts Council.

26 December 1979

Mummers Troupe opens eighth production of the *Traditional Newfoundland Christmas Mummers Play.*

March 1980

Mummers Troupe opens *Just a Postal* at LSPU Hall in St. John's.

24 March 1980

Assassins tied to the right-wing ARENA party shoot Archbishop Oscar Romero in San Salvador.

20 May 1980

Quebec referendum voters say "no" to sovereignty association.

October 1980

Mummers Troupe opens *West Moon* at LSPU Hall in St. John's.

26 December 1980

Mummers Troupe opens ninth production of the *Traditional Newfoundland Christmas Mummers Play.*

March 1981

Mummers Troupe opens *Makin' Time with the Yanks* at the LSPU Hall in St. John's.

May 1981

Mummers Troupe opens *Billy Max in Progress and Tiln* at LSPU Hall in St. John's.

November 1981

Mummers Troupe opens *Stars in the Sky Morning* at LSPU Hall in St. John's.

26 December 1981

Mummers Troupe opens tenth and last production of the *Traditional Newfoundland Christmas Mummers Play.*

March 1982

The last ship-based whitecoat seal hunt takes place off Newfoundland. EEC ban on seal products to be in force within 18 months.

6 April 1982

Brian Peckford wins provincial election and promises that henceforth in Newfoundland "the sun will shine, and have-not shall be no more!"

April 1982

Mummers Troupe tours five provincial Arts and Culture Centres with *Makin' Time with the Yanks.*

9 June 1982

Yves Langlois, last member of the FLQ exiled since the October 1970 crisis, returns to Canada from France.

September 1982

Mummers Troupe closes.

Appendix II: Mummers Troupe Productions 1972-1982

Traditional Newfoundland Christmas Mummers Play, December 1972

John Doyle, Lynn Lunde, Kevin Pittman, Tom Sexton, Chris Brookes.
Author: traditional. Director: Brookes

Newfoundland Night, May 1973

John Doyle, Lynn Lunde, Diane Olsen, Sandra Cantwell, Chris Brookes.
Author: collective. Director: Brookes.

Newfoundland Night (touring version), June-August 1973

Mary Walsh, Donna Butt, Christopher Knight, Paul Sametz, Andrew Thompson, Chris Brookes.
Director: Brookes.

Punch and Judy Show tour (concurrent with Newfoundland Night), June-August 1973

Chris Brookes, Andy Thompson.

Gros Mourn, August-October 1973

Mary Walsh, Donna Butt, Christopher Knight, Paul Sametz, Andrew Thompson, Chris Brookes. (Lynn Lunde replaced Mary Walsh on tour).
Author: collective. Director: Brookes.

Traditional Newfoundland Christmas Mummers Play, December 1973

Jan Henderson, Bembo Davies, Lynn Lunde, Bob Pot, Chris Brookes.
Author: traditional. Director: Brookes.

Once a Giant, February-March 1974

Bob Pot, Judy Marshak, Marsha Coffey, Lynn Lunde, Chris Brookes, Michael Fahey.
Author: Steven Bush. Director: Brookes.

Gros Mourn (school tour), May 1974

Donna Butt, Rhonda Payne, Rick Boland, Heather Earle, Paul Sametz, Chris Brookes.
Director: Brookes.

Buchans a Mining Town/Company Town, August-September 1974

Donna Butt, Bembo Davies, Howard Cooper, Allen Booth, Lee J. Campbell, Connie Kaldor, Chris Brookes. (Rhonda Payne replaced Connie Kaldor on tour, September).
Author: collective. Director: Brookes.

Once a Giant, Punch and Judy (tour of Nova Scotia), September 1974

Donna Butt, Bembo Davies, Howard Cooper, Allan Booth, Lee J. Campbell, Connie Kaldor, Chris Brookes.

Traditional Newfoundland Christmas Mummers Play, December 1974

Donna Butt, Bembo Davies, Rick Boland, Lee J. Campbell, Chris Brookes and Don Wherry (musician).
Author: traditional. Director: Brookes.

Company Town, May-June 1975

Connie Kaldor, Bembo Davies, Donna Butt, Lee J. Campbell, Allen Booth, Derek Butt, Howard Cooper.
Author: collective. Director: Brookes.

East End Story, July 1975

Madeleine Williams, Steven Bush, Jane Foster, Rick Boland, Wayne McNiven, Rhonda Payne, Ron Hynes.
Author: collective. Dramaturge: Alan Filewod. Director: Brookes.

Dying Hard, August-September 1975

Donna Butt, Rick Boland, Ron Hynes, Rhonda Payne.
Author: Elliott Leyton. Director: Steven Bush.

I.W.A., October-November 1975

Donna Butt, Ray Landry, Jeff Pitcher, Pamela Morgan, Rhonda Payne, Ron Hynes, Rick Boland.
Author: Rick Salutin with collective. Director: Brookes.

Traditional Newfoundland Christmas Mummers Play, December 1975

Rhonda Payne, Chris Brookes, Rick Boland, Judy Parsons, Ron MacEachern.
Author: traditional. Director: Rick Boland.

I.W.A., March 1976

Wayne McNiven, Rick Boland, Ron Hynes, Ray Landry, Donna Butt, Rhonda Payne, Jeff Pitcher.
Director: Brookes.

What's that Got to do with the Price of Fish? (Canadian tour), April-June 1976

Madeleine Williams, Donna Butt, Wayne McNiven, Rick Boland, Ron Hynes, Jeff Pitcher.
Author: collective/Susan Perly. Director: Brookes.

What's that Got to do with the Price of Fish? (Newfoundland tour), August 1976

Madeleine Williams, Donna Butt, Wayne McNiven, Rick Boland, Don Walsh, Jeff Pitcher.
Author: Susan Perly with collective. Director: Dudley Cox.

Irregular Entertainment, October 1976

Jeannie Becker, Judy Parsons, David Ross, Terry Reilly, Brenda Devine, John Doyle.
Author: collective. Director: Brookes.

Traditional Newfoundland Christmas Mummers Play, December 1976

John Doyle, David Ross, Chris Brookes, Terry Reilly, Geoff Butler.
Author: traditional. Director: Brookes.

Silakepat Kissiane: Weather Permitting, April-May 1977

Terry Reilly, Jeff Pitcher, Jane Dingle, Judy Parsons, Chris Brookes. Author: collective. Director: Brookes.

The Bard of Prescott Street, August-September 1977

Mary Walsh, Bob Joy, David Ross, Janet Michael, Brian Hennessey, Ron Hynes, Jane Dingle.
Set: Michael Kerney. Author: collective. Director: Brookes.

Traditional Newfoundland Christmas Mummers Play, December 1977

Kelly Russell, Jim Payne, Mavis Penney, Kent Barrett, Sheila Zisman.
Author: traditional. Director: William Roberts.

They Club Seals, Don't They? March-May 1978

Donna Butt, David Ross, Rhonda Payne, Terry Reilly, Glenn Tilley, Jeff Pitcher, Pierre Beaupre.
Author: collective. Director: Brookes.

Stars in the Sky Morning (tour), October-November 1978, co-produced with Mollygrub Productions.

Rhonda Payne, Jane Dingle.
Author: Rhonda Payne. Director: Jan Henderson.

Traditional Newfoundland Christmas Mummers Play, December 1978

Kent Barrett, Charles Tomlinson, Gay Hauser, Wanda Crocker.
Author: traditional. Director: Mark Manson.

Some Slick, April 1979

Paul Steffler, Mac Furlong, Brian Downey, Denis Parker.
Author: collective. Director: Brookes. Set: Warren Brownridge, Derek Butt.

Punch and Judy Show (Canadian tour), May-June 1979

Lynn Lunde, Chris Brookes.

Some Slick (Newfoundland and Labrador tour), November 1979 (Canadian tour), January 1980

Paul Steffler, Mac Furlong, Brian Downey, Denis Parker.
Author: collective. Director: Brookes. Set: Derek Butt.

Traditional Newfoundland Christmas Mummers Play, December 1979

Beni Malone, Glen Rockwood, Charles Tomlinson, Greg Thomey, Colin Quigley.
Author: traditional. Director: Rhonda Payne.

Just a Postal, March 1980

Greg Thomey, Rick Boland, Caroline Ford, Charles Tomlinson.
Author: collective based upon series of lithographs by Frank Lapointe. Director: Rick Boland.

West Moon, October 1980

Ed Keilly, Janis Spence, Sherri Smith, Greg Thomey, Pat Byrne, Sheilagh Guy, Judy Parsons, Rick Boland, Jim Payne, Clyde Rose, Kevin Noble.
Author: Al Pittman. Director: Rhonda Payne. Set: Gerry Squires.

Traditional Newfoundland Christmas Mummers Play, December 1980

Beni Malone, Colin Quigley, Greg Thomey, Sherri Smith, Pip Lewis.
Author: traditional. Director: Thom Sokolovsky.

Makin' Time with the Yanks, March 1981

Kay Anonsen, Brian Downey, Paul Stefflet, Janis Spence, Rick Boland, Jane Dingle.
Author: collective. Director: Mary Walsh.

Billy Max in Progress, May 1981

Rhonda Payne, Ed Keilly, Boyd Norman, Jeff Pitcher, Sheilagh Guy.
Author: Arvo MacMillan. Director: Rick Boland.

Tiln, May 1981

Ed Keilly, Rick Boland.
Author: Michael Cook. Director: Rhonda Payne.

Traditional Newfoundland Christmas Mummers Play, December 1981

Merle Matheson, Mary-Lynn Bernard, Charles Tomlinson, Geoff Butler, Michael Wade.
Author: traditional. Director: Ian Wallace.

Makin' Time with the Yanks (provincial tour), March 1982

Kay Anonsen, Brian Downey, Paul Steffler, Janis Spence, Rick Boland, Jane Dingle.
Author: collective. Director: Mary Walsh.

Appendix III: A Mummer's Creed

INSTRUCTIONS TO ALL YE A-MUMMERING WILL GO

Just as time runs out for civilised man, time is running out for the theatre. Neither will survive without radical adjustment. It is no longer possible to politely impel a static audience to higher consciousness. What is required is a vibrant responsive theatre form that will spur a community's active development of its own new order. A form that demands reaction. If necessary out of self preservation to protect themselves from a howling mass of theatricians about to knock inspiration down their throats.

How does one extract from a group of people the permission to drastically and irrevocably alter their lives? The theatre needs a license to attack fearlessly and imaginatively, to root out complacency and destroy old thought forms. Such license is provided by the traditional Newfoundland Mummers Play. It is a 'must' for any theatrician seeking to invoke genuine change.

The process is easily initiated. When charming their way into a house, Mummers must at all times justify their actions and presence in the name of tradition. From the moment one Mummer foot has secured the doorway however, all pretence of good behaviour and humility can be dropped.

None of the customary theatrical acting aesthetics need apply to the mummer. Concern for believability, economy of movement, logic, consistency, etc. is a hindrance to the real work at hand. More useful are the primal bodily functions and the introduction of parasites. Nothing quite punctuates a dramatic moment like the itchy crotch. Only as a mummer is gross sexual humour not untamed manners but quaint humour.

There are two considerations in choosing a playing area: high mummer mobility and maximum inconvenience for the mummed. Priority is always given to the second. Think nothing of having the couch moved all the way across the room only to then change your mind. Furniture is to be leapt from, grandchildren make imposing weaponry, an evening gown can provide a hiding place. When objects prove too substantial to move, full theatrical resonance is often achieved by a vigorous unsuccessful attempt. Note that the audience is also to be considered as objects. If you are going to spend the next five minutes as a corpse, you may as well expire upon a row of squiggling laps. Permanent maiming, while well within the mummer tradition, is however bad for community relations.

The other "super-objective" for the mummer is to eat and drink as much as possible. Additional credits are given if one holds up the play's action while doing so. Under the guise of folk art it is usually possible to scavenge all the best food at fancy parties. Every digestive tract has its limit however, and it is not always possible to do justice to a particularly lavish buffet. In such cases a sock-foot placed tastefully in the potato salad during the course of the action may be high art.

All in the name of tradition, of course. Who dare defy tradition?

– Formulated Christmas 1974 by Bembo Davies (Doctor).

References

Alinksy, Saul 1971 *Rules for Radicals.* Random House of Canada.

Antler, Steven 1979 "The Capitalist Underdevelopment of Nineteenth-Century Newfoundland." In Robert J. Brym and R. James Soucouman (eds.), *Underdevelopment and Social Movements in Atlantic Canada.* New Hogtown Press.

Artaud, Antonin 1958 *The Theatre and its Double.* Grove Press.

Beck, Julian 1972 *The Life of the Theatre.* City Lights Books.

Berger, John 1959 *A Painter of Our Time.* Simon and Schuster.

_______ 1972 *Ways of Seeing.* British Broadcasting Corporation and Penguin Books.

Boal, Augusto 1979 *Theatre of the Oppressed.* Pluto Press.

Brecht, Bertolt 1964 *Brecht on Theatre.* Hill and Wang.

Brice-Bennett, Carol (ed.) 1971 *Our Footprints are Everywhere.* Labrador Inuit Association.

Byrne, Cyril 1981 "Some Comments on the Social Circumstances of Mummering in Conception Bay and St. John's in the Nineteenth Century." Paper presented to Canadian Association of Theatre History Colloquium, Halifax, June 1981.

Carpenter, Edmund 1973 *Oh What A Blow the Phantom Gave Me.* Holt, Rinehart and Winston.

Chambers, E.K. 1903 *The Medieval Stage.* Oxford University Press.

_______ 1964 *(1933) The English Folk-Play.* Russell & Russell.

Cox, Harvey 1969 *The Feast of Fools, A Theological Essay on Festivity.* Harvard University Press.

Davis, R.G. 1975 *The San Francisco Mime Troupe.* Ramparts Press.

Galeano, Eduardo 1981 An Address to the Writer and Human Rights Congress. Toronto, October 1981.

Grotowski, Jerzy 1968 *Towards A Poor Theatre*. Odin Teatrets Forlag (Denmark)

Guevara, Ernesto Che 1960 *La Guerra de Guerillas*. MINFAR (Havana).

Gunn, Gertrude 1966 *The Political History of Newfoundland 1832-1864*. University of Toronto Press.

Gywn, Richard 1968 *Smallwood, The Unlikely Revolutionary*. McClelland and Stewart.

Halpert, Herbert and G.M. Story (eds.) 1969 *Christmas Mumming in Newfoundland*. University of Toronto Press.

Hunt, Albert 1976 *Hopes for Great Happenings*. Eyre Methuen Limited.

Ladurie, LeRoy 1979 *Carnival in Romans*. George Braziller Inc.

Leach, A.F. 1896 "The Schoolboys Feast." *Fortnightly Review*.

Mackenzie, Neil 1987 "Boy into Bishop." *History Today*.

Mao, Tse-Tung 1940 "On Culture—Address to the Yenan Forum." *Chinese Culture No. 1. Yenan*.

Maylam, Percy 1909 *The Hooden Horse, an East Kent Christmas Custom*. Cross & Jackman.

Mercer, Paul 1974 *The Ballads of Johnny Burke*.Newfoundland Historical Society.

Murphy, Michael P. 1976 *Pathways Through Yesterday*. Town Crier Books.

Noel, S.J.R. 1971 *Politics in Newfoundland*. University of Toronto Press.

Piscator, Erwin 1978 *The Political Theatre, A History*. Avon Books.

Prowse, D.W. 1895 *A History of Newfoundland*. Macmillan.

Schlegel, A.W. 1808 *The Second Lecture on Dramatic Art*. George Bell and Sons.

Shawn, Wallace and Gregory, Andre 1981 *My Dinner with Andre*. Grove Press.

Sider, Gerald 1977 *Mumming in Outport Newfoundland*. New Hogtown Press.

Smallwood, J.R. 1969 *A Short Message from Your Premier*. Action for Joey Campaign.

_______ 1975. *I Chose Canada*. Macmillan of Canada.

_______ 1979 *No Apology From Me*. Newfoundland Book Publishers.

Wordsworth, C. 1901 *Ceremonies and Processions of the Cathedral Church of Salisbury*. Cambridge University Press.

Newspapers and Periodicals

Atlantic Insight (Halifax)
The Evening Telegram (St. John's)
The Globe and Mail (Toronto)
The Chronicle Herald (Halifax)
Macleans (Toronto)
Mayday Magazine (Vancouver)
The Citizen (Ottawa)
The Public Ledger (St. John's)
Saturday Night (Toronto)
The Toronto Star
The Vancouver Sun
The Winnipeg Free Press

Government Documents and Publications

Hansard (Official Proceedings of the House of Commons).
The Canada Council Annual Report 1979-80.
Provincial Archives of Newfoundland and Labrador, GN 2/2, Danson and Buckingham to Colonial Secretary, 14 January 1831.
Provincial Archives of Newfoundland and Labrador, GN 2/2, Danson and Buckingham to Colonial Secretary, 21 January 1832.

Glossary

longer a pole, a fence rail.

upalong mainland Canada.

Term 29 the 29th term of Confederation whereby the Government of Canada pays an annual grant, called the Transition Grant, to the provincial government. Was discontinued amidst much acrimony, by Prime Minister Diefenbaker in 1959, but restored indefinitely in 1965 by Prime Minister Lester Pearson.

Bas (Jamieson) a local Newfoundland open-line radio show host.

Figgy Duff a Newfoundland folk-rock band.

ISER BOOKS

Studies

36 **A Public Nuisance: A History of the Mummers Troupe**—Chris Brookes.

35 **Listen While I Tell You: A Story of the Jews of St. John's, Newfoundland**—Alison Kahn

34 **Talking Violence: An Anthropological Interpretation of Conversation in the City**—Nigel Rapport

33 **"To Each His Own": William Coaker and the Fishermen's Protective Union in Newfoundland Politics, 1908-1925**—Ian D.H. McDonald, edited by J.K. Hiller

32 **Sea Change: A Shetland Society, 1970-79**—Reginald Byron

31 **From Traps to Draggers: Domestic Commodity Production in Northwest Newfoundland, 1850-1982**—Peter Sinclair

30 **The Challenge of Oil: Newfoundland's Quest for Controlled Development**—J.D. House

29 **Sons and Seals: A Voyage to the Ice**—Guy Wright

28 **Blood and Nerves: An Ethnographic Focus on Menopause**—Dona Lee Davis

27 **Holding the Line: Ethnic Boundaries in a Northern Labrador Community**—John Kennedy

26 **'Power Begins at the Cod End': The Newfoundland Trawlermen's Strike, 1974-75**—David Macdonald

25 **Terranova: The Ethos and Luck of Deep-Sea Fishermen**—Joseba Zulaika (in Canada only)

24 **"Bloody Decks and a Bumper Crop": The Rhetoric of Sealing Counter-Protest**—Cynthia Lamson

23 **Bringing Home Animals: Religious Ideology and Mode of Production of the Mistassini Cree Hunters**—Adrian Tanner (in Canada only)

22 **Bureaucracy and World View: Studies in the Logic of Official Interpretation**—Don Handelman and Elliott Leyton

21 **If You Don't Be Good: Verbal Social Control in Newfoundland**—John A. Widdowson

20 **You Never Know What They Might Do: Mental Illness in Outport Newfoundland**—Paul S. Dinham

19 **The Decay of Trade: An Economic History of the Newfoundland Saltfish Trade, 1935-1965**—David Alexander

18 **Manpower and Educational Development in Newfoundland**—S.S. Mensinkai and M.Q. Dalvi

17 **Ancient People of Port au Choix: The Excavation of an Archaic Indian Cemetery in Newfoundland**—James A. Tuck

16 **Cain's Land Revisited: Culture Change in Central Labrador, 1775-1972**—David Zimmerly

15 **The One Blood: Kinship and Class in an Irish Village**—Elliott Leyton

14 **The Management of Myths: The Politics of Legitimation in a Newfoundland Community**— A.P. Cohen (in North America only)
13 **Beluga Hunters: An Archaeological Reconstruction of the History and Culture of the Mackenzie Delta Kittegaryumiut**— Robert McGhee
12 **Hunters in the Barrens: The Naskapi on the Edge of the White Man's World**— Georg Henriksen
11 **Now, Whose Fault is That? The Struggle for Self-Esteem in the Face of Chronic Unemployment**— Cato Wadel
10 **Craftsman-Client Contracts: Interpersonal Relations in a Newfoundland Fishing Community**— Louis J. Chiaramonte
9 **Newfoundland Fishermen in the Age of Industry: A Sociology of Economic Dualism**— Ottar Brox
8 **Public Policy and Community Protest: The Fogo Case**— Robert L. DeWitt
7 **Marginal Adaptations and Modernization in Newfoundland: A Study of Strategies and Implications of Resettlement and Redevelopment of Outport Fishing Communities**— Cato Wadel
6 **Communities in Decline: An Examination of Household Resettlement in Newfoundland**— N. Iverson and D. Ralph Matthews
5 **Brothers and Rivals: Patrilocality in Savage Cove**— Melvin Firestone
4 **Makkovik: Eskimos and Settlers in a Labrador Community** — Shmuel Ben-Dor
3 **Cat Harbour: A Newfoundland Fishing Settlement**— James C. Faris
2 **Private Cultures and Public Imagery: Interpersonal Relations in a Newfoundland Peasant Society**— John F. Szwed
1 **Fisherman, Logger, Merchant, Miner: Social Change and Industrialism in Three Newfoundland Communities**— Tom Philbrook

Papers

18 **To Work and to Weep: Women in Fishing Economies**— Jane Nadel-Klein and Dona Lee Davis (eds.)
17 **A Question of Survival: The Fisheries and Newfoundland Society**— Peter R. Sinclair (ed.)
16 **Fish Versus Oil: Resources and Rural Development in North Atlantic Societies**— J.D. House (ed.)
15 **Advocacy and Anthropology: First Encounters**— Robert Paine (ed.)
14 **Indigenous Peoples and the Nation-State: Fourth World Politics in Canada, Australia and Norway**— Noel Dyck (ed.)
13 **Minorities and Mother Country Imagery**— Gerald Gold (ed.)
12 **The Politics of Indianness: Case Studies of Native Ethnopolitics in Canada**— Adrian Tanner (ed.)
11 **Belonging: Identity and Social Organisation in British Rural Cultures**— Anthony P. Cohen (ed.) (in North America only)
10 **Politically Speaking: Cross-Cultural Studies of Rhetoric**— Robert Paine (ed.) (in Canada only)

9 **A House Divided? Anthropological Studies of Factionalism**– M. Silverman and R.F. Salisbury (eds.)
8 **The Peopling of Newfoundland: Essays in Historical Geography** – John J. Mannion (ed.)
7 **The White Arctic: Anthropological Essays on Tutelage and Ethnicity**– Robert Paine (ed.)
6 **Consequences of Offshore Oil and Gas—Norway, Scotland and Newfoundland**– M.J. Scarlett (ed.)
5 **North Atlantic Fishermen: Anthropological Essays on Modern Fishing**– Raoul Andersen and Cato Wadel (eds.)
4 **Intermediate Adaptation in Newfoundland and the Arctic: A Strategy of Social and Economic Development**– M.M.R. Freeman (ed.)
3 **The Compact: Selected Dimensions of Friendship**– Elliott Leyton (ed.)
2 **Patrons and Brokers in the East Arctic**– Robert Paine (ed.)
1 **Viewpoints on Communities in Crisis**– Michael L. Skolnik (ed.)

Mailing Address:

ISER Books (Institute of Social and Economic Research)
Memorial University of Newfoundland
St. John's, Newfoundland, Canada, A1C 5S7